Praise for D.W. Buffa's novels

Evangeline

"Ever since *Moby Dick* we fear that the ocean treats human beings by its own rules. Marlowe, a worthy successor of Captain Ahab, was the only one who knew these rules."
- *Lufthansa Exclusive Magazine*

Trial by Fire

"The fast-moving dialogue and fine sense of characterization keep the reader hanging on for the ride."
- *Publishers Weekly*

"Haunting, memorable...will be considered a classic in years to come."
- *Midwest Book Review*

"D.W. Buffa would be a household name in a perfect world. Meticulously plotted...with unforgettable characters. Very highly recommended."
- *BookReporter.com*

Breach of Trust

"Another well-crafted legal thriller from one of the genre's best practitioners."
- *Calgary Herald*

"Political intrigue abounds...a truly surprising end,"
- *Publishers Weekly*

"Maddening suspense, captivating courtroom scenes, and a marvelously twisted ending"
- *Booklist*

"If there's anybody who can mount a challenge to John Grisham's mantle...Buffa's the most sure-footed guy to do it. A crisp, first-rate read...a tightly wound thriller. A richly textured cast of characters."
- *Edmonton Journal*

"D.W. Buffa continues to show great intelligence and erudition. There's nobody else like him."
- *San Jose Mercury News*

"Littered with plot twists and land mines that explode when least expected...A novel with wide appeal. A fast-moving tale that jolts and veers enticingly off track, but also stays comfortably in sight of the main objective. Well-developed characters and a rich milieu add depth to this excellent thriller."
- *Publishers Weekly*

The Defense
"A gripping drama...made up of not just one but several exciting trials...More satisfying still, it ends with a couple of twists that are really shocking. And it leaves you wanting to go back to the beginning and read it all over again."
- *The New York Times*

"An excellent legal thriller."
- *USA Today*

"Stunning legal reversals...fine, flowing prose...[a] devastating impact."
- *The New York Times Book Review*

THE
DARK BACKWARD

D.W. Buffa

BLUE ZEPHYR

Published by Blue Zephyr
Copyright © 2011 D. W. Buffa

www.dwbuffa.net

ISBN-13: 978-1463777296
ISBN-10: 1463777299

THE DARK BACKWARD

"But how is it
That this lives in thy mind? What seest thou else
In the dark backward and abysm of time?"

Shakespeare, The Tempest, Act I, scene II

CHAPTER ONE

William Darnell thought he had seen every kind of human conflict, every type of human tragedy, seen them in all their immense variety: murder done from envy, murder done for revenge, murder done for money, murder done for love, murder done after careful planning, murder done in a moment's rage. He had known, and defended, every kind of murderer: some of them intelligent, some of them stupid; some of them people who would almost surely kill again, some of them people who would never be able to forgive themselves for what they had done; all of them, despite their differences, driven by the same desire, known since Cain slew Abel: the need to kill because, in their twisted imaginations, it was the only way their own lives would be worth living. He had known them all, and if there was something he had missed, it was in all probability now too late. He was at the end of what might be the last case he would ever try.

The last case he would ever try. He laughed when he thought about it. From the first time he stood up in a court of law and announced that he was the attorney for the defense, he had known what a great many lawyers never learned: that the case, this case, the one he had right now, was the only case; that this trial, the one he had right now, was the most important thing he would ever do. Darnell had understood that, understood with all the certainty of instinct that the only way to begin a new case was to think that it might be the last case he would ever have. He had become one of the most successful lawyers in the country, a court-room legend in San Francisco, but every case was still like the first case he had ever tried, the last case he might ever have. The only difference was that now it might actually be true.

No one was supposed to do what he did at his age. Trial work was too strenuous, too intense; there was too

1

much pressure, too many demands. Some did it past fifty, a few past sixty; no one did it when he was in his seventies and Darnell was at least as old as that.

"I wouldn't be this old," he often reminded himself, "if I had ever stopped doing what I do. I would have died years ago, like most of the people I used to know."

It kept him alive, he was sure of it: the trial, the story that got told, the story about what had happened and why it happened; the story that he had almost always been able to tell better than the other side. That was why he loved it: the plot, the characters, the way he could use them to create, like some work of fiction, a separate world, showing through the dialogue he had with the witnesses – the questions he asked and the answers he forced them to give – how the story he was telling, his version of events, was the only story a jury could reasonably believe. And the law, the rules that decided what was right and what was wrong, was never as straight-forward as it was commonly thought to be.

Darnell could always find a question, a doubt, about whether the law everyone was bound to follow was quite adequate; whether there was not something missing, some-thing that could not have been foreseen, something that would make what at first seemed like an act of violence, a crime, the only thing that in those particular circumstances could, and should, have been done. Whether in the given instance it had been human frailty or human strength, he would somehow find the human element, the element that every juror could understand, that had made the defendant do something that might on some narrow interpretation have broken the strict letter of the law, but that no sane person would call unjust.

That was the issue: the question of what drove people to do what they did – part of the mystery of human exis-tence, if you will – that had for more than half a century had driven William Darnell. A courtroom was a stage, every trial a new and different play, each of them with its own beginning, middle, and end. He remembered that now as he watched the members of the jury file into the courtroom and take their places in the jury box. After all these years, after more trials than he could count, he still felt the same sensation he had in that first trial, a lifetime ago, when he had waited as a jury came back from its deliberations, ready to announce a verdict. Or, rather, the lack of sensation, the absence of any feeling at all; a strange detachment, as if none of it had any longer anything to do with him. He might as well have wandered in, a casual spectator without any connection to the trial. It was the knowledge that the decision had already been made, that whatever the verdict, the trial was over. He had done what he could and there was nothing more for it but to wait.

The twelve jurors, seven men and five women, people he had not known before the trial started and, unless he should run into them on the street sometime, would never meet again, sat quietly in their chairs. Some of them looked at the judge while he glanced at the verdict form, some of them looked down at their hands; none of them looked at the defendant, a young woman charged with the murder of her husband.

Darnell had put her on the stand, the last witness in the trial, to admit that she had killed him, but only because it was the only way out, the only way to save herself from the physical and sexual abuse to which she had been subjected for years. Why had she not gone to the police, why had she not run away - the questions he had first asked her when she had begged him take her case, he had asked her under oath. When she replied that she had tried both those things and that they had only made matters worse, when she had fought back the tears as she described the unspeakable things that had been done to her, when the jury looked at her with more than idle sympathy, with something of the sense of the terror with which she had had to live, he thought she just might have a chance.

The judge handed the verdict form to the clerk who in turn returned it to the foreman of the jury, a balding bespectacled middle-age man.

"Has the jury reached a verdict?" asked the judge.

"We have, your Honor. We find the defendant not guilty."

Darnell was not surprised, but neither would he have been surprised had it gone the other way. It had seemed to him a close case, one that in the end depended on what the jury thought of her, a woman who insisted that she was more a victim than the man she killed. They believed what she told them about the things her husband had done, but they would not have believed her if they had not felt sorry for her. If she had been just a shade less likeable, a bit less sympathetic, she would be on her way to a lifetime spent in prison instead of walking out of the courthouse free to do as she liked. If this was the last case William Darnell would ever try, it was perhaps entirely fitting, given how often he had tried to search through the moral ambiguity of what people sometimes did, that he was not at all certain that, had he been a member of the jury, he would not have voted to convict.

"The judge would like to see you, Mr. Darnell."

Darnell looked up from the counsel table where he was putting the last remaining papers in his brief case. He knew the clerk, a woman with sad eyes and a kind smile who worked in Judge Pierce's courtroom on the floor above.

"Judge Pierce?" he asked, just to be sure. He could not imagine the reason. "Now?"

"Yes, if you have the time."

They left the courtroom and started down the long hallway to the stairs. Darnell stopped in front of a bank of elevators.

"Do you mind if we take the elevator?" asked Darnell. "It has been a long trial."

"You won another one," said the clerk, staring straight ahead as the elevator doors closed in front of them.

"It was an interesting case."

The clerk smiled to herself, the way a woman does in the presence of young children or old men for whom she has developed a certain fondness. She turned to him and nodded.

"The trial is always interesting, Mr. Darnell, when you're the attorney for the defense."

They had known each other for years, casual acquaintances in the courthouse where he often tried cases and she worked all the time. He touched her gently on the arm and gave her a knowing look.

"That is an extremely kind thing to say. Next case I have in Judge Pierce's courtroom I'll ask that you be on the jury."

She had spent too much time in a courtroom not to have learned something about a lawyer's give and take.

"You might be disappointed, Mr. Darnell; you always make things interesting, but sometimes your client deserves to go to prison."

The elevator shuddered to a stop and the doors creaked open.

"Lucky for me you didn't become a prosecutor. I'd never have a chance," he laughed as she opened the door to the chambers of Judge Evelyn Pierce.

Somewhere the other side of sixty, though much younger than Darnell, Evelyn Pierce had slate gray hair which she almost always wore pinned back and steely blue eyes that were set a little too far apart. She had the broad shoulders and large hands of a sharecropper's daughter, a woman who had worked in the fields until she finished high school and then, while other young women spent their summers swimming and dancing and falling in love, spent every one of hers working in a cannery to put herself through first four years of college and then three years of law school.

Darnell had liked her the first time he met her, almost thirty years ago, during a trial in which she had presided with an even hand and a sometimes caustic wit. His admiration had grown with the years. Some judges never changed, never became any better, and sometimes became much worse as they settled into what they considered a lifetime position; Evelyn Pierce seemed to get sharper, to know more about the law, and to become even more determined that everyone who appeared in front of her was treated fairly and given the best possible chance. It was a measure of the intensity, her involvement in everything that was going on, that she could usually control her courtroom without any obvious effort. A lifted eyebrow or a slight, sideways motion of her head was enough to signal her displeasure with something a lawyer had done and make him stop. On those rare occasions when it was not, she could explode in a way that was volcanic, overwhelming, a visitation from an angry god; but then, as quickly as it had come, it would vanish into a silence so complete, so profound, the poor unfortunate who had incurred her wrath would think for a moment that he must have been rendered deaf by her outburst as he watched her smile gently and gesture for him to continue, certain that he would not break the rules again.

She was on the telephone when Darnell walked in. She pointed to the chair in front of her desk. The windows in her chambers faced east toward the bay, seen in the distance through the tumble of office buildings that bordered the narrow city streets. Darnell had lived in San Francisco all his life but every day he seemed to see it in a way he had not seen it before, see it like he did now, from a different perspective, a different point of view. He was in love with the city and could never get enough of it. There was scarcely an evening when he did not stare out the living room window of his apartment in Pacific Heights, watching as the sun fell burning into the sea and the sky change a dozen different colors until there was nothing but the darkness left and the Golden Gate came alive with the moving lights of a thousand cars.

"Sorry," said Evelyn Pierce as she hung up the telephone. She leaned back and bent her head to the side as if to study him closer. With a wry grin, she shook her head. "Everyone thought you would lose for sure this time." Suddenly, she remembered something. "They used to say that when you don't have the facts on your side argue the law; and when you don't have the law, argue the facts." The grin on her heavy, round face grew broader and deeper as she pondered the idiocy of trying to put in a formula what only the genius of a great trial lawyer could teach. "But from what I hear, you didn't have either the facts or the law and so you did – what – told a story?"

"But that's all a trial is," protested Darnell with a subtle grin of his own. He folded his arms across his narrow chest and rocked back and forth in the wooden straight back chair as he took the question under further advisement. The grin slipped away, replaced by a look of bafflement, as if he could not understand why everyone seemed to have so much difficulty recognizing the simple truth of it. "That's really all a trial is," he repeated in a quiet voice, "a story."

"And some tell stories better than others." She was not going to let him get away with it. He might tell whatever story he liked at a trial, but this was just between the two of them and she had known him long enough to insist on the truth.

"It was a close case," he admitted, meeting her candid gaze with his own. "Thirty, forty years ago, she would have been convicted." He said this with a certainty that immediately yielded to a doubt. He bent forward and tapped two fingers on the edge of the judge's desk. "But then, again - maybe not. For all our talk about equal rights and the rights of women, there was not so much toleration for violence back then, when I was just starting out. A man beats his wife, subjects her to this kind of degradation – gives her to friends of his – No, I think a jury would have said a man like that deserves to die."

Evelyn Pierce narrowed her gaze. She had a question that went right to the heart of the matter.

"How many times did she shoot him?"

"Emptied the gun, I'm afraid; shot him six times."

"Emptied the gun, all at point blank range?" Her eyes were full of knowing mischief. She knew exactly what had happened; everyone in the courthouse, everyone in San Francisco, had heard about it.

"Only the last two," replied Darnell with some mischief of his own.

"While he was crawling away, from what I understand," she drawled.

"Which proved, you see," he said with the same earnest conviction with which he had made his point to the jury, "that not only was she scared to death of him, but that the only thing she knew about violence was what it felt like to be on the receiving end of it."

"Or so the jury believed; or rather was led to believe by the way you told the story."

Darnell looked at her without expression. Did she think he should apologize, or feel some kind of remorse for saving a woman from prison who, in the hands of some other lawyer, might have been found guilty? He knew Evelyn Pierce too well to believe that, but then why was she making such a point of what he had done and the way he had done it?

"Well, whether she should have been acquitted or not," she went on, "I'm glad you won, William Darnell - very glad."

"Thank you, your Honor – but why?"

"Because it was your last case, your last trial; I wouldn't want you to end such a long and distinguished career on a bitter note of defeat. That's not the sort of memory you should carry into a much deserved retirement."

She paused, pondering something; or, rather, as was quite obvious to Darnell, pretending that she did. But why, what was she leading up to? Darnell could not guess.

"On the other hand," she added suddenly, "it isn't clear that winning a case you probably should have lost is the best memory to carry into retirement either, is it? By the way, what are you going to do, William Darnell, after you give up the practice of law?" She asked this with a strange, almost mocking laughter in her wide-set eyes. "How are you going to fill up all the hours you would otherwise be in court convincing juries to ignore the evidence of their senses and let another criminal go free?" With each word the sparkle in her eyes became brighter, more pronounced. She was toying with him, playing a game he did not understand, driving at something, something that she wanted, but would not yet tell him what it was.

"I'm not sure what I'll do when I retire; perhaps I'll write a book and tell the world how the system is broken, bankrupt, and needs to be replaced."

She gave him a significant glance.

"Someone should, before it's too damn late; but I don't think you should do it," she added quickly. "Not yet, anyway; not before you have at least one more trial."

A smile flickered at the corners of her mouth. She looked at him with the shared nostalgia of an old friend.

"When was the last time you took a court-appointed case, William Darnell?"

"I never did. Perhaps I should have, but I always wanted to decide for myself if I was going to represent someone. Is that what you're asking me to do? Is that why you wanted to see me, because there is some case you think I should take? It must be an unusual case, if you decided to ask me; you've never asked me before."

"Officially, I can't ask you now. The defendant doesn't have any money -" She shook her head in amazement and then said in a way that made matters seem even more mysterious, "He may not even know what money is. The case has been assigned to the public defender's office. They're perfectly adequate; they do a reasonably good job in the normal case – but this case....This case requires someone who can see it for what it really is, someone who won't feel bound by all the usual conventions in the way it gets tried; it needs someone who understands that it's a case that probably should not be tried at all."

There was something strange about her tone of voice, something enigmatic about the look in her eye. There was more involved, more than what she had hinted at, but what she said next only added to the mystery.

"It is a case that goes far beyond what we normally understand by the law."

Slowly, and with an effort, Evelyn Pierce rose from behind her desk and walked with measured step across to the window. Her threadbare blue suit had the kind of square shoulders and heavy lapels that had once made spinster principals seem stern and unforgiving. A black judicial robe hung limp on a coat rack next to the door that opened into her courtroom. Standing with her thick legs shoulder width apart and her hands clasped behind her back, she stared down at the busy city streets below.

"You remember the story of Pitcairn Island: Fletcher Christian and the men who mutinied on the Bounty; how they set the tyrannical Captain Bligh and some of the other officers adrift in a lifeboat, then went back to Tahiti; how they searched for a place where no one would ever find them, discovered an island, not more than two miles square, out in the middle of the Pacific, thousands of miles from civilization?"

"Yes, of course…vaguely; I read it years ago, and I saw the movie, the one with Clark Gable and Charles Laughton. I think I also saw the one with Marlon Brando, but I'm not sure. I really don't remember. But why? What does this…?"

Evelyn Pierce looked at him over her shoulder, a question in her eyes.

"You were in the war, weren't you? In the navy, the war in the Pacific, correct?"

The question surprised him, but even after all these years he could not repress a residual pride. A courtroom trial was nothing compared to what he had experienced then. The war, not any verdict he had later won, was the one important thing he had done; it had been, in a way that only made sense to someone who had been there, the best part of his life. There had been an absence of ambiguity, a certainty about things, and, through it, a discipline that, oddly enough, had made him feel freer than he would ever feel again.

"Yes, I was in the navy." He hesitated, wondering whether he should tell the truth. He laughed at his own timidity. "I lied about my age; I was only sixteen, but I looked older."

"Which is probably the reason that you can still lie about your age now," she remarked with a shrewd glint in her eye. "People who look older when they are young often look younger when they get old. How old are you anyway? You don't look a day over seventy. Well, never mind. You were in the war in the Pacific. Good. You have some idea of the distances involved, more than someone who has only seen the movie or read the book. You know how easy it would be to get lost in that vast ocean; how easily a place that size, far away from the main lines of transit, could remain isolated and unobserved, just another bleak, uninhabited place, a distant shore no one would notice. It was nearly seventy years before a ship, an American ship, first noticed Pitcairn. So it's not impossible," she said, turning back to the window and the jostling crowds on the city streets below, the familiar strangers, as she now thought of them, each in a hurry to get to where they were going, where they did not question they had to be.

"What is not impossible?" asked Darnell when she did not explain.

She continued to stare out the window, but she was not thinking about what her eyes could see.

"That the same thing could have happened and not been discovered until now. Strange, isn't it?" she asked, a distant smile on her lips, "that in this modern world of ours, when we think we can map the universe, there are still things we do not yet know about the earth."

She left the window and with a brooding expression on her weather worn face came over to Darnell and put her hand on his shoulder.

"Take the case; it's the only way I'll know there is at least a chance that there might be some justice to come out of all this."

Her hand stayed on his shoulder while she looked down at him, telling him through the troubled sincerity of her gaze that this was no idle request, that she had pondered the question long and hard and would not ask him if she was not convinced that he was the only one who could do it right.

"This case – whatever it is – has to do with something that happened on an island somewhere in the Pacific," said

Darnell as she took her seat the other side of the desk. "An island no one has heard of, an island that apparently doesn't even have a name. Then why is it being tried here?"

Evelyn Pierce gaze shifted past him into the middle distance. A look of weary cynicism moved relentlessly across her strong, broad mouth.

"Haven't you heard?" she asked as her eyes came back to him. "We now have the God-given right to charge anyone with anything, wherever we happen to find them. The situation we now have – the situation you have, if you agree to do this – is one in which someone is charged with crimes that may not have been crimes in the place where they happened."

Darnell caught at the suggestion. He could guess what the government would argue.

"But they should have been crimes, because there are certain things that are always wrong."

"Yes, precisely; which is all the more reason you need to take over the defense. You're old enough to remember that these standards people talk about are not nearly so absolute as they think; and, more importantly, that their own standards, their own beliefs, are scarcely immune from challenge. Still, I have to warn you, the charges against the defendant are serious. The burden of proof will be all on you. The government won't have much difficulty persuading people that what happened out there was clearly a crime, a violation of human rights that has to be punished."

Darnell moved forward onto the edge of the chair. "What exactly is the charge? What is that the defendant is supposed to have done?"

Evelyn Pierce bent her head to the side, a somber expression in her eyes.

"Murder, rape, and…." She seemed not to want to tell him the rest, which puzzled Darnell. After rape and murder what could be so bad as to make her hesitate like this?

"And?" he asked.

"You had a case a few years ago: a sailing ship went down and…."

"The ship was called the Evangeline and it was the most difficult case of my life. What the captain, Marlowe, did – what he had to do – so that some at least might survive…."

"Cannibalism," she remarked, remembering what she had heard about that trial with as vivid a memory as if it had been tried in her own courtroom. "One of the two great taboos, one of the two things that human beings are never supposed to do, one of the two things that are never forgivable."

"Yes, perhaps; though in Marlowe's case, what he did was nothing short of heroic."

"And tragic, too; as you know better than anyone."

"Yes, tragic; the worst tragedy of any case I ever had. But you said two taboos. What is the other? What is the other thing that, beyond rape and murder, seems to be so disturbing?"

"Incest – that is what the young man is charged with; and how you defend against that, I swear I do not know."

CHAPTER TWO

William Darnell unbuttoned his shirt and pretended to be annoyed while Summer Blaine pressed the cold stethoscope against his bare chest.

"Aren't you supposed to get that thing to room temperature before you use it?"

"I do, for all my other patients." She pushed gently on his shoulders until he was hunched forward and then pressed it against his back. "But for you, the worst patient I've ever had, I put it in the freezer first." She listened for a moment, moved the stethoscope farther up his back and listened again. "In my ignorance I thought it might be a way to get your attention," she said as she put the instrument in her black bag.

Darnell's gray eyes danced with laughter, but at the same time with sympathy for the way she worried about him. He did not want her to worry about him; there was really no point to it. But he was glad she did and knew that he would lose something irreplaceable should she ever stop.

"You always have my attention," he said in his most courtly manner. "I listen to everything you say."

Summer Blaine had been through this before. She glanced around the Pacific Heights apartment they shared on weekends and whenever else she could get away from her practice in the Napa Valley. Shaking her head in frustration, she took him by the hand and led him to a living room window and his favorite chair.

"Why don't you just sit down? I'll get a blanket to cover your legs and you can die peacefully in your sleep."

"I know I'm not a very good patient," he began to protest.

"Not a very good patient? You're not a patient at all, in any serious sense. A patient is someone who at least thinks there might be something wrong with him."

14

William Darnell sat in the chair and for a moment looked out the window to the Golden Gate, burning orange in the light of dusk. With surprising agility he jumped back up.

"I'm going to have a scotch and soda," he announced. "What can I get you?"

"A scotch and...? You're impossible," she said as she followed him into the long, narrow kitchen.

He got two glasses from the cupboard next to the stainless steel sink.

"Scotch and...?"

"Yes, all right; but just a small one," she replied.

A table and two chairs sat next to the only window. Alcatraz loomed shadowlike halfway across the bay.

"Every day this week, while you were up in Napa, I did exactly what you told me. I took those damn pills, every morning when I got up and every evening when I went to bed."

She stared back at him, looking for some sign of deceit, knowing that it was not any use.

"You have the most honest face I've ever seen, William Darnell. I should know better than to trust you to tell the truth. I'm not some witness in a trial, I'm..."

"Witness? I thought you were interrogating me."

"Don't try that with me," she replied. She stared harder at him now, smiling in a way that told him that what he could do with juries he could never do with her. "You didn't take your pills every day, did you? You probably didn't take them at all."

He sipped on the scotch and then told her something a little closer to the truth.

"I honestly...," he started and then realized it was a mistake. No one ever told the truth with that beginning. "I really don't remember if I did or not. I think I did, some of the time at least. But during a trial...."

"During a trial you don't think about anything except the trial. Yes, I know all about that. Half the time you sleep – if you can call a short nap sleep – in your office." She took a drink and suddenly felt like a fool. "You didn't even remember I was coming today."

"That's not true. You said you would come as soon as you could on Friday and...."

Her eyes glittered with triumph. It proved her point.

"When you walked in and found me here, you were surprised."

"I was delighted," he said with genuine, and almost boyish, affection.

"But surprised. You didn't know it was Friday, did you? You...."

"I won."

"I know you did."

"You know? But it was just a couple of hours ago. The jury came back with a verdict at four o'clock. You couldn't possibly have heard."

Summer Blaine bent her head to the side and smiled softly. She touched his hand with the warmth of a woman and the confidence of a physician.

"I knew the trial was over, and I knew you had won, the moment I saw you. I know that look, I know what it means, when you have nothing more to worry about, when everything went the way you hoped it would."

No one had ever understood as much about what the work meant to him or how far he got lost in what he did. Sometimes when he looked at her he thought he saw himself, or rather that part of himself that until a few years ago he had not known he had. He told her things that, though he might have spoken the same words when he was younger, when his wife was still alive, held a different and, as he believed, a deeper meaning, a meaning closer to the truth.

"You're right about that look, but it's more a sense of relief. The one thing I know for certain when a jury brings back a verdict of not guilty is that my client won't have to pay the price for all the mistakes I've made."

He stared at the crystal glass, amber colored from the scotch, wondering why he still worried so much about what might happen if a verdict went the other way. Summer was saying something, but he was so caught up in his own thought that her voice seemed to come from far away.

"If you ever made a mistake in a trial, no one else would know it."

"A strange thing happened today. I was sitting there, waiting for the jury, remembering back to the first trial I had, all those years ago, and how nothing had really changed. It's still the same feeling, the sense of watching it all from the outside, as if none of it had anything to do with me."

"That isn't so odd; it's what happens every time I deliver another baby. Once it's over, once the umbilical cord is cut and the baby starts to cry and you know the child is healthy and safe, you've done your part and the rest of it is in the hands of God or nature."

Darnell took another drink. The scotch burned slow and warm against his throat. It gave him a sense of satisfaction, the illusion, if it is an illusion, that the present was all that mattered, that tomorrow and the day after that would somehow take care of themselves.

"I kept thinking that this might be my last trial, the same thought I've had at the end of every trial for a while now, and that if it was that would probably be the end of it, that there wouldn't be anything else; my life would be pretty much over. That would be all right, I think; I wouldn't want to hang around, become a doddering old man, a burden...."

"You'd never be...."

"Of course I would. We've talked about this before," said Darnell with an impatience he immediately regretted. "I'm sorry; I don't mean to be so damned irritable. But it's true. You know, what we've talked about. The work is what keeps me going; take that away and...."

The words echoed into the silence, and as they did so his gaze drifted away as if for some reason he could not any longer look her straight in the eye. Summer knew what it meant, she was sure of it. She did not say a thing, she just waited. It would not take long, it never did. He would turn to see if he could keep going, continue with the story she knew he had rehearsed: all the reasons why what he wanted to do, what he was going to do, was the only intelligent thing to do; what she would want him to do once she understood how important it was to his own well-being, even to his own survival. She started to laugh.

"What...? Why are you...?" he asked with a sharp turn of his head.

"You've decided to take another case. Why don't you just say so instead of mumbling about what might happen if you don't, how your life will be over, how that will be all right, how you don't want to be a doddering old man, how you...."

"I know I promised, and...." he said with the sheepish look of a thief caught red-handed. "But it isn't entirely my fault."

Summer sat back with her arms crossed, enjoying every minute of his latest attempt to explain why he had always meant to carry out the promise that they had both known was nothing more than a serviceable lie, the myth of a future they both understood would never exist. There would be no easy, peaceable descent into old age and death for either one of them.

"It isn't entirely your fault," she repeated in a teasing voice.

"No, it's not. The trial was just over. I was getting ready to leave when Judge Pierce – Evelyn Pierce; you've heard me talk about her – sent her clerk to get me. There's a case she wants me to take. She's never asked me to do anything like this before. It's a very unusual situation."

Darnell got up, went over to the counter and started to pour himself another drink. He looked at Summer with a question in his eyes.

"You think half a drink more would be all right?"

He stood there with a tender, irrepressible smile on his mouth, waiting, as it seemed, for her permission; willing, as it seemed, to follow her direction in all the small matters of daily life.

"God, you make me a little crazy at times," she said.

He brought the half-filled glass to the table. Leaning

forward on his elbows he folded his hands against his chin.

"I know, and I wish I didn't. I owe you everything. I would have been dead if you hadn't been there, that day in court when I had the heart attack...."

"The second heart attack," she reminded him. She ignored the fugitive tear at the corner of her eye and then, with an awkward laugh, wiped it away. "The second heart attack."

"And there hasn't been another. It's the work," he insisted.

She could have replied that the work had almost killed him, the tension of the trial, the erratic hours he kept, the almost total lack of sleep. He was right when he said that if she had not been there when he collapsed, if she had not been a doctor who knew that he had to get to a hospital and surgery right away, he would have died. But she also knew that while medical science had saved him, it was not science that was keeping him alive.

"Why don't we go to dinner and you can tell me all about this new case that has you so excited."

They went down the street to the quiet neighborhood restaurant where they had been going now for years. Their favorite table was somehow always available. There was a vague familiarity, a settled routine, a set of expectations, the way seasoned actors play a part they have played a thousand times before. Invariably, the waiter smiled, led them to their table, and watched with a kind of gentle benevolence as William Darnell, every inch the well-bred gentleman, carefully and with a conscious appreciation for the simple elegance of the act, pulled out Summer Blaine's chair. Then, when Darnell came round to the other side of the table, the waiter would start to reach for the chair and Darnell would tell him not to bother, he could manage.

"Tonight we have that red wine that you...."

"Yes, that will be fine."

And then, no matter how crowded the restaurant, the two of them were alone. Nearly everyone knew the famous William Darnell, and those who did not could tell simply by looking at him that he was someone of importance, but no one bothered them, no one came up to the table to introduce themselves, much less to ask for an autograph. Perhaps it was his age, perhaps he seemed too distant and remote, or perhaps it was the way all his attention stayed on the woman he was with, the woman with the lovely eyes and the graceful beauty that age, instead of diminishing, seemed only to have enhanced.

"Tell me about the case."

A sly grin started onto his small pear-shaped mouth.

"The new one, the one I haven't taken yet, or the one I just finished, the one where the woman who killed her husband is now free to spend all his money?"

"Is that what you argued to the jury? 'If she goes to prison all that money will be wasted'?" She paused. "How much money was there, anyway?"

"Enough to make divorce unattractive. It's strange. Tell a woman – or a man, for that matter – that she'll split ten thousand in a divorce and she won't think twice about it; tell her she'll split ten million she thinks of murder. Makes you start to think we were better off when marriages were all arranged and divorce was all but impossible."

Summer bent forward, her blue eyes clear and lucid in the candlelight.

"Are you telling me you think she was guilty?"

"I'm telling you it was one of the closest cases I've seen. It could have gone either way. The only reason it went the way it did was because she never told the truth in her life." Darnell held up the wine glass and, looking at it, narrowed his eyes. "That isn't the same as saying she's a liar."

Summer thought she understood.

"You mean she doesn't know the difference. She believes whatever she says and says whatever she has to say to get what she wants. Yes, I've known a few people like that, women and men both. They never lie about facts, things that can be proven one way or the other; but they've never known how to tell the truth about themselves, their feelings, their real intentions. Yes, I think I know what you mean."

Darnell was astonished, but then realized he should not be. It was not the first time she had put into words something he had felt but had not been able to express adequately even to himself.

"She doesn't think she did anything wrong." Pausing briefly, he reconsidered. "She blames him for what she did. He was the one who started it, made her life a living hell, and so the question of whether she could have just walked away, filed for divorce and put an end to what she suffered was for her no question at all. Why should he get away with what he had done? They used to build statues to people who had the courage to kill a tyrant; they didn't put them on trial for murder. What happens to a tyrant is always the tyrant's fault. Which reminds me," he asked, suppressing a grin, "have you ever read Mutiny on the Bounty?"

Summer grasped one connection and immediately guessed at another.

"The tyrant that deserves his fate, Captain Bligh and what happened to him. And that has something to do with this next case of yours, doesn't it, the one you can't wait to start?"

Darnell had the look of a frustrated conspirator whose perfect plan has just come unraveled.

"I'd never win a case if you were on the jury, would I? Yes, you're right, as usual. It has something to do with the case; maybe everything for all I know at this point. Not Bligh, but what happened later: Fletcher Christian and the rest of them, the mutineers who settled and, if I remember the story, died, most of them, on Pitcairn's Island. But you've read it?"

She had indeed, and not once, but several times, most recently a few months before.

"You were in a trial," she explained when he seemed confused that he had not remembered. She sipped on the wine, a look of teasing affection in her eyes. "And during a trial, William Darnell, I could be reading War and Peace out loud in Russian and you wouldn't notice."

"You don't read Russian."

"Are you sure?"

"But you read it, Mutiny on the Bounty? Read it again that recently?"

"And the other two as well."

"The other two?"

"It was a trilogy: Mutiny on the Bounty, Men against the Sea – that was about Bligh's voyage in that open boat, thousands of miles, the longest such voyage in history. An amazing story of seamanship; no one had ever done such a thing; no one but Bligh could have done it from what you're led to believe. He was greeted as a hero in England and…. Did you read it – the trilogy, I mean?"

Darnell shook his head. He was anxious for her to continue.

"But you read Mutiny on the Bounty? she asked.

"Yes, but a very long time ago. I think I did, anyway; I may have just seen the movie – one of the movies – and now think I did. But that doesn't matter. Tell me – there was a third novel?"

"Pitcairn's Island. What happened there, how things fell apart, how they ended up, many of them, killing each other."

A distant smile, a strange enigma, played on her mouth. She was about to say something when the waiter began to serve dinner. The conversation turned to other things, what she had done that week at the hospital, what they were going to do together during this, the first weekend in months that he did not have to prepare for another week in trial. It was only when they were walking home that Summer spoke again about what had happened on Pitcairn's Island.

The night was clear and cool, the air fresh and clean, the city shining like a rich man's dream, bridges made of gold and silver, the streets lit up like money. The shop windows were filled with fine clothing and finer jewels, things dug from mines deep inside the earth, things made in places with exotic names somewhere the other side of the sea, all of it brought here to catch the eye of those who never had to ask how much things cost and whether they could afford to buy. Summer stopped to gaze at a long blue dress draped on a manikin.

"It was all about a woman, or at least I think it was." She turned from the window and faced Darnell. "And then, afterward, it was all about women."

"What was...?"

"The mutiny. I don't think you read the book, or you read it when you were too young, when you were only interested in the adventure. The movie has it wrong. Bligh is this terrible tyrant who brutalizes his men. He's insane. All he cares about is getting these stupid plants – breadfruit – delivered safely. The men have no choice. Fletcher Christian has no choice. They'll all die; they'll all be killed by Bligh's cruelty, if Christian doesn't do something to save them."

She said this with the kind of concentrated intensity she often had when she was trying to describe a feeling or a belief that went against the grain of settled opinion. The phrase Captain Bligh may have become synonymous with the worst kind of oppression, but words, or what other people thought, could never stop her. It was one of the things Darnell had liked most about her, one of the reasons why he trusted her perhaps more than he had ever trusted anyone.

"But Christian doesn't think about mutiny until after they've been to Tahiti, until after he has met the girl, the chief's daughter. He doesn't think about mutiny until they've left Tahiti and he knows he won't see her again. He had put up with Bligh's insults, with his severity, for months before, but now, suddenly, it becomes intolerable, more than he can bear." Summer gave Darnell a knowing glance. She was certain she was right. "It's the girl. He can't admit that to himself; he's a British naval officer, sworn to his duty. But it's the girl. He seizes on something Bligh did and rouses the men to mutiny. They take over the ship and put Bligh and those who wish to go with him in the long boat – and nearly all of the officers choose to do so. In fact, there isn't room for everyone who would have gone with him, gone to an almost certain death in an open boat in the middle of the Pacific thousands of miles from civilization. And where does Fletcher Christian go after he has the ship? To Tahiti and the girl."

They started walking up the street, passing other restaurants where other couples sat across candlelit tables talking about their own lives and dreams, and not many of them, it is safe to say, much concerned with something read in a book or said about the past.

"You said it was about a woman, and then you said that later it was about women."

"They went to Tahiti, but they knew they could not stay there. The British navy was certain to come after them. The girl was in love with him, and he was in love with her, and she was going to go with him. But there were other men as well and while some of them found women to take with them, not all of them did. There were also a few native men who went along as well. Don't you see? This was the beginning of all the trouble. They sail off in the Bounty, a small group of people, more men then women, to start a new life in a place where no one, including the British navy, will ever find them. What did they think was going to happen? It's hard to know. They finally discover this speck of land, an island two miles long and only one mile across, burn the Bounty and like something out of Genesis begin a world of their own. Or try to. Because before long the men without women decide it isn't fair."

"And that led to jealousy, and jealousy led to murder," said Darnell, picking up the thread of the narrative. "Is that what happened?"

"Yes, but with a strange conclusion."

"A strange conclusion?"

"There was open warfare, and the men killed each other off until there was only one of them left. He was, according to the story, a decent man, filled with guilt over what they had done to Captain Bligh and the others that had been set adrift. He was the only man; all the rest were women. Some of the women had children, and those who didn't have them wanted them."

"And the one man...?"

"Fletcher Christian had given them what law they had, decided that instead of a captain's order on a ship, everyone should decide on everything together. In a way, that is what led to all the trouble, the belief that each man should have what every other man had. But when there was only that one last man, he did what he could to give them religion. He could barely read, but he had learned enough to teach himself more, and he had a bible. He did not see the use in teaching the children about hellfire and fear; he taught them only those verses that spoke about loving others more than you love yourself.

"And the strange and beautiful thing is that it seemed to work. At the end of the book, when a British vessel first comes to Pitcairn, the children, some of them grown to be young men and women, were said to have an intelligence and to move with a grace and charm that reminded those who saw them of what it must have been like when the world was young and the children had all been fathered by gods."

Grasping the handle of the front door, Darnell stared down at the sidewalk until she finished. When he looked up, he shook his head at the almost uncanny way it fit together, what had happened all that time ago out on an island no one had heard of, and now, on another island no one could find on a map.

"That's almost exactly what the judge, what Evelyn Pierce, said about this client of mine I haven't yet met. She said the only way she could think to describe him was that he looked like he was born to be a king, with the lithe body of an athlete and a mind of pure intelligence."

CHAPTER THREE

William Darnell pushed away from the counsel table, crossed his right leg over his left and began to swing his foot back and forth. Suddenly, and for no apparent reason a favorite line from Hemingway came to him, a line no one now remembered from a book no one any longer read. 'The great thing is to last and get your work done and see and hear and learn and understand.' There was nothing else now, Darnell understood, nothing but that – to see and hear and learn and understand. If he had not been certain of that before, the four months preparing for this trial – or trying to prepare because he still had more questions than answers – had convinced him that it was true. He had poured over documents, read things he had not read in years, studied things he had not studied before – done everything he could think of to make sense of what, the further he got into it, did not seem to make sense at all; or rather to make all the sense in the world if you could only manage to credit the possibility that nearly everything you had thought before might just have been wrong.

It had been difficult enough to do himself, but how was he going to persuade twelve members of a jury, ordinary men and women who had never had a reason to question the validity of their own beliefs, to see the world in a way that was not just different but in important respects the opposite of everything they had known. He would certainly get no help from the prosecutor. She was going to do everything in her power to convince the jury that the case should be judged as if the crime had been committed here at home instead of in a place none of them had ever heard of and none of them would ever see.

The bailiff drew himself up to his full height and, as the door at the side of the courtroom opened, announced that "Court is now in session, the Honorable Judge Evelyn Pierce presiding."

Her eyes fixed straight ahead, Evelyn Pierce walked with measured steps across the front of the courtroom to her place on the bench. Clasping her hands in front of her, she leaned forward.

"Let the record reflect that we are here in the matter of People v. Adam. Mr. William Darnell is here for the defense. Mr. Darnell, for purposes of the record, is it indeed the case that the defendant has only the one name – Adam? No other, second, name? Adam is not his first, or his last, name?"

Darnell rose slowly, but not because of his age. He had always done it this way, slow, unhurried, as if, whatever the question, whatever the situation, he would determine the pace at which things were done.

"That is correct, your Honor; though I should also point out that Adam is not his real name."

"Not his real name?"

"No, your Honor. Adam was the name given him by the people who found him on the island and brought him here."

"And they did that because they didn't know his name?"

"I assume so. They didn't speak his language, couldn't understand it, and so they gave him a name of their own."

"Adam. Interesting choice."

"I thought so, your Honor. As for his real name, if he has one, I'm sure I couldn't tell you either."

"I'm not sure I understand, Mr. Darnell. You're the attorney for the defense. Adam, as we're calling him, has been your client for some months and you don't know his real name? You have been able to communicate with him, haven't you? Forgive me, Mr. Darnell, I shouldn't have asked you that. The court knows you well enough to know that if you hadn't been able to communicate with the defendant you would have advised the court of that fact. But you just said that he was given the name Adam because those who discovered him on the island couldn't speak his language. He speaks English now, though, doesn't he? He spoke it in court before, when he appeared at his arraignment."

"His English is quite good; better than my own, I think," replied Darnell with a thoughtful and slightly whimsical look. "Far better, to tell the truth; he speaks it the way it should be spoken."

Judge Pierce wore a puzzled expression. "But he didn't speak it before? Well, never mind, that isn't any of the court's business. Just so long as he can follow the proceedings and assist in his own defense." She started to turn away. "But if he speaks such good English, why can't he tell you his name?"

"He has," said Darnell, staring off into the distance.

"Then why shouldn't we use that instead of Adam?"

"Because I can't tell you what it is. It is a sound I can't decipher. It seems to be all consonants. I couldn't even attempt to spell it."

Evelyn Pierce wondered if Darnell was playing with her, trying to draw attention, right at the beginning, to how different, how strange this trial was going to be. She lowered her head and gave him a warning glance.

"Your client supposedly speaks English as well or better than you do. Have him spell it."

"He can't."

"Can't spell?"

"Can't read or write, your Honor."

"Can't read or write?" she asked, astounded. "He learned English in a few short months – and he can't read or write?"

Her gaze moved from Darnell to Adam, sitting quietly at the counsel table. He was not anything like what she had first expected. Instead of a dark-eyed, brown-skinned native of some tropical island the young man was blonde with fair skin and, whether or not he could read and write, the most astonishingly intelligent blue eyes she had ever seen. They seemed, those eyes of his, to take in everything at once, to

grasp in an instant not just the physical objects they saw
but what each of them meant in all their various relations.
Watching him that first time when he was brought to court
for the arraignment, she had had the sense that nothing
confused him, that at the end of those few minutes he could
have explained better than any of the lawyers who had been
there what had just happened. He had seemed almost to
enjoy it, as though he were there to observe the way things
were done and that none of it had anything very much to do
with him. And now she was being told that this young man
with the brilliant eyes could neither read nor write.

"Can't read or write? You're saying he's illiterate?"

Darnell stroked his chin. His eyebrows shot straight
up and stayed there.

"Only in the most narrow sense." A grin cut across
his mouth. "The most literal sense, your Honor. My client
cannot read or write, but I can't think of anyone whom I
would be less inclined to call illiterate. I believe I'll leave it
at that, your Honor. For the time being, anyway," he added
with a sly, cryptic glance.

"Yes, very well," said Judge Pierce. With a sideways
gesture of her hand, she let Darnell know she had heard all
she needed. "Now, then, where were we? Yes, this is the
case of People v. Adam. Mr. William Darnell is the attorney
for the defense. Miss Hillary Clark is the attorney for the
prosecution."

Darnell glanced to his right, to the other counsel table,
the one closest to the jury box. There was a time when he
would have been afraid to look at Hillary Clark, afraid that
the look would become a stare, and that, seeing it, the jury
would think that he was not sufficiently interested in the
case. Even now she almost took his breath away. Tall and
angular, with dark, flashing eyes, aware of the effect she had
on men and despising them because of it, she was at once
both sensual and detached. She was the kind of woman that
any man would love to have and then, having her, learn to
hate. The thought of it made Darnell want to laugh.

Evelyn Pierce was talking now to the crowd of

prospective jurors that filled up the first few rows of the courtroom, explaining what was going to happen next. Twelve of them would be chosen at random. The lawyers would ask questions. When one was excused another one would be called to take his or her place in the jury box. Darnell kept looking at Hillary Clark, watching the way she concentrated on the jury questionnaires like a student cramming for a test, but a student, mind you, who did not have a doubt that she would pass with the highest grade in the class. It was part of the reason she could have such disdain for men who only noticed how she looked. They learned their failure soon enough, once she made them subject to that brittle smile that insisted she was light years ahead of them and that razor sharp tongue that seemed to prove it.

Darnell sighed. For just a moment, he wished he were younger, much younger, closer to her age, and he could teach her a lesson of his own. Logical, precise, and analytical, as well as arrogant and dismissive, Hillary Clark was the kind of woman who never read poetry and would stamp her foot with impatience at the first mention of anything as vague and meaningless as the mysteries of existence. Darnell did not like her; he did not like her one bit.

Slowly, one by one, twelve prospective jurors were called to the jury box. Judge Pierce tried to impress upon them the serious nature of their responsibilities.

"The defendant has been charged with the crimes of incest, rape and murder. He has entered a plea of not guilty to each of these charges. That means that you are to consider him innocent of all of them, unless and until the government has proven him guilty beyond a reasonable doubt. Let me be more exact. You are to consider him innocent no matter what the government proves and you are to consider him innocent when you enter the jury room to begin your deliberations. In other words, ladies and gentlemen, you are to consider him innocent until you have listened to all the witnesses, not just for the government but also for the defense; listened to the closing arguments of the attorneys for both sides; listened to the instructions I will give you on the law; and then listened carefully, each of you, to what each of the other jurors has to say during your discussions. Then, and only then, after you have weighed all the evidence, are you to decide whether the government has proven its case beyond that famous reasonable doubt you have so often heard mentioned."

Evelyn Pierce paused, making sure they understood what she had said. She bent forward, emphasizing the importance of what she was about to say.

"This is not a question of probabilities. It is not a question of whether you think the defendant is likely to have been guilty. This is a question of certainty. The jury instruction, which I will give you at the end of the trial, says that you may find the defendant guilty if, but only if, the case against him has been proven 'beyond a reasonable doubt and to a moral certainty'- a moral certainty, ladies and gentlemen, a moral certainty."

The words, heavy enough on their own, were given more weight by the deadly earnest in her eyes. She held them with her gaze, binding them by the sheer presence of her authority to do exactly what she told them.

"Ms. Clark, you may examine the first juror."

Darnell turned his chair so that instead of facing the judge he was looking directly at the jury box. The prosecution might be asking questions, but Darnell wanted everyone to know that he was interested in the answers. If years of practice had taught him nothing else, it was that everything that happened in a courtroom was important and that the smallest detail could make all the difference. It was the reason he always wore dark blue or gray pinstripe suits. The jury had to believe that he was someone they could trust, a man too respectable to tell them anything but the truth. He had always had an honest face and even as a young man had been able to stop a heated argument by the soothing quality of his voice. Moreover, anyone who looked at him, unless they were too caught up in themselves to notice, could see the wisdom in his eyes. Age, instead of diminishing, had only made the overall effect stronger and more prominent.

What reason would someone of his advanced years have to lie? What prosecutor would dare suggest that the venerable William Darnell would ever do anything but tell the truth? Instead of a disability, his age had become, as he well understood, a very great advantage.

"Could you repeat the question?" he suddenly half-shouted. "I'm afraid I'm not quite sure I heard you right."

Startled, Hillary Clark turned and looked at him, wondering if he was serious or was rather trying to throw her off balance.

"Would I...?"

"Repeat the question," said Darnell calmly.

"I was asking Mrs. Arnold whether as the mother of a daughter she thought she could serve as an impartial juror in a case involving rape and incest."

"Yes, thank you. I did hear it correctly." He waited until she turned back to the juror and started to ask her next question. "I heard it correctly, but I still don't understand it."

Hillary Clark spun around, glared at him and rose from her chair.

"Your Honor, I protest! This is voir dire. I'm entitled to ask my own questions in my own way without interruption by counsel."

Judge Pierce did not hesitate.

"She's right, Mr. Darnell. You're not to interrupt."

"I'm sorry, your Honor," said Darnell as he got to his feet. He looked from the bench to the jury box. "Sometimes my hearing isn't as good as it used to be and I wanted to make sure that I hadn't misunderstood the question Ms. Clark was asking. I'll try harder to follow what she says – difficult as that may sometimes be."

"That will do, Mr. Darnell. If you have difficulty hearing, advise the court instead of interrupting. Ms. Clark, please continue."

Darnell watched the way he had before, with complete attention, listening intently to every word. Or so it would have seemed to anyone, including those among that group of prospective jurors who let their own attention stray from

Hillary Clark to glance across at him. In fact, his mind was already racing ahead to the questions he was going to ask, questions that would serve a purpose far beyond the answers they might elicit.

Hillary Clark asked the usual, predictable questions, questions that, in one form or another, tried to discover any latent reluctance to punish, any potential resistance to the idea that everyone should be made to pay for the wrongs they commit or the injuries they inflict. Then she asked the question that distinguished this trial from all the others.

"And do you feel that way – that people should be held accountable for what they do – even if they happen to live in a place where the laws against things like rape and murder haven't been written out in some kind of legal code?"

Claudia Arnold hesitated. She was not certain how she should answer a question like that and said so.

"What I mean, Mrs. Arnold, is that there are certain things we know are wrong, things that are wrong in them-selves. In this country we drive on the right side of the road; in England they drive on the left. A choice has to be made and it doesn't matter what that choice is, so long as there is a rule everyone can follow. But no one would say that about murder, would they?"

Mrs. Arnold, a decent woman, had to agree: Murder was always wrong.

"And so the question, again, is whether even without a formal code, even without written laws, someone can commit murder and not have to face punishment for what they've done."

The question seemed to answer itself, but Darnell, when it was his turn, asked it again himself. He asked it, moreover, in a way much more extreme than the prosecution had dreamed of doing.

"I imagine we would both agree, Mrs. Arnold, that if a husband killed his wife, or a father killed his daughter, and then defended what he had done on the ground that the woman had been raped, he ought to be punished with at least life in prison if not the death penalty, and that whatever was done to him it would not be punishment enough. You would agree with that, wouldn't you?"

The poor woman was shocked to the depths of her soul. Speechless, she could only stare at Darnell, who now nodded emphatically.

"Yes, we agree, absolutely! That's exactly what should be done about it. He ought to be executed, boiled in oil - made to suffer all the torments of hell!"

A soft, sympathetic smile - barely discernible, but no less effective for that -drifted across Darnell's lips. His eyes moved down the line of jurors, down the first row, then back across the six faces in the second. He let them think about the awful thing he had just described and the just severity of what he had said should be done about it.

"But there are places in the world - countries in the Middle East, for example – where the family of a woman who has been raped has what they believe a moral, and a religious, obligation to have her killed. What we find barbaric – what we call murder – they think the only way to save their honor and win the grace of God."

Mrs. Arnold's eyes grew wider. There was no answer for this.

"And so the question I have, Mrs. Arnold, is whether you think you can put aside, for purposes of this trial, what you normally believe about what is and what is not murder – or for that matter, any crime – and follow instead whatever instructions Judge Pierce may give you about what the prosecution needs to prove to convict the defendant of murder or the other crimes with which he has been charged?"

Put that way, there was only one answer Mrs. Arnold could give. There was no reason to think that she understood the question in all its implications, no reason to believe that she had any very clear idea how much she was being asked to give up of her own common sense view of things, but she knew – everyone called to jury duty knew – that whatever else they did, they were supposed to do what the judge told them to do. Still, she had her doubts.

"Are you asking me whether in the situation you

describe I wouldn't think it murder?"

"No, Mrs. Arnold. I only used that as an example, an extreme example, of how the law in one place can be completely different than it is in another place. Sometimes," he added as if it were a commonplace observation, known to everyone who had ever thought about it, "the law in the same place can change and be completely different than what it was."

Voir dire started on a Monday morning and lasted all week. Everyone lied about what kind of juror they would be. They seldom did it consciously; to the contrary, they almost always thought they were telling the truth when they said they could base their verdict on the evidence and on nothing else. The lie was more insidious than that, a belief that though they had probably never acted that rationally before - pushed aside all their emotions and based a decision solely on the facts – they could do it now, and do it easily, because that was what they had been taught from childhood the members of a jury were supposed to do. He asked those questions about whether they could be fair - whether they would follow the instructions of the judge, whether they would return a verdict of not guilty if guilt had not been proved - not because he thought they would do this on their own, but to make them understand that the law applied as much to them as it did to the defendant. He wanted to bind them to a promise, a promise made in public, so that what-ever they believed privately, they would, despite themselves, do in the presence of each other what they thought they were supposed to do.

The questions that were most important, however, were the questions he asked about them, what they did, where they had lived, what they liked to do. Other lawyers hired jury consultants, psychologists with an expertise in averages, what most people of a given background could be expected to do. Darnell would have none of it. He made his own judgments based on what he learned about each indi-vidual, on the sense he got about them, whether they were someone he could outside a courtroom respect and trust and whether, inside a courtroom, they were likely to think that way of him.

Of the twelve people first summoned to the jury box, eight were excused and half of those called to take their places were found unacceptable as well. Each side, the prosecution and the defense, had a limited number of challenges they could use to get rid of jurors they did not want. Darnell waited until eleven jurors had been selected and Hillary Clark had just finished her examination of the twelfth before he raised the issue on which he believed everything might depend.

"I wonder, Miss Wilkins, if you have ever had occasion to read the Supreme Court opinion in the famous case of Roe v. Wade."

A short, round-faced woman in her late twenties, Sheila Wilkins was a college graduate who had listed on the jury questionnaire reading as her favorite hobby. She wore thick glasses and had a tendency to fidget with her hands when, as now, everyone was watching her. She seemed to relax a little when Darnell took over the questioning.

"I'm not asking your view on abortion, Miss Wilkins. That, of course, is none of my business. But assuming that, like most people, you haven't read the court's opinion, I only want to know whether you are aware that Roe v. Wade was the case that upheld what is sometimes called a woman's right to have an abortion. May I assume that you know that?"

"Yes, I know what Roe v. Wade was about," she said as she blinked several times. A smile started onto her lips and then fled behind an awkward mask.

"You're doing fine, Miss Wilkins. There's nothing to worry about," Darnell assured her with a warm, benevolent glance. "It's good to be a little nervous, all these people sitting here. I'm a little nervous, and I've spent most of my life in a courtroom."

He paused to let her see that he meant it, that there was nothing to be afraid of, that everyone felt nervous when they had to speak in front of others.

"The reason I asked you whether you had read that famous Supreme Court opinion was because – and I know this will strike you as strange – I want to get at something that will be decisive in whether you, or anyone, can see the defendant with an unbiased eye. In Roe v. Wade the Supreme Court cites as one of its authorities on the question of abortion the Greek philosopher Aristotle. What the court doesn't mention – what I suspect the court didn't know – is that in the same place where Aristotle says that abortion is morally permissible he also approves of the killing of a newborn infant – infanticide – where the child is born diseased or deformed, or even as a necessary means by which to limit population. I mention this because, again, what may seem to us barbarous and wrong may not be seen that way by others. I mention this because you will hear testimony in this trial that may offend you, testimony that may go against everything you believe. All I am asking at this point, Miss Wilkins, - all that I am asking everyone on this jury – is whether you honestly believe that you can suspend judgment, wait until you have heard all the evidence, wait until you have heard closing arguments and the judge's instructions before you even begin to make a final decision?"

He was looking at her as if they were the only two people in the room, giving her all the assurance he could in that calm, reasonable voice of his that all he wanted was a promise that she would at least try to do the right thing. When Sheila Wilkins agreed that she would, that she would reserve judgment until the very end, she said it as if the keeping of that promise had now become a point of personal pride. There was a reason William Darnell almost never lost.

He was not finished. All through jury selection, without anyone becoming quite conscious that he was doing it, Darnell had challenged the everyday assumptions, the supposedly unshakable standards, of civilized behavior. He had done it easily, with the relaxed authority of someone who studies history, not because he wants to condemn what happened in the past, but because he wants to learn from it. Whether reminding the first juror about the way rape and murder were seen in two different parts of the world, or telling the last juror that even infanticide had once been considered something other than a crime, he gave the appearance of someone who was only searching for the truth of things. Because of that, he could now, at the end of his questioning, make a remark that left little doubt that this was to be a trial like no other.

"I should tell you in advance," he said to the no longer nervous Sheila Wilkins, "that you will hear things in this case that I dare say have never been said in an American court of law. In all the years I have been a lawyer, this is the strangest case I have ever seen."

CHAPTER FOUR

William Darnell looked around the shuttered confines of his downtown office. His gaze lingered at the shelves filled with the voluminous reports of cases decided by the appellate courts, the cases that had settled what the law was supposed to mean, cases that had sometimes decided that the earlier decisions had been wrong and that what had once been settled law now meant something entirely different. He glanced at a large rectangular framed photograph of his law school class, all the men in suits and ties, the only two women dressed the way school teachers and librarians dressed in those days. The photograph had been taken seven years after he had left the service at the end of the war. He had spent four years as an undergraduate and then three years studying law across the bay in Berkeley, at Cal.

Like the other photographs that hung in the few places the shelves did not cover, it had become a part of the background, something he seldom noticed while he hunched over his oversize mahogany desk, writing a brief or pouring over a case file as he got ready for a trial. Lately, however, he found that he was gazing at it more and more often: the captured memory of all his early expectations. He thought he could still see in his eyes, recorded forever on a photographer's film, the youthful and fervent belief that no one he defended would ever be convicted of something they had not done. Had anyone ever been more innocent than that, to think that only the guilty were sent to death or prison after a trial by a jury of their peers? He had been lucky, he told himself, the luck of fools, that he had lost so few times in his career and that there had been only that one occasion when he had been certain that the jury had got it wrong. Somewhere, at the bottom of a desk drawer he always kept locked, he kept the file, now yellow with age, of the murder case he lost and the innocent man who had now been more than forty years in prison.

"He was almost your age," he said without meaning to.

Adam looked back from the window where he was watching the traffic on the street below.

"My age?"

"Sorry, never mind. I was thinking about something else, a case I had a long time ago. Someone I tried to defend was convicted of a crime he did not commit. He was about your age - intelligent, too; extremely so, in fact – a gifted musician, in addition to everything else. I don't remember half the people I've represented, but I've never forgotten him. But enough of that, tell me what you thought about today, - what you think about the things that go on in a courtroom."

Adam took a last look out the window and then came over to the chair in front of Darnell's desk.

"I wouldn't have imagined there could be so much noise."

"Really? I thought things were fairly orderly."

"I didn't mean in the courtroom; I mean out here, in the city, all these machines." He smiled self-consciously as he thought about the words. "Cars and buses, and street cars – I mean trolley cars, yes? It's no wonder everyone seems always in such a hurry. They're trying to get away from it." A look of puzzlement entered his eyes. "But then, when they do get away from the streets, they go inside and turn on noises of their own – those pictures that flicker on a screen, saying things that, as near as I can tell, make no sense."

"Television," said Darnell. "I hadn't quite thought of it like that, but I suppose you're right. Most of it doesn't make sense, just a lot of noise. But are things really that quiet where you come from?"

Adam laughed. "Compared to this, what isn't?"

"I'd suggest you visit New York when this is over, but I don't think you'd much like it. But really," he went on, leaning back in his chair, "tell me what it's like on this island where you live."

"Quieter than this."

Darnell picked up a pencil and tapped it on the desk. It made a hollow echo in what he had always thought the silence of the room, but which now, as he listened, seemed a restless hum, the sound of the city just outside.

"We've known each other for several months now, and yet whenever I ask you to tell me something about the place you lived, the place where you were born, you never give a direct answer."

Darnell bounced the eraser end hard against the desk and caught the pencil in mid-air. The fact that he could still do it, move that quickly, pleased him immensely. Bent forward on one elbow, he gestured toward his law school class photograph.

"I had to go to law school three years to learn how to be as evasive as that. You're on trial for your life - don't you think it's time you started answering my questions? Don't you think it's time you told me the truth?"

"I haven't lied to you – or to anyone – Mr. Darnell. On my honor, I haven't."

"Is there a reason you won't tell me anything about the island, anything about the place you're from?"

"Yes," said Adam with a candid glance. "It's not allowed."

"Not allowed? Not allowed by whom?"

The question seemed to take Adam by surprise, as if the mere statement that something was not to be done was all the answer necessary.

"We're not allowed," he repeated. "We have no dealings with strangers, with those that might come from other places. It's forbidden."

"If I don't understand more about where you're from, about the way you live, you may never get back there. You may never see that island again. You understand that, don't you, that this could happen?"

A strange look passed over Adam's eyes, a look that suggested a deeper meaning in Darnell's question than Darnell could have known.

"I'm not going back – I can't go back – whatever

happens here."

He said this with an air of indifference that, as Darnell grasped immediately, was not because Adam did not care about going home, but because he knew he could not, and, knowing that, accepting that, he saw no point in dwelling on what he could not change. There was a kind of frightening simplicity about the way Adam seemed to look at the world, a strange resignation in the face of whatever might happen. Darnell had the feeling that if Adam had been told that he was going to die the next morning it would not disturb his sleep. And yet, at the same time, if he had been told that he was about to be attacked by a dozen or more armed men, he would have looked forward to the fight.

"Why?" asked Darnell. "What you did – was it considered a crime there as well?"

Adam's eyes, usually so curious and alive, had a haunted look, a semblance of something that, though it was not guilt, was close to it.

"Was it a crime?" Darnell repeated. "Would you have been punished for it if you'd been caught?"

"Caught?" he asked with a surprised, almost scornful glance. "If I had been...?" He realized that he had gone too far, said something he had no right to say. "I'm sorry, Mr. Darnell. You couldn't have known. Caught, you ask. That suggests that what happened was secret, that no one knew; but everyone knew, Mr. Darnell. That's the reason I can't go back. The punishment I received was life in exile."

None of it made sense. Darnell threw up his hands.

"I don't understand any of this. How could you have been sent into exile? Where could you have gone? And for what? You were found on the island, living with several hundred others. The crimes you say you committed happened only after that. They saw what you had done, what you had done with that child. That's the reason you're here. But you're talking about something different, something that must have happened before that. What was it? What is it you think you did?"

Darnell knew that Adam would not tell him. He

would not talk about anything that had happened on the island where he had been born and raised, the island he never would not have left if he had not been forcibly removed, taken prisoner and sent to America to be tried for his crimes. But even this did not make sense.

"If you were punished, as you put it; made to spend the rest of your life in exile, wouldn't that mean that you no longer have a loyalty to the country, the place, that has rejected you, turned you out, told you that were not to be a part of them anymore?" Darnell twisted his head to the side, searching in Adam's expression for something that might help him understand what made Adam think the way he did. "Then why won't you tell me what I need to know if I'm going to have any chance to save you? The only defense we have is that these crimes you're accused of weren't crimes at all, that what you did wasn't prohibited by the laws – the customs, if you will – of the place you lived."

Adam's eyes were so filled with sympathy as to be almost insulting. He seemed actually to feel sorry for Darnell and his inability to understand. It was all Darnell could do not to lash out, the way he would have with a normal client, an American who could appreciate how much he had to lose if he did not answer fully every question his lawyer asked. Darnell got up and walked over to the window, watching the way Adam had earlier the movement on the street below. What would it be like, he wondered, to see all this with Adam's eyes; see it, as it were, not like someone who simply had not stood at this window before, but like someone who had never seen a paved street or a car before, never known electricity, never entered a well-lit room, never known the speed and efficiency of modern life? Never known, a voice deep inside him added, the ease with which we rid ourselves of obligations, or the absence of belief in anything more important than ourselves.

"Do all your trials take as much time as this one?"

Darnell turned around.

"But we've only just started. Why would you...? Of course, I keep forgetting. This is the only trial you've ever seen, and....And I don't imagine you have trials were you're from and –"

"Why do they take all this trouble asking questions of the people who are going to serve on the jury? And why do you have a jury in the first place? Wouldn't it be better to have one of your wisest citizens, like this woman, the judge, Evelyn Pierce, be both judge and jury? A trial is a simple thing, isn't it? The one accused tells everyone what they did."

Darnell was never quite certain when Adam asked him a question whether he was more interested in the answer or in the way that Darnell would sometimes have to struggle to explain something that, because he had always taken it for granted, he had not really thought about.

"For a great many people, telling the truth would be the same as pleading guilty. When you're charged with a crime here, you aren't required to testify. As you must have heard the judge tell the jury, the –"

"'The defendant has been charged with the crimes of incest, rape and murder. He has entered a plea of not guilty to each of these charges. That means that you are to consider him innocent of everything, unless and until the government has proven him guilty beyond a reasonable doubt.'"

Darnell stared in astonishment as Adam went on, repeating word for word Evelyn Pierce's warning instruction to the jury.

"'...then, and only then, after you have weighed all the evidence, are you to decide whether the government has proven its case beyond that famous reasonable doubt you have heard mentioned so often.'"

Adam's eyes seemed to take on another glow, filled with some light of their own. He sat straight, balanced on the edge of the chair as if he did not need the chair at all, but could have stayed in that position, or any position, for as long as he wished and not felt the least bit tired or cramped because of it.

"I understand, at least I think I understand, the reason

for this insistence that an accusation isn't the same thing as proof; I understand why you have a trial. It isn't so clear why you seem to have turned it into a game."

Darnell was still staring at him, trying to take in the prodigious act of memory he had just witnessed.

"A game you say?" His narrow chest rumbled with laughter. He nodded twice emphatically. "Yes, I suppose you could call it that – two combatants, two sides, each of them trying to get a jury to see things their way."

He moved quickly to his desk and dropped into his comfortable well-used chair. Narrowing his eyes, he tapped his fingers together and then, quite abruptly, stopped.

"That's what I was trying to do – get the jury to see things my way – when I asked all those questions during jury selection. Do you remember – I can't recall exactly what I said, but the first thing I said to that first juror -?"

"'I imagine we would both agree, Mrs. Arnold, that if a husband killed his wife, or a father killed his daughter, and then defended his action on the ground that the woman had been raped, he ought to be punished at least with life in prison if not the death penalty….'"

Adam paused. Darnell thought it was because he was not quite certain what had been said next, but he saw the look of confidence in Adam's eyes and knew that was not true. Then he remembered that this was the same place that he had paused himself, and paused for just that same split second.

"'…and that whatever was done to him it wouldn't be punishment enough.'"

Darnell showed no expression, did nothing to suggest that what Adam had done was in any way extraordinary.

"Yes, I believe that's what I said. I have to get them to think that there might be other standards, other laws, than our own. I have to make them believe that it wouldn't be fair to subject you to rules you had no way of knowing."

Pursing his lips, he looked away. For a few brief moments he again tapped his fingers together. A thin smile like a shared secret stole across his aging, parchment colored lips. "Which is why I made that remark – I don't quite remember all of it – about Aristotle. Perhaps you remember…."

Eager to help, Adam bent forward.

"The Supreme Court case: Roe v. Wade? You said: 'In Roe v. Wade the Supreme Court cites as one of its authorities on the question of abortion the Greek philosopher Aristotle. What the Court doesn't mention – what I suspect the Court did not know – is that in the same place Aristotle says that abortion is morally permissible he also approves of the killing of a new-born infant – infanticide – where the child is born diseased or deformed, or even as a necessary means by which to limit population.'"

Darnell nodded, again as if there had been nothing unusual in what the young man had done. He pointed to a shelf behind where Adam was sitting.

"Would you be so kind? Up there, on the top shelf – could you reach it - the first one on the left?"

Adam got the volume, an old leather-bound edition of Blackstone's Commentaries on the Laws of England. There was a thick layer of dust on the cover.

"I don't think I've looked at this since I moved in here," Darnell remarked as he opened it carefully in the middle. "This is what lawyers used to read before there were law schools." His eye moved back to the rough-cut page. "Here is something you might find interesting."

He began to read a long passage from Blackstone's discussion of trial by jury. Near the end of the page, still speaking the words, he glanced at Adam, listening with an attention so complete you might have thought he had been hypnotized. He was sitting perfectly still, no movement of any kind. His lips were slightly parted, his eyes open and unblinking. He stared at Darnell, listening as much by what he saw, the steady movement of the reader's mouth, as by the sounds of what he heard. Darnell turned the page and went on.

"That was interesting, didn't you think? – How the jury system started and what it was meant to do."

He closed the book and held it on his lap. His gaze moved without his conscious intention to that photograph of his law school class. How hard they had studied, how much work there had been, the constant effort each day to remember half the things they had been taught. He shut his eyes and listened in the silence to the dim echo of voices from his own, distant past. All of his former classmates, most of them veterans of the war, had been intelligent, motivated and hard-working; some of them had gone on to highly distinguished careers. But no one with whom he had gone to law school, no one he had ever met, could have done what Adam did.

"Remind me, Adam. Help an old man remember what he just read. Repeat it, word for word, just the way I read it – if you would."

And Adam did. He repeated all of it, and not just the words; he repeated it the way Darnell had read it, with each change of intonation. It was like listening to that rare musician who has perfect pitch, except that instead of music, it was grammar. Darnell studied him intently.

"You can do this, but you never learned to read or write?"

"If you write things down, make those marks – letters, you call them – then what you've learned you have to learn again."

"I don't understand. I write things down so I won't forget them." He pointed toward the book-lined shelves. "No one could remember everything that is in them, and even if there were someone who could, there has to be a record that everyone can consult, a way to keep track of everything that has happened."

"That's what I mean: whatever you write down you have to learn again. You hear something, someone tells you something, you write it down – which you couldn't do if you didn't remember it; but then, because you have it down in writing, you forget what it was, and then, when you want to remember it, you can't."

"But we have the writing -"

"Which you read to learn again what you've forgotten. But, you must forgive me, I know nothing, though I'm starting to learn, about the way you live in this – what is the phrase I hear so often – 'modern world' of yours. There are so many things going on all at once, so many voices, so much noise - perhaps you have to make those marks, write things down, to decide what is worth keeping and what should be thrown away. Still, it seems to me that what I said before is true: that what you've learned doesn't belong to you - it hasn't been made your own possession - unless you can remember it. That's one of the reasons, though not the only one," he added with a glance cryptic and full of meaning, "that nothing worth remembering is ever written down."

Darnell seized on it.

"You mean, where you're from? So some things are written down, some people do know how to read and write?"

Adam looked away.

"Yes, some things; and yes, a few."

"But everything you were taught – whatever that might have been – all of it was told to you, things you heard that you then had to memorize?"

"Yes, of course. How else should you do it? We were taught to run by running, taught to swim by swimming; we were taught to learn by listening."

"Listening; yes, I understand." Darnell sank back in the chair and shoved his hands into his jacket pockets. He fixed his gaze on a point at the far side of the room, now buried in shadows in the late afternoon. "And that's the way you were able to pick up English – by listening to what you heard?"

"When they first came; not so much when they tried to talk to us, but when they talked among themselves."

Darnell was not sure he understood, but he did not doubt that this was the way Adam had done it. The phrase 'perfect pitch' kept going round in his brain. He imagined that Adam could imitate anything he heard. No, that was wrong, he told himself; it was more than imitation. Adam did not just hear a sound, he could get inside it and, in some way Darnell knew he could never fully grasp, make it into something that belonged to him. A lot of people could imitate the sound a particular bird was known to make; he could imagine Adam doing that but with the difference that when he did it he would know exactly what a bird like that would feel.

"So that's how you learned the use of words?"

There was something disconcerting in the way that, despite the great disparity in their age, Adam could seem not just his equal, but at times something more than that. It was more than the sympathy that was often in his eyes, more than the simple, unassuming way he could his recite whole paragraphs from a courtroom dialogue Darnell, who prided himself on his own ability to recall things said in court, had all but forgotten; it was the uncanny feeling that this astonishing young man had lived before, that he had been born with a soul that had been in being through all the ages, that in some strange sense Adam had been here since the beginning. It lasted only a few brief seconds, but when he found himself under the watchful scrutiny of Adam's eyes the feeling was so certain, so profound, that he could not doubt that it was true. But then, moments later, when he broke away from Adam's gaze, the spell was broken, though the memory of it never quite disappeared. It lingered in his mind, the certainty become a question, a different kind of doubt, a kind of wonder whether what he had always believed about the rationality of the world might be incorrect.

"So that's how you learned the use of words?' he heard himself repeating.

"Isn't that the way that every child learns, and not from books? But, yes, that's how I learned to speak English with the English-speaking people; the same way I learned numbers and their meaning." Adam remembered something that made him laugh. "That goes too far. I learned mathematics, and geometry – I could remember what I was taught – but I can't say I ever quite understood the secret of irrational numbers and what their meaning meant."

"What their meaning meant?" Darnell's voice faltered

and became faint. He was just about to grasp what Adam meant when it slipped away, taunting him, as it were, with his inability to see what he thought must be right in front of him. "To look through a glass darkly," he mumbled to himself.

"That's always the difficulty, isn't it?' asked Adam, who had heard. "To get beyond the obvious to what you sense is there."

"Get beyond the obvious to what you….And you don't read or write?" Darnell suddenly realized the time. "We'd better go. Mrs. Hammersmith will be here and she is not a woman who likes to wait."

Darnell got to his feet, but Adam did not move.

"What is it? They're treating you all right, aren't they – Mrs. Hammersmith and her husband? I've known them both for years. I'm sure there can't be anything wrong. But, well – what is it?"

"No, there's nothing wrong. They've done everything they could for me, shown me everything there is to see. No, it isn't that." His eyes drew in on themselves as he sat, hunched forward, a sudden look of despair and loneliness on his face. "It's the girl," he said presently, his voice not quite as strong and confident. "It's been months now, and no word about the girl. I need to see her, to know that she's safe."

Darnell put his hand on Adam's shoulder.

"We've talked about this before. Nothing has changed; there's still nothing I can do. The only way I could keep you from being locked up in jail the months we waited for trial was on condition that you would have no contact of any sort with her. She's the victim, the one they say you raped. I'm sorry, but the only time you're going to see her before all this is over is when they bring her into court, a witness for the prosecution."

CHAPTER FIVE

Whatever their point of view, everyone seemed to agree that what was about to unfold in a San Francisco courtroom was a strange case, perhaps the strangest case anyone had ever seen or heard about, stranger than any made-up story, stranger than any lie. No one could have invented what had happened; no one would have had either the imagination or the nerve to try. Incest, rape and murder, than which nothing could be worse, if you believed the prosecution; a tragedy of tremendous proportions, a clash of civilizations, a crime that was not a crime at all and a trial that should never have taken place, if you believed the defense.

Hillary Clark did not have the slightest doubt she was right. What had happened was, as she put it to the jury in her opening statement, "monstrous, as clear a violation of human rights as it is possible to imagine, acts of violence without any conceivable justification."

William Darnell watched with grudging admiration as she told the jury what the prosecution was going to prove. She was good, better even than he had been led to expect, and that was good enough. Wearing a blue silk dress, her golden brown hair pinned at the top, she stood in front of the jury box talking in a smooth, quiet voice. There was none of the false emotion, none of the false bravado, with which less experienced prosecutors try to condemn the accused before the first witness has even been called to testify. Hillary Clark was much too certain of herself to need any courtroom theatrics.

Darnell turned his chair toward the jury, just as he had during voir dire, to make them think he was paying strict attention to everything the prosecutor did. He was fascinated by the way Hillary Clark could be so much different in a courtroom than she was in real life. Most of those who

51

had ever had to work with her did not like her. The lawyers who had to try cases against her, cases they almost always lost, positively loathed her. Judges who thought themselves entitled to absolute respect did not particularly appreciate how often she appeared to contradict them. Jurors on the other hand – those twelve strangers who would only see her in open court – liked the way she talked to them. She did not condescend to them the way she did to judges who were not quite up on the law; she did not make cutting remarks the way she did about lawyers who had the misfortune to stumble over a word or forget for a moment the next question they wanted to ask. In front of a jury she was a different person altogether. The six men and six women that sat in the jury box liked everything about her, the pleasant manner, the easy affability, the way she explained in clear, understandable language everything the prosecution was going to do.

Twice-divorced and not yet forty, Hillary Clark seldom lost a case and thought it someone else's fault on those rare occasions when she did. But if you had asked that jury to make a guess at who and what she was, there would not have been one among them who would not have said that she was probably happily married with two or three wonderful children and more friends than she could count. They were watching her now, listening to everything she said, more than willing to believe that every word was true. She took her time, describing exactly what the defendant, "the one known as Adam," had done and how the prosecution was going to prove it.

Darnell was intrigued by the effect she had. It was really quite remarkable. Hillary Clark was a stunningly beautiful woman, and beautiful women were often resented and usually disliked by those who did not know them. It was a form of jealousy, of suspicion, a belief that there had to be a flaw, if not an arrogance born of vanity, a lack of character or intelligence. In a single sentence, a few words of no consequence, she had disabused them of any thought that she was different from the unassuming, completely average, person they thought everyone should be.

They liked her. That was a fact that Darnell would have to deal with. They liked the slow and meticulous way she outlined in advance what each witness for the prosecution would say and how, "like the links in a chain," it would all tie together and prove beyond that famous reasonable doubt every element in the case against the defendant. But, as Darnell had begun to grasp, there was something else that they liked as well: the marvelous clarity of her mind, the logical precision with which she constructed what she made to seem an iron-clad case for the prosecution.

Darnell leaned back, his eyes half-closed. With a brooding look on his face, he tapped his fingers against each other, thinking about what it meant. Logic, precision, the seeming certainty of every well-structured sentence that came out of her mouth, as if the world was ruled by reason and reason itself did not require an act of faith. She could start from a premise and march like a Roman general to the only possible conclusion, but the premise – that she did not think about, that she did not know; although, like nearly all of us, she thought she knew it as well, or better, than she knew anything. The premise – whatever one she had seized upon – was to her mind the only principle any sane person could have. Darnell's eyes opened wide. He bent forward, watching her now with a different level of interest. That certainty, that dependence on the logic of her position, precisely what she thought her greatest strength, was in fact her greatest weakness.

Still, listening as she came to the end of her hour long presentation, he knew that his chances of turning that weakness to his own advantage were remote at best. Her summary of the case that the prosecution was about to prove was nothing short of devastating.

"The defendant is charged with incest, rape and murder. But it's worse than that, worse because taken all together, what he did is more than the sum of his crimes," said Hillary Clark as she turned and pointed at Adam. "Incest has always been one of the worst things anyone could do. It destroys the family, breaks the sacred bond that is supposed to exist between parents and children and among the children themselves. It destroys all trust. Rape takes away – destroys – what it only belongs to a woman to give and, as in this case, all the innocence of a girl. And murder – that can never be excused, but if there are any murders worse than others, it has to be the murder of a child. The defendant did all these things, and did them in a way that is almost beyond belief. He committed incest with his own sister, incest when he raped her, a girl not yet fifteen years of age; and then, in this chronicle of horrors, when he discovered that she was pregnant with his child, took the baby, only hours old, and in an act of infanticide almost without precedent, killed it, strangled it in cold blood."

Darnell had in his time witnessed the reaction of a good many juries to a prosecutor's indictment of the crimes of the defendant, crimes the prosecutor promises to prove, but he could not remember anything quite like this. They were looking at Adam, all twelve of the jurors, with something close to hatred in their eyes and something close to fear.

The silence in the courtroom when Hillary Clark returned to her chair at the counsel table was heavy and oppressive, burdened with a judgment that had already been made. Adam, the strange creature sitting there undisturbed, his head, unaccountably, still held high, was guilty, as guilty as anyone had ever been.

Whatever the jury might think, whatever the feeling of the crowd that had watched, transfixed, the closing moments of the prosecution's opening statement, Evelyn Pierce had not changed expression. Crying, screaming, cries for mercy, cries for revenge – she had seen it all during her long years on the bench and if she had ever been moved by anything no one had ever known it. She looked at Darnell with the polite interest with which she generally invited an attorney to take his turn.

"Mr. Darnell, does the defense wish to make an opening statement at this time?"

Darnell stood facing the bench. Then he turned and

looked straight at the jury. His eyes were full of such confidence that they had to wonder what he knew. What was he was going to tell them that would make them change their minds or at least begin to doubt the validity of what they had just heard? With a look of grim defiance on his mouth, he nodded slowly twice, drawing their attention away from the prosecution and back to the defense, dominating the silence in a way that made them remember that the trial, far from ending, had only just begun.

"Mr. Darnell...?"

"Yes, your Honor. With the court's permission, the defense would like to reserve its opening statement until the prosecution has finished its case and we can start to put on ours."

That night at dinner he tried to explain to Summer Blaine that there had not been any choice. They were in a restaurant down a brick lined alleyway two blocks from his office. Full of dark tables and white tablecloths, it was frequented by lawyers, bankers and other members of the commercial class whose work often kept them downtown at night. Everything about the place had the understated tone of people who were used to money and all its advantages. Tourists and other idle pleasure seekers did not know of its existence.

"There was nothing I could do," said Darnell. He broke a piece off a roll and buttered it. "Nothing." He took a bite and with a white linen napkin wiped the crumbs from his lips. "Not a single, blessed thing." He lapsed into a long silence, marveling at what he had witnessed. "She's good," he said finally. "And that's a serious understatement."

"But you're the best, William Darnell," replied Summer, smiling her encouragement. "There's no one better."

He did not hear her. He was listening to the voice of Hillary Clark charm the jury. With his elbow on the arm of the chair, he placed his thumb under his chin and slid two fingers along the side of his face. His head began to bob back and forth, keeping time to the impatience of his mind.

In a gesture of abject helplessness, he flung his hand off to the side.

"If she's that good at closing, I'm finished. There won't be anything I can do to save this boy. You should have seen her. No man could have done what she did. She made them think she was just like them, a next door neighbor, someone who might watch their kids and they'd watch hers. They didn't think that at first, when we first started voir dire. She looks distant, unapproachable, a woman too good-looking to feel anything but her own superiority. But the moment she started talking to them in that calm, quiet voice; the moment they realized – or thought they realized, because as far as I'm concerned it's all an act – that it had never occurred to her to think they were anything but equals, they couldn't get enough of her. It was like watching people meet their favorite movie star only to discover that all this time the movie star had just been waiting to meet them! I'm beginning to believe that people will believe anything."

From the moment he met Summer outside the restaurant he had been full of himself and the trial. He realized that now and was embarrassed.

"Sorry," he said with a chastened grin that barely broke the line of his mouth. "You come all the way to the city to keep me company and all I do is talk about what I've been doing."

Summer Blaine may have lost some of the beauty of her youth, but she still had the most wonderful eyes of any woman Darnell had ever known, filled with light and laughter and a sympathy that never went away, eyes that, whatever might have happened, always made him feel better. It was as if, in her presence, nothing could ever really go wrong. The day he had suffered a massive heart attack in court, she had been there, kneeling over him, and the last thought he had had before he woke up hours later in a hospital room was that even at the moment of his death he could find comfort in her eyes.

"Tell me what your week has been like."

Summer threw back her head and laughed. She put

down the wine glass before she had taken a drink.

"It's only Monday, Bill; the week has barely started." Reaching across the table she placed her hand on his. "This isn't Friday. I wasn't here this weekend, and you didn't come to Napa."

He shook his head at his own confusion and started to stammer a reply.

"Yes, I know; but you know how I am – the days just before a trial. I can't do anything, think about anything; I'm perfectly useless. I would have been terrible to be around; I would have -'

"You needed to be alone," she said matter-of-factly. "I know that. But I did miss you – a little," she added with a coy glance.

"And I missed you, too."

"Liar!" she cried softly in a voice full of laughter. "Give that 'eyes wide open, I'll never tell you anything but the truth' look to a jury, if you like; but I wouldn't try it on me. Don't you think that by now I've learned all your lawyer's tricks, the way you manage somehow to convince even yourself that what you say must be the truth, simply because you say it?"

Darnell sat straight up, enlivened by the challenge.

"It's the absolute truth that I missed you and there's no lawyer's trick in that. I miss you every day you're not around." He raised his round chin a bare fraction of an inch, a comic look of promised retribution in his larcenous gray eyes. "Which only proves the sacrifice I made when, know-ing how unbearable I can be the last few days before a trial starts, that I decided I had to spare you all that."

Summer's fine drawn mouth quivered with radiant pleasure at the sheer duplicity of what she was quick to point out was the biggest lie anyone had ever told her.

"But it's true, you know; I am a bear to be around," said Darnell with a look of injured innocence. "I wouldn't subject you to that for anything. And, you might remember, I called, not just once, but several times each day."

Listening to himself say it out loud, he remembered

how often, as he was trying to make sense out of what had become an impossible case, he had wished she were there. She was the one person whose judgment he fully trusted, and the only person he always liked to be around. Remembering that, he felt awkward, as if he really had been discovered in a lie, or rather, had discovered within himself a failure to tell the truth. He had loved his wife all the years he was married to her, loved her until the day she died, loved her even longer than that; but he was not sure that he had ever loved her quite as much as he now loved, and needed, Summer Blaine.

"I don't know what would have happened," he told her quite honestly, "if we'd met when we were younger and were both still single. All I know is that now, for as many years as I have left, I want to spend all my time with you – including, whether you believe it not, even the weekend before a trial."

They exchanged a glance that said everything. Summer picked up her menu and ordered dinner.

"You started to tell me that you didn't have a choice; but you never told me what you meant," said Summer as they lingered over coffee. "What didn't you have a choice about?"

"I didn't have any choice but to reserve my opening. I didn't like doing that. The jury is going to listen to each witness for the prosecution and think to themselves that it's exactly what Hillary Clark said they were going to hear. That's the only point of reference they'll have. They won't have in the back of their minds the kind of questions I would have tried to raise, the reason they ought to view with suspicion, or at least some reservation, what they're told. But there wasn't anything else I could do. After she finished with them, they would have looked at me as if I were a criminal myself if I had suggested that Hillary Clark might in some important respect be wrong."

"Yes, but you still have your chance, after she's through and it's your turn to put on a case."

Darnell sank lower in his chair.

"If I have a case to put on," he grumbled. "The only

case I had was that the law – our law – shouldn't apply;
that it was unreasonable and unfair to subject someone to
punishment for what, where he lived, might not have been
a crime at all. It's a little hard to argue that, however, when
we're dealing with incest, rape and murder." Darnell sat
up, looked around the restaurant and then leaned forward.
"At first I thought I saw a way. These people – there can't
have been many, though how many no one seems to know –
living together on an island through God knows how many
generations? How could incest be avoided? But you won't
hear Hillary Clark making any concessions to that possibility. She made it sound like the boy was…."

"But what is he, really?" asked Summer, searching his
eyes. "Uneducated, illiterate, a boy in a man's body."

"Illiterate? Only in the most narrow sense. That's
what I tried to tell Judge Pierce when she wondered how he
could speak English so well if he couldn't read or write. But
now I'm not so sure that to call him illiterate in any sense
doesn't take all the meaning out of language. After all, why
should he read or write? It would only slow him down."

The thought of Adam and what he was capable of
made Darnell forget the trial and his own fatigue. A distant
smile came unknowing to his face.

"He came with me, to my office, the end of the day on
Friday, after we had finished voir dire. I tried again to get
him to talk about the island, how they lived, whether what
he did was considered right or wrong, and the damn thing
is that after all these months he still won't tell me anything.
I might as well ask a priest what was said in the confes-
sional as ask him anything. His only answer is that it isn't
permitted, it isn't allowed. He's on trial for his life and he
won't do a thing to help, except to tell the truth about what
he did." Darnell shook his head in reluctant admiration at
Adam's honesty. "He asked me why the trial was taking so
long – we'd only just finished jury selection, the trial hadn't
really started – he asked why we even had a jury, why we
didn't have one of our wisest people sit in judgment about
what should be done after he told them everything that had

happened!"

"The kind of questions a child – an intelligent child – might ask," observed Summer, a thoughtful expression in her eyes. "The child who always wants to know why."

Darnell agreed, but only to a point.

"A child might ask them, but a child doesn't make you feel inadequate when you try to answer, and there isn't a child anywhere could do what he did, sitting there, the other side of my desk, reciting word for word questions and answers he had heard in court."

"He has that good a memory?" asked Summer. She was interested, but scarcely astonished, by what she had heard.

"You don't understand. I'm not talking about a question here and a question there; I'm not talking about some short, yes or no answers. He has perfect recall, whole paragraphs – pages – at a time. I think he could have repeated everything said in court, every question, every answer, during a week of voir dire if he had wanted to, if we had had the time. And it wasn't something he had worked on, struggled with, something he had kept repeating until he had it right. It all came back to him spontaneously as soon as I said something about a question I had asked the first juror."

Darnell put his hand over his mouth and for a moment his gaze turned inward. He felt a strange sense of pride, the vanity of secret knowledge. He had witnessed something extraordinary, so far beyond the range of normal experience that most people would think it impossible, or, if possible, some kind of aberration, a narrow genius, a natural gift that no one can explain and no one else can learn.

"I thought…well, I'm not sure what I thought," continued Darnell. "I had him get me a book, a very old book – Blackstone's Commentaries. I started reading out loud about the beginning of trial by jury and what it meant. I've spent most of my life in court, and I've seen, I think, every kind of witness. I've watched the way they concentrate, or try to concentrate, afraid that if they don't understand a question, if they miss a word, they'll make a mistake. But

I've never seen a look of such perfect concentration, such total absorption in what was being said. It was almost physical, as if instead of just listening, the act of hearing caused the words to make their sound." A flash of intuition lit up his eyes. "I hadn't thought of that before; but, yes, that's exactly what it was like. He sat there, so still he might have died, except of course for those eyes of his, shining firm and steady, greedy with possession."

"Greedy with possession?" asked Summer, struck by the novelty of the phrase.

"Yes, that eager to hear, and hearing, to have what he did not know. I read a page, then I read another, and then I asked him if he could repeat it back to me. And he did, every word; but more than that, he did it exactly the way he had heard it, exactly the same emphasis."

Darnell paused. He sipped on his coffee.

"He doesn't read or write and so we think him uneducated. But it isn't true. Whatever they do on that island, whatever they teach their children, they do it by the spoken, and not the written, word." Darnell raised his eyebrows. "He told me he had learned mathematics, but that he had had some difficulty with irrational numbers."

Summer Blaine spilled her coffee.

"Irrational numbers? Out there, on this island no one had ever heard of until a year or so ago? How is that even possible?" Then she remembered. "On Pitcairn's Island they had the Bible and the one man left after the others had all been killed learned to read it and then taught the children the lessons he thought would help them live a decent, loving life. Maybe something like that happened here. The survivors, whoever they were, whenever they landed on that island, had a few books with them and those became the basis of what they taught and what they know. It would have been handed down, generation after generation, and without the means to print or to make new copies it would had to have been done through an oral tradition. That might explain Adam's powers of concentration and his ability to remember so much of what he hears."

Darnell remained skeptical.

"An oral tradition that passes on the higher mathematics?"

Though Summer moved with a smooth, graceful elegance that made her seem younger than her years, she had the habit of a quirky, inward smile whenever she became convinced that she had suddenly discovered the truth of something.

"Why not? You don't have to know how to read to be able to count, and how do you learn geometry except through diagrams and pictures?" Her mouth turned pensive. "It would be interesting to know what kind of numbers they used."

"What kind of numbers?"

"Arabic, Roman; or some other kind: something of their own invention. But never mind. That isn't important. What's important is the case, the trial. When you were talking about Hillary Clark you seemed to have given up. You've never given up. You always think you can win."

Darnell shrugged his shoulders as if to say that nothing he had been able to do in the past had any bearing on this.

"I don't see how this time." He pronounced this as a serious judgment, the simple truth that he would not hide from himself nor conceal from her. "He might have a chance if it weren't for the murder."

With a worried glance, Summer acknowledged the force of Darnell's observation.

"Infanticide – The papers are full of it; it's all they're talking about on television. We debate abortion all the time," she said, growing more animated. "But killing an infant, a new born child – there's no debate about that."

Darnell hunched forward. He spoke in a low, thoughtful, probing voice.

"You deliver babies – thousands of them in your career. Has there ever been…?"

She understood what he was asking. She was too close to him, and much too decent a physician, to be shocked by the question.

"No, I never have. I'm not sure I could...."

"You're not angry with me, are you? I only ask because there must be some situations where...."

"No, I'm not angry - of course not. It's not a situation we encounter that often anymore. I suppose you could say that the new technology has saved us from that kind of dilemma. Now we know during the pregnancy whether there's any substantial risk of birth defects or other potential problems. And when there is, the mother can make her decision. But when I first became a doctor, before there was any way to know, I'd sometimes hear stories from some of the older nurses, the ones who were getting ready to retire and liked to talk about things that had happened, years before, when a baby was born with some horrible condition and might live only a few weeks or months and be in constant pain. Today they'd call it murder; back then it was thought an act of mercy. But I never had to face that situation and I'm not sure what I would have done."

Darnell stared past her, remembering things he had heard in the early years of his own career, things done privately that no one talked openly about. The law stayed out of it and those who had lost a child could try to put back the broken pieces of their lives.

"You're right," he said presently. "Today they'd call it murder."

"Is that what happened here?" she asked, quietly alarmed. "Is that why the boy, Adam, did what they say he did?"

CHAPTER SIX

Judge Evelyn Pierce seemed to move a little more quickly to the bench the next morning. She looked directly at Hillary Clark.

"Are you ready to call your first witness?"

Hillary Clark continued to study a document that had engrossed her attention. Or rather, as Darnell suspected, pretended to study it; a gesture, foolish in his judgment, meant to show the jury that while the judge might be presiding over the trial, the prosecutor was the one to watch.

"Your first witness?" repeated Evelyn Pierce, anxious to get started. "Now, Ms. Clark, if you would."

Hillary Clark waited a few seconds longer before she raised her chin and threw back her shoulders. Darnell caught the look of triumph in her eyes. He had suspected earlier, when they first met in chambers to discuss certain procedural issues before the trial started, that she did not like Evelyn Pierce, but he was sure of it now. It was not because of anything that had happened in court; she had not been treated unfairly. It was not anything Evelyn Pierce had done; it was what she was: an older woman who had made it in a man's world by becoming, in Hillary Clark's uncharitable estimation, just like one of them. Evelyn Pierce had failed to understand that the real imperative was to change the world, not accept it with all its prejudices and limitations. That Hillary Clark might not have been admitted to law school, and would certainly never have been hired as a prosecutor, had it not been for women like Evelyn Pierce was beside the point.

"The age of assumptions," Darnell thought to himself. "The generation that believes whatever it does is right simply because they do it."

He found that he liked Evelyn Pierce even more than he had before, and Hillary Clark even less. He could not help himself. He stared up at the ceiling, a lethal smile on his lips.

"Yes, are you going to call a witness, or did you think your opening statement so compelling that you wouldn't need to add anything as tedious and troublesome as a little evidence?"

Hillary Clark spun around.

"I...what? Your Honor, I object!" she cried with a scathing glance at Darnell who suddenly sat straight up and turned directly toward her.

"I take it then, that you do have a witness. It's all right to let the judge know that, Ms. Clark."

She looked at him in open-mouthed astonishment; he looked at her, and at the jury behind her, with all the appearance of affable good-will.

"It really is all right," he said in the practiced, cultured voice with which he had charmed juries for years. "Call your first witness. I've been looking forward to his testimony for weeks."

She looked to the judge for help, but Evelyn Pierce was now busy with some papers of her own.

"Your Honor!" she exclaimed, stamping her foot in protest. But there was no answer. The silence began to be uncomfortable. Finally, Evelyn Pierce raised her half-closed eyes and looked right through her.

"Call your first witness, counselor; the court doesn't have all day."

No fool, Hillary Clark quickly collected herself.

"The prosecution calls Eric Johansen."

The double doors at the back opened and a gaunt-looking man in his late fifties entered the courtroom. His long gray hair curled up over his jacket collar and swept back over his ears. His mouth was straight and fine; his eyes, though bright and curious, were also watchful and cautious. There was something enviable in the way he seemed to move within his own, separate space, like a stranger in a foreign port surrounded by hundreds of prying eyes. He stood straight, his shoulders squared, as the clerk administered the oath, and then, as if he had been in and out of courtrooms all his life, turned and took the witness stand.

"Mr. Johansen, would you please tell the court what you do?"

A modest smile creased Johansen's weathered face.

"I'm the captain of a cruise ship, the Stargazer."

"Owned by a Norwegian company, if I'm not mistaken?"

"Yes, that's correct."

"You're a citizen of Norway?"

"Yes, I'm Norwegian."

"But you spend most of your time...?"

"I don't get home much anymore," he said without apparent regret. "If that's what you're asking."

He had not let her finish her question. She hid her irritation behind a quick, glittering smile.

"You spend most of your time at sea?"

"Yes, you could say so; mainly in the south Pacific."

"As captain of the cruise ship?"

"More on my own boat, which I do for pleasure."

Hillary Clark stood directly in front of him, less than ten feet away. She did a quarter turn and took a step toward the jury.

"A sailboat, from what I understand."

"It may sound strange, that someone who spends his time on a cruise ship likes to sail, but on the Stargazer we carry two thousand passengers. It's like a floating city. When I have the chance, I like to get closer to the sea."

"And this sailboat of yours, does it have a name?"

Johansen's eyes lit up with something close to affection and not far from pride.

"Solitude."

"Solitude," said Clark, raising her perfect eyebrows in a gesture of appreciation. "After taking care of that many passengers, I can imagine you might want to be alone. But tell us, if you would, where you keep it, this sailboat of yours?"

"Tahiti. It's where I live now."

"You said you sail her for pleasure, but you've gone on some fairly long voyages, haven't you?"

Johansen's feet were spread apart, his elbows rested on the arms of the witness chair. His shoulders were hunched forward, and he held hands in front of him, his fingers loosely intertwined. His eyes stayed fixed on Hillary Clark as she walked to the far end of the jury box and placed her smooth, white hand on the railing.

"All over the Pacific, South America in one direction, Australia in the other. You've gone as far as Indonesia; you've gone as far as -"

"As far as the moon, for all that matters," cried Darnell, throwing up his hands in impatience. "We'll stipulate to the fact that Captain Johansen has sailed everywhere in the world if Ms. Clark will finally ask a question!"

Judge Pierce gave him a searching glance, a warning that he had better be careful.

"I believe she was about to, Mr. Darnell, when you interrupted her."

"Thank you, your Honor," said Hillary Clark. "Perhaps counsel for the defense has forgotten there is such a thing as cross-examination!"

Darnell laughed out loud. His eyes became, on the surface, sympathetic.

"I'll be the first to admit that I've forgotten quite a lot, but I do remember that if you don't ask the witness a question there won't be anything to cross-examine him about."

"Your Honor?' Clark asked plaintively.

With singular indifference, Judge Pierce twisted her head to the side and turned up her palms.

"Ask your question, counselor. Let's get on with it."

Clark bit her lip, and then, turning to the jury so Pierce could not see, raised her eyes in the common gesture of those who have to deal with errant children or hopeless fools. An instant later she was looking straight at the witness, asking the next question.

"Now, Mr. Johansen – or rather Captain Johansen – you sail all around the Pacific, when you have the chance.

Would you tell us in your own words what happened a year or so ago when you came across an island, one you didn't know about?"

"A year ago last September. I had a lot of leave time coming – vacation days I had accumulated, nearly three months. And so I set out in the Solitude, with no destination in mind, just to go where the wind might take me. I'd left Tahiti the end of July, and as I say, there was no particular place I wanted to go, except that I wanted to get as far away as possible from the routes the cruise ships follow. I'd seen all they had to offer, visited those same famous islands so many times that in the last few years I would sometimes forget which one we had just been to and which one we were going to stop at next." He looked at the jury with a half-embarrassed expression. "It's a little like a bus driver who takes a vacation. He loves to drive, but not along those same city streets. He gets in his car and explores the country, any place he can find a new road."

He seemed to like the analogy but to have some doubt whether it adequately explained how he felt. He would have thought about it, tried to find a closer parallel, but Hillary Clark urged him on.

"Yes, we understand, Captain Johansen. You wanted to explore the Pacific, parts of it you hadn't seen, and that's how you happened to discover -?"

"The early part of September; the morning of the sixth, to be precise."

"And where exactly were you?"

"Well, there's a question, I must tell you," he said, scratching his head. "Where exactly was I? Not where I thought I was, that's for sure. Or rather, I was, but that island wasn't."

Perplexed, Hillary Clark took a step forward.

"This is all a little confusing. You were where you thought you were, but the island wasn't? Perhaps you could explain what you mean by that."

Johansen flushed with embarrassment. He was a modest, unpretentious man who preferred his own company.

What made perfect sense inside his own mind sometimes came out all twisted up and garbled when he tried to put things into words. He felt safe with the brief commands he had to give on ship, and the occasional short comments he made with passengers, but whenever he started to describe something that had happened to him, or what he had been thinking about, every sentence was like a dead end road on which he always had to turn around and start off on another one. Human society was a thicket full of mystery and the words that held it together a hopeless tangle.

"What I mean? I see. The coordinates – the longitude and latitude – seemed to be accurate. It's just that there wasn't supposed to be anything there, nothing but open water, and yet there it was."

"The island?"

Johansen stared straight ahead, a look of wonder in his eyes, as he ran his long, bent fingers through his thick gray hair.

"It shouldn't have been there." As soon as he said it, he changed his mind. "I'm not sure why I say that. My own arrogance, I imagine; the belief that we know everything that's out there, that there's nothing more to discover. And after all, it isn't a part of the Pacific that is ever traveled much."

This seemed to satisfy him, this belief that for all the movement of ships upon the sea, the sea still had secrets, more of them than anyone could guess.

"And if you would, Captain Johansen, just what part of the Pacific is that? Where were you when you found the island?"

The question brought him back to himself. This was something he could answer without any danger of losing his way.

"My exact location was longitude -"

"I'm afraid we don't need anything as exact as all that. I don't know about the members of the jury," she said with a glance toward the jury box that bragged about the things that like any normal person she could not be expected to know, "but I can never keep straight which way either longitude or latitude runs, only that they go in opposite directions. Perhaps you could just tell us how far you were from land, some place all of us have heard of."

"You don't want to know where I was, where the island was? You just want to know how far it was from land?"

He thought he must have misunderstood. What was the point of saying where you were if you couldn't be exact? But as he searched her blank, impatient eyes he realized that like too many of the tourists on their first and only cruise, she could only grasp a distance if it was measured from the certainty of a place she knew.

"Quite a ways from here," he said with a droll expression.

"Could you be a little more specific?"

"I tried, but you wouldn't let me."

She gave him a look to remind him where he was. He remembered why he had never married.

"All I want to know, Captain Johansen – all the jury wants to know -"

"Objection!" Darnell jumped up with an agility that caught everyone by surprise. "The prosecution doesn't speak for the jury. If she did, she might credit them with enough intelligence to want to know the exact location – longitude and latitude – of this island we all want to know more about!"

"I'll ask my own questions in my own way, if you don't mind. I don't need -"

"Enough!" Judge Pierce glared at both of them. "No more. Rephrase the question, counselor. Ask the witness where he was, where the island is, and let him answer."

The eyes of Hillary Clark grew cold and intense. She spun on her heel, ready to lash out at the witness. She caught herself just in time, wiped the anger from her face and tried to laugh away her own mistake.

"I'm sorry, Captain Johansen; my question wasn't very good. I wasn't very clear. All I wanted to find out was where the island is in relation to some place those of us who don't sail the seas might know."

"About fifteen hundred miles off the coast of Peru, give or take."

"And you came upon this island the morning of...?"

"The sixth of September. I hadn't seen land in weeks, and I wasn't expecting to see any. But there it was, and much bigger than it should have been."

"I'm not sure I understand." Hillary Clark stood next to the jury box, drumming on the railing with the fingers of her right hand. It was a gesture of impatience, one she was not conscious of. "If you didn't expect to see land that morning, how could you have had any expectation with respect to how big it was?"

"You're right of course; I didn't." He shifted position, leaning now on his right elbow as he stroked his chin with his left hand. He liked things to be exact but the words were still the problem. "It wasn't supposed to be there, nothing was. But, as I tried to say before, not everything has been discovered. Still, it seemed strange that an island this large – a good twelve miles in length and part of it rising up as high as that, I...."

"Yes, we understand," said Hillary Clark. She was still beating her fingers on the jury box railing. Suddenly, she stopped, and, as if to keep herself from doing it again, clutched her arm across her chest and stepped away. "Tell us what you did next, after you sighted the island in the distance the morning of the sixth?"

"I went ashore. There was a long, sandy beach. There were no reefs or other obstacles."

"And what did you do when you got there?"

"Nothing."

"Nothing?"

"I thought it was deserted. What else should I have thought, an island no one had ever heard of in a place there should not have been one? It had to be deserted. It was quite beautiful, that island: tall palm trees lined the beach and, farther on, thick foliage and tropical flowers, and the only sound the gentle pounding of the surf. The last thing I expected to find was another human being." Johansen sat forward, a look of eager nostalgia shining in his eyes. "I didn't find one either; he found me. A young boy tumbled out through the undergrowth, chasing a wild pig. I was standing maybe thirty yards away when he broke into a clearing near where a creek emptied into the sea. He didn't see me; he was too intent on the pursuit. It was only after he killed that pig in its tracks that he noticed I was there. Strange thing, he didn't seem at all afraid. He was maybe twelve or thirteen – fourteen at the outside – but you would have thought I'd been living there for years and that he had seen me every day. He smiled, shyly, the way you would expect a boy to do with a man my age, but a man, mind you, that he knew and didn't fear. Then he went about his business."

"Went about his business, Captain Johansen? What do you mean?"

"He went about his business, did what he would have done if I hadn't been standing there, by this time not more than a dozen steps from where he worked, gutting the pig, getting it ready to take back to where he lived."

She waited, expecting Johansen to tell the jury what had happened next. There was a long silence. She was having trouble getting him into a rhythm in which his testimony would become a flowing narrative. Either he went on too long, drifting off into pointless digressions, or his answers were too short, ending abruptly somewhere in the middle. She forced herself to take a deep breath.

"What happened next, Captain Johansen? You followed this boy and you discovered there were other people living there, didn't you? Tell us about that, if you would."

Johansen nodded earnestly.

"I followed him, yes; but it was not like I was following him. I mean, he told me to. He didn't say that – I wouldn't have understood if he had. Their language is different from my own, different from any language I've heard. He told me with his eyes. When he was finished, when he had slung the pig over his shoulder, he looked at me and I knew what he expected. That's the only way I can explain it: He looked at me and I followed him. It was not far, a quarter mile down the beach, then another quarter mile or so inland, in a clearing behind that first layer of foliage and just this side of the river."

"Good. Now, what I want to get to, Captain Johansen – what's important for this case – is what you can tell us about the people who lived there. What were they like? Were they savages who preyed on each other?" she asked, casting a harsh glance at the defendant. "Did they spend their time murdering each other and raping the women?"

Johansen seemed more offended than shocked at the suggestion.

"To the contrary, they were as decent and orderly as any group of people I've ever seen. There must have been two or three hundred of them; men, women, and children all living together in a well-kept village. Each family had a house of its own; everyone seemed perfectly content with what they had." He rubbed his chin with the back of two fingers, a puzzled look in his eyes. "No, it was more than that. Grateful, is what I'd call it. Yes, that's right: grateful for what they had; not the things they had, but for life itself. Yes, that's right: they were grateful for the gift of existence. Grateful. That's what drew me to them, what made me like them all so much, though the only way I could decipher anything they said was through the gestures they used to make me understand."

"Would it be fair to say, then, that these people you found there, on that island in the middle of the Pacific, were peaceful, and not at all inclined to violence?"

"As peaceful as any I've ever seen. More peaceful than most of those I've known, if you want to get right down to it."

"So if someone committed rape or murder there it wouldn't be because everyone did that sort of thing? It wouldn't be because that was simply the custom, the way they lived their lives?"

For the first time, Johansen looked directly at the defendant. Perhaps he saw something that reminded him of what he had seen that day when he stepped on shore and read in that other, younger, boy's eyes all he needed to know. He turned back to the prosecutor.

"I can't imagine anyone there ever doing anything they shouldn't do."

It was not the answer she had expected, but she pretended that it was.

"Which would make it all the more inexcusable, wouldn't you agree?"

Darnell was on his feet, waiting, as Hillary Clark glanced one last time at the jury and with a knowing smile announced that she was finished with the witness.

"Captain Johansen, I have only a few questions. First, and just to get this out of the way, you have no knowledge of anything the defendant in this case may, or may not, have done, do you?"

Johansen appeared to relax, to be more at ease, less self-conscious. He seemed fascinated by Darnell. Hillary Clark had drawn every eye to her when she was questioning him, but everyone started to listen more closely the moment Darnell took over.

"No, I know nothing about it."

"And that's because you weren't there when any of these supposed crimes took place, were you?"

"No, I wasn't."

"You were there, on this island you discovered, for less than a week, if I recall correctly."

"Five days."

"You've never gone back?"

"No. I'd like to sometime; but no, I haven't been back."

Darnell had pushed his chair up against the table. He rested his hand on the top of it.

"You didn't get close to it on the cruise ship, and, as I believe you testified, no one sails that part of the Pacific.

During the time you were there were you able to determine how long these people had been on the island or where they might have come from?"

"No, but I had only a limited ability to communicate and….Well, that was part of it, you see: the language they spoke was so unusual, if I can say a thing like that about something I didn't understand, that there were times I thought they hadn't come from anywhere."

Darnell nodded as if he understood completely, not that he agreed with that possibility, but that it would have been easy to have had that thought.

"Language changes over time. Compare Chaucer with the way we speak English today. Were there any artifacts, any books or other objects that might have been brought by the people who first came there?"

"Nothing that I saw." He seemed to hesitate, as if there were something he wanted to say but was not sure he should.

"Please, go on. Anything you can tell us about the people who live on that island, the better."

"In a way, it didn't make sense. There weren't the kind of things you asked about, but you'd think there would have had to have been."

Darnell gave him a look of encouragement.

"Had to have been – yes, go on."

"There were no books, no papers, nothing like that; but more than that, there were no signs of how they made the things they had -the spear, for one."

"The spear? The one the boy had, the boy who killed the pig?"

"Yes, exactly: It wasn't some wooden stick sharpened to a point, the kind used by natives on some jungle island like New Guinea. The shaft was wood, a fine, polished hardwood like oak or ash, but the point was metal, smooth and sharpened with machine-like precision; and it was not simply stuck on at the end: it was fastened with a metal screw or rivet. And the clothes they wore, they weren't like anything I've seen on any other islands. The men wore leather sandals, laced like leggings from the ankle to the knee, and short white skirts with leather belts and sleeveless blouses. The women wore longer, ankle-length gowns. But the fabric – and this is just one of the mysteries I never solved – was of such high quality, a silken linen finely spun, that it did not seem possible they could weave it there."

Darnell moved around the counsel table and came close to the witness stand.

"What else, Captain Johansen? What else did you think was odd?"

"Nothing, really: a thought, a feeling - nothing tangible."

Darnell did not say a word. He stood there, waiting until Johansen was ready.

"Yes, well, all right. It was a feeling, nothing more; but it was a feeling I had from the moment that boy looked at me, a feeling that never left me, a feeling that they had been expecting me, that my coming was not a surprise. I don't mean me, personally; but that they had been expecting someone to come."

Lowering his eyes, Darnell began to pace slowly in front of the jury box. He did not know what he wanted to ask, only that he wanted to know more. He did not have a defense. That was the truth of it. His only chance was to stumble upon something – anything - that might help. He stopped suddenly.

"You testified that this island was as much as twelve miles long, isn't that what you said? How much of it did you see?"

"All of the part that's inhabited, not very much of the rest."

"Why not, why didn't you explore the rest?"

"It's almost impossible. I mentioned that the settlement was bounded on one side by a river. The river runs along the base of a cliff, a sheer drop of perhaps a thousand feet. That's where it starts as well, a waterfall three miles upstream. The other side of the river is virtually impassable."

"In other words, they live on a few square miles, but with tools and clothing they couldn't have made on their own?"

"I didn't say couldn't; only that I didn't know how they did it."

"Just one or two more questions, if you don't mind." But instead of asking them, Darnell went back to his place at the counsel table and sat down. Judge Pierce was just about to ask if he was finished with cross-examination when he bent forward.

"You were there, on the island, for five full days – isn't that what you said?"

"Yes, that's right."

"And you estimate there were anywhere between two and three hundred people living there?"

"Correct."

"And during your time there do you think you saw them all?"

"I don't know why I wouldn't have. They all live pretty much out in the open, and they were certainly quite friendly."

Darnell looked at Johansen and then looked at Adam.

"Tell me, Captain Johansen, before you walked into court today, had you ever seen the defendant, the young man sitting right here next to me?"

"No, I've never seen him before in my life."

"You're sure of that? You're sure you didn't see him on the island when you were there?"

"I didn't see him there. I'm sure of it. He wasn't on the island."

CHAPTER SEVEN

If Adam was not on the island when Johansen was there, where had he been? Was that what Adam meant when talked about being sent into exile as punishment for something he had done? But if he had been sent away, made an outcast by his own people, how had he managed to come back when he had also said he could never return? There were a dozen different questions Darnell wanted to ask, but even had Adam suddenly been inclined to answer them, there was not time. Hillary Clark was already calling the next witness for the prosecution.

Leland Phipps had the complacent look of a public servant of a certain kind, one who acquires a reputation for sound judgment by listening to everyone else's opinion and seldom giving one of his own. He was always weighing alternatives, examining possibilities, commissioning studies, doing everything he could to get all the facts. If Leland Phipps had never made a decision of any consequence, he had come to every meeting thoroughly prepared.

Hillary Clark stood next to the jury box, examining her nails.

"Mr. Phipps, would you please tell the court how you are employed?"

He started to reply, but remembering his own importance, paused to clear his throat.

"I'm the High Commissioner for the Western Territories." Leland Phipps leaned forward, the quiet glow of his own achievement marked plainly in his eyes, listening as the words echoed into nothingness. "I have the responsibility for the various trusteeships in the islands of the Pacific," he explained. This did not sound quite as impressive as his formal title. He looked around to see if anyone noticed.

"And is it in that capacity that you first visited the

island…?" Hillary Clark furrowed her brow. "Does it have a name yet?"

The commissioner's voice had an unusual quality, a kind of background noise, something like the sound of an electric razor. It was almost as if he were humming to himself, a habit he may have picked up listening to the endless discussion and debate that never led to anything but more discussion and more delay. It sounded like a stifled yawn.

"There has been no decision yet. These things take time. There is some consideration for the one who first discovered it, but there is also the issue of the indigenous population – what name they may have given it. These things aren't easy."

"I'm sure not," she agreed. "But in the meantime, they must call it something."

"Well, on a purely interim basis, without prejudging the question of what it should finally be called, we've simply used the name of the man who discovered it: Johansen's Island. But, as I say, that's strictly for the time being."

Hillary Clark tugged on her ear.

"How did the island come to be under your – that is to say, American, jurisdiction? Captain Johansen is Norwegian. Why not Norway instead of the United States?"

Phipps fairly bristled at the suggestion.

"We have numerous territories in the Pacific. It's a small island no one else would care about. It's our responsibility to help these people make the transition to modern life."

"And was that the reason you first visited the island – Johansen's Island – to start that process?"

"Yes. I wanted to see for myself, determine what had to be done. I knew of course that there were certain things that had to be done right away. I knew that they would need medicine, sanitation, the things that modern science can provide, and of course there would have to be some rules of governance, some -"

"Objection," said Darnell in a weary voice. "I'm at a

loss to see what any of this has to do with the case at hand. It doesn't matter what the commissioner went there to do; it only matters what, if anything, he witnessed concerning the crimes with which my client has been charged."

A scornful look raced across Hillary Clark's rose-red lips.

"He couldn't have witnessed what he did if he hadn't been there, your Honor. Even Mr. Darnell must understand that!"

"I'd be surprised if there was anything Mr. Darnell didn't understand," replied Evelyn Pierce with a look that rivaled Clark's own. "I think what Mr. Darnell was objecting to was…." But Darnell had changed his mind, or rather was on the verge of doing so.

"A question in aid of an objection, your Honor."

"Yes, Mr. Darnell; go ahead."

Darnell turned to the witness. "You say you brought medicine?"

"Yes, medicine and other things that -"

"And someone to administer it, a doctor perhaps?"

"Yes, of course, we -"

"Withdraw my objection, your Honor." He started to sit down, but then he remembered. "Sorry for the interruption," he said to the waiting Hillary Clark. "Please go on."

She was not seduced by false pleasantries, but neither did she forget that a jury was watching. Her instinct was to fix Darnell with a withering glance and then turn away, but that, as she well understood, was a luxury she could not afford.

"Thank you, Mr. Darnell," she said with exquisite politeness. "I'll be glad to go on, if you'll let me."

Darnell had just taken his seat. He bounced right back up.

"It's always a pleasure to watch a good lawyer do her work; especially," he added with cheerful malice, "when she has so much work to do."

She seemed to enjoy it, trading lessons in contempt.

"It won't take long, Mr. Darnell, to finish what I have

to do. I think I can promise you that." She did not give him the chance to reply. She spun around and faced the witness. "Tell us, Commissioner Phipps, on that first visit of yours to the island – did you see the defendant?"

"Yes, yes I did."

"Would you tell the court exactly what you saw?"

"It was on the evening of the third day I was there. I saw a thin spiral of smoke coming from somewhere a few hundred yards from the village. It was a fine evening, the sun was just setting. I decided to see what was going on. I thought some of the natives might be cooking a meal out on the beach. But when I got there, that wasn't what I saw at all."

"What did you see, Commissioner?"

"I saw that one there," he said, pointing at Adam. "He had a fire burning, and he was carrying something wrapped in a white cloth, holding it in both arms. I didn't think much about it at first. I was new on the island and didn't know its customs. Then, as I got closer, I realized what he was carrying and I was horrified. It was a child, a baby, and he was taking it to the fire. I called out, tried to stop him, but it was too late. He didn't hear me, or if he did, he ignored me. He placed the baby on top of the fire, stretched out his arms like someone praying to heaven and then stepped back and watched the fire consume the child's body."

Hillary Clark stared at him with anguished eyes

"What did you do then?" she asked in a whispered voice.

"Strange as it sounds now, I thought to offer him condolences. I assumed that I had just witnessed a burial ritual, that the poor child must have died of some disease – a disease we might well have cured – and that he must be suffering awful grief. I was surprised that he spoke some English. When I started to offer my sympathies, he stopped me with a look. And then he said something that even now makes me shudder."

Hillary Clark took a half-step forward, slowly, like someone about to open a door, afraid of what they will find inside.

"What did he say? What did he tell you?"

The commissioner's head snapped up.

"That he hadn't had any choice: that he had to kill it."

"'Kill it'? That's what he said? That he had to kill it?"

"It's something I'll never forget. He said it without remorse; he said it as if not only was there nothing wrong with what he had done, but that it was – not right, exactly, but, well, for lack of a better word – fitting."

"Fitting?" The look of surprise on Hillary Clark's face was genuine. She was not sure what to make of it. "I see. Yes, of course: he told you that he hadn't had a choice, and that's because….What else did he tell you?" she asked with sudden urgency. "What did he tell you about the mother?"

The commissioner did nothing to hide his sense of moral outrage at what he had heard. It had shocked him to the core, as it would have shocked anyone with normal, western, sensibilities.

"He said that she also knew that there wasn't any choice. He said she was his sister."

It was as if the air itself was infected with evil and things unspeakable. No one moved, no one spoke, everyone afraid to breathe, as the courtroom waited for what would happen next.

"Did he tell you how he did it, how he killed the child?"

"Strangled it, strangled it to death."

With a mournful glance, Hillary Clark turned to the jury.

"Strangled it, strangled it to death," she repeated, as if, even now, she could not believe it possible that anyone could have done something so awful and barbaric.

The silence in the courtroom had become heavy and oppressive, broken only by the sound of a throttled cough. Darnell got to his feet, but, instead of immediately asking a question, walked slowly to the other side of the counsel

table, a pensive expression in his eyes. He started toward
the jury box, but then stopped and looked at the witness.
Phipps curled his fingers around the arms of the chair and
got ready. Darnell only shook his head and moved within
arm's distance of the jury box railing. He gazed at each
juror in turn.

"That is a very grim scene you've described to us, Mr.
Phipps," he said as his eyes continued to move down the two
rows of jurors. "It's not the kind of thing any of us are likely
to forget. The body of a child, an infant, placed on a funeral
pyre – that's what it was, wasn't it?" Darnell turned his head
just far enough to see the witness. "It wasn't just a fire burning on a beach, the way you first described it. It wasn't that
at all, was it?"

Darnell turned until his shoulders were square in front
of the witness stand. He stood there, one foot half a step in
front of the other, his hands shoved into his jacket pockets,
boring in on Leland Phipps as if he, William Darnell, were
the prosecutor and Phipps the one who had done something
wrong.

"It was a funeral pyre, a place where this child's last
mortal remains were to be disposed of, offered to whatever
gods these people pray to."

"I doubt that's what -"

"You said – I can have the court reporter read it back
to you – that you saw the defendant place the body on top of
the fire. That has to mean that there was something there,
material of some sort – a structure, if you will – that would
support the body. Not just a fire, then, but a funeral pyre –
That's what you saw, isn't it, Mr. Phipps?"

"I suppose you could say that," Phipps replied,
unconvinced.

"You suppose? But you're the one who told us, Mr.
Phipps – and I'm quoting you again – that the defendant then
'stretched out his arms like someone praying to heaven.'
That's what you said, isn't it?"

"Yes, but that isn't what it was, not after -"

"You said, 'I assumed that I had just witnessed a

burial ritual.'"

A thin, condescending smile stretched tight across Leland Phipps' proper mouth.

"Precisely: I assumed. But, as you will also remember, I soon realized my mistake, when I heard from his own mouth what he had done."

Darnell smiled back.

"Words that made you forget the evidence of your own senses!"

"He confessed to murder!"

"No, he confessed to doing what you just testified he thought fitting – necessary for some reason we have yet to understand!"

Darnell marched back to the counsel table, hesitated, and turned around.

"You had him arrested, taken into custody, brought here, to America, because of what he said and because of what you thought it meant?"

"He admitted he murdered a new-born baby. Would you suggest that is something that ought to go unpunished?"

Darnell's eyes were cold, immediate.

"I would suggest that in this courtroom, sir, you don't ask questions, I do."

They stared at one another until, finally, Phipps looked away.

"Let's begin at the beginning. You graduated from Yale University some thirty years ago, correct?"

"Yes," replied Phipps, curious that he would ask.

"And you went to law school at Yale as well, correct?"

"Yes, I went to law school there as well," he said, as he shifted position in the chair.

"But you didn't practice law, did you?"

"I pursued a career in public service." Phipps turned to the jury, expecting, as it seemed, some show of approval for the sacrifices he had made, a man who could have been rich, but instead was only comfortable. The jury did not seem to understand.

"And did that include any military service?" asked

Darnell with a blank expression. "Were you in Vietnam?"

Phipps turned to Darnell with anger in his eyes.

"No, I wasn't in the military."

"That must surprise people."

"I'm afraid I don't understand."

"You've written a number of articles about the use of military power, have you not?"

"I've held various positions in both the State and Defense departments. I wrote those articles to broaden the discussion about certain policies."

"Articles with titles like…." Darnell reached for a document he had left on the counsel table. "'The Use of Power in the American Century;' 'The Role of the Military by a Dominant Superpower,' 'The Rule of Law in Lawless Places.' Or titles like 'Changing Autocracy: Three Strategies to Introduce Democracy.'" Darnell tossed the list of titles back on the table. His eyebrows shot straight up. "I'm afraid we've all become a little too familiar with the effort to establish democracy at the point of a gun. But tell us this, Mr. Phipps: your appointment as High Commissioner, that wasn't exactly a promotion, was it?"

"I'm sure I don't know what you mean."

Darnell began to thumb through a thick file of newspaper clippings.

"Would you like me to read into the record the stories written at the time, stories about how you had been sent to the Pacific to get you out of Washington, stories about how the appointment was just another indication of the failing influence of the people with whom you had long been associated?"

"Everyone has an opinion in Washington, Mr. Darnell. Anyone can say what they like." He said this with an air of defiance, but he said it without the arrogance, the sense of entitlement he had had before. He had not suddenly become a beaten man – he had too much vanity for that – but he could not any longer pretend that his life and career had always been a steady march from one success to another.

"You must have gone out there, out to the Pacific,

more determined than ever to prove that you were right. That's what a man of your background and intelligence must have thought. You would have taken it as a challenge, a way to turn banishment – because that's what everyone thought it was – into redemption, a new opportunity to show what you could do. Isn't that the reason you were so intent on turning this unknown speck of land, this island no one had ever heard of, into a part of the great American experiment?"

Hillary Clark was on her feet.

"Defense counsel isn't asking questions, he's giving a speech. Worse yet, he's giving a speech that doesn't have anything to do with the trial."

"It has everything to do with the trial, Ms. Clark, everything," replied Darnell. "But you're right: I sometimes do have a tendency to get a little carried away." He looked from Clark to the bench. "May I proceed, your Honor – if I promise to stay on point?"

With a smile that seemed to say that she knew what a lawyer's promise was worth, Evelyn Pierce told him to move things along.

"What I want to know, Mr. Phipps, is whether that was the reason you made that first trip to the island: to make it over in the image of America?"

The commissioner did not disagree.

"I believe we have an obligation to bring progress when we can."

"Progress? I wonder. What is it you thought these people were missing?"

"Missing?" asked Phipps with a caustic laugh. "Everything was missing. They had no education. They couldn't even read a newspaper."

It was Darnell's turn to laugh.

"You consider that a disadvantage? What news exactly is it that you think they missed?"

"What news? - News of the outside world, news of what is going on, news of all the changes that are taking place."

Darnell remained steadfast. His only chance at a

defense was to challenge assumptions.

"I'll repeat the question: What news have they missed? Let me be more specific: What news have they missed that would have somehow improved their lives?"

"Everyone is better off if they know more about the world."

Leland Phipps said this with complete and unyielding conviction; only a fool would think differently about something so obvious. The world, the western world, ran on information. Everyone needed it, and everyone had a right to have it. In the passion of the moment he had forgotten the failures of his own career, forgotten how many of the grand schemes with which he had, if always in a supporting role, been associated had ended in disaster, forgotten how many people had been told that the price they had to pay, the sacrifices they had to make, was worth it because of the bright prosperous future it was sure bring, if not for them, for their children. He looked at Darnell, incredulous that anyone could question what he had always tried to do.

"You wouldn't want them to remain in ignorance, would you?"

"And to cure that ignorance you were going to bring them – in fact you did bring them, as I recall – the wonders of modern medicine. Is that correct?"

"Yes, absolutely – These people, living out there like that….That was the first thing we worried about, the kind of diseases they must be carrying. So, yes, of course we brought medicine, and a team of physicians."

"Are you trying to tell us that these people – two or three hundred of them – had no doctors, no medicine of any kind?"

"They were isolated, cut off from civilization. They were -"

"Cut off from civilization, you say. But that doesn't mean they didn't have a civilization of their own, an organized way of life. It doesn't mean that they didn't know how to deal with the sort of accidents and illness everyone has, does it?"

"Yes, perhaps; but only in the most primitive sense. The Indians of the Orinoco know the use of herbs, for example, if that's the sort of thing to which you're referring."

Darnell nodded as if in agreement, but still seemed not to understand.

"But no doctors, in the way we know them; and certainly nothing in the way of medical technology. Is that what you're saying?"

"Yes, exactly right; which is the reason –"

"So none of these people would know whether when a woman was pregnant she was going to give birth to a healthy child? No way to know, Mr. Phipps, whether the child she was carrying might be born deformed or in some serious way impaired. Correct?"

"Yes; I mean, no, there wouldn't be a way to know that. I see where you're going with this, but -"

"I'm not going anywhere with it, Mr. Phipps. I'm only trying to establish the facts of what happened, the facts to which you were a witness."

Darnell paced rapidly in front of the jury box, three steps one way, three steps back, his gaze fixed on a point straight in front of him as if he were making an effort to concentrate his mind. He suddenly stopped moving, nodded quickly as if he had just come to some agreement with himself and stared hard at the witness.

"You said you thought at first that you were watching a funeral, that the defendant appeared to pray to heaven. It was only after he told you that he had killed the child that you changed your mind, that you interpreted those same facts – what you actually saw – in a different way. But if it's possible, as you've just admitted, that the child had been born with a condition that with us would have meant the end of the pregnancy, a condition that would have made it impossible for the child to live, you're forced, are you not, to go back to your original interpretation and view this for what you thought it was: a grieving father doing what he had to do? What you yourself said was what he seemed to think 'fitting.'?"

Leland Phipps jumped forward to the edge of the chair and jabbed the air with his finger.

"You forget! That wasn't the reason he used that word. It was 'fitting' because the child he fathered was the child of his sister. What he clearly meant was that it was fitting that a child like that, a child born of incest, not be permitted to live."

Angrily, Darnell stepped closer.

"He never said any such thing and you know it! That's only how you chose to take it."

Phipps drew back. His hands rested in his lap. A look of satisfaction filled his eyes.

"He said the mother of the child was his sister," he said quite calmly. "That's not something I made up."

Darnell shoved his hands deep into his pants pockets and for a few short seconds stared gloomily at the faded hardwood floor.

"There were how many people living on this island?" he asked, barely lifting his eyes.

"Nearly three hundred."

"Living there for how long?"

"It's hard to say, we really don't know. We've only just begun to study them, but hundreds of years, I imagine; perhaps even longer."

"All alone, isolated, generation after generation?"

"Yes, I don't see any other possibility."

Darnell placed his hand on the back of his neck, a puzzled expression on his face.

"Did you ever read Mutiny on the Bounty, Mr. Phipps?"

"Yes, I'm sure I did, as a boy." He seemed as much amused as surprised by the question.

"It's the first in what became a trilogy. Did you know that?"

"I'm not sure I did."

"It's very interesting, the way the story ends. After a very long time – seventy or eighty years – Pitcairn's Island is discovered along with the descendants of Fletcher Christian and the other mutineers. What is particularly interesting, Mr. Phipps, is how many of the children had the same father but different mothers. Now what do you suppose would have happened, out there in that isolated place, if it hadn't been discovered by the outside world? What do you think would have happened when, in just a few short years, those children, all of them at least half-brothers and half-sisters, had become of an age to have children of their own? Tell us, Mr. Phipps, would you have arrested all of them on charges of incest and brought them here for trial?"

"Your Honor!" cried Hillary Clark as she sprang from her chair. "That's an outrageous thing to ask!"

"It's what's been done here that's the outrage," said Darnell before the judge could say a word. "The prosecution objects to a question about a work of fiction – why? Because the only permissible outrages are the ones she and the witness commit themselves?"

Suddenly the courtroom was alive, everyone talking at once. William Darnell was a legend, known to push the limits as far and as often as he could, but no one had seen him go this far before. Evelyn Pierce hammered her gavel.

"Silence or I'll clear the courtroom!" She turned a withering glance on her old friend. "Mr. Darnell, you have exactly two seconds to apologize!"

"But your Honor, I -"

"Two seconds, Mr. Darnell!"

"I apologize, your Honor, to the court and to Ms. Clark. I shouldn't have said what I said."

Evelyn Pierce was barely satisfied.

"This isn't like you, Mr. Darnell. I think you know me well enough to know I won't tolerate this kind of thing in my courtroom."

"Age, your Honor; I'm afraid it's catching up with me," he explained with a boyish, puckish grin.

"It isn't your age that the problem, Mr. Darnell; it's the fact that your mind works so fast your mouth sometimes gets impatient."

This cut the tension. The courtroom crowd relaxed.

The jurors who had been sitting on the edge of their seats sat back. Darnell shook his head in wonder at a public reprimand that seemed more a backhanded compliment.

"Mr. Phipps!" he exclaimed with a burst of energy that riveted everyone's attention. "Let's leave aside Mutiny on the Bounty. Have you read the Bible?"

Phipps nearly fell off the witness stand.

"Have I read...? Yes, I've read the Bible, not as thoroughly as perhaps I should, but -"

"Genesis. You've read that, it's something you're familiar with?"

"Yes, reasonably so."

"The story of Adam and Eve?'

Laughter rippled through the courtroom. Leland Phipps could only stare.

"The story of Adam and Eve, Mr. Phipps. It's a simple question."

"Yes, I know the story."

"Tell me if I have it right. God created Adam, and then, out of one of Adam's ribs, God created woman. He created Eve. Is that correct."

"Yes, perfectly."

"Then Adam and Eve had two children, Cain and Abel, and we all know what happened to them. Cain slew Abel. My question, however, is simply this: If God created Adam and Eve, and if they had two sons....well, what then?"

"What then? I have no idea what you're talking about."

"How did the children of Adam and Eve have children? You see the difficulty, Mr. Phipps. In the beginning, whichever way you look at it, without some form of what you so quickly and easily denounce as morally and criminally wrong, without incest, Mr. Phipps, there would be no human race!"

Hillary Clark immediately objected, but Judge Pierce overruled her.

"Go ahead, Mr. Darnell."

"Only one more question, your Honor. Mr. Phipps,

you testified that the defendant made these admissions to you; confessed, as you would have it, to having had relations with his sister and having been responsible for the death of their child. Is it still your testimony that he said these things to you?"

"Yes, absolutely; there is no doubt at all. That is exactly what he said."

"And he did this freely, of his own free will? He wasn't subjected to coercion or anything like that?"

"No, I told you. He was there, by the fire, when he told me what he had done."

"In other words, Mr. Phipps, the defendant made no attempt to conceal anything that he had done. The fire, the statements he made to you – everything was done out in the open. Tell me, Mr. Phipps, does that sound like someone with a guilty conscience, someone who thinks he has something to hide?"

CHAPTER EIGHT

The next ferry did not leave until half past five. Darnell did not mind the wait. It would give him a chance to wander around, lost in the anonymity of the crowd; a chance to forget, or try to forget, the trial. He could not quite remember the last time he had come down here, to the Ferry Building, or the last time he had taken a ferry across the bay. For years the building had been an eyesore, an aging relic of the distant days when San Francisco had been a bustling commercial port. He remembered coming here as a boy, when the ships were unloaded by hand and sweating long-shoremen shouted eager obscenities as another huge cargo net was lowered onto the dock. Born in the city, Darnell had grown up dreaming of ships and sailors, great adventures and exotic places, certain that all the excitement in the world was waiting for him out at the edge of the horizon, some-where just beyond the Golden Gate.

William Darnell leaned on the railing, gazing across the bay. It was Summer's idea to meet for dinner in Sausalito, her idea that instead of driving over he take the ferry instead. He scuffed his shoe against the thick block of wood that kept paper and other debris from falling off into the water below. There were always people here now, crowds of them, come to shop for gourmet foods or to eat in one of the fashionable restaurants that had changed one of the city's most famous landmarks from a shipping center into an upscale urban market. Darnell thought about going inside to look around at what the vendors had to offer, but the late day sun felt too good against his face.

It was odd, the way those boyhood dreams had changed. He had not had to wait that long until he was sailing on a ship to adventures in exotic places, but the war had taught him all he wanted to learn about the sea. The last time he had passed beneath the Golden Gate was the day he had sailed home. The only sailing he had done since had been on small boats that belonged to his friends, and the trips he had taken had never gone beyond the bay. He wondered now if that had been a mistake, whether he should have seen more of the world, but for a long time after the war the last thing he had wanted to do was leave the city. And he never did. His life had been here, in the city, the only place he had ever wanted to live.

A few feet from where he stood, an old woman wearing a large, bulky flannel shirt sat on a bench, tossing bread crumbs to the seagulls wandering fearlessly about her feet.

"I used to come here with my father," she said, somehow aware that Darnell had turned to watch her. "I was just a little girl, but I remember what it was like here, before they built the bridges and the ferries ran back and forth all day between here and Oakland, bringing people to work. I remember when all the men dressed like you, in suits and ties." She threw the last bread crumb over the railing and laughed as the few seagulls still remaining flew off to get it. "I'm glad they brought the ferries back," she said as she ambled to her feet and dusted off her hands. "It's the best way there is to see the city, especially this time of day, with the sun going down over the bridge and the shadows start to move. It always reminds me what a mystery the city has always been."

Despite her rumpled clothing and unkempt gray hair, the woman spoke with a lucid precision that matched the bright clarity of her eyes.

"But I'm sure I don't need to tell you that, Mr. Darnell. You've lived here at least as long as I have." With a hand gnarled with arthritis she touched him gently on the arm. "I'd wish you good luck with this case of yours, but all the years I've been reading the papers you always seem to win. Luck doesn't seem to have much to do with it." She smiled in the way of older people who, though they have never seen each other before, have much in common. "I'm glad I finally had a chance to meet you. You're the last great one we have left."

The last great one: Words not just of praise, but of affection, and, as he well understood, words that carried with them their own finality. Darnell had his doubts whether he had ever been as good as she had said, but he liked that she had said it, liked the fact that in the city he loved, he had become, in the minds of at least some of those who lived here, a part of the fabric, a part of the legend, of the place. He tapped his knuckles three times on the metal railing and then walked across to the ticket window.

He bought a ticket and then bought a newspaper and joined the line that had begun to form. The ferries did not bring cars across anymore, only passengers, and they did not look like the squat open-mouthed ferries he remembered as a boy, more like sleek white coast guard cutters. But this was California, and this ferry went to Sausalito in Marin, and a dozen different passengers had bicycles to bring. A few of those who boarded with him took a second look, but no one bothered him; no one came up to introduce themselves or offer an opinion about the case. The bicycles were neatly stacked on racks just inside, and the passengers quietly took their seats. Darnell sat on the open deck on top.

As soon as the ferry started to move, Darnell admitted to himself that Summer Blains was right, and so was that old woman. "Old woman," Darnell laughed to himself. "She's probably younger than I am." He shook his head at his own strange vanity. "A good deal younger, if you want to be honest about it." But never mind, the point was not age, but the truth of what they had said, though the woman he had just talked to was the one who really had it right. This was the best way to see the city: on a ferry going away from it. You could see it the way you remembered it, the first time you saw it whole, glistening in the morning sun or, like now, in the faded light of early evening, with the sky a solid azure blue and the Golden Gate turning deeper shades of reddish orange. Even for someone who loved the city, it was easy, if you had lived here all your life, to forget the sense of wonder you got when you saw it like this, rising up from the water like an island in the bay. Even the great steel bridge that connected the city to the northern shore seemed to float like some disembodied dream designed to make the place seem more magical.

A line Darnell had first read as a boy drifted chance-like through his mind: "That City of Gold to which adventurers congregated out of all the winds of heaven." Robert Louis Stevenson had written that and, as far as Darnell was concerned, it was still the best description of the city and its character. More than that even, it was still the best description of the way he felt, the pride he took in being part of a place that had from its very beginnings laughed at convention and whenever possible ignored the law.

The farther the ferry moved away from it, the closer the city seemed, as if the more of it you could see - the more of it you could take in – the more it became your own possession. There were times Darnell wished he had been a writer so he could put it all down in words, even though he knew somehow that words would always be inadequate. He remembered the day, years ago, when half the city had turned out to say good-bye to Herb Caen, the newspaper columnist who for half a century had given everyone who read him the sense that the city was the only place to be. Dying of cancer, Caen said that he had had a dream in which he found himself wandering around heaven and that St. Peter had come up to him and asked him how he liked it. To which he replied, "It's not bad, but it isn't San Francisco!"

But still, Darnell told himself, he should have seen other places, seen more of the world, traveled, spent summers in Italy or the south of France, and seen a bullfight in Spain. He was lying to himself, pretending a regret he did not feel, enjoying for a moment the luxury of a disappoint-ment he had not had. He had been lucky beyond measure and he knew it. Travel, see other places – it was like being married to the most beautiful woman he had ever seen and wondering what he might have found had he stayed a bachelor. See other places – where would he have gone to see something like this, the Golden Gate glowing in the evening sun, and there, just on the other side of it, billowing hundreds of feet above, like the curtain in a theater, a thick, impenetrable fog, shielding behind it all the mysteries of the sea. The mysteries, Darnell reminded himself, of that island where Adam had been found.

He tried not to think about the trial. He had read enough Hemingway to know that the best preparation was sometimes to let your mind do its work undisturbed by conscious thought. He watched the fog spiral higher and the sunlight shining on the bay and he watched the long white wake stretch out in the distance and listened to his own brief stories about the past, the voice inside his head that still remembered who he had been and who he was.

Summer Blaine was waiting for him on the dock. He waved, but she did not see him. He smiled at the eager look in her eyes as she searched the crowd, and smiled even more when she finally found him and ran the last few steps and kissed him gently on the side of his face.

"Shall we find a cheap motel, or would you rather have dinner first?" he asked with his best imitation of a scoundrel's glance. Summer took his arm and walked beside him with an easy, swinging gait.

"Why waste money on a motel when we can always use the backseat of my car?"

"In other words, you want dinner." He sighed as the look in his eyes became more mischievous. "And then, when dinner is over, you'll tell me that I need my rest and send me off to my room alone." Summer gave his arm a squeeze and became serious.

"How is the trial going?"

"Awful. I haven't done anything right. I'm trying not to think about it."

She could tell he meant it, though she could not quite believe that things could be as bad as that. They walked in silence for a while, down the street and around the corner to the breakwater and the view of San Francisco across the bay.

"It was a good idea to meet here and then go into the city together. You were right about the ride. It brought back a lot of memories, seeing the city from the bay. I remembered – the line suddenly came into my head – that quote from Robert Louis Stevenson: 'That City of Gold to which adventurers congregated out of all the winds of heaven.' The winds of heaven - that sums it all up; everything, not just the city, but my life, this case, the way that things come together here that couldn't happen anywhere else." He chuckled under his breath. "I'm not making any sense, am I?" He stopped walking and looked right at her. "It does make sense, but only if you're here. That's the point. It's that line – winds of heaven. When you live here, when you've lived your life here, you're used to the strange, the exotic, the kind of mysteries that hint at their existence only long enough to make you think they're real. The things that happen here aren't dry as dust and all logical; the things that happen here don't all make sense. That's the reason everyone dreams of coming here and no one dreams of leaving."

Summer laughed. "This trial is making you poetic."

"Which is another way of saying this trial is making me insane. But never mind that now - where would you like to go for dinner?"

They walked a little farther and then crossed the street to a small Italian restaurant they had visited before. Nearly everyone was dressed in casual clothing.

"I didn't have time to change," he explained, though Summer had not said anything about it. He ordered a bottle of wine and told the waiter they wanted to take their time before they ordered dinner. "Its' Friday," he said when the waiter left, "and there's nothing I have to do. I have the weekend free."

"In the middle of a trial?"

"Sure, why not? There's nothing more I can do. It's been two weeks, two weeks of listening to witnesses say the same thing: that Adam did what the prosecution says he did and that what he did was, on any understanding, unfor-givable. All I can do is try to catch the inconsistency, the contradiction, the implied assumption in what they say. It wasn't too bad at the beginning. Captain Johansen, the one who discovered the island, helped when he said that Adam wasn't there. Not that I have any idea where he may have been, you understand; but it raised a question, or might have if the next witness, the High Commissioner, hadn't been so certain that Adam was the one he saw and the one he heard confess. That was the end of any small chance I might have had to argue that there wasn't sufficient evidence to prove that Adam did it."

The waiter poured the wine. Darnell looked at it as if he had been waiting all day for the chance to drink, but as soon as he took a sip, he put down the glass.

"That isn't the mystery: that he did what they say he did. It never was. The mystery is why he did it and why he won't talk about it, why he won't tell me anything. But he expects me to tell him everything," he added with a rueful, puzzled glance.

Summer had learned enough about Adam to guess at what had been left unsaid.

"And about more than just the trial, I imagine."

Darnell threw up his hands, the antic measure of his own frustration. He had never seen anything like it, the way that Adam could at times seem indifferent to the trial that might lead to his death, but intensely interested in learning more about the mundane details of other people's lives.

"There was a witness, beginning of the week, a cultural anthropologist from Berkeley, a man supposed to be a specialist on the island peoples of the South Pacific. He was a specialist, all right: someone who has spent his life learning more and more about less and less. He was a throwaway, a witness whose only contribution was to make it seem that everyone who knows anything thinks the prosecution is right: that there isn't any set of circumstances – 'no known belief system in the South Pacific' is how he put it – that would have permitted relations between a brother and his sister or approved of infanticide. Adam wasn't interested in any of that. He wanted to know about his credentials, what it meant to have a Ph.D., what a modern university did. He talks me into things and I'm not even aware of it until I realize later what he's done. That day, after trial, I drove him over to Berkeley and showed him around. Do you know, I can't remember ever doing a thing like that for someone I was defending, certainly not while the trial was going on. And yet, when he asked me if we could, it didn't occur to me to say no."

Summer's eyes lit up in that way she had when something suddenly came to her.

"Rousseau!" She said it as if it explained itself; as if, should Darnell have any doubt about her meaning, he had only to look more closely into how she was looking at him. "Rousseau," she repeated. "You remember, the 'noble savage,' man as he was, or could have been, outside all the burdens of civilization. Man in his grand simplicity, fearless, compassionate, born with great intelligence but with no greater ambition than to enjoy all the pleasures of existence, of being alive. I've been trying to think what Adam reminded me of, the way you describe him, and just now I remembered. It's been years since I read Rousseau, probably not since I was in college."

"There's no question Adam is all of that," said Darnell. He was not quite satisfied; the picture was not complete. "But civilization – that's where it goes wrong. I don't think he's savage in any sense; I don't believe for a minute that he just sort of fell out of the trees, that he lived some primitive existence. You remember what he said about his education, the things he learned, including, for God's sake, higher mathematics and irrational numbers. Not civilized? I think he could have gone into any classroom that day I took him to Berkeley and understood anything they were teaching. But don't ask me how. I've spent weeks now listening to testimony about that island and the two or three hundred people who live there and it simply doesn't make sense. Something is missing. They have no books, no records – there is nothing written down – and yet the clothes they wear, the tools they use, to say nothing of the things Adam was taught, are only possible at a much higher stage of development."

The more he spoke, the more involved he became in the very mystery he had been trying so hard to forget. One thought led not just to another, but to a myriad of possibilities, all of them plausible, logical explanations, but only if you first divorced yourself from reality.

"I even started to wonder whether instead of one undiscovered island there might be two. He told me, remember, that he had been made an exile, punished for something he shouldn't have done. Of course he wouldn't tell me any more than that, not the crime he supposedly committed or who had the authority to decide what should happen because of it. Though, come to think of it...."

Darnell narrowed his eyes, as he concentrated on what Adam had told him in his office, or rather one of the questions he had asked about the trial. His eyes snapped open.

"He asked me why we had this complicated and elaborate procedure, why we spent all this time asking questions before deciding whether someone was fit to serve as a juror. But he only asked that question because he had a point of reference, something with which to compare it. He asked why we didn't simply choose one of the wisest – that was the word he used – wisest people to decide everything. He didn't say 'chief' or 'elders' or any of the other things that if you didn't know him you would expect some Pacific islander, a native member of a tribe, to say."

Darnell moved his glass off to the side and leaned forward on his elbows. Summer held her glass steady, taking only an occasional drink. She did not need to say anything to encourage him to go on.

"That suggests a degree of civilization superior to our own, if you want my honest opinion. But the question then of course is where was it, this place where only wise men rule and the higher mathematics is taught by word of mouth? It's clear it isn't that island where Adam was found placing the body of that dead baby on a funeral pyre. And then, remember, Adam wasn't there a year earlier when the island was first discovered. Captain Johansen was sure of it. Adam wasn't on the island, but he had to be somewhere; he hadn't just vanished into thin air. He had been sent into exile for something he had done before. But where?

There had to be a second island, somewhere he could go. But when you think about it, that doesn't make any sense either. He lives on the island, then he's banished; but the life he describes, the things he learned – that couldn't have happened there. And if he did live on the island and was sent into exile – he said he could never go back – what was he doing there?"

Darnell slapped his forehead and with a bleak expression stared into the middle distance. Summer tried to help.

"You could still be right about a second island. What if there was a second one and that was where this other, higher civilization was? Wouldn't that fit? Then Adam would have been exiled to this island where he was found." She thought about what she had said and realized what was wrong. "Except that Adam said he lived there, and it seems to be a point of honor with him never to say anything unless he can tell the truth. And besides," she added as an afterthought, "if there was a second island, how would he have gotten from one to the other?"

Darnell picked up his menu, glanced at it with impatience and set it down again. Scratching his head, he marveled at something he had heard.

"He stays, you know, with the Hammersmiths. They did it as a favor to me, though now they seem to think that I've done them one. I think they're both in love with him, the way they talk about the things he does. They take him everywhere - museums, galleries, concerts – and to hear them tell it, two people who have spent their lives on the boards of those places, he has an eye that takes in everything and doesn't forget any of it. Endless curiosity – that's what they say about him. It doesn't surprise me, of course, given what I've seen him do. Henry Hammersmith actually said to me that if he didn't know Adam had come from an island, he'd almost be willing to believe that he was a visitor from another planet! Henry Hammersmith, the most practical, sober man I know; hard, realistic, proud of what he's got and of the work it took to get it; and he talks about Adam with all the excitement you might expect from some half-crazed archeologist who had just discovered the lost tomb of Solomon. It's unbelievable the effect that boy has on anyone who comes in contact with him. Even that witch…," he said as he started to laugh.

Summer gave him a droll look.

"Well," he said without apology, "she is, you know."

"That's what you keep telling me, and it isn't just because she's the prosecutor in the case. You've spoken highly of other prosecutors you've faced. But this one has really managed to get under your skin, hasn't she?"

He started to deny it, but under Summer's watchful eye, he was forced to admit that she might not be entirely wrong.

"Perhaps she has, a little."

"Because you think she's winning?"

"Think she's winning? I know she's winning. More to the point, I know I'm losing. I've been losing since the day we started."

The restaurant gradually filled up and those waiting for a table congregated at the bar. Darnell signaled the waiter and while Summer glanced at the menu, poured her another glass.

"Losing since the day we started," he repeated once the waiter left. "And nothing I can think of is likely to stop the slide. I've lost before. It isn't that. It's the smug certainty that she's right, this refusal to so much as consider the possibility that things aren't always black and white or right and wrong, that there is such a thing as a moral dilemma, that what we insist is right may not always be right after all. This business about incest, for example." Darnell reached for his glass, held it at eye-level watching the way the color changed as with each slight movement of his wrist the light hit it from a new direction. He kept watching, mesmerized, and the longer he watched the more subdued he became, until, finally, he seemed to have shifted mood altogether, become self-doubting and introspective. He put down the glass and looked at Summer.

"Forget that it's illegal, forget that everyone thinks it's

wrong - what's the real reason that we feel such repugnance just at the mention of the world? Incest, the great taboo, what everyone would tell you is this terrible violation of something that even people without religion consider sacred. But tell me – why? Is it something we're supposed to feel naturally, a part of the human condition, or is it just another one of the things we've been taught not to question?"

Summer was not shocked, or even taken aback, by the question; but she was surprised, now that she thought about it, that she had no answer. It was wrong, immoral, a violation of the duty every parent owed a child, if you were talking about that kind of incest, and a mistake, a tragic error, a psychic wound that would likely never heal, when it happened between a brother and his sister.

"It's wrong. I'm not sure I can do any better than that. More wrong, in certain respects, than killing someone, don't you think?" She searched his eyes, wanting to know what he really thought, not what he hoped to be able to use at trial. "There are exceptions, situations like self-defense, when killing someone isn't wrong; but there aren't any exceptions to this, are there, times when it would be all right?"

"I would have agreed with that before this case, but now...I'm not so sure. I know it must sound ludicrous, but if you take the story of Adam and Eve seriously...."

"The question you asked that witness. The papers were full of that. 'The Adam and Eve defense,' they called it. But you weren't really serious were you? You don't believe Genesis is an accurate historical account?"

"The more interesting question might be why Genesis was written the way it was, because if you start with -"

"Perhaps, but however you want to look at it, the most you could say is that it shows that incest happens, not that it is ever right. If Hillary Clark were as clever as you say, why hasn't she brought up the most famous story about incest ever written, Oedipus, and used it to show how abhorrent it has always been thought to be?"

Darnell's eyes flashed with new interest.

"Maybe I'm the one who should," he mused aloud.

"Bring that in to show that things like this happen as a tragic mistake. Oedipus didn't know it was his mother, it was the last thing he wanted to do. Perhaps -"

"That's what happened here? Adam didn't know?"

"That's the problem: Adam won't tell me. But if he didn't know she was his sister, he knows it now, and from the look he gets whenever she's mentioned, I have to tell you that being with her is nothing he regrets."

Dinner was served and Darnell promised that he would say no more about Adam or the trial, though Summer would not have minded if he had. She knew that it was a promise he made at least as much for himself as for her. On this, more than any of his other trials, he seemed at times almost desperate to get away, to free his mind from the stark confusion that seemed to greet him everywhere he looked. She wished she could help him, but as she had come to learn in the time they had been together, close friends and companions in what they both knew were their twilight years, when Darnell was in a trial he was never more alone. He made an effort to keep up his end of the conversation, but as the evening wore on she found herself filling in the empty spaces while he lapsed into a silence, distant and remote. She laughed softly, and with affection, each time he came back to himself and, as quickly as he could, caught the sense of what she was saying and with a cheerful grin tried to add a few words.

It was almost dark when they left the restaurant and began to walk to where Summer had parked her car. The last few sailboats were coming back, floating like white-winged moths across the bay. Darnell stopped and pointed toward one of them.

"That was the other thing Henry Hammersmith couldn't get over. He owns a big one, a sailboat with a double mast, sails it whenever he has the chance. Last Sunday he took Adam out with him, and he said that Adam moved around that boat like a cat, like someone who had sailed all his life. But the strangest thing, the thing that Henry couldn't get over, was the way that Adam almost seemed to be talking to the wind, telling it what to do."

Darnell took Summer's hand and they walked slowly down the street, safe in the knowledge that whatever happened they had each other. Far in the distance, the lights on the Golden Gate cast a mystic, eerie glow on the fog that now covered both the city and the sea.

CHAPTER NINE

Science is the modern prejudice. Darnell could not
remember where he had read it, but he was now more than
ever convinced that it was true. Only what could be seen
and touched, measured, weighed and analyzed, taken apart
and put back together again, tested by some known hypoth-
esis, could be granted the privilege of being knowable and
only what was knowable could be said with any certainty to
exist. After hours of testimony by another expert witness
for the prosecution, William Darnell was ready to scream.
He tapped his fingers on the counsel table and bit hard on
his lip; he crossed one leg over the other and in violent short
bursts kicked his foot. Evelyn Pierce, who hid her own bore-
dom behind a perfect blank mask, noticed what Darnell was
doing and could not suppress a smile.

"Mr. Darnell, do you have a problem?"

Darnell shot to his feet, grateful for the chance to
stand, grateful for the chance to talk.

"Do you mean other than the fact that I may die of
old age before the witness is finished? Which wouldn't be
so bad," he added immediately, "if I could at least die with
some idea what he's talking about or how it has any possible
connection to the case."

Hillary Clark had grown used to Darnell's frequent
attempts to seize attention and make the jury concentrate
more on him than on what a witness said. She had learned
that the worst thing she could do was to get angry or let
anyone think that she had been taken by surprise.

"I can ask the witness to go slower, if that will help
you understand."

With a curt bow, Darnell declined the offer.

"Thank you, but I'd rather die in ignorance than
prolong the ordeal."

Clark had only a few questions left to ask. When she

was finished, Darnell sank back in his chair and stared at the ceiling like someone giving thanks for a reprieve. Then, before she had a chance to object, he was on his feet, heading straight for the witness.

"Don't misunderstand me, Professor Miller, I wasn't reacting to anything you said in response to the prosecution's questions; it's my own impatience with my own impatience." He nodded in puzzled tribute to his own apparent confusion. "My own impatience at my own impatience! You see what all these years of listening to courtroom testimony have done? It's a little like what I imagine must happen to you, teaching the same course over and over again." His eyes flashed with friendly certainty. He knew they would agree. "You aren't ten minutes into a lecture on comparative law and you begin to wonder if you aren't repeating something you just said. I apologize for that. But you're the last in a series – we've had a whole seminar – on the same question, the rights of women and children in all civilized countries. We've heard from cultural anthropologists – three of them, to be precise; each with a different expertise – two sociologists; even, believe it or not, an economist – though I'm still not sure why, something about labor markets...." Darnell shook his head as if to keep his eyes from glazing over at the memory of it. "And now, finally, at long last, someone who knows something about the law; or rather," he added, as he turned away and began to study the juror's faces, "someone who knows something about the law of several different countries, well-known countries with well-known histories and customs."

Hillary Clark rose from her chair, a look of affected sympathy painted in her eyes.

"Perhaps Mr. Darnell might like to ask a question before -"

"Before you die of old age, Ms. Clark?" Darnell wheeled around and holding both hands behind his back beamed with pleasure. "There's really no chance of that, no matter how long I take. You're much too young to die, Ms. Clark, and, if I may be permitted to add, much too beautiful." He made a courtly bow that, whether from innocent embarrassment or the sense of having been upstaged, made her blush.

"She's right of course," Darnell remarked, turning back to the witness. "I do need to ask a question. It's your testimony that in every legal system that you know of there is a strict prohibition on incest – is that correct?"

"Yes, and that's not a matter of conjecture."

"Not a matter of conjecture? What do you mean?"

In his mid-thirties, Brandon Miller had taught at the Stanford Law School for nearly ten years. A brilliant student, he had been invited to join the faculty the year he graduated. Having majored in computer science as an undergraduate, he brought the use of systems analysis to the field of comparative law. At the beginning of her direct examination, Hillary Clark had spent a tedious quarter of an hour eliciting the list of his various publications. When Darnell asked him what he meant, Darnell knew exactly the kind of answer he was going to receive.

"We've done a computer search, a thorough -"

"Yes, I see. I understand. You used the computer and the computer searched the – what do you call it? Yes, I remember – this data base you have -"

"Every legal system, all the statutes from every country in the world."

"Yes, I see. Thank you for that additional information." Darnell raised his eyebrows, nodded briskly and began to pace back and forth. As quickly as he started, he stopped. An elfish grin cut across his mouth. "I'm afraid I don't even use a computer. Don't know how. I still write longhand with a pen. So you'll have to forgive me, Professor Miller, if I don't quite grasp the full significance of what you've done; though I think I have the gist of it. Your testimony, again, is that every legal system has a prohibition on incest. That much I think I follow. Yes?"

"Yes, that's right. There are no exceptions."

"But you didn't research every legal system, did you?"

Short, compact, with small, quick darting eyes, Miller

had the compressed energy of a man who did not like to be challenged.

"I just finished telling you that that was exactly what I did."

"Yes, but you were wrong," Darnell fired back. "This data base of yours – the legal systems, all the statute law there is – wasn't that your testimony? Wasn't that what you said when Ms. Clark first asked you about it?"

Miller did not see the point of this. It was clear from his expression that he thought the old man was even less up to date than he had said he was.

"Yes, that's what I said."

"All the legal systems now in existence?"

"Yes, every one of them. There isn't any mistake. Nothing was left out."

Mumbling to himself, Darnell walked a few steps away. Miller seemed to think it funny that anyone could be so confused.

"What about the ancient Roman system, or for that matter, the Athenian?"

The humor, and the arrogance, vanished from Miller's eyes.

"What?"

"It's a simple question, Professor Miller. Does this data base of yours, this systems analysis you've done, include any of the laws, any of the legal codes, under which various civilizations lived for hundreds or even thousands of years in the past?"

"That wasn't what I was asked to do," he started to explain, growing red in the face. "I was asked to analyze existing law, I was -"

"The deficiency of your instructions, Professor Miller, is no concern of mine; it's the deficiency of what you did that is at issue here. You testified that incest is everywhere prohibited – part of the prosecution's attempt to argue that even without a specific prohibition it could never under any circumstances be allowed. But all you can really say is that you haven't been able to find any exceptions in the present.

You certainly can't say that there weren't any in the past."

"Well, I doubt very much you'd find an exception no matter how far back you searched."

"Really, Professor – Is that your objective, scholarly opinion? Have you ever read Greek or Roman law?"

"No, but -"

"Have you ever read any ancient history?"

"A little, but -"

"Have you ever read Plutarch, specifically his Life of Themistocles?"

"No, I can't say I have."

Darnell retrieved from the counsel table a page full of scribbled notes.

"If you had, you would have learned something interesting. It turns out that under Athenian law, a law which by your own admission you know nothing about, if a man died and left both a son and a daughter, the son alone inherited."

Miller shrugged it off. "There's nothing new in that. For centuries, only men could inherit. I don't see -"

"You didn't let me finish. The son inherited and endowed his sister, that is to say made some provision for her. But – and I think this will interest you – if they were not children of the same mother, the son, instead of endowing her, could marry her. They may only have been half-brothers and half-sisters, but it still seems like incest to me, Professor Miller. Doesn't it to you?"

Reluctantly, Miller admitted that it did. Oddly, Darnell argued that Miller was wrong to do so, or rather, that he was not entirely right.

"But notice what this example really teaches. Not that incest was allowed, but that it wasn't defined in the same way. He could marry her if she was his half-sister, but not if they had the same mother. Tell me, Professor Miller, do you know anything about the parents of the defendant in this case, or the parents of the young woman alleged to have been the victim of both rape and incest?"

"No, I don't know anything about either one of them. I was only asked to -"

"Yes, thank you, Professor Miller." Darnell waved his hand as if he was through and started back to the counsel table. "One other thing." He stopped and, bending his head slightly to the side, searched Miller's eyes. "I asked another witness about the story of Adam and Eve. I'd like to ask you about Cleopatra. Do you know how old she was the first time she married?"

Miller could only stare. This was way beyond his competence, and farther still from anything in which he had an interest.

"Twelve years old, Mr. Miller. Imagine that, twelve years old." His eyes drifted slowly from the witness to the jury. "Twelve years old, and married to her brother!"

The testimony of Brandon Miller had taken all morning and as soon as Darnell had finished with his cross-examination, Judge Pierce recessed for lunch. The jury filed out of the jury box and the courtroom crowd began to disperse. Henry Hammersmith who, on the days that his wife did not do it, brought Adam each morning to court and usually stayed to watch the proceedings, was waiting near the door. He patted Adam on the shoulder and asked if he would mind waiting outside.

"It's good to see that you still know how to steal all the attention and take over a trial," he said to Darnell.

They had known each other for years and, in the habit of old friends, cloaked their affection with mild words of derision. Darnell was a lawyer, which meant he could always be called a crook; Hammersmith had made a fortune as an investment banker, which meant that Darnell was always talking about all the money he must have stolen. Today, however, there was a serious purpose behind what Henry Hammersmith said.

Darnell was equally serious when he replied, "I'm not sure it will do any good." He looked back over his shoulder at the now deserted courtroom and the empty jury box. "They have one more witness, and then I'm supposed to put on the case for the defense, but the only witness I can call is Adam, and I'm not sure I should call him." He looked sharply at the other man. "Have you ever in your life seen anything like him? I swear I can't make him out."

Everything about Henry Hammersmith, from his tailored English suits to the way his hair was cut, had the feel of money, but money well-spent by someone with a selective eye. He envied a little Darnell's occasional flamboyance, the way he could mesmerize a courtroom and hold a jury in the palm of his hand, but that was not the same thing as thinking that it was something he might have wanted to do. He much preferred the quiet dealings of the boardroom and the nice adjustments of commerce and power. He preferred the things he could touch rather than what he could only imagine. And then he met Adam.

"Seen anything like him? I've seen him nearly every day for months and I'm still not sure he's even possible. But that isn't why I wanted to have a private word. I'm a bit worried."

Darnell put his briefcase down. With no one but his old friend to see him, he dropped the mask of unvanquished and almost perfect confidence he wore in court.

"There's nothing I can do. We're going to lose. I'm afraid it's as simple as that. I'm sorry. When I asked if he could stay with you, I didn't realize that you and Laura would get this close to him. I didn't -"

Henry Hammersmith stopped him with a look. He had very little use for sentimentality; it only got in the way of getting things done. He also was not the kind of man who ever gave up. He thought Darnell was trying to prepare him for what was likely to happen, to let him know that the probabilities were against them, but that Darnell had not meant it literally when he said he was going to lose.

"I'm not worried about that. Remember what you've often told me: that something unexpected always happens in a trial, something that no matter how much you prepared you could never have anticipated, and that more often than not it changes everything? Something like that may happen here. No, I'm not worried about whether you can pull this off. It wouldn't be the first time you've done something no one thought you could. No, I'm worried about the boy."

"Adam? Why? What's happened?"

"At the end of the day yesterday, when Clark announced that she thought they could finish today, that they had only two more witnesses."

"Yes, I remember, but….The girl! Is that what -? He's been asking me for weeks when he could see her. He'll see her this afternoon. Is that what has him upset? He didn't say a word to me."

"Nor to us. It wasn't what he said, it was what he did. Last night, after he had gone to his room, I heard this tremendous wailing sound, like someone driven out of his mind by grief. I went to the door, to see what was wrong and if there was anything I could do, but he must have heard me – he can hear things at a distance I can't hear up close – and it stopped. But I have to tell you, Bill, it was just about the most soul-shattering cry I've ever heard, all the anguish in the world, and then, just like that, the moment he thought someone might have heard, he stopped. And then this morning he was the same as always, completely in control of himself - cheerful, outgoing, eager to help. But last night…. There are things inside him, terrible things, things I think would kill a normal human being."

Darnell picked up his briefcase, looked at Henry Hammersmith and could only shake his head.

"He's in love with her, as much in love as anyone can be. In love with his own sister – I wonder what the jury is going to think about that."

Though Darnell usually spent the lunch recess reviewing the voluminous notes he made in preparation for the testimony of every witness, he was not in a mood to do much of anything except wander around outside and try to clear his mind.

Walking down the street on a sunlit afternoon, Darnell wondered what Adam must be thinking. Did he dream at night of the island and the girl, and did he have any regrets, or even believe he should, for anything he had done? Darnell was almost certain that he did not. Of all the remarkable things about this strange young man, perhaps the most astonishing was how much he seemed to live in the moment and not think about the past. But then that anguished cry that Henry had heard - Was that because of what Adam remembered, the girl, his sister, that he had lost, or the girl he still needed, the one he wanted now?

Darnell walked for half an hour and the exercise did him good. He felt better, more refreshed, than he had in days. By the time he was headed back, he started to get a kind of second wind, a sense that things were not as bad as he had feared and that the odds against him might not be so great. He was standing just across the street from the courthouse, waiting for the light to change when suddenly someone took hold of his arm.

"Mr. Darnell, I wonder if I might speak with you for a moment?"

Darnell had been accosted by strangers on the street too often not to know how to get rid of them. With a look of annoyance, he pulled his arm free.

"I'm sorry, but I don't...."

That was all he got out before he changed his mind. He found himself staring into one of the most remarkable faces he had seen, perfectly balanced with thick gray brows over fine, intelligent eyes, high cheekbones and a tapered chin. The stranger's age was indeterminate, certainly past fifty but very possibly much older than that. There seemed to be a slight accent to his speech, but Darnell had not yet heard enough to know more than that. He was wearing a suit and to the casual observer did not look any different than a great many men seen on the sidewalks of the commercial heart of town, but Darnell, who had an eye for the small detail, noticed immediately that the suit was a shade too large and, judging by the size of the lapels, years out of date.

"Yes, of course, Mr.....?"

The stranger hesitated, as if for some reason he had to be careful about revealing his identity. His eyes moved in a slow, steady arc from one side to the other, making certain, as it seemed, that he would not be overheard.

"Holderlin – Gerhardt Holderlin."

The name defined the accent.

"You're German, Mr. Holderlin?"

"Yes. I came here from Berlin."

The light changed and they started across the street. Darnell checked his watch. He still had a few minutes before he had to be in court.

"What is it you wish to talk to me about, Mr. Holderlin?"

Darnell was impressed and even intrigued by the other man's formal bearing, the strict manner of his speech, the precise efficiency of the way he moved. Holderlin paused before he answered and Darnell was certain that it was because he wanted to make sure that he knew exactly what he wanted to say and the best, most reasonable way to say it.

"The reason I wanted to speak with you is because I think I may be able to help you."

They had reached the other side. Darnell stopped where he stood and turned a skeptical eye on his new acquaintance. It was instinct pure and simple, instinct taught by decades of experience, instinct for the con man, the scam artist, the street hustler. They came dressed like thieves and bums, they came with expensive haircuts and three-piece suits, and the story, for all its endless, bizarre variations, was always the same. They knew something that would help, a piece of evidence the police had not found, a witness who had seen the crime and could testify that the defendant did not do it, it was someone else. Then, because it was a case you were otherwise sure to lose, a case you would have done anything to win, you wanted to know more. What was this lost piece of evidence, where was this witness and when could you talk to her? There were difficulties, you would be told with a lowered gaze in tones of regret. He wanted to help, he really did, but it was going to take money, serious money. There were expenses that had to be paid, and of course, there were his own costs involved....

"You came all the way from Berlin just to help me?"

he asked with a jaundiced grin.

"Please, Mr. Darnell; I'm not what you think I am. I'm not some charlatan trying to take advantage."

Darnell looked at him more seriously, though still with caution.

"How is it you think you can help me, Mr. Holderlin? What is it you think you can do?"

"Perhaps I should have come earlier, when I first heard....But you see, I couldn't really believe it would go this far, that they would actually bring him here and put him on trial."

"You didn't believe...? You're talking about Adam, the young man I'm defending? You're talking about the trial?"

"Yes, of course. Why else do you think I've traveled this distance?"

"I'm sorry, Mr. Holderlin, but how would I have known what you wanted to talk to me about?"

At first he seemed not to understand, to believe for some reason that it should have been obvious was he was there. Then, a moment later, his eyes flashed with embarrassment.

"Yes, of course; you're right - how would you have known? I'm so caught up in what I'm doing, I've been so preoccupied with this, I'm afraid I haven't been thinking too clearly. But the important thing is that I'm here now, isn't it?"

He stood there, waiting, as it seemed, for some sign of approval of what he had done, coming all the way from Germany to help.

"Yes, of course," he said, berating himself. "You still don't know what I've come to tell you. I was there, Mr. Darnell, on the island."

Clutching his briefcase with both hands Darnell bent forward at the waist, trying to search the meaning in Holderlin's unflinching gaze.

"It's true, Mr. Darnell – I've been there. I know quite a lot about it; more, I would venture, than anyone else still alive."

He said this with a hint of mystery, a suggestion that there was some connection between the island and death.

"The island was discovered less than two years ago. When could you have been there?"

Holderlin acknowledged the truth, or rather the apparent truth, of it.

"Discovered by a Norwegian - Yes, I read about it. But I was there long before he arrived," he added with a tinge of melancholy in his voice. "Long before. Forty years to be exact."

Darnell was stunned. He was not sure what to believe. The claim seemed outrageous, but the man who made it seemed not just honest and sincere, but deeply troubled by something that he knew.

"This Captain Johansen," continued Holderlin "seems like a decent man from everything I've read – not some adventurer out to make a name – but he doesn't know what he found. An island, yes – but nothing about the truth."

"The truth?"

"The truth that I discovered forty years ago, the truth that no one would now believe." He made an abrupt movement of his head, reminding himself that there was not much time. "That's why I have to tell you what I learned, because without it you can't possibly understand what this young man you're now defending really did, or what it really meant."

Darnell checked his watch again. He was in danger of being late.

"But forty years ago," he remarked as he glanced at the courthouse steps, trying to calculate how quickly he could climb them. "Adam wasn't even born yet; everything must have been different. Even if you were there – and I'm not saying you weren't – what could you tell me that could possibly help?"

"I lived there, Mr. Darnell. I lived there for a year. It doesn't matter that it was forty years ago; it doesn't matter that I was there before he was born."

A strange, knowing smile cut straight across his mouth. His eyes were filled with what to Darnell appeared to be the perfect confidence of a man who has spent years, a lifetime, protecting some deep secret of his own.

"It doesn't matter, Mr. Darnell, because nothing there ever changes; nothing ever has and nothing ever will. What's on that island has been like that forever."

Darnell fumbled in his pocket for a card.

"Can you come to my office, later this afternoon, after I'm through in court?"

And then Darnell turned and hurried up the steps.

CHAPTER TEN

Judge Pierce had just taken her place on the bench when Darnell rushed through the doors at the back of the courtroom.

"Sorry, your Honor," he apologized as he made his way to the empty chair at the counsel table.

A raised eyebrow and a slight downward turning at the side of her mouth, a look Evelyn Pierce could almost claim to have invented, a look designed to teach lawyers their own inconsequence, was all he got by way of reply. Darnell stood at his chair, lost in admiration.

"That's really quite good," he remarked. "Better, more effective certainly, than any verbal scolding."

She had not expected this. With a sharp glance she was about to warn him of the dangers of insolence, but she could not resist the boyish larceny in his aging eyes, and, more than that, the shrewd judgment passed on her own performance. The quick anger on her lips became wistful and even self-deprecating.

"I'm glad you approve, Mr. Darnell; but now that you've finally graced us with your presence, perhaps we can get on with the trial. Ms. Clark, is the prosecution ready with its next witness?"

Serious, composed, and if anything even more intense than usual, Hillary Clark announced that she was.

"The prosecution now calls -"

"Your Honor," Darnell interjected. "I have a matter for the court."

A matter for the court meant that it was something that had to be discussed outside the presence of the jury. Judge Pierce began to instruct the bailiff to take them to the jury room, but Darnell again interrupted.

"I think this would better be discussed in chambers, your Honor."

Adam was curious. Darnell bent close and whispered that it was all right, that there was a legal question that had to be resolved. But the next witness, the last scheduled witness for the prosecution, was the girl and Adam for the first time betrayed his feelings.

"I have to see her, I have to -"

"It's all right," Darnell assured him; "you will."

That was what he said, but it was not what he hoped. He did not want anyone to see the girl before the trial ended, not Adam, and certainly not the jury. And there was a chance – not a very good one, but still a chance – that he might be able to do that, stop the girl from testifying, and with that, force an acquittal.

Evelyn Pierce sat behind her large, heavy desk, leaning forward on her large, heavy arms. She invited both attorneys to take a seat, but did it in the peremptory way of someone who intended to keep the meeting short. She looked at Darnell and waited.

"The defense objects to the prosecution calling its next witness. Despite repeated requests, we've never been given the chance to talk to her, to conduct the kind of interview necessary to prepare an adequate defense."

The judge's eyes moved immediately to the prosecutor. "Ms. Clark?"

The muscles in Hillary Clark's smooth, sculpted jaw had tightened as she listened to Darnell's complaint. She did not look at him; she looked only at the judge.

"Mr. Darnell is right. He did request to interview the victim in this case. The victim, however, refused; and, as Mr. Darnell is well aware, the victim in a case like this has no obligation to speak to anyone, including the lawyer for the defense, before she testifies at trial."

"That's correct," replied Darnell immediately, "as a general statement of the law, but the question here is whether the law has been fully complied with. As Ms. Clark properly points out, the victim has the right to refuse to speak with counsel for the defense, but in a case like this – where the girl is underage, brought to a country she knows nothing about, spoken to in a language – well, I don't know how much of it she's learned or how much of it she understands. The point is that in a case like this I should have been given the chance to determine for myself that her refusal to speak to me was made with a full understanding of what she was doing and that she was doing it voluntarily."

"Voluntarily? What are you suggesting?" demanded Clark, turning to look at him.

"I'm suggesting that I find it difficult in the extreme, given what I know about the relationship between my client and the supposed victim in this case," replied Darnell with some heat, "that she would refuse to talk to the only person who can help him! Is that clear enough for you?"

"Mr. Darnell!" cried Judge Pierce. "Both of you – that's enough!" She looked directly at Hillary Clark. "He has a point, Ms. Clark. The girl might easily have been confused. Are you sure that she understood who Mr. Darnell was and the reason he wanted to talk to her?"

"Yes, absolutely. We explained to her that the attorney for the defense wanted to interview her. We explained that she could do so if she wanted, but that she also had the right to refuse."

Judge Pierce turned to Darnell to see if he had anything to add.

"Unless you have something else, based on the representations of Ms. Clark that the witness understood her rights, I don't see that I have any choice but to allow her testimony."

"She doesn't explain why I wasn't allowed to see the witness and hear her refusal from her own mouth. Nor, I might point out, has the prosecution provided any documentation to support its claim."

"Documentation?" asked Clark indignantly. "Show me the statute that requires that!"

"I'm afraid I can't do that," admitted Darnell. "I know what the law requires and what the law doesn't; but I also know the difference between a prosecutor who wants to do justice and one who only wants to win." Reaching into his briefcase, he pulled out a copy of a letter and handed it to the judge. "This is the last letter I sent to Ms. Clark on this matter. You'll see that at the end of it I say that if the girl really doesn't want to talk to me I would like to have a signed affidavit detailing exactly what she had been told and the reasons for her refusal."

"Just because you ask for something, Mr. Darnell, doesn't mean I have to give it to you."

"No, but when you don't do something that is easily within your power, it does lead to questions about why you didn't."

Evelyn Pierce subjected Hillary Clark to a long, silent scrutiny. She did not doubt that Clark would bend the rules to win a case, but it was something else again to believe that she would break them.

"You're certain that the witness understood everything, certain that she wasn't in any confusion about Mr. Darnell's request and that she knew what she was doing when she refused?"

"Absolutely certain, your Honor."

"And that this was her own, voluntary, decision – no one tried to influence her?"

"Of course not, your Honor. It was her decision and her decision alone."

It was clear from the way she looked at her, that Evelyn Pierce was not convinced that Hillary Clark was telling the truth.

"I tend to agree with Mr. Darnell that under the peculiar circumstances of this case he should have been given the chance to have her tell him directly that she did not with to talk to him before the trial. But, based on your representations as an officer of the court that her decision was both knowing and voluntary, I don't really see that there is any choice but to let her testify."

Hillary Clark rose from her chair and turned to leave.

"Which is not to say that I approve of the way you handled this, Ms. Clark. It's the duty of a prosecutor to avoid any doubt on a question like this; especially when, as in this instance, it would have been so easy to do so."

Clark spun on her heel, her eyes hot with defiance. Pierce was out of her chair, both hands planted firmly on the desk. A look of stern resolution stopped Clark from the fatal mistake of saying what she thought. Then, with that same firm expression, she forced the prosecutor into the kind of lie that reminded her who was in charge.

"There was something you wanted to say?"

"No, your Honor."

Evelyn Pierce nodded. "Just as well, I think. One other thing," she added, her eyes cold, determined, immediate. "Because Mr. Darnell had no opportunity to interview the witness, the court will grant the defense considerable latitude in its cross-examination. That seems only fair, don't you agree?"

Hillary Clark's chin came up, her face grew red; she made an effort to control herself.

"Whatever the court decides," she replied as they continued to stare at one another.

"That will be all," said the judge abruptly. "We've kept the jury waiting long enough."

She did not wait, as she normally would have, for the lawyers to get back to their places. She marched back into the courtroom first and busied herself with some paperwork as a way to let her anger subside. She was not angry at Hillary Clark; she was angry at herself, angry that she had not made her understand at the very outset that in her courtroom only the highest standards of conduct were acceptable. Shoving the paperwork aside, she drummed her fingers on the cold hard wooden surface of the bench she had occupied for nearly as many years as Hillary Clark had been alive. Her eyes moved in quick, rapid bursts, as she glanced first one way, then the other, examining, as it were, every nook and cranny, all the bricks and mortar, of the stage on which had been played out the human drama of all the trials of the past. She understood, and took a certain pride in the knowledge, that she was the link that connected all of them, the dozens, the hundreds, of trials over which she had presided.

It gave her a sense of not just purpose, but of permanence. When she looked at the empty witness chair just below on her left, she could hear the dead echo of every witness who had either told the truth or lied.

The two lawyers had made their way back into the courtroom, but she did not see them. The courtroom crowd, the audience of which she was, during the intensity of a trial, only dimly aware, now by its very silence reminded her that she still had work to do. Her eyes focused and alert, she looked at Hillary Clark as if no cross word had ever passed between them.

"Is the prosecution ready to call its next witness?"

No amount of backstage bickering could affect Hillary Clark's performance. The sharp-eyed glance, the evil tongue, the pious attitude of barely suppressed superiority – all of it was gone, replaced with a gentle, almost worried look of apprehension. Her only concern, that look seemed to say, was how she could help the next witness, the victim of these awful crimes, get through the ordeal of having to testify against her assailant and the man who had killed her child.

"The prosecution calls Alethia."

Every eye turned toward the double doors in back, straining to get a first glimpse of the young woman who had been so much the subject of their attention. Alethia – the name itself had the sound of something distant and exotic, ancient poetry and the youthful stirrings of a romantic soul. And the moment she entered, the moment she walked inside, she seemed to prove that no matter what might have been imagined about her, none of it had been exaggerated. There was an audible murmur, a heart-stopping pause, as the crowd got its first close look. She was more than beautiful, she was exquisite; a woman, though not old enough to be one, a child still innocent, but far from ignorant of the things a woman knows.

Dressed in a simple shift, a pair of sandals on her feet, she moved with a lithesome grace, ignoring, or oblivious, of all the staring faces, all the prying eyes, until she reached the railing that marked the boundary between the benches reserved for spectators and the area where only those with business before the court could sit. Her hand on the gate, she held her head high, sensing, as it seemed, something, or someone, she had not seen. Then, in an instant, she understood. She turned and with a desperate, wounded look stared at Adam who was on his feet, staring back at her.

Darnell held him fast by the wrist, afraid of what he might do; but Adam did not move. They kept looking at each other, Adam and the girl, with a gaze so strong that, though neither of them took a step, distance seemed to lose all meaning as the measure of separation.

Hillary Clark put her arm around the girl's shoulder and led her toward the witness chair, but the girl, unrelenting, would not take her eyes away. She kept looking back with what struck Darnell as an utterly astonishing combination of anguish and pride, as if, having captured Adam with her eyes, she was afraid that, now that she had found him, if she looked away he might disappear. If Hillary Clark still wore a worried expression, she wore it now for another reason.

"Would you please state your name for the record?"

Instead of looking at her, the girl kept staring at the defendant.

"Alethia."

The same murmur that had swept through the courtroom when she first appeared, repeated itself. The girl's voice was strange, uncanny, almost mystical; a cool, vibrant, rhythmic sound that lingered in your mind, the sound the sirens must have made luring Odysseus to his death, gentle as a feather and as unforgettable as a kiss.

"You have no other name, just the one?"

"Alethia," the girl repeated, a smile, proud and knowing on her face as she continued to stare into Adam's eyes.

Clark had no choice. She had to ask the court's help if she was going to stop it.

"Your Honor, would you please instruct the witness that she isn't to keep looking at the defendant?"

"Miss – Alethia, this is a court of law, and it is expected of any witness that she pay attention to the attorney who happens to be asking her questions. Do you think you could do that?"

The girl tossed her head and looked up at the judge. She seemed to recognize some quality in Evelyn Pierce's eyes – simple honesty, perhaps, or a basic decency – that gave her confidence. A radiant smile exposed a line of perfect white teeth.

"Yes, I think so." The smile faltered, grew faint, and then dwindled into shy reserve. "I'll try." Her eyes darted back to Adam as if asking for his approval, and then, but only then, she looked into the waiting gaze of Hillary Clark.

"Good. Now, Alethia – that's a very pretty name. Is it common where you come from? Do many other girls have that name as well?"

"No."

That was all she said; no explanation, no discussion of where the name came from or what, if anything, it meant.

"No? I suppose if you have a name that pretty it's even nicer if you're the only one to have it."

The girl sat on the very edge of the witness chair, her legs held close together and to the side, her hands folded delicately in her lap. Her eyes, as Darnell noticed, seemed to change color with the light. At first he had thought they were blue, or rather a bluish green, but now they seemed a color he had not seen before, yellow, almost gold.

"Now, Alethia," Clark continued, doing what she could to ingratiate herself, to let the girl know that she was on her side. "I know this is painful, but would you please tell the jury what happened, how you were raped?"

The girl had no idea what she was talking about. The word meant nothing.

"I understand; you still have problems with the language. By raped, I mean when he forced himself on you, had intercourse with you."

"He didn't hurt me."

Hillary Clark tried to be patient. "Yes, Alethia;

but he was bigger, stronger, older – he didn't need to hurt you to have his way. So, please, describe to the jury what happened, what he did to you."

"Made love, you mean?"

"That's usually the way we describe the act of intercourse when both parties engage in it voluntarily and of their own free will; but all right – when you made love."

The girl had a surprising capacity for detachment, an ability well beyond her years to see things the way someone else, someone who did not know the meaning of what had been done, might see them. Slowly teasing a curl in her hair, she smiled at the memory of what had happened.

"I loved him, and he loved me."

There was a short, breathless pause. Something about her seemed to change. The hint of innocence, the sweet possibility that what she was describing was a young girl's infatuation, was pushed aside and banished forever by a second, more certain thought. The look in her eyes had turned seductive.

"He wanted me and I wanted him. Don't you understand? – I didn't want anyone else; I wanted him. He didn't force me; he didn't make me do anything I didn't want to do. I wanted him."

Like a teacher, or a priest, about to lecture a recalcitrant child, Hillary Clark shook her head.

"I understand that's what you think, but I also understand that you only think that because of what he did."

The girl looked at her as if she were completely mad.

"He took advantage of you, took advantage of your innocence and your youth." Clark turned to the jury just long enough to let them know that this was significant. "He didn't have to use physical force, he could dominate you mentally. He's your brother, isn't he? You're his sister."

The girl admitted this without embarrassment and without apology. It was hard to avoid the thought that, whether out of ignorance or some twisted set of loyalties, she refused to think that this was wrong. Or was there some other reason, Darnell wondered as he sat there watching the girl and the puzzled, startled, and yet still entranced expressions on the juror's faces. But if there was another reason, what was it and would it make things any better or only worse? He tugged on Adam's sleeve.

"Is she really your sister? Did you both have the same parents?" he whispered intently. "You need to tell me; I need to know."

Adam, wearing the same dark blue suit he did every day, turned and started to say something, another cryptic response, but when he saw how determined Darnell was to have an answer, he changed his mind and nodded solemnly.

"It's always been the way. No one can remember when it wasn't," he added with a peculiar, stoic glance as if there was something particularly venerable about a rule that made no sense. Darnell caught at it.

"To have…with your sister?"

But Adam had turned back to watch the girl and listen to what she would say next.

"So your brother, who is much older," Clark persisted, "convinced you that it would be all right, that there was nothing wrong – but you weren't old enough to make that decision; the fact that it was incest proves that you didn't know what you were doing, that he used his influence to -"

"Objection, your Honor," said Darnell calmly, as if he only wanted to help. "If counsel doesn't want to ask a question, I have a few I'd like to ask."

"Sustained," ruled Judge Pierce. "Ask a question, Ms. Clark. This isn't closing argument."

Hillary Clark had not moved her eyes from the witness.

"Just to be clear, did your brother – your older brother – have sex with you?"

"Yes."

"On one occasion, or more than that?"

"More than that."

"How often?"

"I don't know."

"You don't know? Because it happened so often?"

"As often as we felt the need."

"As often as you...? Just to be sure, is your brother older or younger than you are?"

"He came into being before."

"Came into being – that's an interesting way of putting it." Clark, afraid that her own witness had become hostile, tried to be friendly. "He was born before you were. And would you tell the court, please, how old you are?"

This was no trivial question and Darnell knew it. Even consensual sex could be rape if the girl was under-age. He was about to ask a question that would have gotten him laughed out of most courtrooms, but with nothing to lose there was no reason not to try it. Besides, whichever way the judge might rule, there was a point he had to make. Before the girl could answer he was on his feet lodging an objection.

"You object, Mr. Darnell?" asked Judge Pierce, doing nothing to hide her surprise. She watched the way he put his hand inside his jacket, straightening his tie like someone about to make a major announcement. That was something that could not be taught, the ability to make everything you did – every word, every gesture – seem important in itself and necessary to what you were trying to do. It would not have worked if he ever had to think about it, worry whether the effect would follow from the cause; it worked because after half a century everything he did seemed natural. It was, she thought, one distinct advantage of getting older.

"You object, Mr. Darnell – to what, exactly?"

"I object to the question about the young lady's age." He said this as if some great principle of the law was at stake.

"You object to...? Could you be a little more specific, because I'm afraid I don't see how that question could possibly be objectionable?

"If I could be permitted to ask a question of the witness in aid of objection, I believe the grounds for my objection will become apparent."

"By all means."

Darnell turned to the witness. His face fairly glowed with good will and benevolence.

"I know this question will probably strike you as strange, but please, if you would, just answer it honestly. The question is this: Do you have any conscious recollection about your birth? In other words, do you remember being born?"

There was an undercurrent of laughter, a sense in the courtroom that it was some kind of joke, a way to break the tension, an attempt by the legendary William Darnell to ingratiate himself with the witness by letting her have a brief respite from the intensity of the trial. But the girl did not laugh, she smiled.

"No, I have to say that I don't."

Darnell turned to Judge Pierce as if that should be the end of it.

"I'm sorry, Mr. Darnell, I still don't…."

"If she has no independent knowledge of her own birth, then she can only know what others have told her, which means that the only answer she can give to Ms. Clark's question about her age would be hearsay and, for that reason, inadmissible."

Hillary Clark was beside herself.

"That's not only wrong, it's ludicrous. Everyone is presumed to know how old they are."

"Presumed, Ms. Clark?" Darnell looked at her with a quizzical eye. "Presumed by whom?"

"By the law, Mr. Darnell. Witnesses are all the time asked to state their age."

"In an American courtroom?"

"Of course in an American courtroom," she replied, rolling her eyes at the sheer temerity with which he had introduced something as monumentally irrelevant as this.

"In America, where in every county we have a complete and accurate record of births and deaths? In America, where anyone can upon demand - for purposes, for example, of a judicial proceeding in which age is a crucial element of the case - produce a copy of their official birth

131

certificate – Is that what you mean?"

Now, too late, she saw where this was going. She cast a pleading eye upon Evelyn Pierce, but the judge, ignoring her, bent forward, eager to take up the argument.

"Is it your contention, Mr. Darnell, that in the absence of an official record proving the victim's – the alleged victim's – date of birth, the prosecution is barred from introducing any other evidence about her age?"

"No, not quite. The prosecution could certainly introduce the testimony of the parents, or of the doctor – if there was one - who delivered the baby; anyone who was there and has direct knowledge of the date the witness was born. That testimony would not be hearsay; this testimony is."

Judge Pierce studied him with new admiration. In a desultory fashion, she scratched the side of her neck.

"I've been on the bench a long time, but that's one argument I've never heard, and I must say, it's difficult to see what's wrong with it. Ms. Clark, do you have anything you want to say about it?"

"There's a reason you haven't heard that argument before. No one in their right mind would make it, no one -"

"Careful, Ms. Clark," warned Judge Pierce. "You better make sure you can win an argument before you start questioning the sanity of someone by whom you might be defeated!"

The courtroom burst with laughter. Hillary Clark's cheek turned red. Darnell, quite on purpose, seemed mildly amused.

"What I meant, your Honor," Clark insisted, "was that whether or not there are available official records, everyone knows their own age. In the same way, I might add, that everyone knows their own name. Or would Mr. Darnell try to argue that a witness couldn't testify to that unless he could produce an official document to prove it?"

"I certainly would," replied Darnell with a quick, decisive nod, "if one of the central elements of the case, one of the things the prosecution had the burden to prove, was the witness's true identity. But let me, in my turn, ask Ms. Clark a question: If the witness wasn't here, if you didn't have her on the stand to testify, would you argue that you didn't have to produce some official document to prove her age, if her age was, as it is here, essential to the case?"

"No, of course not; but we have the witness, and I will say it again: her testimony on the question is sufficient."

To everyone's confusion, Darnell seemed almost to agree with her.

"I suppose my objection is a bit radical. Very well – withdrawn."

"Withdrawn, Mr. Darnell?" inquired Judge Pierce. "It's a rather interesting question, one that -"

"Very well, I won't withdraw it. Would your Honor care to rule on it?"

For one of the few times anyone could remember, Evelyn Pierce laughed in court.

"'Hoisted on my own petard,' as the saying goes." Pursing her lips, she pondered her decision. "It is an interesting issue, but one that requires the time and expertise of an appellate court. So I'm going to overrule the objection and you can reserve it, should you need it, on appeal. Now, Ms. Clark, please continue. You were asking the witness how old she was."

"Seventeen," announced Alethia before Hillary Clark could even ask. "Seventeen last month."

"Which means that two years ago, when your brother made you pregnant, you were only fifteen years of age," said Clark in a voice full of pity. "Only fifteen," she repeated with a scornful glance at the defendant. "No more questions."

Darnell seemed surprisingly indifferent to the court's ruling on an objection to the girl's testimony about her age. Stranger still, his first question on cross-examination was to ask her to repeat it.

"How old again did you say you were?"

"Seventeen," she replied with the same, eager smile she had shown him before.

Darnell was practically bouncing up and down on the

balls of his feet.

"Fifteen, from what you said in response to Ms. Clark's question, at the time you conceived your child. Is that correct?"

"Yes, fifteen."

It is the first rule of cross-examination never to ask a question to which you do not already know the answer the witness is going to give. What set an attorney like William Darnell apart from the rest was the knowledge, or rather the instinct, of when to break it.

"But would I be wrong in assuming that where you come from, on that island where you lived, it's considered normal for a young woman that age to bear children?"

"No, you wouldn't be wrong. Fifteen, as young as thirteen even – whenever a girl becomes a woman."

Darnell cast a cautious glance at the jury.

"Yes, I think we understand. Now, just so there is no confusion on this point, you admit you had relations with the defendant and you insist that they were consensual, that he didn't in any way force you?"

"Force me? It's what I said: He's the only one I ever wanted."

Something about the way she said it, something in her voice, made Darnell look more closely.

"The only one you ever....Yes, I see. Well, never mind for now. I have only one or two more questions for the moment. You weren't forced to have sex with the defendant, but you became pregnant, and then, for some reason, shortly after the baby was born the baby died. I don't want now to discuss the circumstances of the baby's death; all I want to know is – whatever happened, whatever Adam did – was that also with your knowledge and consent?"

The courtroom stiffened. There is no other word for it. The reaction of two hundred people was identical to what any one of them would have done had they been left alone to hear and confront that dreadful question. The girl appeared to feel sorrier for Darnell, who had to ask it, than she did for herself.

"I knew what would happen; I knew there wasn't any choice."

"Thank you, my dear; that's all I have." He had taken only two steps before he turned back. "There is one other question I have to ask. Did you know that I first wanted to talk to you weeks ago, long before the trial started?"

"No, no one told me that."

"No one told you that the lawyer for the defense in this case had asked to interview you, to hear from you directly about what had happened?"

The girl remembered. She thought it was her fault.

"No, I mean yes; they asked me if I wanted to talk to Adam's lawyer. I asked if I could see Adam instead. Did I do something wrong?"

"No, you didn't do anything wrong. But someone did," he added, shaking his head at the way both he and the court had been lied to.

"Your Honor!" cried Hillary Clark as she tried to explain.

"Not now, Ms. Clark; but later – you can be sure of that – later we'll listen to what you have to say. Are you finished with the witness, Mr. Darnell?"

"Yes, for now; but I reserve the right to call her as a witness for the defense."

With a weary, dispirited sigh, a commentary on the way the prosecution had abused the rules, Carolyn Pierce glanced at the clock on the wall in back.

"It's getting late, Ms. Clark. I believe this was to be your last witness. Do you plan to call another?"

Embarrassed and momentarily chastened, Hillary Clark said she did not. She took a deep breath to steady herself and then, in the formal phrase that always ended the first phase of a trial, announced in as strong a voice as she could muster, "The prosecution rests."

Judge Pierce began to remind the jury that they were not to discuss the case, but Darnell was already on his feet, waving his arm.

"I have a matter for the court, your Honor."

Evelyn Pierce was tired, but not too tired to remember what Darnell was asking her to do. She told the bailiff to take the jury to the jury room.

"I take it you wish to make a motion, Mr. Darnell," she said as soon as the door shut behind the last juror.

Darnell made the motion always made at the end of the prosecution's case, asking that the charges be dismissed on the ground that, even if left uncontroverted, the evidence offered was not sufficient to prove the guilt of the defendant. He knew he did not have a chance on the charges of incest and murder – both had been as good as admitted – but rape was a different matter.

"The girl herself testified that while they had relations, those relations were entirely consensual. In the absence of any evidence that the girl was forced, the only thing left to the prosecution is to prove rape by statute, that the girl was too young, and the boy too old, for there to have been consent. Far from proving this, the prosecution hasn't even offered evidence on it."

"That's absurd," replied Hillary Clark. "The testimony of the girl was admitted over Mr. Darnell's objection. She testified she was only fifteen when this occurred, when her brother began to molest her."

"I object to the use of that word, your Honor; it's just another example of the prosecution's willingness to confuse accusation with proof. Yes, the girl's testimony was admitted. Yes, under the evidence admitted the girl was only fifteen. But the prosecution has managed to forget the most important element in any case of statutory rape: the existence of a statute. There is no applicable statute in the case – none that has been introduced – specifying the age below which a female cannot give consent. And even if, as unfair as this would be, the prosecution wants to say that we should apply our own statute – a statute these people could have known nothing about – that statute, which sets the age of consent at eighteen, requires that the age difference between the male and the female be at least three years. In other words, your Honor, the prosecution, to make its case, has to demonstrate not just that the girl was fifteen, but that the defendant was more then three years older. The prosecution can't call the defendant to testify against himself, and, as Ms. Clark admitted just a few minutes ago, in the absence of the direct testimony of the person in question, a birth certificate, some official record, is required. I don't remember seeing one, your Honor."

Hillary Clark was quivering with rage. Evelyn Pierce looked at her through half-closed eyes and in a cold, clear voice announced her decision.

"In the absence of any evidence about the defendant's age, the charge of rape is dismissed. With respect to the charges of incest and murder, the motion to dismiss is denied."

CHAPTER ELEVEN

Henry Hammersmith was waiting in the hallway just outside the courtroom. He looked at his old friend Darnell with the gloating confidence of a gambler about to collect on a sure thing, a bet he had known he could not lose.

"I told you I knew you'd pull it off. You really put the screws to her in there, the way you trapped her into admitting that she had to have a document if she didn't have someone's testimony." He shook his head in admiration for what, had he been on the other side of it, or had it been another one of Darnell's trials, he would have dismissed as just another shyster's trick, a piece of legal legerdemain that, even if effective, was still a scandal. "She didn't know what hit her! And you got the charge thrown out!"

"Thanks, Henry, but don't let's get carried away. We've done some good, that's all."

Along with Adam, they were making their way out of the courthouse. Darnell was still thinking about the trial, watching the scene all over again, what he had said, what Clark had answered, how it had all played out. He had set a trap, just like Henry said, but what Henry did not know was that it had been a trap without a plan. There had not been any thought, nothing like a developed strategy; it had come to him on the moment, the sudden realization that if Hillary Clark insisted that a witness knew her age, she would not think twice before agreeing that in the absence of the witness, age could only be proven by some sort of official documentation.

"You know, Henry," he said in confidence, "someone told me once that among the many writings of Aristotle there is a work called 'Sophistical Refutations.' I've never read it, and I doubt I'd understand it if I tried, but I like the title. It reminds me a lot of what I do – and what, you old bastard, you always accuse me of doing – attack an argument in a way that isn't quite legitimate. What I did in there – the safest thing to attack is what someone believes in most. It's almost always the thing they've thought about least. Why should they think about it? They know it's true. No one has ever questioned it."

They chatted for a few more minutes on the court-house steps. The air was cool and crisp and after a long day in court felt good against Darnell's face. He listened to Henry's words of encouragement, but out of the corner of his eye he watched the way Adam looked all around with the keen interest not of the idle tourist but of the well-informed traveler, someone who comes not to have a good time but to learn everything he can about each new place he visits. Seeing the girl, seeing Alethia, had made a marked differ-ence in the young man's attitude and demeanor. Busy with all the details of the trial, Darnell had not noticed any change before. He had not seen any sign of the wounded anguish that had worried Henry Hammersmith, but he saw it now in reverse reflection: the added quickness in his movements, the new intensity in his always eager eyes, and a greater confidence, to say nothing of the burnished glow upon his cheek.

"Yes, thank you Henry," said Darnell in reply to an earnest compliment he had barely heard. "I'll see you both in the morning." He turned to go, but then remembered. "Adam," he called after him, "tomorrow, after trial, I'll need you in my office to go over some things before you testify." Adam waved and then set off with an easy loping stride that forced Henry Hammersmith to take two steps for one of his.

The streets were crowded, everyone stuck in traf-fic. Blaring horns, shrieking brakes, the creaking, cranking sound of buses rounding corners, the tin bell charm of cable cars groaning on uphill iron rails, the city was a screaming welter of shouted noise and - every single discordant note of it - music to William Darnell's ears. He walked along, lost in the anonymity of the crowd, grateful for the privacy and the chance to clear his mind. He was only a half a block from his Sutter Street office when he remembered. He began to walk faster, afraid he might be late.

Gerhardt Holderlin was sitting in one of the large, overstuffed chairs in Darnell's outer office doing absolutely nothing. The daily newspapers and the latest editions of a half dozen magazines were arranged in perfect order on the square glass coffee table in front of him but he had not bothered with any of them. He seemed content to wait quietly, without the need to find some diversion from himself. To the contrary, he was so lost in thought that he did not know he was not still alone until, standing right in front of him, Darnell asked how long he had been there waiting.

"Not long, not long at all," he said with an eager smile.

Whatever the thought that had so preoccupied his mind, he was now outgoing and civil, assuring Darnell that he had not minded waiting at all; it had given him a much needed rest from all the noise and commotion of the city outside. Darnell led him into his private office and shut the door.

"This looks like a perfect place to think and work," remarked Holderlin. Not content with a cursory glance, he walked over to the book-lined shelves and began a closer inspection. He stopped in front of the photograph of Darnell's law school class and, with his hands clasped behind his back, studied it for a moment.

"Front row, fourth from the left." He looked back at Darnell, so much older now, for confirmation.

Impressed, as well as surprised, Darnell stood next to him, examining the picture, wondering that someone could pick him out so easily. Did he really still look like that serious and rather too intense young man with the confident, too confident, perhaps even arrogant, eyes? Darnell scratched his head and emitted a short, nostalgic laugh.

"It's been so long, I'm not sure I could have picked me out. You have an unusual eye, Mr. Holderlin. But, please, sit down."

Moving past him, Darnell dropped his briefcase on the floor and sank into the familiar comfort of his chair. He sat there a moment, letting the tension of the trial run out of him, a way to trick himself into thinking that it was all the rest he needed. Full of false energy, he sprang forward, pushed a button on the intercom and asked his secretary if she would mind bringing him a cup of coffee before she left for the day. He hesitated, glanced across at his visitor, and asked if she would mind bringing two.

"Do you want me to wait, Mr. Darnell?" asked his secretary after she brought the coffee. She had been with him for nearly thirty years and knew his habits better than he knew them himself. Almost as much as Summer Blaine, she understood that without someone to badger him into it, he would not do any of the things he was supposed to do for his health.

"I'll be fine. You can go," he said, his eyes fixed on Holderlin, wondering what this interesting European was going to say.

"Are you sure?" she asked doubtfully.

His eyes moved away from Holderlin and reached her full of willful guile.

"I promise I won't do anything I shouldn't. I won't drink more than a fifth of whisky and I won't smoke more than two cigars!"

"You're impossible, you know."

His gaze became gentle and considerate, a look with which he often let her know that he did not doubt she was right but that there was nothing either one of them could do about it. She understood that, accepted it, but still felt better – they both felt better - for reminding him just how incorrigible he was.

"Now, Mr. Holderlin," he said when the door shut and they were left alone, "you've come all the way from Berlin because you think you might be able to help me. You said you had been on the island forty years ago, and that there were things I should know. Why don't you tell me first how you found it, how you discovered it? And then perhaps you might explain why no one knew what you did – Why no one else seems to have known this island existed before Captain Johansen found it just two years ago?"

Holderlin sipped slowly on his coffee and then held the cup and saucer in his lap. He listened to Darnell, nodding in agreement with what he said, but seemed reluctant to begin, as if the answers to those few short questions would take an endless telling.

"It was forty years ago, but it began longer ago than that, when I was still a boy, if you want the whole truth of it. My father was an archeologist who spent more time in Egypt than he did at home. He told me stories about ancient civilizations that had been buried for thousands of years before their ruins were first discovered. He told me about the Egyptians and the Persians; he told me about the Sumerians and the Greeks, about all the oldest, lost civilizations, but the story that most astonished me, the one that, once I heard it, stayed in my mind, was how Schliemann discovered Troy. Schliemann – how he discovered....Do you know that story, Mr. Darnell, the curious thing that Schliemann did? A thing so obvious that...which is the reason no one had thought to do it before. Do you know how remarkable it is to think something possible that no one else believes?"

Holderlin's voice was like a dark echo, everything he said coming back on itself. The words ran together, then stopped, as if each time he started he knew he could not finish, the thought to which he was trying to give expression that elusive.

Darnell was not quite sure what he remembered about Schliemann and the discovery of Troy, only that he remembered something.

"Schliemann – the name; yes, I think....I might have read...but no, I can't recall anything now."

"Schliemann read Homer. That was not so remarkable; a hundred years ago everyone – everyone in Germany - did. It was part of every schoolboy's education. But Schliemann took it seriously; that is to say, he left open the possibility that this great work of poetry, a work that was supposed to be nothing more than a fiction based on legend, was real and that the ancient city of Troy was in the very place Homer said it was. So he looked, tracing the descriptions in the Iliad, and found it exactly where it should have been. Astonishing! Schliemann discovered Troy by reading Homer. And that's how I found Atlantis, or what was left of it."

"How you found -?" Darnell now realized that Holderlin was not a fraud, a sly adventurer, some con-man trying to sell a made-up story for money; Holderlin was demented, insane, living in a world of his own invention, a would-be modern day Columbus who instead sailing across an uncharted ocean had fallen irretrievably into an imaginary past.

"You asked why no one knows what I found forty years ago – because of that: your reaction," said Holderlin, triumphant in the certainty of his knowledge. "The reaction anyone of intelligence would have had. Discover Atlantis? What proof could I offer?   I had none, but even if I had there were reasons I could not – did not – tell anyone what I had found. It's a secret I've never shared with anyone – until now."

He looked across the book-lined room to the window and the city lights outside. There was a long pause as he steadied himself, as it seemed, for what he had to do.

"I don't blame you for not believing me. There have been times during all these years when I've wondered whether I should believe it myself, whether it isn't some strange delusion that took possession of my mind; times when I have asked that question that casts doubt on my own sanity: whether the madman ever knows he's mad. It's a question I can't and won't pre-judge for you, Mr. Darnell. Let me tell you what I did, and what I found, and then you can decide whether what I've said is the truth or the ravings of some lunatic who ought to be put away.

"Schliemann read Homer and discovered Troy. The story, as I said, made a great and lasting impression on my boyish mind. That isn't to say it became an obsession, or anything like that; in fact, I didn't think much about it while I was growing up, a child in my father's house, nor did it form the basis for what I finally decided I wanted to be. My father told me all those stories, but of course he only did that when he was home, which, as I grew older, was less and less all the time. There had been a gradual estrangement between my parents, which, when I realized it later, explained much about the way we lived. One effect was that, in terms of my mental development, I went my own way." Holderlin hesitated, went back to the thought and started again. "That isn't true of course; we none of us ever really do that – we're always dependent, except for a very few of us, and then only when we're much older, on the influence of others. My point is that without my father's constant presence I was much more open to what I heard in school, what my teachers taught about what was important and what was of only passing interest. By the time I went to university I had no doubt that the only subject worth study-ing was philosophy.

"I studied all of it, ancient and modern, but I was drawn most of all to Plato. At first, it may have been the way he wrote; not the sometimes mind-numbing treatises of Aristotle, to say nothing of the scholastics, but in those wonderful dialogues that make even the most difficult ques-tions come alive. The problem, which I did not understand until much later, was that Plato wrote at different levels, disguising what he really meant in words that, if you looked closely, had a double meaning and sometimes more than that. He had such a genius for concealment that he could hide what he wanted to say by not appearing to hide it at all. You can spend a lifetime trying to find out what he really means."

Holderlin lapsed into a long silence. He sipped some coffee; then, very carefully, afraid he might break them, put the cup and saucer safely on the edge of Darnell's large ornate desk. He seemed to disappear inside himself, trying to recall with exact precision what it was important for Darnell to know: the extraordinary thing that had happened to him and the utterly accidental way it had occurred.

"I must have read it who knows how many times – a dozen, more than that? And not in German, mind you – in

Greek. One of the most difficult of the dialogues – not as difficult, I admit, as the Parmenides, but difficult enough – the dialogue in which Plato takes up the not unimportant question of the origin of the world, or rather, whether it has an origin, whether it has come into being or has always been. Someone said that we are all born metaphysicians, all those questions we ask as children about the why of things, but that we grow out of it. Perhaps I never did – grow up, I mean; perhaps I always remained a child – because once I read the Timaeus I knew I had to try to master it, had to understand every nuanced word of it. I decided to write my doctoral dissertation on it.

"Strange I didn't see it, didn't think of it right away, the first time I came upon that passage, instead of a year later, when I was going through the dialogue for what I thought might be the last time; the last time, I mean, before I finished writing and was ready to take my degree. It was always there, in plain sight, the story of what happened to Atlantis."

A tiny, shrewd smile creased Holderlin's mouth. It was the look of someone who had stumbled upon something no one else had known; it was the look of someone who now believed in chance.

"I had considered myself so independent-minded, fully able to make my own judgments, but I was still under the influence of others; the 'spirit of the age,' some might call it, the belief that we did not have to understand Plato as Plato understood himself, that we knew him better than he knew himself because we had the advantage of history and could understand the assumptions of the age in which he wrote. It is always the arrogance of the present to look down upon the past. That was the reason I paid so little attention, why I did not take seriously what Plato wrote about Atlantis. It was just another fable, a contemporary myth he could use to explain a point. Then, late one night, as I sat reading through it for what I thought would be the last time, I suddenly remembered – I could hear my father's voice – that story about Schliemann and how reading Homer he found

Troy. What if everything Plato said was true?"

He expected some reaction, an acknowledgement of the breath-taking possibility this opened up, but Darnell was forced to tell him that, beyond the blunt assertion that Plato had written something about Atlantis, he had only the vaguest idea what any of this meant. He motioned toward the bookshelves that towered to the ceiling.

"I'm afraid that my life and education have been more limited than yours. I'm a lawyer, Mr. Holderlin – that's all I know. The last time I read anything Plato wrote was when I was an undergraduate, and apart from a feeling that it must have done me good, I couldn't tell you much, if anything, about what it said."

There was nothing superior in the broad smile that suddenly crossed Holderlin's fine, straight mouth. It was the look, rather, of genuine good-will; of approval, if not outright admiration, for a man who did not hide his ignorance behind a cloak of self-importance, dismissing ancient learning as irrelevant to the more pressing issues of the moment. If children were born metaphysicians, men like Darnell when they got close to the end sometimes greeted death that way as well. Holderlin got up from the chair and walked over to the window. He stood there for a moment, watching the busy, endless movement on the streets.

"No one has time to waste," he observed out loud; "and so they waste all of it." He turned back to Darnell. "I'll tell you what he wrote. It's a story that was told to Solon, the famous lawgiver, the wisest of the Seven Sages, a story that was passed down through four generations before someone called Critias told it to Socrates. I've studied it so often, gone over it so many times, that I know it now by heart, but I won't recite it to you – it would take too long and I know you have things you need to do. I'll try to give you a brief summary, but in a way that gives you a feel for how it was written in the dialogue that Plato left us.

"Solon traveled to Egypt, to the city of Sais in the Delta, a city founded by the goddess Neith, who, the Egyptians claim, is the same goddess the Hellenes call

Athena. Solon talked to the priests, who kept track of ancient things, and tried to draw them out by telling them about the most ancient things in his part of the world, about the great Deluge and how long ago it had occurred. One of the priests, a man of very great age, laughed and said that the Hellenes were all children without one old man among them. Solon and the other Hellenes talked about the 'great Deluge' as if there had been only one of them, when in fact there had been many.

"'There have been, and will be again,' he said, 'many destructions of mankind arising out of many causes; the greatest have been brought about by the agencies of fire and water, and other lesser ones by innumerable other causes.' There have been great conflagrations upon the earth, fires that recur at long intervals, and when they happen many of those who live on the mountains and in other dry places perish, and only those who live near the rivers or the sea survive. There have also been great floods and then those who live by the rivers and by the sea are destroyed and only the herdsmen and the shepherds who live on the moun- tains are left alive. But neither fire nor flood destroys the Egyptian because the Nile saves them from fire and the river's flood is always self-contained. That is the reason that though all other civilizations have vanished and not left any record of their existence, the Egyptians have remembered. 'And whatever happened either in your country or ours,' the priest told Solon, 'or in any other region of which we are informed – if there were any actions noble or great or in any other way remarkable, they have all been written down by us of old and are preserved in our temples.'"

Holderlin searched Darnell's eyes to make sure he grasped the full significance of what he was being told: how easily, and how often, the past had been forgotten.

"What Solon knew, or thought he knew, about the origins of his own people was, according to the Egyptian, no better than the 'tales of children.' The priest tells him: You remember only a single deluge, but there were many. And then he tells him that far beyond the memories of any

Athenian then living, there had been another Athens which contained 'the fairest and noblest race of men which ever lived,' and that 'you and your whole city are descended from the few survivors of this race of men.' That city, that ancient city, was the best governed and the best in war of any city that ever was. Solon of course wants to know more about this, and among other things, how long ago this was. The priest tells him that this ancient Athens, which none of the Athenians now remember because of the great Deluge that destroyed it, came into being a thousand years before Egypt and Egypt is eight thousand years old."

"Nine thousand years ago?" asked Darnell, following intently.

"Nine thousand years when Solon was alive, which was four generations before Critias tells the story to Socrates nearly twenty-five hundred years ago. The Egyptian is describing an Athens that existed nearly twelve thousand years before you and I were born, an Athens of which we have no record, but in which the Egyptian claimed to believe. If you think that impossible, ask yourself why. This country, for example, isn't even two hundred fifty years old, and even without the kind of cataclysms that wipes out the memory of things, how much has already been forgotten about what happened at the beginning?"

Darnell's eyes moved to the photograph of his law school class. He was struck by how little he could remember of the once familiar faces that he had seen almost every day for three full years. In the absence of the kind of brilliant single-minded concentration Adam had – though where he had gotten it remained a mystery - human memory was at best a feeble instrument.

"Twelve thousand years, Mr. Holderlin. Yes, go on."

"As I say, Solon wanted to know more, wanted to know everything: the laws they had, their way of life, what made them as great as the Egyptian said they had been. The priest tells him many things. He tells him that the best of the Egyptian laws are the counterpoint of the ones Athens had in what he calls the 'olden time,' when everything was dedicat-

ed to supremacy in both wisdom and war. He tells him that
their histories contain the record of a number of great things
the city did, but that one of them stands out as the greatest
thing of all, the war that Athens fought against Atlantis."

Holderlin leaned forward, eager to go on, to share with
someone, finally, after all these years, the secret, or rather
the beginnings of the secret, he had uncovered, the great
discovery he had made.

"A mighty power – that was how the Egyptian
described it –invaded all of Europe and Asia. He means
Europe around the Mediterranean and what we call the
Near and Middle East. This power came out of the Atlantic
Ocean – and the narrator is compelled to point out that the
Atlantic was in that distant time navigable, which has to
mean that at the time Critias is telling this story the Atlantic
was not navigable. There was an island in front of the
Pillars of Hercules, an island larger than Libya and Asia
put together. He doesn't meant Libya the way we know it
today; he means the whole of North Africa. This island had
to have been enormous. Even more noteworthy is the fact
that, according to the story, the island served as the way to
other islands and that from these islands you could pass to
the opposite continent. Do you see the significance of this?
- Islands, a chain of them, easy navigation to another continent, what today we call the Americas, and Atlantis, this
great empire, controlling all of it.

"Atlantis had already subjected parts of North Africa
and Europe and was on its way to conquering everything,
ruling, for all intents and purposes, the entire civilized world
as it was known at the time. Only Athens stood in her way,
but Athens, by her strength and virtue, drove Atlantis back
beyond the Pillars of Hercules and saved from slavery both
Europe and Asia. And then, at the very moment of its greatest strength, Athens, along with Atlantis, disappeared.

"It was one of those great cataclysms, perhaps the
greatest one of all, tremendous earthquakes and floods. The
priest, according to the account of Critias – the account,
remember, that Plato has written – tells Solon that 'in a

single day and night of misfortune all your warlike men
in a body sank into the earth and the island of Atlantis in
similar fashion vanished in the depths of the sea.' Then he
adds an interesting remark that parallels something he had
said earlier: The sea that had once been navigable is now
'impassable and impenetrable.' When the island sank below
the sea a great mud shoal was created, blocking the entrance
to the Mediterranean."

Staring straight ahead, Holderlin concentrated on what
he had learned and what he was now trying hard to explain.
Suddenly, he extended his index finger and with a quick,
slashing movement began to trace over and over again the
outline of a triangle. The significance of this, if there was
any, was lost on Darnell, but not the urgent sense of imme-
diacy. Once, twice, three times - that same intense motion,
the movement of a conductor with his orchestra or a teacher
of geometry with his class. Then it stopped.

"So, you see, Mr. Darnell, there it was, right in front of
me, the story of Atlantis and where it was."

But Darnell did not see, or rather what he saw was
no different than the common myth or legend everyone had
heard: an ancient island that had sunk beneath the waves,
a civilization that had once existed and then disappeared,
leaving not the slightest trace of what it was or where it had
been.

"But you must see, Mr. Darnell. It isn't that Atlantis
once existed; it's what the story tells us about where it was,
and something more than that, something, I confess, I hadn't
noticed, hadn't thought about, all the other times I had read
it. Atlantis wasn't just an island in the normal sense; it was
larger than 'Libya and Asia put together.' It was more the
size of a continent than an island and, remember, there were
other islands on the other side, stepping stones, if you will,
to the continent that formed the western boundary of the
sea."

Darnell still did not understand. "But even if all of
that was true, Atlantis disappeared. 'In a single day and
night' – isn't that what you said? – and it vanished beneath

the sea."

Holderlin beat his knuckles on the edge of Darnell's desk.

"Yes, precisely! It vanished, but in that day and night how many people got away? How many of them were living somewhere on the western edge, how many of them made it to that bridge of smaller islands that led eventually to what we call the Americas? - None at all? Remember what the Egyptian priest told Solon, that whatever happened, fire or flood, there were always a few survivors? That was the possibility that finally caught my attention and ultimately became my obsession. Because, you see, if Atlantis had simply vanished and left no trace behind, how was it that Plato, in another place, described the way these people lived?

"We do not have all of the dialogue called Critias, but we have enough to know that Plato did this. Of course, Plato might have created it entirely out of his own remark-able mind, but I could not let go of the possibility that he might have written about Atlantis the way Homer had writ-ten about Troy, not from the things he may have imagined, but from some authoritative source, those records that had once been kept with such painstaking devotion by the caste of priests in Egypt who had preserved them through eight thousand years. What if Atlantis was real, and what if some part of it had not been destroyed? What if the survivors had found their way across the islands, islands which themselves later disappeared, across to the safety of the western conti-nent, to South America and then, perhaps....Well, that's what I could not let go of once I decided that Plato, who believed absolutely in the truth, might not have been lying, and that just as Schliemann found Troy I could find Atlantis – not the island that sank in the ocean, but the new Atlantis that might have been brought into being by the survivors of the old one. And I did."

CHAPTER TWELVE

"Two thousand years after Plato wrote those astonishing dialogues of his, there were reports that seemed
to confirm what I now suspected. There was an island,
Antillia, called by the Portuguese the Island of the Seven
Cities. The earliest etymology connected the name with
Atlantis, and the island itself is marked on an anonymous
map of 1424. You can imagine the excitement I felt the first
time I examined it in the ducal library at Weimar. Whoever
drew that map had done so with all the exactness the knowledge of the age permitted, which, while it may not have been
the same as the precision cartographers can now employ,
was certainly sufficient to give a likeness of the shape,
proportion and relative distance among the things known
to those who had seen them with their own eyes or listened
to the trusted reports of others. What reason would anyone
have to distort the truth, pretend that something was there
that was not? What reason would anyone have had to invent
such things, to tell such lies? It was the Middle Ages, how
could the existence of an island make any difference to the
Church?"

Darnell could think of no reply, but it did not matter.
The question was not one that had, or even needed, an
answer; it was a question, one of the questions, that had
driven Holderlin on what the world would have thought a
mad pursuit, a search for a legend, a legend that he alone
believed was true.

The afternoon had turned to evening and evening
was on its way to night. The lamp on Darnell's desk cast an
eerie, yellow glow, and, with each movement of Holderlin's
delicate, expressive hands, shadows pale and insignificant
danced against the wall. Darnell watched in quite wonder
as Holderlin became more animated, more excited, the more
he told about the way that something he had learned from an

ancient writing had led to what, if he were telling the truth, was one of the great adventures of modern times.

"That map was dated, as I say, in 1424, but that was not the only time Antillia was located in the middle of the Atlantic. Beccaria the Genoese put it on a map in 1435, and the Venetian, Andrea Bianco, did so a year later in 1436. There were other maps, in 1455 and again in 1476, that did the same thing. On most of them Antillia is accompanied by three smaller islands: Royllo, St. Atanagio, and Tammar. What is most interesting is the way they are classified. They aren't called legendary or mythical; there is not the slightest suggestion of any doubt about their authenticity." Holderlin's whole body seemed to tense; his head became so rigid it shuddered. There was a brilliant intensity to his eyes, as if his mind was filled with fire. "They are classified, these islands that are supposedly only the stuff of legend, as 'insulae de novo repertai,' newly discovered islands. Newly discovered islands, Mr. Darnell, newly discovered! Do you see what this means? They were real!"

Suddenly aware of his own intensity, Holderlin threw up his hands and laughed with embarrassment. He jumped out of the chair and started toward the window, but then changed his mind and came back. Instead of sitting down again, however, he stood with his hand on the back of the chair in the idle posture of someone not quite certain how to compress into a few words of intelligible speech what it had taken him years to understand.

"Maps, I must have looked at hundreds of them – and then there were all the other documents: charters, royal commissions, the records of journeys that never got started, journeys that were begun but never finished, the ships and crews never heard from again, lost somewhere in the vast reaches of the Atlantic. I visited libraries all over Europe, public libraries, private libraries, libraries in universities, libraries in monasteries. I found in one of them the letters of Paul Toscanelli, a Florentine, who had written to both Columbus and the Portuguese court. It was 1474, the height of the Renaissance, and Toscanelli was no fool. He does not just assume that Antillia exists, he takes it to be the half-way mark between Lisbon and the island of Cipango or Zipangus, the island we call Japan. But more curious even than that is the globe made in Nuremburg in 1492 by the geographer Martin Behaim. According to him, in 734, after the Moors had conquered Spain and Portugal, the island of Antillia was colonized by Christian refugees led by the archbishop of Oporto and six bishops. The inscription in the globe adds that the island was sighted by a Spanish vessel in the year 1414.

"Others dismiss all this as legend, the workings of the far too credulous medieval mind, but to me it made perfect sense. It was just what Plato said, what he put into the mouth of that Egyptian priest – what he may have first learned from an Egyptian priest – that in every great deluge the only survivors were the ones who lived on mountains. Atlantis was larger than Libya and Asia, not so much an island as a continent. When the earthquake came, when Atlantis sank beneath the sea, some of the mountains must have become the islands that remain there, in the Atlantic, to this day. But that would mean that there were survivors, that Atlantis did not vanish without a trace; that the memory of what Atlantis had been survived, and could, somewhere else, live again. And then there was the word itself – Antilles – traced back all those thousands of years ago to Atlantis, and then identified as the land Columbus discovered in what is now called the Gulf of Mexico. Everyone assumes that this only proves that Atlantis had been a legend, that the islands said to have been 'newly discovered' in the 15th century had always been there, and that the name 'Antilles' was a giant misunderstanding, the result of having confused myth with reality. I believed on the contrary that the movement of the name traced the movement of a people, the remnant of what had once been, twelve thousand years ago, the greatest and most powerful civilization in the world. Any doubt I may have had vanished when I made my way to South America and traveled to Peru."

"To Peru?" asked Darnell. But Holderlin was already

thinking of something else, a crucial piece of information that, in his hurry to tell his story, he had forgotten to add.

"So much happened, there were so many possibilities I explored, so many different conjectures about what might have happened twelve thousand years ago, that is isn't always easy to recall the sequence in which one thought followed the other, much less how each thought led me to take a certain action. There were so many false beginnings, promising starts that came to nothing and had to be abandoned so I could start again. Forgive me, if you can, for being sometimes less coherent than I should. There was something vital I forgot to mention, something that made me think first that the islands I spoke of had been the mountain tops of Atlantis, and that at the same time seemed to prove it. And once again it was something I read in Plato, in that dialogue of which we have only the first part. In the Critias, describing the geography of Atlantis, he tells us that the island 'was famous for its encircling mountains, more tall and beautiful than any that exist today.' These mountains contained many villages that were wealthy and, moreover, had on them 'timbers of different kinds in quantities more than sufficient for every kind of manufacture.'

"'Every kind of manufacture' – that fact seemed decisive. It meant they could build anything; ships, for example, that would have let them sail anywhere – west to the safety of the other islands, and, beyond them, to that other continent, when the earthquake and the great Deluge destroyed everything. But what really sent me in the right direction, what sent me to South America and Peru, was the description Plato gives about the things they built in Atlantis: the sheer size and grandeur of their palaces and other buildings; the way they cut canals, some of them a hundred feet deep, some of them a hundred feet in width, to make the island a series of concentric circles of land and sea, to protect themselves from any threat of invasion; the magnificence of its temples all coated in silver except for the statues that were covered in gold. Plato writes of what these people accomplished, that 'it sounds incredible that any work of human hands should be so vast by comparison with other achievements of the kind.'"

Holderlin shook his head in amazement, but whether at what Plato had written or the strange consequence it had had for Holderlin himself, Darnell could not guess. Still standing, Holderlin turned away and looked around the darkened room the way someone on the open deck of a sailing ship might gaze up at the stars, more for what he remembered about other places and other nights than for anything he saw. The lines in his forehead deepened and grew broader, and with each passing moment the further back in time he seemed to go.

"You were about to tell me something about South America," said Darnell, his voice in the silence the whisper of a reminder that the present, still existing, had not been buried in the past. Holderlin blinked his eyes.

"South America? – Yes, of course," he said, coming back to himself enough to remember where he was. A shy, almost bashful smile moved with deer-like feet across his mouth. "I never thought I would tell anyone what I'm telling you; and telling it, saying it out loud instead of seeing it in my mind the way I have so often over the years, takes me back, brings me closer, to the way I was when much of what I'm telling you was still ahead of me. Perhaps I should have written it down, kept a journal; I could probably tell it better if I had. But then, if I had done that, I wonder if I wouldn't have changed things, altered them a little, to make what happened seem more logical and coherent, to give it, the way we do any story, a sense of inevitability, when I can assure you, Mr. Darnell, there was nothing inevitable about it. To the contrary, when I look back on it, without any written record to convince me otherwise, I'm struck by how much of what happened on that strange voyage of discovery happened by chance. Peru, for example: It wasn't reading Plato that sent me there; it was a soldier in the war."

"A soldier in the war?" asked Darnell, wondering if he had heard him right.

"Yes, in every sense of the word; a survivor, if you

can call him that, of Germany's twelve year nightmare."
Holderlin looked at Darnell with the grim nostalgia foreign
to most Americans and known at once by older Europeans.
"You were in the war? You were old enough for that?"

"Yes. Toward the end of it; the war in the Pacific
against the Japanese."

"Then you have some sense of what war does to
people, the memories they have to live with when it's finally
over."

"But you weren't in the war; you must have been just a
child."

"That's true of course; I wasn't old enough to be a
soldier, like Jurgen Reinhardt, my teacher and my friend.
But whatever age you were, if you were in Germany, you
were in the war."

"Jurgen Reinhardt – He was your teacher and he was
the one who...?"

"I was a student at the Free University of Berlin in
the 1960s when Berlin was a divided city. Reinhardt was
a professor of history with a special interest in classical
architecture. He was a strange man, or perhaps I should say
he was not strange at all: there were a lot of men like him
in Germany after the war, desperate to lose themselves in
something – anything – that would keep them from thinking
about what had happened. Many of them turned to business, to the work of putting the German economy back on
its feet, to rebuilding everything that had been destroyed.
They used the future to shut out the past. Some others, men
who had had some serious training, men who could not
forget themselves in a swirl of activity, men who knew too
much for that, tried to reconstruct something of Germany's
previous dedication to music, the arts, and the life of the
mind. Jurgen Reinhardt tried to overcome the past by taking
himself much farther back in time, making himself a home
in the ancient histories of other people.

"Did you ever have a teacher when you were in
university who almost overnight made you change the way
you thought about precisely the things you had always taken

most for granted; made you question – and not just question, completely revise – all the basis assumptions of your life? It is the greatest gift anyone can give, and Reinhardt gave it to a whole generation of German students. I wasn't one of them; that was my misfortune. If I still say he was my teacher, it is because in the most serious sense it's true. I only came to know him when, upon the successful completion of my doctorate, I joined the faculty and began my own career, one which still continues. Reinhardt was very much my senior – one of the lecture halls is now named after him – but in addition to his brilliance he was exceptionally kind. It was, as I came to understand later when I learned of what he had gone through as a soldier in the war, one of the few who survived Stalingrad, the kindness of a man who, if I can put it like this, had no more life to live. When I first knew him, he was not yet fifty but he was already a relic, old before his time, hobbling down the hallway on a single crutch and one good leg.

"Reinhardt was the only one I trusted, the only one I knew would not laugh when I told him my conjectures about Atlantis and the possibility of survivors. A man like Reinhardt – after what he had been through: Stalingrad, the long Russian winter, the brutal carnage he had seen...the awful things he had suffered, the unspeakable things he had been forced, ordered, to do – what would seem impossible to him? He listened, just the way you are doing now, with a thoughtful expression. He did not feel the need, as so many others would have done, to take the side of convention, of what others believed, and insist that it was all too absurd, that everyone knew that Atlantis was a fable, an invention of ancient poets and story-tellers, no more to be taken seriously than the story of Jason and the Golden Fleece."

This last phrase brought a pause as Holderlin suddenly realized why had used it. A mirthful look of shrewd curiosity passed through his eager eyes. With the back of his fingers, he scratched the side of his face.

"The fable of the fleece was no more a fable than Atlantis. That was the first thing Reinhardt told me, the example he used to encourage me to go forward with what I planned to do. The Golden Fleece – sheepskins dipped in a Thracian river to collect the tiny particles of gold that washed down from the mountains. With perfect patience, Reinhardt explained the solid ground on which that, and other so-called legends, came to be. He listened to everything, the summary of all my research, the different conjectures, the various contradictions, the inconsistencies, the false starts, the false hopes, and through it all, the single thread that had never quite been broken, the belief that all of it made more sense than the alternative; that Plato had been right, that Atlantis had not been a dream, and that instead of vanishing entirely it was still there, islands above the surface and God knows how many tribes of men.

"Reinhardt was not sure he could go that far. As I say, he had seen too much to dismiss anything as impossible, but, for the same reason, he was cautious in his judgments. I can still see him sitting there, in that small, Spartan office of his; a cubbyhole, really, barely big enough for his small desk and two wooden chairs; everything, all his papers, his few books, neatly arranged, nothing ever out of place. It was late in the afternoon, in January, just after the Christmas holiday, and so bitter cold we wore coats and sweaters inside. When I finished telling him what I thought I had discovered, after he told me that it was an interesting line of speculation and that I should follow my instinct and pursue it, he lapsed into a profound silence. I remember glancing out the window at the falling snow, thinking how quiet everything had become. And then, finally, Reinhardt spoke.

"'That would explain something I've never understood. If you're right, this may be a way to prove it, or at least to lend what you say some tangible support, and perhaps, more importantly, give you an idea where you need to go next. You know about the Incas?'

"I didn't know much: indigenous natives of South America, an unusual religion; a cruel, violent, and barbarous people, I guessed. With his usual kindness, Reinhardt showed me how truly ignorant I was." There was a sparkle

in Holderlin's eyes as he recounted Reinhardt's subtle procedure. "He didn't tell me what he knew; he pulled a book off
the shelf behind him as if he was himself not quite sure. He
read aloud about 'cyclopean ruins of vast edifices, apparently
never completed,' about works that 'appear to have been
erected by powerful sovereigns with unlimited command
of labor, possibly with the object of giving employment to
subjugated people, while feeding the vanity or pleasing the
taste of the conquerors.' Reinhardt then looked right at me
to repeat the next line he read: 'Of their origin nothing is
historically known.'

"You can understand how intensely interested I
became. No one knew for certain how these great works
had come into existence. Someone had built them, or started
to build them, but why they were built, what their purpose
was – it was all conjecture. What was known was that the
Incas – the 'People of the Sun,' as they called themselves
– had conquered the region and, to provide against attack,
occupied the mountains that surround the valley of Cuzco
and Lake Titicaca at an elevation of twelve thousand feet.
Would anyone do that who wasn't used to living on mountains? Would anyone do that who didn't feel a need, passed
down through the generations, to be as close as they could to
the sun, the god they worshipped? The more Reinhardt read
from that description of the Incas, the more certain I was
that he was right, that I had to go to Peru and see for myself
what they had done.

"There were other things that Reinhardt told me,
other things he read from that book of his, which gave me
encouragement and hope. When the Incas first come into
history, that is to say, when we first have any record of them,
they already were in possession of a considerable civilization. Their empire extended from north of Quito to the river
Maule in the south of Chile, a region which they ruled with
a system of roads and post-houses over mountain ranges and
deserts, and an attention to administrative detail that included the use of accurate statistics. Where did this learning
come from? Was it possible that it just sprang up, by itself,

in the midst of a primitive people? And then there was this –
and when Reinhardt read it to me, I knew I was right. I later
borrowed his book and went over every line of it. This is
what was written about the things they built:

'The edifices displayed marvelous building skill, and
their workmanship is unsurpassed. The world has nothing
to show, in the way of stone-cutting and fitting, to equal the
skill and accuracy displayed in the Inca structures of Cuzco.'

"That isn't all, Mr. Darnell. In a few short words,
a few astonishing words, a comparison is drawn between
what the Incas did and the achievements of contemporary
Europeans:

'As workers in metals and as potters they displayed
infinite variety of design, while as cultivators and engineers
they excelled their European conquerors.'

"Yes, conquerors: at the beginning of the 16th century,
when Francisco Pizarro and the Spanish came. The question
then would be whether the survivors of Atlantis, the generations that had kept moving west, had moved again. But first,
I had to go to Peru, to find out what I could. Six months
later, when I ended my classes for the year, I took a leave
from the university and began my journey. I did not come
back until two years later."

At the mention of how long he had been gone, how
long that fateful exploration had taken, Holderlin straightened his shoulders and, as if he did not need support of any
kind, let go of the back of the chair. He stood there, tall and
proud, his perfectly balanced face shining with the faded
brilliance of his own achievement, an achievement more
impressive because it had all these years remained a secret.

"I had no money; not the kind that someone would
need to mount a serious expedition. I was alone, a young
scholar who had never expected more than to live a life of
what used to be called shabby gentility. There are, however,
certain advantages to being relatively impoverished. It did
not occur to me that I could not travel as cheaply as I lived.
Nearly every summer I had gone on long walking tours of
Germany and France; I could certainly find my way around

South America. I wonder, Mr. Darnell, if the key to human progress isn't human ignorance. If we knew in advance all the trouble, all the hardships we would face, would we ever try to do anything? I didn't have money to book passage on an ocean liner; I worked my way across the Atlantic on a tramp steamer."

Holderlin stared down at his feet, an expression of wistful mocking, the felt affection for the lost certainties of his vanished youth, dancing softly in his eyes.

"It was the hardest work I'd ever done," he said, laughing. "But I got there, the western shore of South America, and made my way into the mountains, up to Cuzco and the Inca ruins, where I was disappointed. Disappointed? I was depressed. There were ruins all right, and even my untrained eye could see that there must once have been something that was truly monumental; but I wasn't trained, an archeologist who can tell from a few broken shards of pottery what a whole culture might have looked like. In my eager desire to find the proof of Atlantis, I had expected some clear sign of the thriving civilization Reinhardt had described to me: buildings shining gold and silver in the sun-drenched mountain air, projects that dwarfed the imagination of what Europeans had ever tried to do, even, I suppose, the ghosts of engineers and warriors still at work; but instead I found, among those crumbling ruins and pathetic excavations, a few rumpled Indians with flea-bitten llamas selling trinkets in the square.

"Had I been wealthy, had I come there at the head of some well-financed expedition, I would have done the intelligent thing and simply gone home; but I didn't have money and, worse yet, I was young and didn't worry that I was wasting time. I was also, to give my youth more credit, resilient; which only means that I still knew how to forget my initial disappointment. I taunted myself with my arrogance, my unreasonable expectations. What had I thought would happen? That someone would run up to me and tell me that everyone there knew all about how the Incas first arrived and had only been waiting for me to show up so they could tell me? I began to make inquiries."

Holderlin searched Darnell's eyes for common ground, the sense that men of their age shared for the travesty of logic that formed the unwritten biography of their early lives. A huge grin engulfed his buoyant face.

"Inquiries? Like I was some careful, methodical researcher, sent to South America on a grant to make detailed observations of a native culture! I talked to native Indians in their own idiom – I had a certain gift for picking up any language I needed – about the everyday necessities of finding a place to eat and a place to sleep. I spoke to the local authorities with their drowsy manners and their eyes full of calculating avarice. I ate bad food in dirty taverns and drank things that, if I drank them now, might cause blindness. And all the time I learned more about how these people thought and the myths, the legends, that had become so much a part of who and what they were, so much a part of their language and the way they spoke, that they didn't know it."

"Didn't know it? I'm not sure I...?"

"It's not that difficult, Mr. Darnell. A quick example: How often do you hear it said that someone has embarked on some odyssey of his own? People who have never read a line of Homer, who don't even know who Homer is, tell his story in their language every day. It is the way in which the language of the present, if you consider it closely, can throw a light on ancient origins. At any rate, that was what I tried to do: Discover in the speech of these people, during the months I stayed there, some hint about the past. I found certain words, variations of what in English is called Antillia. Buried at the bottom, so to speak, of what they claimed to know about the early gods of the Incas were words and descriptions invoking a place beyond the clouds, high up in the sky. That seemed to suggest that the Incas – or perhaps the men who conquered the native tribes and formed then into what became the Inca civilization – had come from other mountains far away; mountains that became islands when Atlantis sank, if all my conjectures were correct.

"But if that were true, had it all come to an end here, in the mountains of Peru, when the Spanish conquistadores destroyed a civilization for the sake of gold and in the name of God? I could not believe that had happened, not if those same people, the descendants of Atlantis, had survived the worst disasters the world had ever seen. Some of them must have gotten away. No, that wasn't what I believed. They were too bred to a different discipline, a way of life we can scarcely imagine, to be caught waiting by some foreign force of mercenaries. It was just a feeling, but a feeling produced by long familiarity with what, I was certain, were the main tendencies of a superior civilization. I was convinced that for a long time – maybe since Atlantis, but for thousands of years – these people were a lost tribe that instead of settling in a single place, kept moving. I don't mean changing places all the time, but with some frequency, every few hundred years perhaps; that like a race of visiting gods they would first subjugate a population, then teach it the rudiments of their own, advanced civilization – the science and the arts needed not just to live, but to live well – and then, after mixing some of their own blood with theirs, move to another place and lay the foundations for another sudden, otherwise inexplicable, appearance of a high culture. All the history books are full of the story of the European conquest of the western world; I was convinced that story had started thousands of years earlier and that, in recent times, there had on occasion been a convergence, if usually a violent one, between what the new Europeans were bringing and what the descendants of Atlantis had left behind."

"And you found something?" asked Darnell, following every word. He had reached the point of certainty. Holderlin was either telling the truth or was completely insane. There was no middle answer to explain the utterly astonishing claims he was making. Darnell had seen, and examined, every kind of witness, and had developed an instinct for knowing when someone was trying to deceive. Holderlin was not lying. Darnell was certain of that. But that did not mean that Holderlin was telling the truth, only that Holderlin thought he was doing so.

"You found something," Darnell repeated, this time not as a question, but as a symbol of his confidence, the assurance that he would not have listened to as much as he had if he had not become convinced of the importance of what Holderlin was saying. "You found the island, the one that, forty years later, Captain Johansen rediscovered. But how - How did you get from the mountains around Lake Titicaca to an island more than a thousand miles out in the Pacific?"

Holderlin slipped back into the chair in front of Darnell's massive desk. He sat, as he always did; the way, Darnell noticed, Adam did; the way that any man of noble lineage and good breeding did: with easy elegance and razor straight.

"Yes, I found the island; though it may be more accurate to say that the island found me. How did I get there? – Chance, chance in the form of a brazen adventurer with the euphonious name of Alberto Lopez Rodriguez. I had left Cuzco and wandered westward, down to the sea, where I took my time learning what I could about whatever local legends I could uncover, the stories old men tell each other and that get embellished with time, but that, like language itself, carry within them the first seeds of their development. Nothing much happened in those days along the Peruvian coast and news of a young European with an interest in what others had heard of the sea traveled ahead of me, news that Alberto Lopez Rodriquez thought he could turn to his own advantage.

"You should have seen him. He might have been a distant descendant of the lost tribe of Atlantis, with his blazing black eyes and glowing bronze skin. He wore a thick black mustache of truly epic proportions and had a dazzling smile of immaculate teeth. It was a smile that made you think he knew what he was talking about precisely on those occasions when he was almost totally confused. He had heard, he informed me with the measured look of a born conspirator, the very legend he had heard I wanted to learn about, an ancient tribe, the Incas – no, the grandfather's of the Incas was the way he put it with that voice of his that whatever he said always seemed to whisper danger – that had left the Andes and disappeared somewhere in the Pacific. He had heard more than that, Rodriquez assured me; he had heard from his father, who had heard from his, about an island where this ancient tribe had gone. It was, he insisted, a difficult, treacherous voyage, but one that he had made before. Others were afraid to go there, and, he admitted, they were right to have their fear. There were rocks and whirlpools and other obstacles, and, some said, even fire that came down from the sky. No one would go there; no one would even admit that such a place existed – 'Lest their cowardice be revealed,' he put it with that glittering smile of his. But even though he was honor bound to advise me against the risks of such a journey, he had respect for bravery and would take me if, knowing of the dangers, I still insisted. He owned a boat and made his living from the sea."

Holderlin's eyes sparkled with the memory of the false bravado of Alberto Lopez Rodriguez, a man who, had he been a general, would have been so entranced by martial music that he would have marched into battle and only remembered too late that he had forgotten to bring any weapons.

"I do not know if he meant to steal the little money I had, or if, with his crazy dreams of grandeur, he believed in all the stories that by his own description had terrified other men, and thought that, with this one voyage, he would make his mark as the permanent local hero, the man who finally sailed to this island full of mystery and made a safe return. We sailed due west, in that tiny fishing boat of his, the captain and a crew of three, each of whom seemed to look at me with one eye full of distrust and suspicion and the other full of greed. We had been out for ten days, moving at what seemed a steady pace, and we had not had any sight of land. The weather had been perfect, the sky a constant radiant blue, but then, that afternoon, the clouds began to gather, and before we knew it we were in an awful storm. The men began to grumble, and, as the storm got worse, Rodriguez began to panic, afraid that he might lose his boat. He decided to turn back. I protested. He got angry, demanded payment. I reminded him that we had agreed he would be paid only upon the successful completion of the voyage. This infuriated him. I tried to reason with him, but finally, to keep his good will, I relented and gave him the money, nearly everything I had. I told him that I expected that he would now, as a man of honor, continue on the route he had planned. A hero in his dreams, Rodriguez was insulted and did what he thought any man of honor would do, which, as sometimes happens, was the very course of action a murderous thief would choose. He hit me as hard as he could, knocked me off my balance and pushed me over the side. Rodriguez had my money and the sea now had my life."

CHAPTER THIRTEEN

Darnell had work to do before the morning and the next day in trial, but he had forgotten all of that, listening to Holderlin tell the story of his exotic and inexplicable adventure. He would have experienced no greater sense of charm and wonder if, instead of this strange European, a Saudi prince had suddenly materialized to tell him that the stories of the Arabian nights were true and that he himself had lived every one of them. With every word the story became more fabulous and impossible; with every word it became more plausible and convincing. Darnell sat quietly, staring at his hands folded in his lap, as Holderlin described how he had miraculously been saved from the sea.

"I struggled for a short while in the water, the natural instinct of anyone who wants to live, but with every stroke I tried to take, I only took in more water. There was no point to it; nothing could prevent my drowning. I stopped trying; I stopped trying to swim and became the curious observer of my own impending death. It was, I decided, not the worst way to die, still young with all my powers, doing what I had thought important. It seemed better than wasting away, an old man with nothing left to live for. Odd, how much we're given to vanity even at the end.

"I was floating, a bubble on the surface of an endless sea, a speck of nothingness in the infinite reaches of the universe. There was darkness everywhere, as if, in the last and greatest of all the great disasters, the earth and everything on it had sunk below the surface and vanished beneath the waters of the ocean. Then, suddenly, driven by the waves and current, I was pushed beyond the darkness and out into a circle of light that was like a rainbow except that instead of bending in an arc rose straight up, a bright colored column, a solid fire, hurled from heaven into the sea. That was what I remembered, the last thing I saw, before I lost consciousness, before I thought I drowned.

"But I didn't drown, of course; I was pulled out of the water, as I later learned, by the islanders, or rather, those who were forced to live on shore. Alberto Lopez Rodriguez never knew how close he had come to realizing his dream. When he shoved me off his storm-tossed boat, we were less than a mile from the island, that place of mystery and legend that would have made his name."

Darnell looked up, waiting for an explanation that did not come.

"The straight light, like a column – was that...?"

"My imagination, the light some people claim is seen just before death, the light of heaven? No, that light was real. The island is often surrounded by a thick fog, a heavy, impenetrable mist. It's dark as night when you're inside it, but then, when you come through it on the other side, the brightness of the sun – and the sunlight there is brighter than any I have ever seen – takes the form of a column, or perhaps more accurately, the inside of a cylinder. The mist that surrounds the island has something to do with the mountain, a weather pattern that the mountain makes, if you assume that it is only nature at work and not the hand of man."

"The hand of man? Are you suggesting that...?" Darnell's voice trailed off. He read in Holderlin's expression that there were things that could perhaps never be explained, things beyond the range of what was considered human capability. "Yes, I understand," he added, the vague assurance that he knew things could happen that no one would believe. "But you said something else – you were rescued by the islanders, those 'forced to live on shore.' What did you mean, 'forced to live on shore?' That's where Adam and the girl lived, where the village is, on the shore."

Holderlin bent forward, quick to agree.

"Exactly right. Has he told you why he lived there? Has he said anything about having done something he should not have done and been punished for it?"

"He said he was an exile, and that he could never go

back. It didn't make any sense to me because he was on the island when the island was discovered – or perhaps I should say discovered for a second time, after you had done it first."

Holderlin was far too interested in what Darnell had been told to care about the question of discovery.

"That is what exile means: living in that village on the shore. The punishment for breaking the laws is banishment from the city."

"The city? What city?"

"The city on the mountain, the city neither your Norwegian captain nor any of the Americans who have since gone there know about."

Darnell's eyes opened wide. He remembered the courtroom testimony describing the island. Only part of it had been explored.

"They said everything the other side of the river was impassable, a sheer wall of rock thousands of feet high. You're telling me that somewhere on top of that mountain there is a whole city?"

Holderlin seemed almost to feel sorry for him, as if there were such an enormous disproportion between what Darnell could possibly imagine about what had just been revealed to him, this city no one knew existed on a mountain no one had explored, and the truth of it, that trying to explain it would be like trying to teach the laws of physics to a child. Darnell caught the hint of condescension, the air of superiority, but he also grasped that it was not meant to be offensive and that, far from a slight on his intelligence, it was a comment on the limits of how far any man's imagination could comprehend another man's experience. Darnell began to ask questions.

"How large is this city?"

"Three thousand - sometimes a little more, sometimes a little less. They control it as best they can. They have to, you see. They can't allow too many people; they have to live within their means. But it's more than that, more than the need to make certain they always have enough food and other resources; they think it important, even vital, that each child they bring into the world be capable of full development, capable, each of them, of the requisite human excellence. Every one in the city is regarded, and regards himself, as part of a whole. It's how they've managed to survive these last twelve thousand years."

Darnell's mind raced back and forth between Holderlin's description of the city and Adam, facing charges of incest and murder.

"When a child is born who, because of some disease or deformity, isn't capable, then the child is put away?"

"As you yourself pointed out – I've read the accounts of the trial – it is an age-old practice, one approved of by your Aristotle, as I believe you reminded the jury."

It seemed to Darnell that 'your Aristotle' was a strange way to put it, but then everything about Holderlin was strange. He lived in another world, the only man alive, until he told Darnell, who knew about a city that was not supposed to be there and a lost tribe that, instead of being lost, was not supposed to exist.

"Infanticide, in other words, is the common practice, much like abortion is here today?"

A look of scarcely veiled contempt passed quickly through Holderlin's eyes, a scornful dismissal of the parallel Darnell had tried to draw.

"Every child's death is considered a tragedy. It isn't less painful because it is unavoidable, Mr. Darnell; it may be more so. It's a tragedy precisely because it is neces- sary, a condition of existence, something which, if it wasn't done, would lead to the end of everything. They don't share our belief that there is nothing more important than life; they believe that life, existence, is not an end in itself but a means, a means to live the life that nature intended, to achieve perfection, or as close as any can come, of the specific excellence of human beings, what distinguishes us from all the other animals: the very reason that allows us, or some of us, to grasp the nature of the world."

Darnell tapped his fingers briskly on the desk. There was more than one question he wanted to ask.

"But Adam never learned to read; no one ever taught him. Or was that part of the punishment, the reason he was sent into exile."

Holderlin raised an eyebrow and then, a moment later, raised his chin. He seemed to think the answer was plain on the face of it, if Darnell would only examine a little more closely what he was sure Darnell must already have known.

"Do you believe that Adam couldn't teach himself to read? Do you think that if he tried, there might be something he would forget; that the task would be too great, take too much time and effort?"

"I haven't told you anything about him," replied Darnell, wondering how he knew about Adam's gifts. For a brief moment, Holderlin seemed confused, as if, now that he was challenged, he did not really have an explanation.

"I've seen him, in the courtroom, the last few days in trial. I didn't want to approach you before I was certain that he was one of them, one of the ones chosen to lead."

"Chosen to lead? You just told me – what he's told me himself – that he was exiled, banished, for something he had done. But never mind that. You could tell just by looking at him - what, exactly? That he could learn to read, write, could learn anything, if he chose to do so?"

"Yes, I could tell that. He has the look, the look the most gifted ones have, the ones born with god-like minds, the ones who have the quickest apprehension, the ones who can listen and remember everything they're told."

Darnell cupped his hand over his mouth and chin. He nodded thoughtfully.

"A memory like nothing I've ever seen. But that doesn't explain why he wasn't taught to read or write."

"No one is," said Holderlin with a shrug of indifference. "No one before they are fifty years of age, and then only those, like this young man you call Adam, who will eventually be entrusted with the mysteries, the rituals, and the records that have been kept through all the time that Atlantis and the descendents of its survivors have been in existence. There isn't any reason for anyone else to read and every reason why they should not. It weakens the memory, reduces concentration, and does not allow error to be corrected. You seem shocked, Mr. Darnell, but you shouldn't be. You put a witness on the stand so both sides can ask him questions and the jury, watching the way he reacts, can decide whether or not he is telling the truth. Would you have the same assurance if the only way to get his testimony was to have him write it down while he stayed somewhere out of sight? But in any event, I'm not here to defend what they do, only to tell you what it is. I would add, however, that they are the best educated people I have ever seen."

"The best educated...? But how, if almost none of them can read or write? Are you going to tell me that they all have memories like Adam?"

"I said he had the look of one of those with the quickest apprehension, one who can listen and remember everything they're told. That makes him different than the others of his generation, but different in degree, not in kind. It is remarkable how much a human being can do, how much he can learn, when there are no distractions and when every-one of every age believes that nothing is quite so important."

Any other time, Darnell would have been ready with a dozen different questions about how the children of the island were taught and what they learned, but right now Adam was his only concern.

"If Adam had such unusual powers, if he were one of those who would eventually be taught the mysteries you referred to – he must have done something awful to be punished like that, made an exile for life."

"Not for life, Mr. Darnell; though that almost certainly is what he would have been told. It's all part of the test. But you asked what he did. The answer is simple: the girl."

"The girl? You mean because of what he did, had relations with her, his own sister?" Darnell was visibly disappointed. "So the law there isn't that much different than what it is here." He suddenly remembered. "And that was the reason the girl was also punished, sent into exile as well, because even though she was much younger she should have known better than to break that taboo?"

Holderlin lowered his gaze and gathered his thoughts. When he looked up again, Darnell was struck by the change of expression in his eyes. A kind of gentle wisdom suggested a different understanding, a way of seeing things beyond the narrow limits of a given time and place.

"It wouldn't have been anything like what you think. They weren't sent into exile, Adam and the girl, for what they did; they were sent into exile for what they wouldn't do."

"What they wouldn't do? So what they did was all right? Relations between a brother and sister aren't forbidden? Incest is not a crime?"

"It may be better if I go back to the beginning and tell you something more about the city. I did not see it, did not know it existed, until I had been some weeks in the village by the shore. They weren't allowed to speak of it, even among themselves. That is the first thing you need to understand. The people of the village – it's part of the punishment, the price they have to pay for having disobeyed the rules, the curse for disobedience, driven out and sworn never to mention home, like fallen angels who can never speak of heaven."

"But from all reports," protested Darnell mildly, "there is nothing violent about these people. Captain Johansen speaks of them as the most gentle-souled men and women he has ever met."

"They're not criminals, Mr. Darnell; not as you understand the term. They didn't hurt anyone; they just didn't live like everyone else. They only hurt themselves. It is their example that could not be tolerated. That is the reason they have to be removed. You'll understand this when I tell you what I learned.

"As I was saying, I was there, in the village, several weeks, and then one morning there was a great commotion. Everyone was running around, getting everything in order. Each family stood in front of its small house, ready, as it seemed, for some kind of inspection. Two men dressed the same way as the villagers except for the gold wreaths they wore on their heads, came across the river on a raft. They greeted everyone by name, but no one said a word in reply, and, stranger still, no one dared looked either one of them in the eye. By now I had learned enough of that most difficult of languages to understand most of what the two men said. They had come to see for themselves the stranger and to invite him to visit the city. At this there was a murmur of excitement which, as I was later brought to understand, was because this meant that what they had done in saving me from the sea had met with approval. They were exiles, banished from the city, but they were still a part of it, responsible for discovering the first sign of trouble from the other world, the one beyond the ocean.

"The two men, sent by the city's elders, treated me with every courtesy. They led me back across the river which we then followed on the other side for about half a mile, until we came to a waterfall. To my astonishment, they headed right toward it. But then, as we got closer, I saw that there was a rocky ledge just behind it. I thought it was a bridge back to the other side, a path that would take us around the mountain that towered high above us, but it was not that at all. A dozen steps across the ledge and we were inside a narrow, crooked cave, a labyrinth so dark I could not see. My two guides knew every turn by heart, and with each of them holding onto one of my arms, I stumbled through the pitch-black darkness until, after more than an hour, we came out the other side and into the most magnificent sight I had ever seen: great rolling valleys, lush with every kind of healthy vegetation, enormous cultivated fields, vast well-tended orchards, and, high above it, a distant plateau with a city shining like a chimera, all gold and silver, a mirrored reflection of the vanished Atlantis I had imagined for so many years.

"I was greeted not as a stranger, but as a long-lost friend, almost as a conqueror come back from a distant war. Children threw flowers at my feet, women looked at me with

modest eyes; everyone of every age applauded my arrival.
I was taken immediately to a stately apartment where my
every need was met. That first evening I sat guest of honor
in the largest of the city's dining halls."

Holderlin rubbed his chin, his face a study in nostalgia
so pleasant he had to shake himself to get back to what he
knew he had to explain. He bent forward, but only at the
waist; his head, his shoulders, did not move.

"That was the beginning of my education, that dining
hall, the fact that they all ate together, took all their meals in
common. I say that was the beginning of my education, but
of course I did not understand immediately what it meant.
I was too intrigued, too full of exuberance for what I was
seeing, Atlantis come to life – I was certain now that I had
discovered it – to think about the implications, to think about
anything except the moment. I was struck most of all by the
absence of curiosity. No one was pulling at my clothes, or
pinching my skin; they did not look at me as if I were some
alien being. It was almost as if they had been expecting
me," said Holderlin with a significant glance. "And perhaps
they had. At least that's what I thought at the time, that the
news of my arrival had been brought to them the day of my
rescue and that they had had time to think about the kind
of reception they wanted to give me. Later, I realized that
was not true, that it went deeper than that, that it was a part
of their history – their story, the one that every child grows
up with, the one that the men they call poets, the rhapsodies
who recite from memory the saga of their adventures in the
same way Homer told his story to the Greeks – that there
were on rare but regularly repeated occasions, once every
century or so, visitors, someone who happened by chance to
come along. I was not the first, as I no doubt would not be
the last, to discover them. It was part of the story, part of the
adventure, how they treated each of them. Some of course
they had to kill."

"Had to kill?" asked Darnell. "That must have given
you a moment's pause."

"There was no occasion. I only learned this later,

and by that time I had every reason to think I would be safe. Also, every reason to think I would never leave, that I'd spend my life in a kind of exile of my own, a permanent visitor to a city no one knew existed. At first of course I was too excited to think about such things. I was particularly excited when I discovered that no matter how much I wanted to learn about them, they wanted to learn even more from me. They wanted to know everything, not just about where I came from and how I got there, but all about my education, starting when I was a child. Every day, for months, I sat with the city's elders, answering, or trying to answer, questions about the art, the sciences, the industries, the peaceful pursuits, the wars, of what we in our ignorance call the civilized world.

"I was of course more than willing to tell them every-thing I knew. I tried not to disappoint them, they seemed so eager to hear all that was happening, all that had taken place, in that other world of which they had no part. I was so concerned with making certain that everything I said was accurate, and not my own suppositions, that I only gradually began to realize that nearly everything I told them seemed to do nothing more than to confirm what they had expected, their own conjectures about what would likely happen from what they knew of what had gone before. There were frequent comments, made with growing confidence, that the continued democratization of the world, the emergence of mass politics, was inevitable after the French Revolution; that the invention of the steam engine meant that industrial-ization, aided and abetted by modern science, would threaten the world with extinction. They were very certain of every-thing, and none of it, I'm afraid, very good with respect to what we might expect in the future.

"None of that seemed to bother them, however. They wanted their own way of life and to be left alone. I was there for a full year, and every time I noticed something I thought could be improved by the use of modern technique they expressed an interest, marveled at the simple ingenuity of it, and then, after telling me they would certainly consider it, promptly forgot everything I had said. As I became more comfortable, and more certain that there was very little chance I would ever leave, I began to ask what I thought were some penetrating questions of my own, questions about their arts and sciences, what they taught to each succeeding generation. What I discovered astonished me. They had mastered all the sciences, and rejected most of them as too devoted to what one of the elders called the arts of preservation – of extending life – and not enough to what makes a life worth living; too much to the trouble of existence and not enough to what, taking a page from the Greek, I might call the 'grandeur of nobility.' They are not a people of the modern world. The one science they treasure, the one they study all the time, is mathematics, which includes for them geometry."

"Yes, Adam told me. He said he had some trouble with the theory of irrational numbers, though I think he was just being modest."

Holderlin seemed surprised. "He told you that? He must trust you quite a lot to tell you anything about what happens there. They're taught from the cradle, so to speak, to view one another as all members of the same family and everyone else a potential threat to their existence. But he told you that? What else did he tell you?" asked Holderlin with great interest.

"Nothing, which is one of the problems I'm having. He won't explain anything; nothing about why he was being punished, why he was made an exile; nothing about whether there might be some explanation of his actions that would make what he did something other than incest and murder. If you hadn't come to see me, I never would have known that in this city you're describing the practice of infanticide is apparently not only permitted but, in the instances you mentioned, required."

For some reason, Holderlin seemed to approve of Adam's continued refusal to help Darnell with his defense.

"I wouldn't have expected anything less. If he had been taken prisoner in a war – and those ancient histories

are full of such examples – he would have been thought
a coward if he told anything to his captors, whatever the
consequences might be. The city is what matters, more than
any of the citizens. That is the reason for the dining hall,
for the fact that they all eat meals in common and never,
any of them, in private. That is the reason they do not allow
marriage."

"Don't allow...? What are you saying?" asked
Darnell.

"That nothing there is private, that everything belongs
to the city. Whether it started on Atlantis, or only some
time later, I can't really say; but at some point they came to
believe that their survival depended on the complete dedication of everyone to the common good and that the best, and
perhaps the only, way to achieve this was to make it impossible for anyone to withhold anything of his own from the city.
That meant an absolute communism, not just of property,
but of women. Everything belonged to everyone; nothing
belonged to anyone. The family did not exist, because if
it did there would be a conflict of loyalties, a tendency to
favor your own over what belonged to someone else. Parents
could not know their children; children could not know their
parents. Children were all raised together, brothers and
sisters, whoever their biological parents might actually have
been. And then, when they reached the age when they could
have children of their own, they were allowed to co-mingle,
but never to make the choice themselves about whom to have
intercourse with, and never to have the same partner twice."

"What you're describing sounds like indiscriminate
promiscuity, random sexuality, no different than the copula-
tion of beasts in the field," said Darnell, furrowing his brow
in disapproval.

"I can assure you that it is anything but that. These
things take place only at set times and places, once a month
during the full moon; and far from a random choice, the
pairings are determined by a mathematical formula that is
said to reflect the ordered movement of the heavens. One of
the elders in charge of procreation, tried to explain it to me,

but it was far beyond my capacity to understand. There is a whole ceremony, a set of rituals that take place, burnt offerings asking that each of these one-time unions be blessed with a healthy child. They have one god whose face is the sun, a god that presides over a world that has always been and will always be. There is no belief in an act of creation. Their religion is completely different than the revealed religions of the last few thousand years."

Darnell had barely heard. He was thinking about what Holden had said just moments earlier.

"If no one knows his parents, if all the children are raised together, if they all consider one another brothers and sisters – then incest, as we know it, is impossible!"

"To the contrary, Mr. Darnell, it would seem to be inevitable."

"Yes, but in the end it comes down to the same thing. No one can really know whether someone he calls sister had the same mother or father; he can't know – Adam can't have known – whether the girl he sleeps with is really his sister or not. But if they weren't in trouble because they had relations with each other, why were they sent into exile, why were they being punished?"

"This isn't easy to understand without first understanding how ingenious the lawgiver must have been, the one who established the arrangements of pure communism under which these people live. He knew it was the only way to prevent the divisions, the partial interests, that destroy a city from within; but he also seems to have known that it wouldn't work, that the communism of women, or for that matter – because it was just the other side of the same coin – the communism of men, presupposed a kind of equality that could not exist. Women, whatever their other merits, are not all equal as the object of men's desire, for the simple reason that some women are more beautiful than others. That was the crime of Alethia, and Adam's crime as well: they were drawn to each other in a way that made them not want to be with anyone else. They were obsessed with this need they had to be together, separate and apart. They had to be driven out, sent into exile, so their example, their flaunting of the law, could not harm others.

"That was the provision that had been made by which to deal with the exceptional ones, the ones like Adam with the most erotic natures; the ones who, because of their remarkable intelligence, would never be content with living life in the average, a part of the herd; the ones who would always question the way things were and, by that questioning, come to understand the reason, the necessity, for the very rules they had once broken. Adam was sent into exile precisely because he had the kind of nature needed to become one of the island's leaders. Exile is a testing ground to see whether he will become the greatest friend of the city or its enemy, a man who will learn to subjugate his own desires for the common good of all, willing to sacrifice everything for the city, or someone the slave of his own emotions who could never be trusted with power. That is what he's doing here, though he doesn't know it – being tested, to find out what he's made of; that, and to see how much he can learn."

It seemed to Darnell a peculiarly curious thing to say.

"Being tested? You make it sound like it was all deliberate, that it was their decision – these elders you speak of – to have Adam taken away, brought here, to America, to stand trial for what, as it turns out, weren't crimes there at all."

"Not the particular specifics of what happened – how could they have known anything about that? – But the general situation, the possibility that someone would come, and that something would have to be done about it. We're always being tested, Mr. Darnell; it's only chance that decides the occasion."

Darnell had a great many questions still to ask, questions about the island and the rigid customs that contradicted every western notion of the rights of individuals. They talked, the two of them, late into the night, and though they once or twice suggested they might stop for dinner, the conversation always proved the greater need.

"How did you finally get off the island, how did you finally leave?" asked Darnell a few minutes after midnight when they had nearly finished. "You said at one point that you thought you would probably be there the rest of your life."

"After they introduced me into the mysteries, the secret of their worship; after I came to understand their teaching that the world was not created, neither by God nor any process like evolution, but that – as your Aristotle thought he proved – the world is eternal; after I understood that the world is intelligence, the source from which even a god who created things would have to draw the image of what he wanted to do. When I understood all this, they told me I could go. They knew they could trust me to keep secret all that they had taught me."

"Yes, but how did you get back? There was no one to take you, was there?"

"They took me, two of those men, two just like the ones who had brought me from the village. After twelve thousand years, they know something about sailing vast distances on the sea. They brought me to within a hundred yards of the shore, the same place from which I had first started out, a little more than a year earlier. I stayed at the same dilapidated inn I had stayed before, and the very next day went to same dusty tavern and found Antonio Lopez Rodriguez bragging about another doubtful adventure of his. I bought him a drink, thanked him for doing more for me than he would ever know, and then, as he stared at me with speechless eyes, I walked out of the bar, left South America and in forty years never went back."

Holderlin was on his feet, mumbling an apology for taking up so much of the lawyer's time.

"But I thought there were things you might want to know. I hope this proves useful, what I've told you, and that it will help you do something for the young man you call Adam."

He paused. It was obvious that there was something he wanted to ask. Darnell, standing right in front of him, urged him not to hesitate.

"I wonder if it might be possible to have a few words with him. It might do him good to speak to someone in his own language. I still remember enough of it, I think, to carry on a conversation. And it would of course do me good as well, to learn just a little of what might have happened to some of the people there I came to know."

Darnell said he would arrange it the very next day, here in his office, immediately after the end of that day's proceedings.

"I'll want to talk to you again, in any event – to go over the testimony you're going to give."

Holderlin seemed almost panic-stricken as he recoiled from the possibility of any public statement.

"There's nothing I can testify to! It's been more than forty years! And who would believe it, a story about Atlantis and a lost tribe of survivors? If I told a jury what I've told you, they'd laugh me out of court and start proceedings to have me committed to an asylum somewhere. And even if there was a chance someone might believe me, I gave my word, forty years ago, when I was initiated into their mysteries, that I would take their secrets to the grave."

"But you've told me, Mr. Holderlin; so why not tell it in a court of law, under oath, to help the young man whose life you came here to help me save?"

"I told you, Mr. Darnell, because you are old enough and, as it seems to me, wise enough, to understand the harm that would come if this were ever to get out. What chance do you think they would have, these last descendants of a vanished civilization, one that, if you consider carefully what they have done, is so much better than most of what now exists? How long do you think it would be before every half-wit explorer, every would-be adventurer, descended upon the island with their video equipment and their camera crews, and destroyed for the sake of a moment's celebrity, the oldest thing we have? And if the price of preservation is the life of one of its citizens, isn't that a choice that properly belongs to them? Isn't that what it means for Adam to be tested? No, Mr. Darnell, I am not going to testify; I'm never going to say a word after tonight. I know you know I'm right. Tomorrow, when I talk to Adam - ask him what he would like me to do: Use my testimony to help him save his life or say nothing and keep the city's secret safe?"

CHAPTER FOURTEEN

Darnell looked at the clock. How long had he been sitting here, listening in the quiet solitude of his mind to the echo of Holderlin's eager, absent voice? - An hour? More than that? He shook himself, got up from the desk and walked about the room. He had to think. Tomorrow – this morning, just a few hours from now – he was going to have to stand in front of the jury and give the opening statement he had postponed. The prosecution had rested; it was time for the defense. Hillary Clark had called her last witness; it was his turn to give an outline of what the evidence would, or would not, prove after he had finished calling the witnesses for the defense.

"The witnesses for the defense!" he muttered scornfully. There were no witnesses for the defense, no one who could put things in perspective the way Holderlin could have done. But Holderlin was right: Everything he said would be dismissed as the strange delusions of a harmless crank, a crazy academic who did not know the difference between legend and reality. And even though they laughed him out of court, there was still the danger of which Holderlin was acutely aware, that someone would decide to investigate matters for themselves and the city Holderlin had promised to protect would be revealed and destroyed. Darnell tried to tell himself that it was not his problem and that his only obligation was to do everything he could to save his client, whatever the consequences might be for other people. Would he do it, though, he wondered? – Give up an ancient civilization, force a man like Holderlin to betray his trust, to save the life of someone who, given the choice, would not want to be saved. Put that way, it was Adam's decision, not his. Or was it? Would he let any other client decide that instead of doing everything to win, he would sacrifice himself to some larger cause? That was not what a trial was supposed to be.

The questions kept going round and round in his brain, taunting him with the knowledge that the answers, if there were any, were all beyond his reach. And even if he could answer them, he knew it would not matter: Holderlin would not testify and there was nothing he could do to make him change his mind. That was what made Darnell feel so impotent: He knew the secret, the secret that would prove that Adam had not acted as a criminal, but it was a secret he could not use. His conscience had been easier when he still had ignorance as a guard.

Darnell tried to concentrate on the task at hand. What was he going to tell the jury, what could he tell them when he could not think of anything he could prove? He had only one hope. Every time he stood in front of a jury something always happened. Things would start to make sense, an argument would start to form; words, slow and tentative at first, would begin to build on each other; sentences, short and abrupt, would gradually stretch into smooth, flowing prose; whole paragraphs would come rushing out in a single, eager breath. It was more than experience – there were not half a dozen lawyers in the country who could do this – it was his own practiced genius, as much a part of him as the color of his eyes. He took it for granted, the working assumption of what he did, like the belief of one who knows arithmetic that he can add two numbers without knowing in advance what they are going to be.

Something always happened when he began to talk to a jury, but that did not mean that he did not go a little crazy when he tried to think about it in advance. That was the price he had to pay, the agonizing doubt, the struggle to see clearly how everything fit, the intense preparation, the sense that he would never get it right, his conscious mind a living hell; while all the time, working even while he slept, his unconscious mind was busy organizing everything into a speech that Darnell would not hear until he heard it with the jury.

He tried to think of the witnesses he would call.

Witnesses? Who did he have? Adam, of course; though what he would say, how far he would go to explain what he did and why it was not a crime, Darnell did not know. The girl, Alethia; but after what Holderlin had told him, he wondered if she would go any farther than Adam when it came to anything that might disclose the secret existence of the city, to say nothing of whether anyone would believe her if she did.

"It's hopeless," Darnell told himself. He stood at the window, his hands clasped behind his back, looking down at the street. Even now, at four o'clock in the morning, an occasional car could be seen, a taxi taking someone home from a late night adventure, a delivery truck making a morning delivery. Everyone had their own life, their own settled routine, part of a world they did not need to understand precisely because they had always been a part of it, born into it, raised in it, certain not just that it was the best of all possible worlds, but that it was the only world there was. Darnell found it curious that it had taken until now, when he was old enough to die any day, to start to wonder whether the world had ever been what it seemed. There was a strange irony that it was only when he had to confront his own mortality that he first began to doubt that there had ever been an act of creation, or for that matter, any beginning at all. There was a surprising comfort in that, the idea that he was part of a whole and that, while he would soon perish, the world would always continue. He felt a sudden kinship to Adam and the lost tribe of Atlantis, an attachment born of the certainty that they could see clearly things he could only glimpse.

Darnell stretched out on the sofa and, moments later, fell asleep still thinking about the case and what he would say to the jury. When he woke up, two hours later, it was as if he had only paused between two sentences, the last thing he remembered the first thing he heard.

"Of course I have witnesses," he said in a newly cheerful and rather knowing tone. "How stupid of me not to think of it."

The sound of his own voice, reminding him of what

he had forgotten, one of the first lessons he had learned early in his career, kept him company while he pulled a fresh shirt out of the closet and began to change. He had all the witnesses he needed; the prosecution had provided them. He was going to call them all back, old witnesses, new for the defense, and ask them not so much about what they knew, but about what they did not know. By the time he left the office and started across town to court, he had almost convinced himself that it might even work.

Darnell was not the only one who had spent most of the night pondering over the trial. Evelyn Pierce, as she was prompt to advise both attorneys, had been awake to "all hours, struggling with what to do about this case."

"What to do about this case?" asked Hillary Clark. She had not gotten over what had happened just yesterday, when the rape charge was dismissed. She did not like the judge and never had. Pierce tried to exercise too much control and did not allow enough discretion to the prosecution. Clark sat on the edge of her chair, ready to argue, ready to fight.

Judge Pierce made an expansive gesture toward the law books on the shelves in her chambers.

"There's no law to cover this: applying the criminal law of one country against the citizen of another; there's no _"

"That issue has already been decided," interjected Clark. "You decided it. The question was fully briefed on both sides. The government's position was that the absence of a written law could not excuse what every civilized nation considers the most serious crimes anyone can commit: murder, rape and incest."

"Murder and incest, I think you mean to say," remarked Darnell, staring at a point on the wall behind the judge.

Clark ignored him; Judge Pierce ignored them both.

"There is a difficulty in what we're doing here, a precedent that might be set, that might have consequences far beyond anything we imagine." She looked hard at Hillary

Clark. "You couldn't prosecute someone, a citizen of this country, for something that was not a crime when he did it. How is that any different than what we're doing here?"

Hillary Clark could not believe what she was hearing.

"Because it's murder, and I defy anyone to show me any place where murder hasn't always been a crime, whether or not anyone bothered to write it down!"

Darnell turned in his chair until he was looking straight at her.

"First, what you call murder, the killing of that newborn child, has not always and everywhere been considered murder. Second, even where something is called murder it hasn't always and everywhere been a crime that was prosecuted. The family of the victim was allowed to extract a price – blood money – from the offender. The problem with this prosecution of yours is that you have no idea how the people on that island understood either what murder means or what should be done about it."

"The victim was an infant, Mr. Darnell. Do I need to remind you about that? If they don't think that's murder, then every one of them should have been indicted! We're supposed to end barbarism, not support it!"

"We're supposed to…? Are you sure we any longer know the difference, Ms. Clark? You've seen the defendant. You heard the girl – your own witness – testify. Do you really believe they ended that child's life because they didn't think they were ready to become parents? - Because they didn't want to give up their 'lifestyle'? - They come from a place about which we know less than nothing, less that what we think we know, and you sit in judgment as if they were a couple of self-indulgent Hollywood truants. The only barbarism here, Ms. Clark, is what we're doing."

"Your honor!" she protested. "This is outrageous. How anyone can think that the murder of a child, a child born of an incestuous relationship, could be -"

"I didn't bring you both in here for a shouting match," said Judge Pierce, looking from one to the other. "I'm frankly not interested in what either one of you thinks about the moral dimensions of what the defendant did. What I want to know is whether there is some way this case can be resolved, some way to stop this before it goes to a verdict."

"We'll drop the charge of incest if he pleads to murder," said Clark with cold indifference.

"A plea to manslaughter might be more reasonable," suggested Judge Pierce. There was something so calm and reassuring, so conciliatory, in the way she said this that Hillary Clark began to hesitate. "He would still have to serve some time; it wouldn't mean that he would go unpunished."

She had such an imposing manner, she was so persuasive in her blunt-spoken honesty, that even Hillary Clark, with all her prejudices and suspicions, teetered on the edge of agreeing that it would be the best way to bring things to a decent conclusion.

"That isn't something I could recommend to my client," said Darnell in a somber, thoughtful voice. "Send him to prison, however long or short the sentence, you send him to his death. He couldn't survive confinement; he wouldn't allow it."

Caught by the significance of that last phrase, Judge Pierce searched his eyes, not because she doubted the meaning, but to measure how far that judgment went; whether, as she imagined, that the remarkable young man she had watched and wondered about all through the trial, had too proud a spirit to suffer himself to live for even a day caged like an animal, or whether he would, as some captured animals did, simply waste away.

"Then any time in prison is unacceptable – you'd rather continue with the trial?"

"There isn't any choice, not just because of what I said, but because by the standard that ought to apply – the law of the place he lived – he isn't guilty."

Hillary Clark thought he had misspoken.

"The law of the place he lived? The only law they had was the kind of primitive custom you might expect among people that would do such things."

"Then you admit that what he did had a sanction: the custom – the unwritten law – that ruled their lives, a law that you decide should have been broken?"

"A rule that would allow the murder of a child – you would call that law?"

"One that, had you listened, has been followed in our own, western, ancient history. How could you now decide that this people, about whom the world knows next to nothing, should be punished for what they, for reasons of their own, consider right?"

"I don't pretend to know much about Roman history, but if I remember correctly, they brought law and order to the world two thousand years ago, which is all we're now trying to do."

"And all this time I thought we were trying to bring freedom, to let everyone live the life they choose."

"A chance that new-born child will never have. Murder, Mr. Darnell, is never lawful."

"Death and murder, Ms. Clark, are entirely different things. I hope to make the jury understand that."

"Both of you are determined?" asked Judge Pierce. "There isn't any room for compromise?"

Darnell scratched his chin. He wanted a way out. The only thing that mattered was to keep Adam out of prison, to give him a way to return to the island.

"We're open to anything that doesn't involve confinement in a prison here. If they drop the murder charge, he could plead to incest – if he was given probation and allowed to go back home."

"That's impossible!" exclaimed Clark with a rude, dismissive glance. "We'd never do it."

Evelyn Pierce turned a cold, quizzical eye on the prosecutor and asked why. Clark professed to be astonished that she could even ask.

"He can't just walk away from murder."

Her gaze steady, penetrating and unrelenting, the judge continued to look at Clark.

"Less than six months ago, in this courtroom, you

agreed to a probationary sentence for a young girl, barely eighteen, who had abandoned her newborn baby in an alleyway, where it died. And now you say that this defendant can't just walk away from murder? How is it you draw the distinction – because the one defendant was a woman and this one is a man?"

Hillary Clark stared back a moment longer, but then gave it up and looked away.

"The girl had been abused, raped by her step-father; she was desperate, didn't know what she was doing. There wasn't any point in punishing her any more than she had already been." Clark straightened up. "But that isn't the situation here. He wasn't raped; his sister was – Yes, I know, the charge has been dismissed, but that is what he did: used his power and influence to get his way, and then, when the girl gets pregnant, takes the child and strangles it to death. So, yes, I'd say there was a distinction between the two cases, a very serious one."

With a heavy sigh, Judge Pierce turned up her palms and looked at Darnell.

"It appears that you now get to put on your case. I assume you'll want to start today with your opening statement, which I allowed you to defer. But after that, how many witnesses do you intend to call?"

"Besides the defendant? – Everyone the prosecution called."

It was the unexpected move for which William Darnell had become famous, the one no one else would have thought of; the one that, even after they heard about it, most other lawyers would not understand. There had already been the chance to cross-examine every one the prosecution had called to testify – Why would you want to call them again, as witnesses for the defense?

Evelyn Pierce did not have an answer, but she knew she would not have long to wait. An arched eyebrow, a smile that beneath its slightly jaundiced surface suggested a deep appreciation for the expert way he played the game, formed the silent, running commentary on this, his latest maneuver.

She turned to Hillary Clark to see what she would say, but Clark was too incredulous to speak.

"I would, however, like finally to have the chance to interview the girl, Alethia, before I call her as a witness for the defense," continued Darnell.

With a look that said that on this point there would be no argument, the judge told the prosecutor to arrange it. Clark said she would set up a time for an interview in her office.

"In my office, if you don't mind," said Darnell with quiet firmness. "I would like to see her tomorrow after trial, and I would like to see her alone. I don't interview witnesses in the presence of the prosecution."

"So long as it's understood that she's not to have any contact with the defendant, that he's not to be there, that -"

"I don't agree to anything! You don't put conditions on my right to see this witness, not after you did everything you could to make sure I wouldn't have the chance!"

"I won't have a victim subject to intimidation," she protested, turning to Judge Pierce.

"I have the feeling, Mr. Darnell, that the defendant and the witness both want to see each other. Can you assure the court that...? No, I don't need to ask you that. I'm sure you won't let any intimidation take place."

"But, your Honor!"

"Ms. Clark, the only improper influence I've seen in this case is what you did when you deliberately misled this same witness into believing that if she saw Mr. Darnell she could not see the defendant. It seems to me only fair that she now have the chance to see both of them if she so chooses!" A warning glance stopped Clark before she could protest again. "As there doesn't seem to be anything else we need to discuss, I'll see you both in court."

Ten minutes later, Evelyn Pierce, with her determined, square-shouldered walk, crossed the front of the courtroom to her accustomed place on the bench and, as she settled into her chair, ordered the bailiff to bring in the jury. She did not look at the courtroom crowd, waiting eager and expectant for what was going to happen next, when the defense finally had a chance to begin its case; she did not look at the two lawyers, occupied with last minute thought of their own; she watched instead the young defendant, with eyes full of bright curiosity, and yet, with seeming indifference to what the trial might mean for him. Adam caught her glance and flashed a smile of assurance, but, strangely, if she read it right, more for her than for him. It was as if he did not want her to worry, that whatever happened he would be all right.

She felt a kind of relief, a sense of returning from a world she did not understand, when the jury entered and took their places. She greeted them with the cheerful, calm demeanor of a seasoned veteran of the bench, a judge who runs her courtroom with a firm and steady hand.

"At the start of the trial, before the prosecution called its first witness, Ms. Clark gave an opening statement, a brief description of what the prosecution intended to prove. The opening statement of the prosecution is usually followed by one for the defense, but Mr. Darnell, as was his right, reserved his opening until the prosecution had finished putting on its case and it was his turn to put on the case for the defense. Before Mr. Darnell begins, I would give you the same caution I did before Ms. Clark began hers. The statements of the attorneys – and that means both their opening statement and their closing argument – are not evidence. They are only their opinions about what they believe the evidence introduced at trial proves or doesn't prove." She turned from the jury to Darnell who was just getting to his feet. "Mr. Darnell, if you're ready."

It would have been impossible to guess that Darnell had scarcely slept the night before, or that the hour or two he did sleep had been on his office sofa. Dressed in a dark blue suit and an understated tie, his short, gray hair parted neatly at the side, he did not look any different than he usually did in court. If anything, he seemed to move with more energy, a greater bounce to his step, as he came up to the jury box, bent his head slightly to the side and fixed each one in turn with that eager, knowing glance of his. Every gesture, every movement, promised something that, though you had not known it, you had just been waiting to learn. They were drawn toward him, those twelve jurors, in ways they could not explain. With close to choreographed precision, they all leaned forward.

"When I was first starting out, years ago, a young lawyer eager to learn his trade, I made a point of spending as much time as I could in the courthouse, listening to the way the older lawyers tried their cases. I didn't have anything else to do – I didn't have any cases of my own. In those days, lawyers weren't in so much of a hurry. They didn't talk as fast as most of them do now, and they didn't spend all their time worried about how much money they were going to make. They liked what they did. Liked it? – It was who they were, what they lived for. They took me under their wing, tried to teach me the craft, the way the law was supposed to work, what a lawyer could do to make sure there was at least a chance for justice. Some of them – all of them at times – were cynical and irreverent, what you would expect from men who had seen how often the promise was betrayed by reality; but they were, in those days, all great readers, men who had a thorough knowledge of not just the law, but literature. One of them – who I think must have read everything – used to quote to me – and if he did it once, he did it a hundred times – a line that summed up the lawyer and his trade. The legal mind, he would quote, his chest starting to rumble, 'chiefly displays itself by illustrating the obvious, explaining the evident, and expatiating on the commonplace.'"

With a wistful glance, Darnell shook his head at the memory of a vanished age. He took a step forward, paused, and then, a broad, boyish grin stretching across his mouth, admitted the truth of they were thinking.

"The language now may seem too formal and ornate, structured, forced, and even artificial, but at the time – and perhaps still, to some of us – it was smooth, flowing, nothing short of perfect, a few short phrases that captured forever the self-importance of the average lawyer and the average way he tried a case. The average lawyer didn't like it; the average lawyer never does.

"I miss the men who taught me, the ones who could quote a line like that and never get tired of it, the ones who knew there is no such thing as an average case, that every case is, or rather would be if you treat it right, unique; the ones who stayed up all night, who never slept, when a man's life was at stake, even if, or perhaps especially if, they knew that there wasn't any chance in the world they would ever get paid.

"I have tried to tell myself that, remember it, every case I get. But this case, there was no need to be reminded; this case every average lawyer would know is like no other, a case without precedent, a case that, whatever your verdict, is a tragic mistake, an attempt to subjugate a people by a law they never made and did not know. We think we know what is good for others when we seldom know what is good for ourselves; we think we know the future when we know scarcely anything about the past. I quoted you a line that, years ago, when I was young, was quoted to me. Let me quote you something that as I grow older seems to teach the limit of what we know. Shakespeare, in The Tempest, has Prospero say to his daughter about something she remembered from her childhood:

'But how is it That this lives in thy mind?

What see'st Thou else In the dark backward and abysm of Time?'

"The 'dark backward and abysm of time.' How much do we know about ourselves, our own history? How much do we know about his?" asked Darnell, turning to the counsel table where Adam sat alone. "How much do we know about this island that, until two years ago, no one knew existed? How long have those people lived there, and where did they come from before that? Are they the remnants of some ancient civilization, some lost tribe, that had managed, like certain tribes of South America, to avoid contact with the outside world?

"I don't ask these questions because I think they have

answers. I ask them because, as I am about to prove from the same witnesses who have already testified as witnesses for the prosecution, the prosecution doesn't have answers for them either. But if the prosecution doesn't know anything about the history of these people, if the prosecution doesn't know anything about their customs, their traditions, then the only basis they have to convict the defendant of a crime is raw power – not the law, because the law of one nation does not apply to the citizens of another nation – but power, the brutal fact that the government of this country can do what it likes because no one on that island has the power to resist!

"So that, ladies and gentlemen, is what we're going to do for the next several days: listen to the prosecution's own witnesses, some of whom bragged about how they were bringing civilization to a backward people, under oath confess their ignorance. And then, once we've done that, shown the thing to be the fraud it is, I'm going to put one last prosecution witness back on the stand, the girl herself, the supposed victim of the defendant's supposed crimes, and have her tell what really happened on that island and why, even under the law the prosecution insists is the only one any civilized people could have, none of it was criminal. There will be only one witness after that, the only one you haven't heard from before, the defendant, Adam, at which point Ms. Clark can ask him anything she wishes." Darnell turned just far enough to see Hillary Clark staring back at him. "One of the things he was taught from childhood in that lawless island where he was raised is that the truth is all that matters and that lying is worse than death."

CHAPTER FIFTEEN

Summer Blaine laughed when she saw the look on Darnell's face.

"You didn't expect to see me in court today, did you?" She took his arm and they headed out of the courthouse into the echoing noise of the city. "I was worried," she explained in a soft, lilting voice. "I tried to call last night, several times, and by midnight, when you didn't answer, I knew you were going to do what you promised you wouldn't do anymore: I knew you were going to work all night, stay up till dawn, preparing for trial."

"If you know me so well, why worry when you know exactly what I'm doing?"

It was antic logic, a complete evasion, a denial of all responsibility. She wanted to scold him, tell him that he was a thoughtless fool to take such poor care of himself, but she knew it would not do any good, that with the blood still racing through his veins, every part of him full of the trial, he would only tell her that he was indestructible and that he had not felt this good in years. Later, when the excitement and the energy had run their course, the tell-tale signs of age and exhaustion would peek out from behind his eyes and the steely defiance on his lips would become more a burden than a badge of courage.

"It's the moment," he whispered as they hurried along with the sidewalk crowd. "What else is there to enjoy? The more I think about it, the deeper I get into this case, the more certain I am of that. Every day is a miracle, a chance to learn something new." He was walking fast, gesturing with his hands, his voice a rising staccato, short bursts of enthusiasm that underscored the intensity of what he felt. "We have a chance; finally, we have a chance. Judge Pierce threw out the rape charge. That still leaves incest and murder, but after what I learned last night, after what Holderlin told me about

198

the island, about who these people are -"

"The island? Who these people are?" asked a bewil-
dered Summer Blaine as she struggled to keep up. But
Darnell was oblivious.

"Yes, what Holderlin told me, last night, in my office;
what I stayed up all night thinking about – how I could use
it, whether there was a way to do it that would make sense.
What Holderlin told me, what...." He stopped walking
so suddenly that Summer was two steps past him and had
to come back. "You don't have any idea what I'm talking
about, do you? I'm sorry; you must think I've lost my mind,
going on about something I haven't even bothered to explain.
Bothered to explain," he repeated with a rueful expression.
"Once I explain who Holderlin is and what he did, once I
tell you what he told me, you really will think I'm mad. It
doesn't matter, I have to tell someone, and if I can't tell you,
I can't tell anyone."

"Why don't we go somewhere for lunch? We'll find
someplace quiet and you can tell me everything about last
night."

"I probably should have something to eat."

"You didn't have dinner last night, did you?"

"Of course I had dinner; I always....Did I have dinner?
No, I guess I didn't. We talked about it, several times as
a matter of fact, but there was always something more
Holderlin wanted to say. So, no - now that I think about it - I
didn't eat." He sneaked a guilty, sidelong glance, as they
walked down the street. "And then, this morning, there was
so much more I had to do that...."

"You didn't have breakfast, either? Then why waste
time with lunch, a man your age who doesn't need food
or sleep? I wonder why I never thought to prescribe that
regime to any of my other patients."

With the puckish grin she had never been quite able to
resist, Darnell tugged at her sleeve.

"Because none of your other patients have ever lived
as long as I have? Besides, if you are all that worried that I
might miss dinner, why don't you stay in the city so you can

make sure I do all the things you think I should?"

"I would, if I thought you meant it; and I might do it anyway, even if you don't. Someone has to take care of you, now that you've proven incompetent to take care of yourself."

She felt better for saying it and, to her surprise, so apparently did he. They had just arrived at the restaurant. He was about to open the door.

"I'd like it if you would. I've missed not having you with me. But can you take the time off from the hospital? I don't want you making that drive every day."

Summer looked at him with the calm certainty of a woman who knows her mind and did not say anything. They knew each other too well for words to matter.

For the next hour, they sat undisturbed in one of those quiet, out of the way places where you have to walk through a long, narrow bar to get to the few tables in back. It was Summer's turn not to eat, or rather, barely to pick at her food as she listened in growing amazement to the astonishing story that Holderlin had told.

"It's impossible!" she exclaimed. That was the judgment of her mind, though her heart, as reflected in the knowing smile on her lips, said she believed every word of it. "But there are so many details, so many connections with recorded events….And the way he started out, that story about the man – Schliemann, was it? – who discovered Troy; the way he reasoned that there might be a parallel between what Schliemann found in Homer and what he thought he found in Plato! And you, – you've had to make judgments about people all your life, and you don't think he's crazy – You believe him?"

Hearing the question from Summer, instead of asking it of himself, as he had done the night before on more than one occasion, Darnell became cautious.

"I don't think he's crazy, and I don't think what he told me is impossible. I believe it could have happened – Atlantis, the lost tribe, all of it; but am I sure of it, the way I'm sure you're sitting on the other side of this table, talking to me? Last night, when he was there, telling me this – I was certain of it, certain he was right about everything; but now, in the cold light of day, thinking back on it…? The only way to know for sure would be to announce it to the world and then someone would go to look; but then, if Holderlin is right, the price for that kind of certainty would be the destruction of what I hoped to find."

Summer believed that there was another way, but that Darnell was too involved in the trial to have thought of it.

"When the trial is over, you might go there yourself. Perhaps Holderlin would go with you. It's been forty years since he's been there, forty years with this secret that he hadn't been able to share with anyone until, last night, he revealed it to you. It might be good for you finally to take a vacation. You haven't been on a ship since the war."

Darnell looked at her with grateful eyes. He thought it a wonderful idea.

"You don't think I'm a little too old to go searching for lost cities?"

"A man who doesn't need to sleep or eat?" she countered with a teasing smile.

Grumbling cheerfully at this last reminder of his truant habits, Darnell signaled the waiter for the check.

"Where shall we go from here?" he asked to Summer's puzzlement.

"Don't you have to be back in court?"

"The hell with it! I'd rather go somewhere with you and have a good time," he said as he helped her out of the chair. She gave him a glance filled with knowing mischief.

"Better be careful, William Darnell - I might call your bluff and where would you be then?"

"I'm always in trouble anyway; what difference would it make? But I'm not bluffing," he insisted as an impish grin fought its way to freedom. "I thought we'd check into a quiet hotel and spend the afternoon."

Summer's answer was a throaty laugh, a suggestion of things that once had happened when they were both much younger and had been drawn together by more than the sunset friendship they now enjoyed.

"You think I can't?" he asked with a look in his eye she remembered quite well.

"I think you won't, when you have to get back to the trial."

Summer walked him back and said goodbye on the courthouse steps.

"I have appointments this evening, and some things I have to do at the hospital in the morning, but I'll be here tomorrow in the afternoon and I'll stay through the weekend and all next week. So you have only one more night of freedom, only more evening to misbehave."

She kissed him on the cheek, turned and started to walk away. She knew, in the same way that she always knew, that his eyes were still on her, and after a dozen steps, she turned around and waved goodbye again. He only smiled, instead of waving back, but that, for her, was better than anything.

Darnell watched the bright, sad, look of affection spread across her lovely, gentle face and remembered how she had become so much a part of him that he often found himself talking to her even when she was not there. He watched her go, watched until he could not see her anymore, and then he climbed the steps and made his way down the long marble corridor, back to the courtroom and the strangest case he had ever known.

Adam, deep in thought, did not notice when Darnell sat down next to him. Darnell touched him on the arm.

"I have something to tell you." Adam began to apologize, but Darnell stopped him with a look. "There is someone who wants to meet you. I didn't have time to tell you this morning with everything that was going on. A man named Holderlin. Does that name mean anything to you? Did you ever hear it mentioned on the island?" Darnell paused, searching the young man's eyes for the first glimmer of recognition, an anticipation perhaps of what he was going to say next. "He was a visitor to the island, before you were born, forty years ago. He was brought on shore, saved from the sea. Have you ever heard of him – any stories you remember about a stranger who once came to the island and stayed there for more than a year?"

"No," replied Adam with a curiosity so genuine that Darnell could not doubt he was telling the truth.

"He didn't stay in the village for a year," Darnell continued as if he were adding a detail of no great importance. "He stayed in the city, the one the other side of the river, high up on the mountain, the one no one knows anything about."

Adam's eyes went wild, darting everywhere at once. It was true! - Every unbelievable word of it. Impossible or not, Holderlin had done everything he said he had. He had been the first to discover the island and the only one to see the city. Adam's eyes kept moving, searching for something – anything – that would tell him what to do, how to defend the secret that was not a secret anymore. Darnell tried to calm him.

"It's all right. Mr. Holderlin has known about it for forty years and never told anyone until he told me last night. He made me understand why no one else can ever know. And even if I wanted to tell, no one in their right mind would believe it. I wouldn't believe it if I hadn't met you and come to know just a little of what you can do; and to tell you the truth, there's a part of me that isn't quite certain that I haven't become delusional."

As quickly as it had come upon him, the fear and the uncertainty left Adam's eyes. He knew that Darnell was a man of honor, and that, now that someone else had revealed it, he could trust him with the truth.

"There is a city, which I was part of, until I was banished for my misdeeds, when I refused, when the girl refused, to…."

But before Adam could say another word, the door at the side opened and everyone in the courtroom was on their feet as the Honorable Evelyn Pierce marched to the bench, gesturing for the bailiff to bring in the jury. With a quick glance and a brief nod she told Darnell to call his first witness.

"The defense calls Captain Eric Johansen," announced Darnell, eager to get started.

Captain Johansen was not certain why he had been called to testify a second time, but he seemed almost glad to see Darnell. Within a few moments of taking the stand, the awkward reserve he felt in the presence of a crowd of strangers had disappeared.

"It's good to see you again, Captain Johansen."

"And you, sir."

"I wanted, now that I have the chance to put on evidence for the defense, to ask you a few more questions about the island and what you found when you first discovered it."

"Any question you ask, Mr. Darnell, I'll do my best to answer it."

"I've gone back over the transcript of the testimony you gave when you were called as a witness for the prosecution. At the very end, when I was asking you questions on cross-examination, you said that though you had become familiar with the two or three hundred people living there, you hadn't seen the defendant. Since you gave that testimony, have you had any reason to change your mind? Has anything happened to make you think that you might have seen him there after all?"

"No, I'm sure I didn't see him there." Johansen looked past Darnell to the counsel table. "That isn't a face you'd be likely to forget."

"So he wasn't there then, but we know," said Darnell, glancing at the jury, "that he was there some months later when the High Commissioner, Leland Phipps, first arrived. Very good. But let me ask you, Captain Johansen – as you look at him today, is there a sufficient resemblance to those you did see on the island to make you believe that he's from the same stock; for lack of a better phrase, a member of the same tribe? In other words, if you didn't know that he had later been found on the same island, living in that same village, would you be able to identify him as one of them?"

There was not the slightest hesitation. Johansen was emphatic.

"No question. I've been all over the South Seas, and the people on that island have a distinctive look. It's more than the high cheekbones with their peculiar slant; more than the blue-gray eyes with their clear intelligence. It's the fluid movement, the noble bearing – It may be a strange way of putting things, but I've never seen people who seemed more alive. They seem to take in at a glance what the rest of us might study for years and still not understand." A shy smile crept across the captain's weathered face. "Sorry if that seems excessive, but it's what I came to feel."

"No need to be sorry for anything, Captain Johansen; we're only looking for the truth. But that leads me to the next thing I wanted to ask you: Where could these people have come from? You testified – and I believe these were your exact words – that there were certain mysteries you couldn't solve, among them how they made certain of the things they used."

"Yes, that's correct. There were signs all around of a different, a higher, civilization, but what it was, or where it was, or even when it was, I have no idea."

"But you did have an idea that these people, the ones you found in the village, were part of some older, more advanced, civilization?"

"Yes."

"And you testified that these people were friendly, peaceful; that there was nothing violent or barbarous about them?"

"Yes, I did; that's correct."

"Which suggests a tradition, a settled way of life, rules, habits – laws, does it not?"

"If by that you mean: Were they orderly, did everyone know what they were supposed to do and did everyone treat everyone else with respect? –Yes, absolutely."

Darnell stared down at the floor, as if pondering the significance of this. The pause grew into a silence and the silence became profound. Finally, but not before the silence was about to become uncomfortable, Darnell raised his eyes.

"The kind of habit that takes generations to instill, a way of life that doesn't need a written law to teach the difference between what is expected and what will not be tolerated. But tell us this, Captain Johansen: Do we know anything more than that? Do we know, for example, whether under their moral code there are circumstances under which it is permissible, and perhaps even mandatory, to allow a newborn child to die?"

"No, I'm afraid I wouldn't know anything about that."

"In other words, Captain Johansen, as far as you can testify as a witness for the prosecution, what the defendant did – whatever we may think of it here, in this country – may very well be exactly what he was supposed to do under the law he had a duty to obey?"

"I can't disagree with anything you've said. I know nothing about their laws."

With a glance at Hillary Clark, Darnell remarked sharply, "And apparently neither does anyone else." He turned quickly back to the witness. "You said something odd, when you first testified. You said you had the feeling that the people on that island had been expecting you; not you in particular, but expecting someone to come."

"I couldn't quite put my finger on it, but there was something….Maybe it was nothing, but they were often talking among themselves, and while I couldn't understand what they said, I had the sense they were discussing what they ought to do. There was one man in particular, – he seemed to be their leader –, he kept pointing to the mountain, where I think they believe their gods dwell, as if the answer would come from there. Perhaps there is something in their religion – many religions have it: a promise that someone will come, along with a warning that, when someone does, they have to be sure it's the one they expect. I'm sorry, Mr. Darnell; I'm afraid all I have is supposition, nothing specific."

"I suspect you're closer to the truth than you know, Captain Johansen. Just one or two more questions, if you wouldn't mind. The island wasn't on any map, and there wasn't supposed to be an island where you found it. When you first approached it, was it perhaps surrounded by a thick, impenetrable fog, or did anything else prevent you from seeing it?"

No, there was no fog at all. The air was crystal clear, visibility was unlimited. But there was something odd, a feeling, a strange sense of urgency when I first saw it, a speck on the horizon. It was as if something was reaching out across the sea, drawing me toward it, telling me I had to go, that I had...." Johansen paused, searching for a better way to describe what he had experienced, but he could not find one. "I'm afraid, Mr. Darnell, the more I learn the less I think I understand about that island. Everything about it is still a mystery to me."

The answer made Darnell begin to reconsider. After what Holderlin had told him, he had thought that the island must always have been hidden in a mist that shielded it from the occasional passing ship and the satellites that in recent years had begun to orbit high above the earth; but there was nothing like that when Johansen first arrived. The question was whether the difference between what Holderlin had experienced and what, forty years later, Johansen had seen had just been the workings of chance, the effect of nature and its ways, or part of some design that involved a feat of engineering atmospherics that could not be explained by modern physics.

"Mr. Darnell, do you have another question?" asked Judge Pierce as he continued to stare in silence.

"What? – Yes, of course. Forgive me, your Honor. Something the witness said made me think of something else." But instead of asking another question, Darnell walked slowly to the counsel table and stood behind Adam. "When you left the island – I assume you were free to do so? No one tried to stop you?"

"No, to the contrary – they helped me."

"Helped you?"

"They helped get my boat safely away from shore.

They gave me food and water. Far from wishing me any harm, they asked me to come back."

"Asked you to come back? I'm afraid I don't quite understand. You said a moment ago that you didn't speak their language, didn't understand anything they said. So how could you know that they -"

"They spoke mine. I don't mean to suggest they were fluent in Norwegian, but in the few days I was there, they managed to pick up a few phrases. They encouraged me to talk and – don't ask me how they did it – they started mimicking the sound, throwing it back and forth, like some children's game. They would look at me with their eager, inquisitive eyes and with deft movements of their hands and arms encourage me to make some gesture of my own that would show them what the words were supposed to mean. Their apprehension was quick, immediate – once you did something, you didn't need to do it twice."

"And so when they asked you to come back they used your language?"

"Yes. And when they said it, they gestured toward the mountain; which meant, I guess, that they had received some sign that the gods approved."

"Thank you, Captain Johansen." Darnell raised his eyes to the bench. "I have no further questions of the witness, your Honor."

Judge Pierce turned to Hillary Clark and asked if she wished to cross-examine the witness.

"No, your Honor. I asked what I needed to when Captain Johansen was called earlier."

Judge Pierce excused the witness. Johansen nodded politely and started to get up.

"There was one other thing," he said, as he sank back onto the witness chair. You asked me whether the island was surrounded by fog. It wasn't, when I first arrived; and there wasn't any on the day I left. The weather was perfect, not a cloud anywhere, the kind of day you can almost see the curvature of the earth when you're out at sea. I must have sailed five or six miles when I looked back to see the island one last time, but when I did, it wasn't there. For an instant I had the strange feeling that it had never been there, that it didn't exist, that everything that I had thought had happened had been the work of my own imagination, a dream from which I had just awakened. But then I realized that the island was still there, only now, because of some phenomenon I can't explain, it was buried behind the densest fog I'd ever seen."

The next witness Darnell intended to call back to the stand, the High Commissioner, Leland Phipps, would not be available until the next day. Cautioning the jury against discussing the case among themselves, or with anyone else, Evelyn Pierce adjourned the proceedings until the morning. Darnell waited while the jury filed out of the box and the courtroom crowd began to disperse. Then he turned to Adam.

"You were going to tell me why you were banished. It was because you wanted only to be with the girl, because the girl wanted only to be with you, wasn't it? You wanted to spend your lives together, but no one is allowed to do that, are they? Everything belongs to everyone in that city of yours, and nothing belongs to anyone, isn't that right?"

Adam sat there, bold and magnificent, proud of what he had done, and prouder still of what he was, a man who obeyed no one but himself. There was no contrition, no regret; if it meant exile from the city and everything he knew, if it meant that he would sometimes feel all the anguish of a home-sick stranger, then so be it. That, at least, seemed to be the verdict in his now defiant eyes. The measured disposition, the balanced emotion, the remarkable equanimity bordering on indifference to whatever fate might have in store, all the characteristics with which Darnell had come to identify him, did not so much vanish as were superseded by the sense that this was someone who knew there was nothing he could not do and that the rules that governed other men could never govern him.

"Alethia belongs to me and to no one else. They didn't banish me, I left. This man you say was once a visitor, he knows a great many things about how we live, but he doesn't know that. They didn't like it; they came after us, told me I had to come back. I refused, said they could kill me if they wanted, but the girl belonged to me and so long as I lived would never be with another. If the child had been born right, it would have been the way it should have been. We didn't need anything but each other. But the child was not born right, and the others came, came to tell us what to do, and now we're here and every day things get a little bleaker. I thought at first that they wouldn't do this, call what we did a crime – call it murder; that they'd realize their mistake and let us go." He peered deep into Darnell's eyes, asking for a promise. "Whatever happens, you have to make sure she gets back. She isn't strong the way I am; she can't live anywhere but there. They'll take her back in the city, if I don't come back with her."

Adam had never asked Darnell for anything, except for the chance to see the girl, and Darnell had grown so attached to him that he could not think to do anything but to promise to do everything he could, should it come to that.

"But it may not happen. There's still a chance we might win this case, and you can go home free."

"It's never how it ends that matters, its how you played your part," replied Adam with a wisdom that astonished Darnell and that he knew he could not match.

"Mr. Holderlin will be waiting at my office," he said as he gathered up his papers. "He can't wait to meet you."

Now that his secret was known, now that he could talk freely with Darnell, Adam's observations became less restrained and more acute. A block from the office, he stood, transfixed, as a cable car packed with breathless tourists came grinding past and cars in all directions hurtled down the street. Men in expensive suits and women dressed to kill paraded by, while a street hustler asked for cash and two homeless men lay bent against a building sunk in an endless torpor.

"There is one way of life in the city and it never changes; there seems to be as many ways of life here as people and nothing stays the same for very long. It's color-ful, exciting, the way you people live; but it's not a life I'd recommend to anyone who wants to keep their sanity."

"You get used to it," replied Darnell, wondering whether, on the whole, he did not think Adam right.

They had barely walked through the door when Darnell heard Holderlin's unmistakable voice speaking a language that not only did he not understand, but seemed completely different from any language he had ever heard. At the sound of it, Adam's eyes lit up, but as he turned to see Holderlin something was said that caused his expres-sion to change. Suddenly rigid and alert, he listened to what Holderlin was saying with what appeared to Darnell to be guarded hostility. They stood there, the two of them, one of them more than twice the age of the other, staring like two diplomats from rival powers.

"What is it?" demanded Darnell. "What are you argu-ing about? What are you telling Adam that's having this effect?"

Holderlin broke into a broad smile. In the most friendly manner possible, he put his hand on Adam's shoul-der and in a far more gentle tone said something that seemed like assurance.

"It's my fault," he explained to Darnell. "It's been so long since I've used the language, so many things I've wanted to know about, I started asking questions about things I shouldn't have."

Darnell looked at him with suspicion.

"Things you shouldn't have?"

"I asked him why he thought he could ignore the law, why he thought he was more important than the city that had given him life. I told him that his father never would have done that."

"His father? How would you know – how would he know – who his father was?"

"Because he looks just like him, the way his father looked –and he sounds just like him, the way his father sounded, too – when I knew him, the best friend I had on the island, forty years ago."

CHAPTER SIXTEEN

"The defense calls Leland Phipps."

The high commissioner was less than pleased about being called into court to testify a second time. Darnell seemed to enjoy his irritation. He leaned against the railing of the jury box.

"You're still the high commissioner for the Western Territories?" he asked, raising his eyebrows as if an affirmative answer would be a source of some astonishment.

"Of course!" snapped Phipps.

"You've held so many different positions, I wasn't sure," said Darnell.

He began to walk slowly in front of the jury box. He paused, scratched his head as if he had lost his train of thought, looked at the witness hoping he might help him out, remind him what he wanted to ask next, and then, realizing that it would not be any use, began to walk some more, while every moment Leland Phipps became more impatient. Finally, with a puzzled expression, Darnell stood still.

"You testified, as a witness for the prosecution, that the reason you first visited the island was – and I think I can quote you exactly – 'to see for myself, determine what had to be done.' Isn't that what you said?"

"I believe so – or words to that effect."

Darnell returned to his position at the railing of the jury box. He glanced at one of the jurors in the second row, nodded as if they were now acquainted, and looked back at the witness.

"And did you?"

"Did I what?"

"Determine what had to be done?"

"I believe I testified that I did."

"No, I'm afraid that you didn't."

"I think you're wrong, Mr. Darnell." Leland Phipps

jutted out his chin. "I remember quite distinctly that I testified to the need for medicine, sanitation, the things – and I can quote myself exactly – 'that modern science can provide.'"

"I remember. You also said – and I believe it was in the same sentence – that 'there would have to be some rules of governance.' But none of that was because of what you found on the island; those were all the things you said you knew in advance the people there would need. You brought medicine and a team of physicians with you. You didn't wait to determine with your own eyes if they were needed; you knew it – or thought you knew it – in advance, didn't you?"

"I really don't understand the question. Yes, I brought medicine and doctors. I wasn't going to wait to first see for myself what kind of diseases they might be carrying, what kind of help they might need."

"Certainly a reasonable precaution," Darnell remarked. "Tell us, if you would, what that team of physicians discovered. What kind of diseases were these primitive people suffering from?"

Leland Phipps fixed him with an icy stare. When he spoke, his voice was hollow, metallic and disengaged.

"They found no disease."

"No disease? They had no doctors, no science, and there was nothing wrong with them?"

"Apparently not, but that doesn't mean that we were wrong to take that precaution, to bring doctors and medicine. What if we hadn't and -"

"You're not on trial here, Commissioner Phipps. No one is questioning your judgment."

A tight smile passed over the commissioner's mouth. The look in his eyes became a shade less hostile. Darnell tapped two fingers on the jury box railing.

"You went to the island to determine for yourself what needed to be done to bring – I think the words you used was 'progress'- to these people. The first thing you found was that they didn't need any of the miracles of modern science – modern medical science – to keep them healthy and able to function. But let me turn that around and ask the question another way. If they had been suffering from the kind of diseases you had feared they might, did you, or the physicians who were with you, find any evidence that they would have been able to treat them? In other words, so far as you were able to determine, did they have any way to treat disease – serious disease – apart from the body's own defenses, the ones we're born with?"

"There was no evidence of any medical knowledge of any sort or description, which is again the reason I took the steps I did, why I brought medicine and a team of doctors -"

"We've been through that. The question was whether they had any way to deal with disease. You said they did not. But that means, does it not, that if a child was born with some debilitating disease - a heart condition, or something that affects the brain - there would have been nothing anyone on that island could have done about it – isn't that true?"

"Not so far as I know," replied Phipps with reluctance.

"Not so far as you know? They couldn't, and you know it. You just said so. When you saw the defendant standing at the funeral pyre, raising his hands to heaven, that was the first time you had seen the child, wasn't it?"

"I hadn't seen either one of them before."

"So you cannot tell this jury anything about the physical condition of the child before its death, can you?"

"No, I can't."

"You cannot tell the jury that it was in good health, free of a disease that would have condemned it to a life of unimaginable pain with no hope of ever getting better, can you?"

"As I say," replied the high commissioner, "the first time I saw either the defendant or the child was after the defendant killed it."

Killed a child that as far as you know was already dying and in pain." Phipps tried to say something but Darnell cut him off. "Let's move on. The doctors, the medicine – none of it was needed, - but what about those rules of governance you thought they would need? Or did you find that they were equally unnecessary?"

"It's really too early to know what kind of changes we'll need to make."

"Changes? From what, exactly?"

"From the way they have been doing things."

"What way is that?"

"As I said, it's too early to tell."

Darnell threw up his hands.

"Too early to tell the way they have been doing things? You were there! You saw how they did things, didn't you? Or is it that you didn't understand what you saw: that they live peaceably with each other and that everyone has a task, something they do to contribute to what is needed?"

"They seem to have their traditions, but the subject needs much more study."

Barely able to contain himself, Darnell bounced on the balls of his feet.

"More study, more time? – Have you learned their language? Has anyone?"

Leland Phipps became defensive.

"It's very difficult; no one yet seems to have been able to learn more than a few words. But we will, with time we will."

"And in the meantime – let me guess! – they've learned ours?"

"Yes, some of them - that's true. They seem to have a peculiar facility for it, a kind of instinctive grasp of sounds and what they mean. Or so at least I'm told."

"Because you yourself...?"

"I couldn't be expected to learn the languages of all the people we have to deal with. I have more important -"

"Yes, I'm sure you do. But let me make certain I understand. When you testified earlier, you told us that these people – people who can now speak our language, while we can't speak theirs – had no education. You told us – the phrase you used was 'couldn't even read a newspaper.' But now it turns out that they learn more quickly than we do?"

"I didn't say that. I said that they seem to have a capacity to learn languages. That's not so unusual, when you think about it. People without a written language often have a better ear for the sound of words. It's a well-known historical fact that people who depend on an oral tradition are often more poetic: They rhyme the words to help them remember what they hear."

"In other words, commissioner, we would all have better memories and would learn – at least learn languages – more quickly if we had not learned to read?"

Leland Phipps grew red in the face. He stared at Darnell with contempt.

"Never mind," said Darnell, dismissing it as a matter of no great importance. "I want to find out more about this question of governance. You assumed that they would need medicine and the help of trained physicians, but they did not. You assumed they would need – or rather, that you would need – to make changes in the way they governed them-selves, but you don't yet know what those changes might be. Is that a fair summation?"

"Not entirely. I said the situation required more study; but obviously certain things are clear already."

It was a trap, and Darnell knew it. He could see it coming in the way that Phipps leaned forward, eager – too eager – to put Darnell on the defensive. It was exactly what Darnell had been waiting for.

"And what are those, Mr. Phipps?" he asked with all innocence.

"Laws to stop the barbarous practice I was forced to witness: the murder of a newborn baby, to say nothing of the incest that led to it!"

"So it's now your testimony that at the time this act took place there was no law that made it a crime? Just a moment ago you told us that you knew nothing about the condition of the child, whether the child had a chance to stay alive without suffering unspeakable pain. And now we learn that not only was there no law to prohibit what was done, but that, for all you know, there could have been a law that required that a child that could not survive not be allowed to suffer!"

Leland Phipps was halfway out of the witness chair.

"I said no such thing!"

Darnell had turned to the jury. He wheeled back and fixed the witness with a lethal stare.

"That's precisely what you said. You said it was too early to tell what kind of change would need to be made because the subject needed more study. You said the language was too difficult, that no one really knew anything about their way of life, except that they had one. You don't know anything about these people – you admitted it – so you can't know – can you? - that they didn't have a law requiring exactly what I said!"

"Even if they did, it's barbarous and it can't be tolerated," insisted the commissioner.

"We're not interested in your opinion, Mr. Phipps; we're only concerned with the facts, and it doesn't seem that you have very many," Darnell shot back. He took a second to calm himself and then tried a different approach. "You've told us about what you observed on your first visit to the island. Did you learn anything more on your second?"

"My next visit is scheduled several months from now."

"That first visit was your only visit? You haven't been back since?"

"I have responsibilities all over the Pacific. This is just one island."

"So you came there, eager to help these primitive people begin the transition to the modern age, and then, when they didn't need your modern science and you couldn't learn their language, you had one of them arrested, forced another one to come here as a witness, and left the rest of them to their own devices?"

Hillary Clark was on her feet, objecting to what she called "a blatant attempt by defense counsel to distort the truth."

"At least you didn't accuse me of distorting anything this witness has said," he retorted. And then, before she could think of a reply, Darnell waved his hand in the air, a signal that he had had enough. "No further questions, your Honor. I'm quite finished with this witness."

One by one, Darnell recalled each of the other witnesses for the prosecution and made them confess their ignorance. No one could say that what Adam had done had been against the laws as he knew them; no one could say, on the contrary, that he had not been required to do what he did. This was Darnell's strategy, the only hope he had, to hammer constantly on a single theme: that the prosecution could not prove that, under the only law that could have applied to him, what Adam did was criminal.

For her part, Hillary Clark did all she could to insist that ignorance cut both ways. Through an artful cross-examination, she got each of the witnesses she had called before to admit that if they did not know if there was a law on that island that allowed the defendant to do what he did, neither did they know, what would seem more likely, that there was a law that prohibited it.

"But even if there was a law that allowed it," she made sure to ask each of them, "wouldn't you agree that a law like that is barbaric and can never be used to excuse what anyone with a conscience would know – that it's never all right to take the life of an innocent child?"

It was an effective, if not quite legitimate, rebuttal; one that, ignoring the obligation of the prosecution to prove every element of its case, played to the emotions of the jury and the belief that the only truly moral principles were the ones they shared. Each time she did it, asked the witness, and through the witness, asked the jury, to judge what others did by what they would have done themselves, Darnell felt a little more of the ground he had begun to gain start to slip away. He was trying to argue logic, but she was pleading passion, and in a fight like that reason almost always loses. Finally, there was only one more prosecution witness he had left to call.

When Darnell had insisted upon his right to interview Alethia, he had done it mainly to give Adam and the girl a chance to spend a private hour together. After everything he had learned, after what he had seen that day in court when she was called to the stand by Hillary Clark and could not take her eyes off Adam, he knew there was not any danger that he might be helping to facilitate the intimidation of a witness. He did not leave them alone, but he let them sit together on the sofa in his office while he worked at his desk. He did not understand their language, but that was not necessary to understand that they were as much in love as any two people could be. It was embarrassing – he tried not to look – he felt a base intruder on a delicate intimacy, each time she reached up to touch with her fingertips Adam's cheek or Adam's eyes. When it was time for her to go, she did not break down in tears or plead for just a few more minutes; she had too much dignity for that. She thanked Darnell for giving them the chance to see each other and asked him if there was anything she could do to help.

"No, nothing," Darnell told her. "Just tell the truth, and when you do, make sure the jury knows how you feel. That's important. We have to make them understand that what happened was not because you were irresponsible, but because you loved each other, and because you loved the child."

"Isn't there anything you want to ask me now, before you ask me at the trial?"

She had the most beautiful eyes Darnell thought he had ever seen, a bluish green that bore a strange resemblance to the twilight water near an island shore.

"No," he had answered, "I know everything I need to know, and perhaps even more than I should."

Alethia came to court in the same outfit she had worn before, a simple shift and sandals on her feet. She stopped when she drew even with the counsel table and looked across at Adam. She was calmer and more composed, and, as it seemed, more certain of why she was there. Every eye in the courtroom was on her, but if she noticed it did not bother her. Like Adam, she appeared to live much within herself, aware of other people and concerned with how they felt, but not dependent on what they thought for what she thought about herself. Watching her, Darnell suddenly realized what he had missed, the comparison that had kept nagging at him and that at times had seemed whisper close, but that until now had always eluded him. He had seen it, years before, a famous painting, part of a touring exhibition that had passed through San Francisco: Adam and Eve in the garden, the story of paradise and lost innocence but, more than that, the dawning awareness of themselves, beings become conscious of their own existence with the power to make a life of their own. That was the real story of Genesis, that the beginning of the human condition was the freedom, and therewith the necessity, to choose what kind of life was worth living. It all came together in Darnell's mind: the things that Holderlin had told him about where they came from, and the way they looked, Adam and Alethia, the last descendants, and the new beginning, of an ancient race. Approaching the girl on the witness stand, he had the uncanny sensation that though she was not yet eighteen, she was the oldest woman he had ever known.

"Do you regard the defendant, the young man we call Adam, as your husband?"

"Yes," she said immediately.

"Do you also consider him to be your brother?"

Again there was no hesitation.

"Yes."

"And you regard yourself as his sister?"

"Yes."

"Would you tell us please the names of your parents?"

"I can't; I don't know."

Darnell pretended to be both surprised and baffled.

"Well, can you tell us the name of Adam's parents?"

"No, I can't do that either."

"Because he's never told you? You've never met them?"

"He doesn't know who they are. None of us do."

"You don't know who your parents are, and your husband doesn't know who his are. Then why do you think

221

he's your brother and you're his sister?"

"We're all brothers and sisters," she explained patient-
ly. "Everyone of the same generation."

"Everyone of the same...? I think you need to explain
that, if you would."

Without any prompting, entirely of her own accord,
Alethia turned to the jury. In a haunting lilt she described
as if it were completely normal an arrangement that shocked
them to the core.

"No one knows who their parents are. When a child
is born it is given to the nursemaids who have the care and
custody of the newborn. The child never knows its mother.
All the children are raised together in what you might call
an orphanage, a single, open structure where everything
they do can be observed. There is no such thing as privacy,
at any age. We believe – or rather, I should say we were
raised to believe, because we – Adam and I – don't believe
it now, that nothing in the education of children should
be left to chance. Every child is taught that she is part of
the same family, that all the other children are her sisters
and brothers, and that every adult is her parent. We don't
belong to anyone as children because, you see, we belong to
everyone."

Darnell stood in front of the witness stand, his shoulders hunched forward, his hands clasped behind his back.
A solemn, brooding expression twisted slowly across his
mouth.

"If no one knows their parents, and if everyone of the
same generation considers themselves brothers and sisters,
what happens when you're old enough to have children? In
this tightly controlled system you've described, where nothing is left to chance, who decides who marries whom?"

A bitter smile brought a shadow to the girl's coun-
tenance. Her eyes darted quickly to Adam, and then,
reluctantly, came back.

"We don't marry; everyone belongs to everyone in
common."

"I'm sorry, I don't quite understand," said Darnell,

as the courtroom seemed to hold its collective breath. "Everyone belongs to everyone in common? What are you trying to say?"

"When it's time, when men and women need to couple, the pairings are determined by lot. No one is allowed to be with the same person a second time until each has been with all the others. It's the way we've always had. Everyone has what everyone has. The men have all the women, and the women have all the men, all of them together the mothers and the fathers of all the children that come of it."

"But you didn't want that, did you?" asked Darnell, encouraging her to go on, to explain what she and Adam had done. "You didn't want anyone else. You wanted only Adam."

"From before I can remember, from the time I was just a child, I could no more stand to be apart from him as I could think to be without my own body. He was more a part of me than I was myself; I wasn't anything without him. It didn't matter, all the things I was taught; it didn't matter, all the things I believed. I knew the way I felt was wrong, what I knew I needed. I tried to fight it, I tried to be like all the others; I didn't want to be a source of shame. But I couldn't do it, I couldn't be what I was supposed to be, and after a while I didn't care. I didn't care about anything except being with him. I decided I would kill myself rather than be forced to be with someone else."

"Did you tell Adam that? What was his reaction?"

"Tell Adam that? He already knew. He knew it before I did. Adam knows everything. He knew what was going to happen before we ever committed sin, before we made love in a place no one else could see us. He told me that we would have to give up everything and live alone, and that if we did that, if we made that our choice, we could never change our minds. But I had made that choice long before, the first time I saw him and thought I was looking at a god."

Alethia's eyes glowed with triumph at what she had done and what she knew. Darnell did not doubt for a moment not just that she would gladly give her life for Adam, but that if anything happened to him, if Adam died, she could no more survive that than Adam could confinement.

"I want to make sure we all understand this. You were required as a young woman to have relations with men chosen by lot?"

She smiled at his modesty.

"It wasn't that one-sided: the men had no more choice about whom they slept with than the women."

There was a surge of nervous laughter in the courtroom, and then, again, the kind of silence in which even the slightest movement of a chair seemed a harsh intrusion.

"In other words, no marriage, nothing permanent; no fidelity – no promise of fidelity – one to the other? And you rejected this? You preferred to live an outcast, you and Adam, alone?"

"Yes, we knew it was wrong; we knew it went against everything we believed, but...."

Darnell could feel the jury staring at her, mesmerized by what they heard, the strange practices that to them seemed so unlikely, so unnatural, so barbaric. It was the reaction he had been hoping for.

"But no one here would think that what you did was wrong. You wanted to be with one person and no one else. And the only way you could this was, as you put it, to live alone, in a kind of exile, away from all the others?"

"Yes, we had to leave the -"

"The others. Yes, I understand."

He had stopped her before she could say something that might have revealed the existence of the city. There was another possibility he had to foreclose. He made it sound trivial, a brief pause before he moved on to the more serious questions he had still to ask.

"And that was the reason...? No, let me ask it this way: You weren't living in the village with the others when Captain Johansen was there, were you? No, of course not. But let me get back to what happened after you and Adam were sent into exile. You were pregnant, and you had a child?"

"Yes, I had a child, a child that could not live." She said this in a solemn voice, but without any sign of regret. It was the candid report of an unfortunate event that, like most of life's tragedies, had to be dealt with as best one could. "It was a blue baby, something wrong with its heart. His breath was like a choking sob. I could not stand to see it suffer so. I would have helped it, ended all its pain myself, but Adam wouldn't let me, said he knew it would hurt me too much."

"You said 'he.' It was a boy, then?"

"Yes, Adam's son. It broke his heart. There were tears running down his face, but he knew what he had to do and that he had to act the man."

"Act the man? How do you mean that?"

"That he had to observe the ritual, after he had ended the child's misery: wrap the body in white linen and then cleanse the body in the fire, return what had, if only for a little while, come into being, to the being that never dies, the eternal god, the one our people have always worshipped, the face of whom you call the sun."

"And is it part of that religion, part of what you and Adam and the people of that island believe, that a newborn child that cannot live should not be allowed to suffer?"

"For as long as time has lasted."

"As long as time...?" repeated Darnell, struck by the perfect equanimity of the way she said it. "Are you telling us then, that what Adam did – the death of the child – was done because the child was suffering and was going to die, and because your religion – your way of life – required that you end a life when all that is left to it is unendurable pain?"

She looked at him, shocked that anyone could think there was an alternative.

"Who would be so inhuman as to let a child suffer?"

"Who indeed?" replied Darnell as he returned to his chair at the counsel table.

Hillary Clark rose slowly and with an air of reluctance, summoned to perform a duty no one would enjoy. At first, those watching imagined it was because she felt sorry for the witness, but they quickly understood that it was because she did not believe anything she had heard.

"You expect us to believe that you and the defendant didn't know you were brother and sister – had one or both of the same parents – because no one knew who their parents were, because in this fantasy of yours everyone is raised in common and the sexual relations among those old enough to have them can best be described as indiscriminate promiscuity, everyone sleeping with everyone else and no one sleeping with anyone twice?"

"When I speak, I speak the truth," replied the girl with simple dignity.

Clark ignored her. She was not interested in the answers, only in the questions that would bring the jurors back to their senses.

"Does everyone there look exactly alike? Do all the young women look like you?" She pointed to the defendant. "Do all the young men look like him?"

"No one looks like him!" replied the girl with guiltless pride.

"No one looks like him? But if there is a difference in the way he looks, if no one looks the same as anyone else, then surely the children must look more like some adults than others. And if that's true, it wouldn't be too hard to guess who your real parents were, would it?" demanded Clark with a hard, caustic glance.

"It's not a question anyone would ever ask," asserted the girl with confidence.

"More likely, not a question anyone needs to ask," retorted the prosecutor. "Even assuming this mythical tale you've concocted was really true. But leaving that aside, by any measure there isn't any question but that your testimony here today has convicted the defendant of the crime of murder!"

"Objection!" bellowed Darnell, as he clambered to his feet. "Ask a question. Don't start telling the jury what they're supposed to think, especially when what you've said is so obviously wrong. She hasn't convicted him of anything, except doing what their religion – which in this case is their law – told him was the only decent thing to do."

"Murder – decent? Not among any civilized people."

"Enough!" ordered Evelyn Pierce, banging her gavel to quiet both of them. "Ask a question, counselor. And, Mr. Darnell, the next time you have an objection, you might want to let me rule on it!"

"I'm almost finished," said Clark, turning back to the girl. "You said the child was a blue-baby, and that it had a heart condition, that its breath was labored - a choking sob, is how you described it."

"Yes, that's right; that's what I said."

"Did it ever occur to you that instead of a heart condition, your baby might just have been choking, that there might have been something lodged in its throat, that there might have been something wrong with its wind-pipe that might have corrected itself?"

"I checked his throat. There was no obstruction. And his choking breath, that came together with a heart beat that was faint, spasmodic. The child was dying - I could look in his eyes and see the pain. You think it more decent – more civilized – to let the life be tortured out of it, than to help it to a peaceful end?"

"I think it more civilized not to take a life that doesn't belong to you!"

"Then I feel sorry for you, and for anyone, that could do something so unnatural and so cruel."

CHAPTER SEVENTEEN

Summer Blaine thought she would go crazy. Every time she looked up from the book she was trying to read, Darnell was either pacing around, mumbling incoherently, or collapsed in his chair, staring out the window with a blank expression. Manic one moment, depressed the next, he was fast becoming a textbook example of schizophrenia.

"What is it, Bill?" she asked, tapping her finger against the closed cover of her book. "You've been like this all weekend. One minute you look like you're ready to conquer the world, the next minute you look like you're ready to give up and die."

He was back in the chair, sitting with his knees pulled up, rocking slowly back and forth, watching out the window with sightless eyes. He had not heard a word she had said. Summer lay the book aside and got up from the sofa.

"Bill," she said, touching him softly on the shoulder. He did not look, he did not move. She bent closer to see his face, closer so he could see hers. Pulling the threadbare gray cardigan close around his throat, he smiled at her and grunted an apology.

"It's this case," he explained as he stood up and glanced around the room as if he had just awakened. He saw the look in her eyes and shook his head in a second apology. "But you knew that, didn't you? When this one is over, perhaps you should do us both a favor and have me committed. Isn't it a sure sign of mental illness when you're convinced that everyone else is insane?"

Summer went back to the sofa. It was getting dark and she turned on the lamp. Standing on the hardwood floor in his stocking feet, his hair pulled in all directions, he looked as confused as a tortured adolescent. She offered him what sympathy she could.

"If you can ask the question, I think it means you're

not insane."

Summer's eyes, the way she looked at him when he was troubled, always made him feel better, but it was the soothing warmth of her voice that made him feel safe. It brought him into a different world, a world in which everything made sense, even a trial that by any other measure made no sense at all.

"I'll bet I'm not the only one who isn't sure of anything anymore. Those twelve people on the jury must be wondering whether, by the time this is over, they'll know the difference between what's real and what isn't. You were there, you saw the way they looked at her, the girl, when she told them what happened."

"They felt sorry for her. Is that what you mean? How could anyone not feel sorry for a woman, especially a woman as young as that, who knows her baby won't live and that it's suffering with every breath it takes? Who can know the anguish of what she felt?"

Darnell was pacing again, moving around the large living room in an aimless circuit. Summer could not take it anymore.

"Could you please stop? Could you just stay in one place?"

Darnell, stunned at first, began to laugh. His whole body seemed to quiver. He shoved his hands into his pants pockets and fixed her with a gentle, irrepressible grin.

"You've caught me! This is how I work, how I get ready for the next thing I have to do at trial. I confess it isn't organized; I know it isn't pretty. I bounce around, keeping time to the things I hear myself saying - what I'm going to say at trial – and then, when I realize how stupid it sounds, I fall into a chair and sink into a deep depression. It works every time!"

Summer had seen it all before. She did not need to have him explain.

"And you sit there, looking dejected and almost suicidal, certain that you've lost not just the case but your ability to ever try another one; but then, suddenly, you think of something else, and you're off on another one of your manic excursions, listening to what you're going to say, mumbling your own applause!"

Darnell nodded decisively.

"Yes, I think that sums it up perfectly. And you don't think I'm ready to be committed?"

"No more than you have been for the last thirty or forty years," said Summer, challenging him not to laugh.

Darnell grabbed a straight back chair and dragged it next to the sofa.

"All right, I'm sitting. I'm not dashing around, applauding my own brilliance. I'm not staring out the window, convinced I'm the greatest fool who ever lived. I'm alert, I'm in control, I'm...? - I'm at a loss to know what to do next." He gazed at her for a moment. "I think I felt better when I felt suicidal."

With a shrug of her shoulders, Summer got up and headed for the bedroom.

"Where are you going?"

"I'm getting dressed. The least you can do before you kill yourself is take me out to dinner the way we planned. In case you've forgotten, our reservation is in half an hour."

They were a few minutes late, but they had come to this, their favorite restaurant, so often they could have been an hour late and the table next to the window would still have been available.

"They always ask the condemned man what he wants for his last meal," mused Darnell with a cursory glance at the menu he knew by heart. "Do you know what I would tell them, if I were on death row? I'd say, 'Dinner in the city.' I wonder if anyone has ever asked. I wonder if they'd do it."

Knowing that he was too distracted to think about food, Summer ordered for them both. She drank a red wine they liked and urged him to do the same.

"What did Adam do this weekend? Was he out sailing again with Henry Hammersmith and his wife?"

"He'd live out there, if they'd let him. Henry goes along, but he says that Adam does all the work. That boat of Henry's is supposed to take at least two people to sail her, but somehow Adam manages everything himself. Henry – it's the last thing I expected to happen – but Henry idolizes him. Adam is the son he never had. Henry – his wife, too, but Henry – poor Henry, he'll be devastated if Adam is convicted and has to go to prison. Every time he sees me, every day when he collects Adam after trial, he keeps telling me in that gruff, no-nonsense voice of his – 'It isn't right, you know it isn't.' If Adam is convicted, I'm not sure he'll never forgive me."

"He won't think that, no one will. Everyone knows the only chance that boy has is you!"

"The jury – you saw the way they reacted. What you said, it's true: they did feel sorry for her; they know the anguish she must have felt. But I'm asking them to say that under certain circumstances it's all right to kill a child. We're not used to that; we think that in a certain sense death is inexcusable, that when anyone dies – but especially if it is a child – it's a failure. All the old beliefs, all the old gods, are dead, and the only thing we now believe, the only thing we have to hang onto, is the idea that life itself is sacred and that, whatever the consequences, it has to be protected and preserved."

Summer finished her glass and asked him to pour her another. She seldom drank a second glass, and never, as far as he could remember, before she had started on her dinner. He felt guilty that he had been so preoccupied, so absorbed in what he did, that he had failed to think about what she might be going through.

"I haven't been very good company. I'm sorry for that."

She blushed when she realized why he said it. She put down the glass.

"First, the wine is as good as any I've tasted; but, second, I've been thinking about my own reaction and what I think it tells me about the duty of a physician. What are we supposed to do, but restore health when someone falls ill and relieve suffering when someone is in pain? That's easy to say when you work in a hospital and have all the best medicines and all the newest technologies. A baby born with a heat condition, struggling in pain with every breath it takes? – Operate, perform heart surgery, administer a pain-killing drug. But out there, on an island, with none of those things available? I would have done what she did, or rather what her husband did. If you can't give the child a healthy life, if you can't stop its suffering – what else are you supposed to do? Just let it lay there, so you can say it died of natural causes?

"We talked about this before. I told you what I was told used to happen, years ago, when a baby was born with a condition that couldn't be cured. And I said I didn't think I could have done anything like that, but the other day, listening to that girl….I kept thinking, what else could I have done? And I had no answer, and the more I thought about it, the more I realized that this girl, this child with the wonderful name, has a greater sense of the tragedy of existence than I'll ever have, and that what she did, what Adam did, was the only decent thing to do, and what I would like to think that I would have done had I been in their place."

Darnell ran his finger around the edge of the glass, shimmering dark and dusty in the candlelight's reddish glow.

"And if you had done that – what anyone with a sense of mercy thinks right – you'd be on trial for murder, because no one wants to think it can ever come to that, where that cruel choice is the only choice you have."

"But everyone knows it can come to that," objected Summer.

Darnell tried to explain.

"No one wants to feel complicit, and every prosecutor – and certainly Hillary Clark – will tell a jury that they're condoning murder if they don't vote to convict. You saw what she did, how effective she was when she cross-examined that girl. That's what she does – why she's so good – she keeps after it, she's relentless. Nothing matters except the fact that it was a child that died and that when anyone kills a child there is no excuse - it's always murder. I suppose I should be grateful that she didn't charge the girl as an accomplice, but, of course, if she had, she couldn't have called her to testify for the prosecution."

"So what are you going to do, William Darnell? How are you going to convince twelve average Americans, all of whom presumably want to do the right thing, that this time, instead of murder, it was what each of them would have done if they had been put in that same impossible situation?"

"Say that again."

"Say what again?"

"You said, what each of them would have done if they had been in that same 'impossible situation.'"

"Yes, but I don't -"

"No, that's all right. I have it now. Maybe that's the best thing I can do, argue that it was impossible and that to say otherwise is to make the law the devil's weapon. I wonder now if I should still call Adam as the last witness for the defense."

"Why wouldn't you? He has the right to tell his story, doesn't he – to tell the jury what he did and why?"

"Because I can't control him, because he isn't some defendant who only cares about being acquitted. Adam has too much pride to care about what might happen to him. He isn't like anyone I've ever known. God knows what will happen if I put him on the stand. On the other hand, I'm afraid I know what will happen if I don't."

"Then you don't have any choice, do you?"

"No, I don't have any choice. I have to put him on the stand."

They did not talk about the trial again that night, but it was always there, just below the surface, giving what they said a forced, artificial quality. Summer spoke about her practice, or started to, but the words died on her lips. They ate in silence, each of them thinking the same thing. Darnell asked her about the book she had been reading and then drifted off into thoughts of his own when she began to tell him.

"I told you," he said glumly, as they left the restaurant,

"I'm not fit to be around when I'm this far into a trial, especially when I haven't been able to figure out how to win it."

There was nothing she could say. There was no point telling him that things would turn out all right. Things did not always turn out all right; sometimes they went horribly wrong and there was nothing anyone could do about it. You did everything you could to save a patient, or to save a client, but patients died and not every defendant walked out of court a free man. It was the beginning of wisdom to know there was a limit to what you could do, but because you could not know in advance where that limit was, it could also, if you were not careful, make you a little crazy, wondering whether you had reached it or had simply made a mistake, forgotten something you should have remembered, or done something you should not have tried.

"We'll go home," she said, taking his arm to give him comfort. "We'll go home and we'll crawl into bed and we'll get a good night's sleep. Things will look different tomorrow. They always do when you're back in court."

Darnell patted her hand. She was right: things always did look different when he was at work in trial.

"I don't have to think about anything then," he remarked as they headed up the fog-bound street. "Everything just happens."

Summer kept her end of the bargain and tried to make him keep his. An hour after they got home, she crawled into bed next to him, read six dull pages and then turned off the light. A few minutes later she was fast asleep. Careful not to wake her, Darnell got up, went into the study and stared out the window, thinking about what he might have forgotten, what he might still try, or whether he had reached the limit of what he could do to save the life of a young man he did not pretend to understand.

When Summer found him sitting there at dawn, she knew he had not slept. She had not thought he would, but she did not want him to know that. He was entitled to his own secrets, what he tried to keep from her so she would take care of herself instead of worrying about him.

"You're up early," she said as she kissed him gently on his forehead. Then she went into the kitchen and made coffee.

Darnell had reached certain conclusions about what he was going to do, conclusions which, though not much different from what he had decided at the beginning, had become more certain, more fixed in his mind, for the struggle he had had with himself. Adam was going to testify, and instead of trying to guide him, step by step, through the narrative of what had happened, he would let Adam take the lead. The more the jury heard things in Adam's own voice, he believed, the greater the chance they would start to see things through Adam's eyes. This was a trial not about facts, but about values, about whether there was something worse than murder.

Darnell walked into court right on time. He had just taken his seat when the bailiff called out the presence of the judge and, as everyone rose to their feet, Evelyn Pierce strode briskly to the bench. The jury was just filing into the jury box, when she noticed.

"Mr. Darnell, is there some reason the defendant isn't here?"

For an instant, he thought she must be mistaken, but then, embarrassed, he realized that the chair next to him was vacant. He fumbled for an explanation.

"I'm sure he's on his way, your Honor. Probably tied up in traffic."

Judge Pierce gave him a look of mild disappointment and then sat back in her high-backed black leather chair. She began to tap her fingers, counting off each passing moment, the rough addition of his negligence. Five minutes went by, and then five more.

"Take the jury back," she finally told the bailiff. "They might as well relax." As soon as they were gone, she suggested that Darnell might want to make some inquiries. "Perhaps you might want to call your office – just in case something has happened."

No one had called his office. Darnell called Henry

Hammersmith at home and was told that he and Adam had left more than an hour ago. They should have been there long before this.

"Probably caught in traffic," Darnell tried to assure Henry's wife. "Road work, an accident – I'm sure they'll be here any minute."

Hillary Clark had another theory. After Darnell reported to the judge in chambers what he had learned, Clark remarked that it would not be the first time someone out on bail had tried to run away.

"And where exactly do you think he would run to?" asked Darnell, angered by her condescending tone. "The only place he's ever been is San Francisco."

Clark raised an eyebrow and laughed.

"Yes, well, he isn't here, is he?"

"He will be," promised Darnell with firm insistence.

An hour went by and there was still no sign of him. Darnell was worried, not that Adam had decided to run away, but that something had happened. He trusted Henry Hammersmith as much as he had ever trusted anyone. Henry had said he would have him here, and that meant Henry would.

"Perhaps I better excuse the jury, send them home until tomorrow. We should know something by then, don't you think?"

Darnell was not sure what to do. He turned to Hillary Clark.

"Could you have someone in your office call the police to find out if there's been an accident? I can't think of any other reason why Mr. Hammersmith wouldn't have had him here by now."

Clark now seemed to share his concern.

"Yes, of course," she said. "I'll do it right away."

But just as she got to her feet, the door opened and the judge's clerk, a small, mouse-like woman who without her glasses always squinted, announced that the defendant had finally arrived.

"He seems to be in rather bad shape," she added. "He

has blood on his face and his clothes are torn."

Darnell dashed into the courtroom and found Adam, seemingly quite calm and collected, in his usual place at the counsel table. The clerk's observation had been correct. He had a gash along his left cheek and the sleeve on his jacket, as well as the front of his shirt, had jagged tears. Then Darnell noticed that Adam was clutching his arm to stop the blood slowly trickling down his wrist and onto his left hand.

"What happened? Are you all right?"

"We had a small adventure," said Adam, who looked as if he had actually enjoyed it. "A car decided to take a shortcut across two lanes of traffic. Unfortunately, we were in the way."

Out of the corner of his eye, Darnell saw Henry Hammersmith standing just inside the doorway at the back. Evelyn Pierce had returned to the bench. One look at Adam and she told the bailiff to get him medical attention.

"I'm all right," Adam told Darnell. "A few cuts and bruises, nothing serious - I don't need any help."

"You're going to get some anyway. You need to get cleaned up. I can't put you on the stand looking like that now, can I?"

Still insisting that it was really nothing, Adam followed the bailiff into another room to wait for a medic to see to his injuries. Darnell caught up with Henry Hammersmith in the corridor outside.

"Adam saved my life," said Hammersmith, his eyes wide with amazement. "Some idiot came flying out of nowhere, ran the light and crashed right into us. I didn't see him coming, but Adam did. He threw himself in front of me, protected me from the crash. It all happened in an instant. He didn't hesitate, didn't think about himself, just did it! Look at me! Not a cut on me, and he was cut all over. Broke his arm, too, I think; but he wouldn't hear about it when I said we had to get him to a hospital to see a doctor. He just kept saying that he wasn't hurt, that he was fine, that we had other things to do. Other things to do? He saved my life, Bill – that's the fact of it, and you'd think he hadn't done anything except tripped and stumbled and scraped his knee."

Within the hour, Adam looked as good as new. The blood was gone and Darnell had found him a clean shirt. With some thread, borrowed from the judge's clerk, the jacket sleeve had been repaired and, at least from a distance, no one could tell it had been torn. Adam seemed amused by all the fuss.

"You were almost killed," Darnell reminded him as they sat at the counsel table, waiting for the judge finally to start the day's proceedings.

Adam turned a glittering eye on the much older man.

"It's the 'almost' that matters, isn't it? Why worry about what didn't happen, when you couldn't worry if it had?"

There was something wrong with that, but Darnell did not have time to figure out what it was. There were only a few minutes left before Adam would have his only chance – his last chance – to convince the jury that what he did had been what any one of them, in the same circumstances, would have done.

"Tell them, not just what happened, but what you felt about it. Tell them that you would have died yourself if that would have given the child a chance to live."

The judge came in, the jury came in; everyone was ready. The courtroom, packed with spectators eager to see whether William Darnell had another trick up his sleeve, one of his famous last-minute maneuvers by which he had won unwinnable cases before, became as silent and self-possessed as a crowded church. Evelyn Pierce looked at Darnell.

"You may call your next witness."

Darnell was on his feet. In a gesture of confidence and encouragement, he put his soft, pale hand on Adam's shoulder.

"The defense calls the defendant, Adam."

The clerk told Adam to put his hand on the bible and repeat after her. The prosecution immediately objected. Both arms on the bench, Evelyn Pierce moved her bulky frame forward.

"You object to the defendant taking the oath?"

"I object to having the witness sworn on the bible. From what we heard the other day from the young woman involved in this case, the bible has no significance for the people of that island. They have a different religion."

"Yes, I see your point," said Judge Pierce thoughtfully. She turned to the clerk. "You don't need to use the bible; it's sufficient that the witness swear to tell the truth."

Hillary Clark was as good as any one Darnell had gone up against. How many other prosecutors would have thought to use a simple technical point, a procedural nicety, to remind a jury that whatever else they might think of the defendant, he was an alien creature who did not believe in either the god of the Christians or the god of the Jews? Darnell tried to repair the damage.

"When you took the oath you understood that, by all you hold sacred, you promise to tell the truth?"

Adam seemed almost offended by the question.

"I never lie."

"I know that. I want the jury to know that. Let's start with something I've never had to ask anyone on the witness stand before. Your name – what is it? You've been called Adam all through these proceedings, but it's the name you were given after you were taken from the island where you live. Your language is difficult, almost impossible, for us; but you've learned English better than most Americans. In English, then, as best you can make the translation, what should you be called?"

A look of gratitude, as of a burden lifted, came into his eyes.

"Lethe," he replied.

"That sounds close to what the young woman is called."

"Our names, like our lives, are intertwined." He said this in a way that made Darnell suspect that this was no passing observation, that there was some deeper meaning involved, but this was not the time to pursue it.

"Lethe, then, is what we'll call you. We've already heard testimony from Alethia about why the two of you were living alone, and what happened when the child was born. Is there anything she said that wasn't true, anything you would like to correct?"

Lethe shook his head emphatically.

"The girl doesn't know how to lie."

"She was telling the truth when she said that you put an end to the suffering of the child?"

"The child couldn't live; it couldn't grow to be a man. There was no choice but to kill it."

The way he said it, the absence of any feeling of regret, much less remorse; the sense that what he had done was no different than putting down an injured animal; made the jury, and not just the jury, look at him as if more than his religion set him apart from what they thought everyone should be. Darnell did what he could.

"But you didn't want to do this, kill your own child; and you wouldn't have, if there had been anyway to save it."

"Of course I wouldn't have done that, if he had been born healthy and able to become what a human being should be. That's what we wanted, a child that could later have children of his own, another link in the generations."

"Was there any way to save the child? Was there anything that could have been done to keep the child from suffering until it died?"

"We know nothing of how to keep alive what is not born strong enough to do it."

"You mean you don't have our kind of medicine, our ability to provide life by artificial means?"

"Yes, all we know is nature; which is the reason, I think, that we hold life in greater respect than it appears to me you do."

Darnell nodded as if he understood, though the truth was that he had no idea what Lethe was going to say next, or even what he should ask him. At this point, all he could do was to let him say what he wanted and hope that something might still be salvaged out of what was quickly becoming a disaster.

"And you say that for what reason?' he asked cautiously.

"Because from what I've been able to observe, you seem to think that the battle against death and disease is more important than the kind of lives people lead. That's what I meant when I said we have the greater respect for life: we believe it means something more than just the fact of staying alive." In deep earnest, he turned to the jury. "The child might have lived for a long time, months perhaps, in agony. If life is the only measure of what you think important, I'm guilty the way Ms. Clark there says I am. But if I hadn't done what I did, I would be guilty of something worse, a kind of cruelty that only a barbarous people could forgive."

There was nothing more Darnell could do, no more questions he could ask. The last answer was the last thing anyone could say. Hillary Clark had a different point of view.

"By your own admission, then, the child would have lived?

"For a while, yes."

"Months, you said."

"Months, perhaps, for all I know."

"Yes – for all you know. Because you don't know, do you? All you know is that the child was alive and you killed it, didn't you?"

"I killed the child – our child – yes."

Clark stood next to the counsel table, drumming her fingers. Her nails were painted a hard, shiny red. She was dressed in black.

"And you say you did this – killed a child - to end the child's suffering?"

"Yes, I did."

"But you would have killed it anyway, wouldn't you?"

"I don't know what you -"

"You would have killed it even if it hadn't been suffering!"

"But it was suffering. You could tell by the way it had to struggle for every breath it took."

"Struggle for every breath – because it wanted to stay alive! It had a heart condition; it wasn't getting enough blood – that's why it was blue. That's what the child's mother told us. A child with a heart condition wouldn't be able to function in what you consider the normal way, and that's the reason you would need to kill it – isn't that true? – Adam, or Lethe, or whatever your name is – a child born with any disease or defect, a child that isn't normal, isn't allowed to live – shouldn't be allowed to live, according to what you and this sun-god of yours believe! Don't try to deny it. You as good as admitted it just a few minutes ago, when your lawyer asked you – tried to get you to agree – that you wouldn't have killed the child if there had been any way to save it. Don't you remember what you said? Do you want me to ask the court reporter to read it back to you? You said that you wouldn't have killed it if it had been 'born healthy and able to become what a human being should be' – whatever that means. And then, moments later, when you tried to tell us how barbaric we were, with our concern for the life of everyone and not just those with some higher claim to be alive, you said that you and the people you come from knew nothing of 'how to keep alive what is not born strong enough to do it.' The point is that as far as you're concerned a child who isn't born perfect shouldn't be born at all, should it? A child who isn't born perfect is, as far as you're concerned, a child you ought to kill!"

Darnell shot out of his chair, objecting as vociferously as he could, but the courtroom was in turmoil, everyone talking at once, and Judge Pierce was too busy trying to restore order to pay attention to what he wanted. He looked across at Hillary Clark, her eyes feverish with excitement at the lethal blow she thought she had struck. He looked at Adam, the name he had used too long to give up, and had to marvel at how little any of this seemed to affect him. The only thing that mattered, the only interest he had, was that he had been truthful in everything he said. He smiled at

Darnell, as if to tell him not to worry, but Darnell could not bring himself to smile back. For one of the very few times in his long career, William Darnell knew for certain that he was going to lose.

CHAPTER EIGHTEEN

Hillary Clark could hardly wait. Ramrod straight, she drummed her hard lacquered finger nails on the table and tapped her pointed shoe. Her long black lashes, heavy with make-up, curved like iron lattice work above the windows of her eyes. She stopped drumming her fingers long enough to cross her legs the other way, and then, changing hands, started doing it again. A tight smile of perfect satisfaction slid serpent-like across her broad, narrow mouth. Her whole life had been a preparation for this, it was the dream she had always had – the prosecutor, eager and aggressive, about to give the closing argument in the case that would make her famous as a leading champion of the rights of women.

Darnell had just come into court, but Hillary Clark did not notice, and if she had she would not have paid any attention. She certainly would not have said hello. She never spoke to the attorney for the defense, unless the attorney spoke first. She did not believe in courtesy and respect; she believed only in winning, especially when the attorney on the other side was a man, and especially when the man was someone as lost in the past as William Darnell. If she had few friends in the profession, that was, far from a source of sadness or disappointment, something viewed with a martyr's pride. As the voice of women, she welcomed the hatred of the people she fought against.

Growing more impatient by the minute, she glanced at the clock on the wall, and then, just to be sure, checked her watch. Ten minutes late. It was disgraceful. But then so was just about everything Evelyn Pierce did. Hillary Clark stopped beating her fingernails on the table and, as if to stop from becoming even more irritated than she already was, began to tap her fingers against her head. That proved not to be quite as satisfying as she had hoped. She stopped doing it, and to make sure that she did not start again, held her arms tight around herself. With an audible sigh, she began to swing her foot.

The door at the side finally opened and Hillary Clark jumped from her chair. But instead of Evelyn Pierce, the judge's clerk came out and asked that both attorneys follow her into chambers.

It was annoying. She had been up half the night going over what she was going to say in her closing argument. She had not memorized all of it – she was afraid that would sound too rehearsed – but she had committed to memory each of the main points she wanted to make, placed them in the right order, and for each of them found the phrases that would best summarize what she thought it important to say. She was organized, ready, and now this! Another change of schedule, another disruption, and all because Evelyn Pierce, overweight and undisciplined, lacked all sense of judicial restraint! Hillary Clark was certain she was winning, and certain that Evelyn Pierce did not like it, but she was still shocked when she learned what the judge, no doubt out of jealousy, had decided to do.

"I was bothered by this case before I heard the witnesses for the defense, and now that I have, I'm bothered even more."

"Bothered, your Honor?" asked Hillary Clark, as she raised an eyebrow, a gesture which did nothing to ingratiate her with the judge.

"As you would be, Ms. Clark, if you were interested in anything more than winning."

"I resent that!"

"But you don't deny it," replied the judge dryly. "Winning this case won't prove anything, except our willingness to make judgments about things we don't under-stand. If I had known what I know now, if I had known the circumstances surrounding what happened, know that far from rape and incest, these two young people wanted to live what I would have thought you would have regarded as a normal, married life – I would have granted Mr. Darnell's motion and thrown the case out for lack of jurisdiction. We have no business meddling in the affairs of other people, people who seem to have lived quite well without anyone's outside supervision."

"Lived quite well? Were we listening to the same witnesses? You just said they wanted to live normal, married lives. What stopped them? – A culture of organized promiscuity in which women, made sex slaves to all the men who wanted them, were denied their most basic human rights!"

"Men, too, from what I remember," remarked Darnell, not wanting to be left out. "And if you're right to call their arrangements organized, you're wrong to call it promiscuity. From what I heard the girl say on the stand, everything was done for a purpose. We might not agree that the purpose was a good one, but it isn't clear to me at least that it's any of our business how these people choose to live."

Hillary Clark did not bother to reply. Darnell was beyond redemption, too old, too much the product of an earlier generation and its discredited ways. She focused all her attention on the judge who, though no more enlightened, had, unfortunately, the power of decision.

"What do you propose to do? The trial is nearly over. After closing arguments, the case goes to the jury."

"I could declare a mistrial, and then, if you decided to prosecute it again, rule in favor of the defense motion that no American court has jurisdiction."

"The island is an American possession. If we don't have jurisdiction, no one has."

"I found that argument persuasive when you first made it; I don't find it persuasive anymore."

"But there aren't any grounds for a mistrial! There hasn't been any misconduct, nothing that would prejudice the jury. You can't just declare a mistrial because you feel like it."

When Evelyn Pierce was thinking about something, her thick neck seemed to shorten and flatten out as her head sunk down to her shoulders. There was a kind of grandeur in her ugliness, the way it made her remarkable intelligence and the solid character that went with it only more apparent.

"The court, as you know, has the inherent authority
to prevent injustice. And as for your point about misconduct, I don't think I need to remind you about the way you
deprived the defense of its right to interview one of your
witnesses – one of the supposed victims in this case – before
she testified for the prosecution. But, leaving all that aside,
I am not going to declare a mistrial. I want to settle this
another way. I want you to offer the defendant a plea – one
count of manslaughter – and, if he agrees, I will suspend the
sentence. The defendant, Mr. Darnell, can then go home."

"You can't -!"

"I can, Ms. Clark - and I will!"

"I won't make that offer – not in a thousand years!
And there's nothing the court can do to make me. A plea
offer is strictly a matter of prosecutorial discretion."

"I had a feeling you might say that, Ms. Clark. And
you're right of course: there is nothing I can do to force you
to do what is right and reasonable."

Clark realized her mistake.

"But you're not going to -?"

"Declare a mistrial? – No, I'm not. I'm going to leave
it instead to the jury's discretion, now that I can't rely on
yours. Among the other instructions I'm going to give them
before they begin deliberations, I'm going to give them
one on lesser included offenses. It will be up to the jury to
decide whether, if he is guilty of anything, he's guilty of
murder in the first degree or manslaughter in the second.
The latter charge, as you know, often results in a sentence of
probation instead of prison time."

Hillary Clark did not doubt for a minute what the jury
would do.

"Do you really think the jury is going to let someone
who murdered a child just walk away?"

Her eyes lit up as she said it. She liked the way it
sounded, the easy way it rolled off the tongue – 'let someone
who murdered a child just walk away' –; she liked the reaction it produced on that hostile audience of two. It seemed to

prove that she had struck a chord. The line kept going round and round in her head, the stark reminder that, on a question this serious, there was only one thing the jury could do. She liked it so much that the last thing she said in chambers was with a slight modification the first thing she said in court.

"Do you really believe – does anyone believe – that someone who murders a child can just walk away? That is the question, the only question you have to decide, because, unlike other murder cases, the defendant in this case has admitted what he did. A child was born alive and the defendant - Adam, or Lethe, or whatever other name he may go by – killed it. He killed it, murdered that child in cold blood, and not satisfied with that, tells you that he did a good thing, that far from being blamed, this murder should be praised. But I for one will not applaud. Nor, I think, will anyone who hasn't taken leave of their senses."

Hillary Clark bent forward and tapped her red painted fingernail hard against the railing of the jury box, daring anyone to disagree. Her eye ran from one juror to the next, extracting a silent pledge to do what they had all sworn they would: follow the evidence and reach the only conclusion the evidence allowed.

"Go back to the beginning. Remember what I told you in my opening statement, what I promised you the evidence would prove, and ask yourself if I failed to do anything I said I would. Was there a single witness who didn't testify the way I had told you he would? But perhaps you're worried that after a lengthy trial like this, you may not remember what every witness said. Let's go back to the beginning together and review their testimony."

For the next hour, never once referring to a note, Hillary Clark summarized the testimony of each of the witnesses she had called to make the case for the prosecution. She left nothing out. There was no distortion, no attempt to emphasize only the strongest points; instead of ignoring a contradiction, she explained it, showed how it was actually consistent with the central argument in the case against the defendant. Talking in a low, confidential tone, pausing frequently to smile when she appeared to stumble over a word – appeared, because it was each time deliberate, a way to make the jury believe that she was as prone to human error as any of them – Hillary Clark told a timeless story of depravity and murder.

"We're told that we can't apply the standards of the civilized world to people that haven't yet been taught the advantages of civilization. We're told that – and Mr. Darnell tried quite ingeniously to use the prosecution's own witnesses to do this – that we don't know enough about these people to know, not only whether the murder of a child was considered a crime under the customs and traditions they might have had, but whether it might not actually have been – if you can believe this! – required."

Throwing her hands in the air, she turned on Darnell with what appeared to be a warning.

"There is a limit how far anyone should be allowed to go. It's a dangerous thing to suggest that murder isn't murder unless you can prove that everyone agrees. What's next? – Let the murderer decide if he should be convicted?" Watching Darnell a moment longer with an eye filled with contempt and derision, she then turned back to the jury. "That really is the sum and substance of the defendant's case. He doesn't say he didn't do it; he says he did, but that it doesn't matter, because as the father of a child he doesn't want he decides whether the child lives or dies. He killed – he murdered – a child, but that is his business and he ought to be left alone. There are no rules, no standards, no requirements of civilized behavior, which can bind him; he has standards of his own – what 'nature' tells him, what he knows is right by some instinct the rest of us don't seem to have!"

Her voice had become harsh, brittle, an echo of revenge. Her dark eyes glittered with eager malice.

"You know - every one of you knows - that what he did was wrong. Look at him, and then remember the girl. You saw the way she looked at him; you saw how much she is still under his spell. She was just a child herself, subject

249

to God knows what kind of strange and bestial practices among that ignorant people, lured away by the promise of something better, a chance to escape the organized promiscuity of that dreadful way of life, caught up in a young girl's infatuation, ready to give herself as often as he wanted to the man she trusted as her brother. Yes, she consented to what was done to her. Yes, she agreed to share her brother's bed. But does anyone – does even the defendant, or the defendant's lawyer – dare to argue that had that happened here, under the laws we fought for to protect the rights of women against violence and abuse, he would not be guilty of rape?"

"Objection!" shouted Darnell as he leaped red-faced from his chair. "This is beyond all tolerance! She can't be allowed to do this – argue a charge that has been dismissed! Even her own witnesses could not prove it, and now she thinks she can act as if the charge were going to the jury? Your Honor, I've seen a lot of things in a courtroom, but never anything like this!"

Judge Pierce brought down her gavel to silence the murmuring of the crowd. Hillary Clark was glaring at her, defiant of anything the judge could do. The judge ignored her insolent smile and turned instead to the jury.

"The court would remind you that when the trial started the defendant was charged with three separate crimes. One of them, the charge of rape, was dismissed at the end of the prosecution's case because the prosecution had failed to provide sufficient evidence that the crime had been committed. It doesn't concern you why the court was forced to reach this conclusion, only that the charge has been dismissed. That means, as a matter of law, that the defendant has been ruled not guilty of that crime. In plain English, ladies and gentlemen, it has been decided that the defendant didn't do it, and it would be a gross dereliction of your duty to assume for any purpose that he did. Your decision with respect to the two remaining charges must be based on other evidence. In the heat of the moment, things get said in a trial that should not be mentioned. In her zeal to make the strongest case she can, Ms. Clark has stepped over the boundary of what is permissible in a closing statement. I'm certain this was inadvertent, and I'm certain," she said, looking straight at an unrepentant Hillary Clark, "that she won't do anything like this again - will you Ms. Clark?"

"May I continue, your Honor?"

Evelyn Pierce narrowed her eyes and leaned forward. "Will you Ms. Clark?"

"No, your Honor," replied Clark with an air of indifference. She turned quickly back to the jury and went on as if she had not been interrupted.

"The defendant and this underage girl – the girl he calls his sister – had a child. The defense tries to make a point that everyone on that island who was roughly the same age called each other brother or sister because none of them supposedly knew who their parents were. But remember, there was no answer for it when I asked whether it wasn't true that they could clearly identify their parents, and therefore their real siblings, by how much they looked alike. The defendant knew who were his real brothers and sisters and who were not. He called the girl his sister. I suggest he did not lie. I suggest that he committed incest and that he knew it when he did. I suggest he committed murder when he killed the child produced by this incestuous relationship and I suggest that nothing anyone can say can change that. Murder, ladies and gentlemen, had been murder since Cain slew Abel and there isn't anyone in this courtroom who doesn't know it."

When she was finished, when she told the jury one last time that the evidence was overwhelming and that the murder of a child should never go unpunished, the silence in the courtroom was electric. She sat down, exhausted but with the glow of victory on her cheek, confident that she had left William Darnell no escape. To her astonishment, Darnell appeared to agree.

He waited for a long time before he stirred from his chair. No one is allowed to applaud or make any overt sign of approval after an attorney makes her closing argument, but that did not mean that there was not a palpable sense

of emotional intensity after Hillary Clark's final performance. Darnell sat quietly, swinging his foot back and forth,
perfectly relaxed, as if what the prosecutor had just done was
the same kind of routine closing he had heard in every case
he had taken to trial. The tension in the courtroom began
to subside, the silence broken by the sound of shuffling feet
as spectators, jammed together on hard wooden benches,
shifted from positions that, mesmerized by Hillary Clark's
oration, had been held beyond the normal terms of endur-
ance. Several of the jurors sank back in their chairs, crossed
their arms and began to glance around.

"Mr. Darnell, are you ready?" asked Judge Pierce
finally.

Darnell looked up as if mildly surprised. He got to
his feet, slowly and to no apparent purpose. He continued to
wear a slightly baffled expression as he approached the jury
box.

"I'm afraid I'm completely unprepared for this," he
remarked, scratching his head like someone who had just
realized that he is in serious trouble. The button on his suit
jacket had come loose, perhaps by Darnell's own design, and
was hanging by a thread. He held it between two fingers,
twisting it back and forth, a kind of symbol - a talisman - he
seemed to say, of the way his case had been picked apart
by the sharp-tongued prosecutor with the sharp-pointed
nails. "I'm not prepared for this at all." With one last, rueful
glance at the button, he raised his eyes and shrugged his
shoulders. "I didn't realize until just now, after the prosecutor finished her speech, that there really is no defense to
these two charges against the defendant. There is no question now but that he's guilty of both incest and murder; and
if I were you I wouldn't even waste the time it would take to
get back to the jury room to reach that verdict."

The jurors looked at him in wide-eyed amazement, not
sure what to make of it, and, when he turned and began to
walk to the empty chair at the counsel table, not sure what
they should do.

"I mean what I say," said Darnell, pausing in his exit

to explain. "Just get it over with. Find him guilty. Go
home. There isn't anything to decide – Ms. Clark has done
all your thinking for you." He waved his pale white hand
in the air, a gesture of the futility of further argument. "It's
decided." He took a single step back toward them. His
gaze became serious and more intense, challenging them to
decide something on their own. "Isn't it? You were ready
to convict him on the spot not five minutes ago. I saw it on
your faces. You were transfixed – every one of you – by the
prosecution's rhetoric. She would have had you hang him
had she thought to bring a rope. He's guilty: incest, murder
– rape, too, because after all what difference does it make
that the prosecution not only could not provide any evidence,
but that their own witness proved it didn't happen? What
difference does anything make when we all know – don't
we? – that he did it."

Darnell shook his head in scorn as he began to search
the eyes of each juror in turn, searching, as it seemed, for
some light of reason, some inner sense that they had a higher
obligation than to serve up vengeance. He wanted them
to feel all the remorse of the lynch mob that, caught in a
ghastly revelry after it has just hung a man it knew must be
guilty, learns that the real killer has just confessed. He stood
there, staring them down, as if they ought, each of them, to
feel ashamed.

"Now, let's talk a little more about this," he said as he
moved closer. "Let's be sure about things before we decide
to convict a man for murder, especially when it is a young
man who never lived a day of his life in this country and
never could have known the requirements of our law. The
prosecution tells you that none of this matters, that murder
is murder, and that since Cain slew Abel everyone knows
what murder is. The prosecution doesn't tell you, though
there was evidence in this trial to prove it, that in other
places and in other times – and in our own country not that
long ago – the killing of a newborn child – infanticide – was
under certain circumstances not considered a crime and
was even thought to be an obligation. This may strike our

modern, more sensitive ears as nothing short of monstrous, a primitive custom no civilized people would tolerate, but it is a fact, and facts cannot be ignored. Adam – Lethe – lived among a people where there was no choice - when a child was born that could not live – but to let it die. Yes, I know, he isn't charged with letting the child die – he isn't charged with neglect –he's charged with murder. But do you have any doubt that if he had let the child die, the prosecution wouldn't have come after him for that? And if that had happened – if he had let the child die of natural causes – the prosecution might well have had a stronger case. They could at least have then argued that he had done nothing to stop a child's suffering!"

Darnell stepped back from the jury box and looked across at Hillary Clark who stared right back. He seemed to draw a kind of strength from the depth of her disapproval.

"Would you really have preferred that the child die in torment, lingering for no purpose in awful, hateful, pain? There was no hope of recovery, nothing anyone could do. Has that kind of cruel indifference become the standard of civilized behavior?"

With smoldering, stiff-necked anger, Hillary Clark stared back a moment longer before she picked up a ball-point pen and, as if she had just remembered something, scratched a note. Darnell did not move. He stood there, as if in silent vigil for something lost, an older sensibility, a feeling for the tragic circumstances of other people's lives.

"It's no use, I suppose," he went on, turning again to the jury, "asking what someone would do in a situation they will never have to face. But still, if we can't put ourselves in Adam's place, how can we know whether what he did wasn't right? Because that is the question – the serious question – you have to ask, and if you can't answer it, then despite what you've been told, the only decision you can make is to acquit, to find him not guilty on the ground that there wasn't any decent choice.

"The prosecution repeatedly insists that this is simple murder, and that everyone knows what that means. But nothing is quite as simple as she would have you believe. Imagine for a moment that you're a soldier in a war and that your best friend, the one person you know you can always count on, had just been shot and is nearly dead and there isn't any way to save him. He lays there, writhing in horrible agony, begging you, his best friend, to put an end to it. What do you do? What would Ms. Clark do? – Let him suffer, die a thousand awful deaths before he finally dies? I don't believe that and neither do you. But this is a child, not a soldier in a war – a child who hasn't learned to talk, to put its suffering into words. The child didn't ask to die. Is that the argument to make a child suffer?

"But let's be honest about more than this. The truth is that if Adam is guilty of the child's murder, so must also be the mother. Remember what she said – Alethia, as remarkable a witness as I've ever seen – remember her confession, that she knew the child could not live, that the child had to die, and that what Adam did he did in part for her, to save her from a necessity that he was willing to face himself, to end the life of the only child they had. Ms. Clark didn't much like what her own witness said, but do you remember what the witness said back? - That she felt sorry for anyone who could be that cruel.

"Why did she say that? Was it only because she understood that neither Ms. Clark nor anyone else Ms. Clark is likely to know will ever be confronted with the awful choice she had to make? Or was there something deeper, something about what she and Adam were raised to believe: that life has a meaning beyond itself and that whatever else that meaning might involve, preventing whatever cruelty and suffering you can is part of it. We know nothing about these people. We did not even know they existed until two short years ago. They're different than the other islanders of the south pacific, a seeming race all unto themselves. Where did they come from? How long have they been there? Is it possible they've been in existence longer than we have - the descendants of some ancient people that time and history have forgotten - people who may once have been, as we are now, a dominant power in some other place on the globe? These are questions we cannot answer, questions that may forever go unsolved, as much a mystery as the question where we ourselves have come from, whether born perfect, the work of some all-knowing God, or something that just started millions of years ago in the mud, a creature only now beginning to understand the world in which he lives.

"It doesn't matter that we have no answers. The questions are important. They remind us of our ignorance and the need for caution in our judgments." Darnell stretched out his arm and pointed straight at Adam. "You've watched him sitting here from the first day you were summoned to the jury box, you listened to him testify. Do you believe for one minute that he would have done what he did if there had been any other choice, any other way to stop the suffering of the child he had with the woman he loved? Do you believe for one minute that what he feels for this girl, for Alethia, is anything like the incestuous perversion the prosecution insists it was? I don't believe that and neither do you. They were living in perfect justice, the two of them, Adam and the girl, until we came along and, like the serpent in the garden, told them that everything they believed was wrong. There will be a day of reckoning for what we've done. Let us hope that nothing we decide here will make that reckoning even worse."

CHAPTER NINETEEN

"How long do you think the jury will be out?" asked Henry Hammersmith.

Sprawled in an overstuffed chair, Darnell peered into his scotch and soda, but he found nothing in the swirling amber liquid to help him read the future. He glanced up at Hammersmith, sitting with his wife on the sofa in the immense living room of their Russian Hill apartment. They looked so earnest, so eager to hear something that would give them hope that Adam might still be saved. Darnell felt a little like a swindler who has suddenly discovered his conscience. A physician, someone like Summer, could tell you with some degree of precision what the chances were that a patient would recover, but a lawyer whose case was now in the hands of a jury? One might as well look to a flight of birds to guess what the verdict might be.

"They could be out for hours, they could be out for days; there have been juries stayed out for weeks and still couldn't come to any decision."

"Yes, Bill, we understand that," said Laura Hammersmith, in the warm, silky voice of a leader of taste and fashion. "But you've been doing this a long time. Surely you can make an educated guess." Like many women who had always had money, she was a stranger to the idea that there were things that could not be controlled. "Adam isn't guilty; surely it won't take them too long to understand that there is only one decision they can make."

Her husband rolled his eyes. He often treated her with impatience. When she was not wrong, she either failed to get to the point fast enough or did not quite express herself in the way he would have preferred. They had been married so long they barely knew each other.

"She's right, Bill – Adam isn't guilty. How long can it take for them to realize that?" Still brooding over it, he got to his feet and took the glass from Darnell's hand. "Here, let me get you another."

"It's almost time for dinner," his wife reminded him, but he paid no attention to what she said. He filled the glass at the small bar at the far end of the room and brought it back. The worried look in his eyes vanished, and with a wine bottle in his hand he teased Summer, sitting in the chair next to Darnell, with how little she had had to drink.

"No, I'm fine," she said, holding her long, tapered fingers over her glass. "Well, all right," she said, relenting under his friendly, gentle pressure. "Just a little."

"What do you think, Summer?" asked Laura Hammersmith. "You were there today, during closing arguments. Didn't you think Bill was magnificent?"

While the two women talked about how well he had done, Darnell sipped on the scotch and soda. The Hammersmith's co-op apartment, which occupied the top floor of one of the oldest buildings on Russian Hill, had a view of the Golden Gate and the headlands of Marin at one end of the bay, down to the Berkeley hills and the Bay Bridge at the other. There was a sense as you sat there that nothing could be better than this, that nothing could ever go wrong. When you looked out at all the lights than circled all around the dark black waters of the bay, you felt the same way you had that first time you had seen it, when you were very young and Saturday nights were still the best nights you ever had.

"I think the chances are not very good," he said abruptly.

"What?" asked Henry, alarmed. "After what you did in there today? You were brilliant. The jury hung on every word."

"They hung on every word of the prosecutor's as well," replied Darnell. "Maybe more so. I appreciate what you say, but you have to understand that the emotion of a closing argument doesn't last. What happened when I finished, when I sat down? The judge took a brief recess and then, half an hour later, when the heat of the moment had passed, when everyone was all settled down, went about the business of giving the jury the instructions they're supposed to follow during their deliberations. And besides – and this isn't false modesty – in terms of closing arguments, Hillary Clark had the better of the exchange."

"She didn't – that isn't true," objected Summer, with both of the Hammersmith's echoing their agreement.

"You're too close – we're all too close – to see it," said Darnell, trying to explain. "If Adam had been tried on that island, tried to a jury made up of people who were brought up the same way – really tried to a jury of his peers – there wouldn't be any question what the verdict would be. The only question would be why anyone would have thought to prosecute him for what he had done. But he wasn't tried there, he was tried here, not to a jury that shared all his assumptions and understands him, but to a jury that is being asked to forget everything they have ever learned, every-thing they have ever believed – everything the only law they know tells them is right. When you cut through everything - all the evidence, all the questioning, all the arguments – that's really what I'm asking them to do: ignore the law and decide on their own that this is a case where the law doesn't work. There's a chance they might do that, but I'd be lying if I said I thought that the chances were very good."

"If he loses," asked Laura Hammersmith after a long, depressing silence; "if they jury does convict him, you can appeal it, can't you?"

The blind assurance that things could always be arranged, that she would never have to suffer any serious misfortune, had disappeared. There was now a pleading quality to her voice. Darnell did not have the heart to disap-point her.

"Yes, of course; we'll certainly appeal. And you shouldn't be too discouraged by what I said. I've been wrong before about what a jury was going to do. I'm just feeling a little let down. It happens sometimes at the end of a trial, before you know what the verdict is going to be – a sense that I could have done more."

He looked at their worried faces and thought it remarkable, the effect that Adam had had. The Hammersmiths had long had the easy attitude of the comfortable upper classes that anyone charged with a crime must be guilty, and now both of them were so convinced of Adam's innocence that all they could think about was what could be done to fight a conviction. No one thought much about fairness when it was just for people they did not know.

"Perhaps I've been too pessimistic," he allowed as the maid came in to announce that dinner was ready. "At least the jury doesn't have to decide between convicting him for murder and letting him go. The judge gave the instruction on lesser included offenses."

"What does that mean, exactly?" asked Laura Hammersmith, intensely interested, as she brushed back a lock of the platinum hair that, until recent years, had drawn attention the moment she walked into a room.

"It means that if they think they have to convict him of something, they could find him guilty of manslaughter instead of murder. And that would mean," he added, his voice vibrant with hope, the way it often was in court, "that he'd be given a suspended sentence and he and the girl could go back to the island where they belong."

Saying it out loud made it seem more tangible, more real, than an abstract possibility in which he did not believe. Hearing it, and remembering the determined look in Evelyn Pierce's eyes when she first advised them in chambers what she was going to do, Darnell began to feel much better. The color came back to his cheek, the bounce back into his step. He began to recall the words of his closing argument with something close to pride.

"Where is Adam, anyway?" asked Summer, as they sat down to dinner in the silver glow of a crystal chandelier. "Isn't he joining us?"

"He went out about an hour ago," explained Henry. "He walks for hours, often misses dinner. I didn't think – especially today, with the case just gone to the jury - that I ought to insist. He seems to like to be alone, seeing everything he can. He has more curiosity, always asking questions about things, always -"

"He's gone to see the girl," said his wife abruptly. A strange, wistful smile, the look of love once remembered, flickered on her fine, cultured mouth. More than nostalgia, it was a kind of defiance, a protest against anyone who did not understand the importance, the value, of a passion that cared for nothing but itself. "He's gone to see the girl. You thought he was out exploring the city, a tourist all alone? He's gone to see the girl. That's what he does every night, once he discovered where she was."

Her husband was not quite sure whether he should believe her.

"And you know this how? Did he tell you that's what he was doing?"

She took a delight in his confusion. Tossing her napkin on the table, she taunted him with the wisdom he did not have.

"What is it they say? Two things, really: A woman always knows when her husband is having an affair; but then, when the situation is reversed, the husband is always the last to know. No, he didn't tell me, Henry; he didn't have to. I know what that look in his eye means. I used to see it, years ago, when I first knew you. And just because I haven't seen that look in quite a while doesn't mean I wasn't able to recognize it again, when I first starting seeing it on that young man's face."

"When you first started...? Probably right after they met together in my office," said Darnell, certain it was true. "Of course she would have told him where she was staying. And once he knew that – you're right – he couldn't stay away." He glanced across at Summer. "Well, good for them – All I knew was that they were keeping her at a small hotel on Sutter. They wouldn't tell me which one."

"You knew this," said Henry Hammersmith to his wife, "and you didn't tell me?"

"No, I didn't tell you."

"And may I ask why?"

"I was afraid you'd feel an obligation to do something about it, try to stop it, or, if you couldn't do that, tell the authorities."

He threw up his hands in frustration.

"Tell the authorities? Why in the world would I do that?"

"You put up his bail, and you promised to make sure he complied with all the conditions of his release, one of which was that he not have any contact with the girl."

"To hell with the money - and to hell with their conditions! He's innocent, he ought to be able to spend time with his wife; and as far as I'm concerned the only people who have done anything wrong are the people who are trying to put him away. You really think I would…?"

For the first time in a long time she smiled at him the way she used to, when they were lovers instead of strangers.

Later that evening, after they had gone home, Summer asked Darnell what he really thought Adam's chances were, but the truth was that Darnell did not know. The case was too unusual, too different, a case without precedent that, as he had kept telling everyone who would listen, should never have been brought to trial.

"We do a lot of things these days we shouldn't do," he confided to Summer as he sat next to her after she had crawled into bed. She tugged at his sleeve, a gentle reminder that he needed to get some rest. "I will," he promised. "In a little while; there are too many things going through my mind right now."

"About the trial? You've done everything you can. It's up to the jury now. All you can do is wait."

"Not so much about the trial, about Adam – Lethe. I wish I knew what it meant, that name of his – or if it means anything at all. Lethe and Alethia: It's almost as if they were named with the intention that they would be together. And perhaps they were, the way everything else seems to have been organized and tightly controlled. I keep wondering what would have happened – I mean if I could have convinced that strange man, Gerhardt Holderlin to testify

– if I had told everyone the truth, that this wasn't just some island, some small speck of land in the middle of the Pacific that for some reason no one had discovered before, but the last outpost – the final outpost for all I know – of a civilization so much older than our own that we're just children by comparison."

Summer placed her hand on Darnell's knee as she searched his anguished eyes with the cool, clear gaze of a physician. He felt better for her touch and tried to seem less worried about what he had done or, rather, about what he had not done.

"Holderlin was right, I suppose. No one would have believed him. Why should they? What proof does he have? – His own unsubstantiated claim that he was there forty years ago? A story he could easily have made up. I'm not sure why I believed him, now that I look back on it, except that there was something about him that made me know that what he said was true. But Hillary Clark would have laughed him out of court. And as for Adam supplying some kind of confirmation – he couldn't prove it, either, even if he had been willing to break what seems to have been a blood oath never to reveal anything about the city and where it is. Prove it? How much does he really know? When I've talked to him about it, asked him what he can tell me about how far back these people go, all he says is that they have 'always been.' He doesn't know anything about their origins, nothing about where the city came from, or how they got to where they are. He doesn't know anything about what happened – or didn't happen – twelve thousand years ago. Why should he? How much do we know, any of us, about ourselves? How many generations can we trace back with any certainty?"

Summer remembered something that, with his mind devoted to the trial, Darnell had forgotten. But before she told him she got out of bed, went into the bathroom and found a bottle of sleeping pills. She handed him one of them along with a glass of water.

"Take this. You need to get some rest. You can't

spend a second night fretting about what's going to happen next."

"There's something you were going to tell me. What is it?"

"Not until you take the pill."

With a show of reluctance, he did what he was told, and then waited for her to keep her end of the bargain.

"Adam has never told you that he doesn't know - has he? You just assumed that because all he would tell you is that it's 'always been.'"

"Yes, but what else....?

"Didn't Holderlin tell you that they learn everything by listening to what they're told, and that they have this oral tradition, this story – history, if you wish to call it that – that is committed to memory and passed down through the generations? If that's true, then Adam knows it as well as we can read what is written in the Bible. He won't tell you because you're an outsider; he can't reveal more to you than what you've already learned."

"That's what he meant, at the end, when I finished my closing. He thanked me for what I had tried to do for him and said he wanted to thank me even more for what I hadn't said. I had kept the secret and he was grateful for that."

Darnell changed into his pajamas and, feeling drowsy, got into bed beside Summer and closed his eyes. Summer kept talking about Adam and the stories he must have heard.

"All the adventures, all the escapes, all the times they must have been threatened with extinction, all the last minute heroics to make sure they weren't. What you said when Judge Pierce first tried to get the prosecution to reduce the charges, when she said that he would have to spend some time in prison – you were right, it's true: Adam could never live a captive, he'll die if he can't be free."

Exhausted, all his energy spent, Darnell slept until noon. The first thing he wanted to know was whether anyone had called, whether the jury had reached a verdict. He knew of course that Summer would have awakened him if that had happened, but he had to be sure. Grumbling that he should not have slept so long, he had lunch and then went to the office where, as he quickly discovered, there was nothing to do. He had not agreed to take on any new cases because, as he had during each of his last few trials, he had thought this case might be his last. It was always a lie, the way he cheated himself into a future. If he got through what might be his last one, then why not do just one more, one more last one before he retired? The stack of letters asking if he would consider taking on the writer as a client had grown thicker by the day. He began to read them.

At five o'clock the court clerk called. After deliberating all day, the jury had decided to have dinner brought so they could continue into the night. They were back at it in the morning and Darnell began to feel a surge of hope. If they had not decided yet, it must mean that they had some serious doubt about what the verdict should be. But a serious doubt meant that in their minds proof of guilt was anything but certain. And that had to mean…. It did not mean anything, and Darnell knew it. A jury could be out for a week and come back with a guilty verdict as if there had never been any doubt at all. Pulling a coin out of his pocket, he tossed it in the air and called out 'heads.' He caught it and slapped it down on the back of his other hand. It was 'heads,' but he still did not feel any better. The grim wait continued.

But not for much longer. At three o'clock that afternoon, the court clerk called to tell him that the jury had reached a verdict. Everyone was to be in court in an hour. Darnell called Henry Hammersmith to let him know.

There was a dead silence at the other end.

"Henry, did you hear what I said? The jury has reached a verdict. Adam has to be in court in an hour. Four o'clock. Have him there a few minutes early, if you would. I want to talk to him."

"He isn't here," finally replied Henry Hammersmith. His voice was cold, distant, drawn in upon itself, as if he were being forced to repeat a fact that was no one's business but his own.

"What are you talking about? Of course he's there. This isn't time to play games, Henry. Quit trying to make me feel nervous."

"He left yesterday. He won't be back."

It was as if Darnell had been struck a physical blow. A hollow, empty feeling was followed by a wave of nausea. He did not want to believe it and he was angry because he knew it was true.

"How do you know -?"

"He has my boat. He sailed away and they won't find him. He's safe and I can't say I'm sorry."

"You knew about this? You knew about it yesterday and you didn't tell me? You just let him go and didn't try to stop him?"

"I let him take the boat out by himself. I didn't know he wouldn't be coming back. But I'm not going to be a hypocrite and tell you that I'm sorry that he got away. Are you?"

"Of course I...," Darnell started to reply, only to realize that the answer was not as obvious as he had thought it would be. "It doesn't matter, Henry; none of that matters now. He's gone, and you're going to have to come to court and tell the judge what happened."

Darnell discovered that he was not the only one disturbed. Hillary Clark was beside herself. With her lips pressed tight together, she twisted her mouth into one contortion after another while her hard-polished fingers beat a harsh staccato on the table. The sad-eyed bailiff stood off to the side, barely able to suppress a smile at the prosecutor's apparent frustration. Then the court reporter walked in, and, a moment later, Evelyn Pierce took her place on the bench. Hillary Clark sprang to her feet.

"Your Honor, I have to report what I think may be a kidnapping. The young woman, the victim in this case, the girl known as Alethia, has been missing for two days. She disappeared from the hotel where she was being kept and no one has seen her since. She doesn't know anyone here. It's difficult to believe she just wandered off alone. Perhaps," she added, turning a suspicious eye on Darnell, "counsel for the defense can shed some light on this."

Judge Pierce did not like the implication.

"What makes you think Mr. Darnell would know anything about this? The girl was your witness. You made the arrangements about where she would stay and the people who would look after her. I don't think -"

"I may know something about this, your Honor," said Darnell, in a tired, weary voice. "I'm afraid the defendant has also disappeared. I don't know for certain that he took the girl with him, but I seriously doubt he would have left without her. They're too much in love for that to happen, too much -"

"No one's interested in that!" shouted Hillary Clark. "The question is where have they gone? They need to be brought back. You need to tell the court everything you -"

"Don't you dare start telling anyone what the court requires!" scolded Judge Pierce. "Don't even open your mouth unless I tell you to." She stared hard at her a moment longer and then, with a much kinder expression, turned to Darnell. "You're sure he's gone, that he won't be back, that he isn't just lost somewhere?"

"Henry Hammersmith, who posted his bail and was taking care of him, is waiting just outside. He can explain what's happened, your Honor. It might be better if you heard from him."

Hammersmith was brought into court and sworn as a witness, but neither of the attorneys was allowed to ask a question. Evelyn Pierce took over.

"I've had you sworn so that there won't be any confusion in your mind that you have to tell the truth, the whole truth. Tell me what's happened to the defendant and why he isn't here."

"He borrowed my boat and -"

"Borrowed your boat? Were you in the habit of letting him take it out alone?"

"A couple of times. I couldn't have sailed her alone, but Adam could."

"And you let him do this knowing that at any moment the jury might reach a verdict and he would have to be in court?"

"No, I didn't. He took the boat out just after dawn, the morning the jury first started deliberations. I thought he would be gone only a few hours."

"When he didn't come back – what did you do then?"

"Nothing."

"Nothing? You didn't advise Mr. Darnell that there might be a problem? You didn't think you had an obligation to inform the court?"

Hammersmith sat on the witness chair just a few feet away, as close as if they were having a conversation across a table in his office. A strange and quite unexpected smile creased the corners of his mouth. It was the only answer he would give.

"I see. You weren't disappointed that he disappeared. You posted his bail, didn't you? You told the court – you told me – that you guaranteed his appearance."

"And he appeared, didn't he? – Every day of this misbegotten trial! He's gone, your Honor, and there is nothing I can do about it."

"With that attitude, Mr. Hammersmith, I should throw you in jail for contempt."

"Go ahead, your Honor, if it will make you feel better. But that won't change the fact that Adam isn't going to be here."

"He should certainly be put in jail for -"

"Enough, Ms. Clark! I've warned you before – I won't warn you again."

She paused, drew back, placed her hands in her lap and appeared to consider her decision. Darnell had the feeling that though she would never show it, she had some sympathy for what Henry Hammersmith had done. She had one more question.

"When you let him take your boat, you thought he was coming back? He didn't say anything that even hinted that he had made up his mind to leave?"

"He said he wanted to sail around the bay, that he knew he might not have another chance."

Evelyn Pierce nodded thoughtfully and lapsed into a prolonged silence.

"Very well," she said presently. "There's no reason to think you were involved. You should have reported it, but I don't see the point in punishing you for that. You did lose the boat, and you won't get back the bail, so it wouldn't be true to say that you haven't paid a price for your neglect."

Henry Hammersmith, unrepentant as far as anyone could tell, was excused. Evelyn Pierce turned to the immediate question of the trial.

"The defendant may not be here, but we have a verdict, and that verdict needs to be announced and this trial brought to a final conclusion."

She ordered the bailiff to bring in the jury. As they took what had now become their accustomed places in the jury box, Darnell had a premonition that his best hopes were about to be dashed. They seemed worn out, as if they had been struggling with something that had in the end defeated them. Their eyes were all averted, afraid, as it seemed, of what others might expect. They had the look of reluctant executioners.

"Has the jury reached a verdict?"

At the sound of the judge's voice, they all looked up, but not one would so much as hazard a glance in the direction of the defendant. They did not notice the empty chair.

"Yes, your Honor," replied the foreperson, a tall, middle-aged woman with a long nose and an angular face. She looked unhappy. "We have."

"Would you please read the verdict."

She started to, but her eyes, drifting to the counsel table, registered surprise when she realized he was not there. She forced herself back to the single sheet of paper clutched in her hands.

"On the charge of incest, we, the jury, find the defendant not guilty."

Darnell did not care about the charge of incest; only

the murder charge was important. Still, they had found him not guilty of it, which meant they were not as blind as he had feared. He sat on the edge of the chair, tightening both hands into fists.

"On the charge of murder, we, the jury, find the defendant...." She lowered her hand and looked straight at Darnell. "...guilty."

In the simple formality with which jury trials end, Evelyn Pierce thanked the jury for their service, waited until they left the courtroom, and then announced that a warrant would be issued for the arrest of the defendant. Sentencing would take place when he was brought into custody.

Henry Hammersmith was waiting for Darnell when he walked out of the courtroom

"I won't ask you what you think, Bill; but I'm glad he got away. There is one other thing you should know. Yesterday, the day after Adam left, a strange man came to see me. He told me that Adam was no thief, that he didn't steal my boat. He had come to pay me what the boat was worth."

There were only a few stragglers left in the corridor from the crowd that had packed the courtroom each day of the trial. Darnell leaned against the cool, white marble wall. For the second time that day he thought he knew what he had not yet heard.

"What did he look like, this strange man who came to see you? Did he have an unusual face, almost perfectly balanced?"

"I wouldn't have thought to put it that way, but yes, exactly. You know him? He said his name was -"

"Gerhardt Holderlin. Yes, you could say so."

"He said he was paying for the boat because he owed the boy a debt. What do you think he meant by that?"

But Darnell was thinking about something else.

"He came the next day, after Adam left? Which means that he knew before you did what Adam had done. And that means that, somehow, he helped Adam do it."

"That must be right, because there was another thing

he said, a message he wanted me to give you. He asked that you not think too badly of him for what he had done. He said he was sorry that he had to lie."

"Lie - about what?" Then he knew, or thought he did. "I'll tell you what he lied about! - Everything! It was all a made-up story, the whole fantastic lot of it. But why?" he asked, though he knew that Henry Hammersmith could give no answer. "Why, for what reason? Holderlin apologized, did he?" he said angrily as turned and started toward the exit. "We'll see what he has to say when I find him and he has to tell me face to face!"

CHAPTER TWENTY

Summer tried to stop him.

"You can't just fly off to Berlin! You're in no condition to go anywhere. You just finished a trial. You're too exhausted – you're too depressed!"

"Depressed? I'm not depressed; angry, maybe, but not depressed. And as for being too exhausted, you were the one telling me that I ought to take some time and travel," said Darnell with the sly grin she could never quite resist. He had been pacing around the living room, trying to work off some of his frustration. He sat down next to her on the sofa. "Why don't you come with me? We can finally see Europe together."

Summer knew him too well to think he would change his mind. He was going and there was nothing she could do about it.

"I would – I'd love to go with you – but I can't. I have to get back to my patients. I've been gone too long as it is." She patted his hand and smiled. "We both have things we have to do. But I still don't understand what you hope to accomplish. What do you think this man Holderlin will tell you that you don't already know or that will do you any good? There's nothing he can say that can change the verdict or bring Adam back."

Darnell got to his feet again. With his hands on his hips he stared out the window at the great bridge, the one known all around the world, shining bright and golden in the mid-day sun. He thought about Adam and the girl, slipping between the steel pillars, early on a fog-bound morning, on their way to freedom somewhere no one would ever find them.

"You're glad he got away, aren't you?" asked Summer, certain from the distant look in his eyes that it was true.

Darnell laughed at how easily she could read his mind.

"Yes, I suppose I am. It's better than what would have happened had he stayed. There would not have been anything anyone could do after the jury came back with that verdict. He would have been sent to prison for the rest of his life. Hillary Clark would have been pleased, but no one else. Evelyn Pierce will never admit it, but I think she was relieved that she did not have to pass sentence and put him away. And we owe it all to Henry Hammersmith, who, when it came down to doing what he thought was right, didn't give a damn about the law. Which proves, I suppose, that not every rich American is a complete idiot."

"Does Henry know you're going?"

"No, I'll tell him about it when I get back. I'm still a little angry with him. I know it sounds hypocritical, but I've been a lawyer too long to approve of what he did, even though I'm glad he did it."

Summer tilted her head to the side the way she did when something was said she thought worth exploring.

"Don't you think he feels the same way himself? - Bothered by what he did, though he knows that he would do the same thing in the same set of circumstances. That's the nature of the thing, isn't it, when you do what you know is right but what everyone else thinks is wrong?"

"Yes, I suppose it is," said Darnell, surprised, as he often was, by how much she understood that he did not.

"But you still haven't told me what you think this man Holderlin can tell you."

"What he lied to me about; whether anything he told me was the truth. Whether he was ever on that island, and, if he was, whether any of the rest of it – Atlantis, what happened to the survivors, the whole history of the last twelve thousand years – was true, or just some fable he invented because for some reason I don't understand he wanted to help Adam and thought he could do it by telling me this incredible story that no one in his right mind would believe – no one but me, that is."

"That's what bothers you, isn't it? - Not that he might

have lied, but that you believed it."

"No, not that I believed it, but that I wanted to believe it." With a rueful expression, he added, "The truth is I still want to believe it. That's the real reason I'm going: to find out what exactly Holderlin lied about so I can know whether Adam is really a descendant of some ancient civilization, someone we can learn from; or whether he is what Hillary Clark kept saying he was: a member of some illiterate tribe that needs to be brought into the modern world."

Three days later, Summer drove Darnell to the airport and, after making him promise for at least the fourth time that he would take his medication and call every night, kissed him goodbye. As he watched the car pull away, Darnell thought she might be crying. He felt a hollow sense of loneliness and began to regret the decision he had made.

When he landed in Berlin he checked into the Adlon Hotel and wandered along the Kurfurstendam, the most fashionable street in the city. He found himself wishing that he had waited until Summer could have come along. The crowds were different here than they were on the streets of San Francisco, the faces more interesting, more defined, drawn, as it were, as much by what they remembered of the past as what they hoped for from the future. Then there were the voices, the intriguing sound of languages he did not understand, and on occasion, to his acute embarrassment, the rising, garish sound of Americans, tourists mainly, who seemed to think that because they were Americans the city belonged to them. He noticed that his eye lingered most often on men old enough to have been in the war. He tried to read in their healthy, prosperous looking faces some sense of guilt or regret, some sign that they remembered the brutal savagery of what had been done. He found nothing, and wondered why he thought he would. The war, the twelve year nightmare through which Germany had lived and died, was too painful to remember. And besides, Darnell reminded himself, the past was always being re-written in the same way that each of us was always re-writing our own lives, changing the meaning of each thing that had happened in light of the things that happened later. The world had always been a fiction masquerading as the truth.

Or was that something we told ourselves to make our ignorance seem reasonable? - The principle of relativity made a convenient means by which to excuse any serious interest in the truth. Darnell did not know, but he thought that there had to be something more solid and lasting than the cacophony of gabbling noise that kept shouting in the modern ear that no opinion was any better than another and that there was no such thing as the truth.

Darnell had arrived in Berlin on a Saturday and spent most of Sunday seeing what he could of the city. On Monday, he took a cab from his hotel to the University of Berlin and, after getting directions from an obliging student, made his way down a long hallway to the philosophy department and his much anticipated visit with Gerhardt Holderlin. It reminded him of Berkeley, the way the students in their shaggy, unpressed clothes looked as if the weight of the world were on their young shoulders. There was the same intensity in their eyes, a reflection of the long struggle to understand Kant or Hegel; the same certainty that what they were doing was the only thing important. Darnell wished he had had the time to have known what that was like, studying for the sake of what he could learn instead of what it taught him about how to become proficient in his profession.

The office of the philosophy department was a small, cramped affair with a bulletin board a tangled web of announcements and two decrepit wooden desks where two secretaries typed the manuscripts faculty hoped to get published as well as the chairman's correspondence.

"Excuse me, but does anyone here speak English?" asked Darnell with a brief, apologetic smile.

The department chairman, a thin, angular man in his forties, was talking to one of the secretaries. When he looked up and saw Darnell dressed in a suit and tie, he came right over.

"Yes, I speak English. How can I help you?"

Darnell introduced himself, explained that he had just

come from San Francisco and wanted to see a member of the faculty, Professor Gerhardt Holderlin. The chairman seemed puzzled.

"Holderlin, you say? Gerhardt Holderlin? I'm afraid there is no one on our faculty by that name. Perhaps he's in some other department. Let me find out."

While Darnell waited, the chairman picked up the telephone and had a short conversation.

"No, I'm afraid he doesn't teach anywhere in the university. Are you sure you have the right name?" He took into account Darnell's age, but was too kind to mention it. "Sometimes when we hear a name in a language we don't understand, it's easy to get confused."

"No, I'm sure that's the name he used. I'm afraid that's the only thing I'm sure of." He thanked the chairman for his help and with a feeling of immense disappointment left the office and started down the hallway.

"Mr. Darnell," someone called after him. The other secretary, an older woman with gray hair and a noticeable limp, was hurrying after him. "There used to be someone here by that name, years ago, when I first started working in the department. He used to come by once in a while, at first to see if he had any mail, but then, later, just to say hello. I haven't seen him in a long time, but I still have his address, though I couldn't tell you if he still lives there. But wait here, I'm sure I've got it somewhere."

Darnell sat down on a bench, wondering what it meant. Holderlin had told him that he was still teaching. Why would he have lied about that? Why would anyone insist he was still at a university when he had not been there in years?"

"Yes, I have it," said the secretary when she came back. The address had been written in ink on a sheet of departmental stationery. Darnell smiled at the elegant precision with which it had been done.

"Thank you," he said as he folded it in half and put it into his jacket pocket. "You've been very kind."

"I always liked Professor Holderlin. I hope he is all

right," she said with a worried, sympathetic glance.

"Do you know why he left, why he didn't stay at the university?"

"I'm not sure. I had just started here; I was just a young girl. He was considered a man of extraordinary promise. It all happened quite abruptly. No one talked about it, but I had the feeling that something had happened, that he had had some kind of breakdown."

What kind of breakdown, wondered Darnell as he made his way to the street outside and flagged down a taxi. How severe? Holderlin had seemed as clear-minded, as little subject to mental disturbance, as anyone he had met. But whatever had happened had happened forty years ago, he reminded himself, the same time he claimed he had gone on that remarkable adventure across the Atlantic and across South America out to a place in the Pacific that no one knew was there. Or had all that just been in his mind? Had Holderlin broken under the strain of all his late night studies? Had he become so convinced of what he imag- ined might have happened to the lost tribe of Atlantis that he believed that he had seen it for himself? Was the man Darnell had thought so intelligent simply an overworked scholar gone insane?

The taxi pulled up in front of a small restaurant on a busy street just off Friedrichstrasse. Darnell was confused. He pulled out the sheet of paper on which the address had been written.

"Just next door," explained the driver. He pointed to a doorway with a buzzer and a set of tarnished brass nameplates.

Gerhardt Holderlin had one of the two apartments on the top floor of the four story building. Darnell hesitated. He was not sure now why he had come. He felt old, tired, a little demented himself for coming all this way to confront someone who probably did not know that his whole life had been a delusion. With a bitter, silent, laugh, Darnell pushed the buzzer.

"Yes?" said a voice through the static of the intercom.

"Gerhardt Holderlin?" asked Darnell.

The intercom went dead and a moment later the lock was released. Darnell pushed open the door. It was not what he expected. Instead of a narrow staircase in a tiny, congested space, the steps were broad enough that four or five people could climb them together. The banister and the doors he passed on each landing were heavy, dark, and ornamental. It was an endless climb for someone used to elevators, the staircase turning back on itself between floors, so that he had to go up the equivalent of eight normal flights to reach the fourth floor. He was out of breath when he finally knocked on Holderlin's door.

It was the wrong apartment. The man who answered was not Holderlin.

"I'm sorry," apologized Darnell, wiping the perspiration off his face. "I must have pushed the wrong buzzer."

Well over six feet tall, with broad shoulders and a rather prominent jaw, the man looked at Darnell with some impatience.

"You asked for Gerhardt Holderlin. I am Gerhardt Holderlin."

"But you're not… I'm sorry, you're Gerhardt Holderlin?" he asked, feeling more confused than he had felt in his life.

"Yes, I'm Gerhardt Holderlin." His impatience was replaced with curiosity. "And you are?"

"William Darnell."

"You're an American, aren't you?"

"Yes, from San Francisco. I came to Berlin to see Gerhardt Holderlin, but you're not…."

"Why don't you come in, Mr. Darnell? It might be easier to discuss this if we were sitting down. And you do look like you could use some water."

Holderlin held a thick book in his hand, something he had been reading, or rather, as Darnell observed, studying, because from the look of things everything that happened in that apartment was dedicated to the same, serious end, whatever that end might be. There were books everywhere.

Bookshelves, the cheap kind, unpainted boards braced against the wall, groaned under the weight of them, all the chairs except the one in front of the desk where he worked, were buried under them. They were stacked on the floor in free standing columns, stacked on counter tops, stacked in closets that could not be closed and in front of windows that could not be opened. It was all chaotic, or so it seemed, because as Darnell looked closer he began to suspect that there was after all some organizing principle at work. Each book was filled with any number of small slips of paper, and from what he could see, each of them were filled with handwritten notes. And then there was the rosewood desk, polished to a hard, gleaming shine, everything on it arranged with a meticulous, one could almost say a regimental, eye for cleanliness and order, three stacks of paper, blank paper on the left, paper covered with a tiny, neatly printed scrawl on the right, and, between them, a page half written, the unfinished product of his latest labor. He wrote in pencil, and just below the shaded lamp there were three of them, each sharpened to a perfect point, enough so that when he sat down to work again he would not have to stop to sharpen another. Another thing caught Darnell's attention. On the wall above the desk, a map of the world had been posted with a line drawn from the Pillars of Hercules across the Atlantic, over to Peru and out into the Pacific. Darnell was more confused than ever.

Puzzled what to do, the man who called himself Holderlin looked for a place where his visitor could sit. Careful to keep them in order, he lifted a stack of books from a chair and carried them to an open spot on the floor in the corner.

"Mainly dictionaries," he explained as he settled into his usual chair. He glanced around the room as one who has just realized what it must look like to a stranger, someone who had not lived every day in these same surroundings. "Dictionaries and ancient histories. I've been working on something – a dictionary, a language no one knows anymore. I've been...." He looked at Darnell. "Why are you looking for someone with my name? It's not a very common name. And how did you happen to come here? I'm not in the telephone directory; I don't have a telephone."

"They gave me your address at the university."

"The university? I haven't been there in years. Someone there still remembers me, and still has my address?"

"A secretary in the philosophy department, where you used to teach."

The lines in Holderlin's high forehead deepened as he drew his sharp blue eyes close together. He was a handsome man for his age, athletic in build, agile and strong, with short-cropped iron gray hair and a ruddy complexion. He did not look the part of the reclusive scholar.

"That was a very long time ago," he remarked with a clear sense of disappointment. "A very long time ago."

"Forty years, if I'm not mistaken."

"Yes, that's about right. I was only there a year or so. I thought I would spend my life there, teaching philosophy to generations of eager students. Instead....But I'm still confused, Mr. Darnell. Who is this other Gerhardt Holderlin and why are you looking for him?"

The dictionaries, the map, the book he said he was working on, the fact that he had been at the University of Berlin – there were too many coincidences, too many things that otherwise would not make sense.

"Tell me, Mr. Holderlin, forty years ago, before you left the university, did you make a trip to Peru, and were you then taken on a boat, your money stolen, and you were thrown overboard? And where you then saved from the sea by what turned out to be the last descendants of the lost tribe of Atlantis, and did you then spend a year among them in that city high up on that mountain on that island no one had yet discovered? And is that dictionary on which you have been working all these years the language of Atlantis that, as you just put it, no one knows anymore?"

Gerhardt Holderlin stood straight up, staggered by what he had heard. His face turned pale white, his hands began to shake.

"How do you know…? How could you possibly know what happened then? I've never told anyone, I've never breathed a word. I kept my promise, I never…."

"The island was discovered – re-discovered, I suppose I should say – two years ago. You didn't know?"

His eyes still wide with amazement, Holderlin gestured toward the cluttered shelves.

"I don't pay much attention to what goes on in the outside world…. But, tell me, how – who discovered it?"

"A Norwegian captain – quite by accident."

Holderlin sat down, placed his hands on his knees and stared straight ahead, pondering what Darnell had said.

"By accident?" he asked skeptically. "Only if they allowed it; only if they wanted to be discovered. But whoever discovered the island didn't find the city, did he?"

"No," replied Darnell, fascinated by the certainty in the other man's eyes, the sense that he had almost been expecting it, that someone else would find the island but never find the city. "No one knows anything about it. I wouldn't know anything about it if someone who called himself Gerhardt Holderlin hadn't come to see me in the middle of the trial."

The reference to a trial was met with a blank stare. Darnell began to explain what had happened, what Adam had done and why he had been brought to America to stand trial. Holderlin stopped him before he went any further.

"Tell me about the man who used my name. How old was he, what did he look like?"

"Difficult to know exactly, but about your age, if I had to guess."

"And what did he look like? What was the first thing that struck you when you saw him – the perfect balance of his face, the clear, penetrating look in his eyes?" he asked with growing excitement.

"Yes, exactly – I'd never seen a face quite like it. Just looking at him you knew you were in the presence of a remarkable intelligence."

Holderlin stared into the middle distance, his face rigid under the pressure of what seemed an overwhelming shock.

"He was my friend, the one who taught me everything the year I was there. Even among that remarkable people, he had an exceptional gift. There was no question but that he would eventually become one of the council of elders, the ones who carry on the tradition and rule the city."

Holderlin sank back in the chair. He seemed suddenly lost, too overwhelmed to know what to do next. Darnell went back to the beginning and described what had happened in the early stages of the trial. Then, careful not to leave anything out, he recounted what Holderlin, or rather Holderlin's friend, had told him.

"Yes, it's all true, every word of it," said Holderlin when Darnell had finished. "He remembered everything I told him, and then, forty years later, repeated it back to you, an exact account of what led me to go on that search for the lost tribe of Atlantis and of how I finally stumbled on the truth. They learn everything by remembering the spoken word, and no one had a better memory than he. What you said about this young man you defended, that was no ordinary thing, that memory of his. It's no wonder they came after him. When his time comes he'll be one of those who rule."

"But Adam -"

"That can't be his name."

"No, that was just what he was called at first by those who found him and then accused him. No one could learn their language, though they don't seem to have much trouble learning ours."

Holderlin glanced at the neat stacks of paper on his desk.

"That's what I've been doing, for forty years; the reason I couldn't go back to the university; the reason there are people who think I lost my mind. I'm writing the dictionary of their language, and not just that, but an etymology in which I try to trace its influence through all the ancient languages, and through them, into ours. It is very difficult work. But tell me, what name did he have? It's important."

"The girl's name is Alethia; his name is Lethe."

Holderlin's eyes lit up.

"That's really quite wonderful! It's Greek. Didn't you know? Lethe in Greek means forgetfulness; Alethia, on the other hand, means truth. Truth and forgetfulness – Do you see the connection? The truth, to be preserved, has to be forgotten; hidden from view, so that only a few can know to find it. The island has been hidden from view for hundreds of years, but now, suddenly, it has been discovered. Do you really believe that was an accident, Mr. Darnell? Do you really believe that after twelve thousand years, they had not prepared for every eventuality; that they hadn't learned, far beyond anything we know, the arts of concealment? There is a reason they let themselves be discovered, a reason why the city is still secret. Think about it, Mr. Darnell – Why did someone come to see you, why did he use my name? - To help you with your defense? What did he tell you that helped? You could not use anything he told you; no one would have believed you if you had tried. He came to see you, Mr. Darnell, because he had to help Lethe escape, and because he wanted you to find me."

"To find you? But why…?"

"Because he wanted me to know what had occurred, that the island had been discovered and that something was going to happen."

"Going to happen? What do you mean?"

Holderlin did not hear him. He was back in the past, seeing everything through his still youthful eyes.

"He told me he would, that one day he would send for me; that I could come back to the island and never have to leave."

"Why didn't you go back a long time ago? Why did you think you had to wait until you heard from him?"

Holderlin shook himself out of his reverie.

"What? Oh, yes – why didn't I go back? I tried. A

few years later, I went back, but the island wasn't there. I couldn't find it." He gave Darnell a knowing glance. "But that won't be a problem now. They want us there."

CHAPTER TWENTY ONE

The village on the southern coast of Peru was not a village anymore. The dusty tavern where Gerhardt Holderlin had forty years earlier made the dangerous acquaintance of Alberto Lopez Rodriquez had been torn down and replaced with a modern hotel. The fishing boats that had once been hauled up on the beach at night were now motorized craft with all the latest electronics, each with its private berth in a protected marina. On their first night there, the two men lingered over a dinner prepared by an Argentine chef in a well-lit restaurant filled with eager-eyed tourists.

"Everything changes," remarked Darnell.

"Almost everything," replied Holderlin. He did not have to mention the exception he was thinking about. For the last week, from the time they left Berlin, to the trip to the ruins of Cuzco in the Peruvian highlands, they had talked about little else than the unbelievable story both of them believed.

"It must have been more interesting then, when you first came here, down the coast of Peru, listening to the stories the old men told, trying to discover something that would tell you where to begin your search."

Holderlin finished off a glass of beer and ordered another.

"When you're that age – young as I was then – you think everything is possible, but you also think that if you live as long as this – as old as I am now – what you did will seem like some distant dream. You must know what I'm talking about. It was forty years ago, but it seems more like forty days, just last month, that I was here. Everything looks different, but that isn't what I see."

"Do you still see Alberto Lopez Rodriguez, the look on his face when you showed up again, a year later, after he threw you overboard and was certain that you had drowned?"

"No, that never happened. I never tried to find him. He tried to kill me once; I didn't want to tempt fate a second time."

"But I thought…. Yes, of course, how would anyone have known?"

"He told you everything I told him, and I told him that as well. I said I was going to do it, find Rodriquez and make him think I had come back from the dead, sent by the devil to get my revenge. I was young, and after what I had found, after the year I had spent, my mind was full of all the adventures I had not yet experienced."

Holderlin's gaze drifted to the crowded bar where a bartender with a sleek graying mustache and black steely eyes flashed a set of perfect white teeth as he took the tourists' money.

"That might be him, old Rodriquez, who may have used what he stole from me to start his first business. Isn't all property based on theft?"

After dinner they strolled down a narrow, palm-lined street, talking about their plans for the morning, when they would start their journey into the Pacific.

"The boat has been chartered; the captain, unlike Rodriquez, is reputable and reliable," said Holderlin, puffing on his pipe. "And the weather is perfect. Look, a full moon and just a few scattered clouds."

"Do you think Adam is there? Do you think he and the girl went back to the island?"

Holderlin stopped at a stone fountain and splashed some water on his face. He looked again at the moon, guessing at the time.

"We leave early," he said, worried about Darnell. "We'd better get back to the hotel." They walked a while in silence before Holderlin ventured an opinion about Adam and the girl.

"I don't think so. I've been thinking about what you told me. They got away, the two of them, on that boat that belonged to your friend - The two of them, Mr. Darnell, not the three of them. My old friend from the island didn't go with them. He waited, and then must have gone back the same way he had come, whatever way that was. But if they were going back to the island, why wouldn't they have all gone together? No, something else is going on, and I think I know what it is. They're moving, the lost tribe, going somewhere else, starting somewhere where they won't be found again. Perhaps not all of them, maybe just those two: Lethe and Alethia - Adam, as you call him, and the woman who is both his sister and his wife. That's all it would take, two people, to start all over, to make sure that they don't die out. Did you ever consider the possibility that the story of Genesis isn't about the beginning of the human race, but about its continuance; that the Garden of Eden was, like the island, just a stopping place, where something that had been going on forever could have a new beginning, another long cycle of existence?"

A warm breeze rustled through the palm trees. Somewhere in the night a bird called out and, in a language only they could understand, another bird called back.

"Come to my room for a moment," said Holderlin when they got back to the hotel. "I have something for you."

Holderlin's gift was a thin, tattered paperback book, an old copy of something published more than half a century before. Darnell's eyes brightened at the sight of what he remembered reading when the book was new and everyone was reading it.

"Kon-Tiki! It's a title I never forgot," he said, fondly turning it over in his hand. "Nor the name of the author: Thor Hyerdahl. Thank you, but why this particular -?"

"Because more than anything else that book told me that I was right, that I wasn't just pulling things out of the air, finding connections were there weren't any. I told my friend on the island most of what led me to go on that search of mine, but I didn't tell him about this. It wouldn't have made much sense to him. I also wanted to hold something back, so as I learned more about what had happened to them

I would have a way to test some at least some of it against what we in the modern world had discovered on our own. Although in this case, it was more what Heyerdahl did not think to ask than what he set out to prove. He wanted to show that people of South America had settled the islands of the South Pacific; he didn't ask where these same people had first come from. When you read it – and I've marked the passages – you'll see how close he might have gotten if he had only, so to speak, looked the other way."

Darnell called Summer when he got to his room. After a long conversation in which he swore he had not once failed to take his medication, he climbed into bed and began to read. He had not read two sentences of the first passage Holderlin had marked before he knew Holderlin was right. At the beginning of the book, Heyerdahl had written:

"The Inca Indians had their great empire in the mountain country when the first Spaniards came to Peru. They told the Spaniards that the colossal monuments that stood deserted about the landscape were erected by a race of white gods which had lived there before the Incas themselves became rulers. These vanished architects were described as wise, peaceful instructors, who had originally come from the north, long ago in the morning of time, and had taught the Incas' primitive forefathers architecture and agriculture as well as manners and customs. They were unlike other Indians in having white skins and long beards; they were also taller than the Incas. Finally, they left Peru as suddenly as they had come, the Incas themselves took over power in the country, and the white teachers vanished forever from the coast of South America and fled westward across the Pacific."

Darnell had read these lines before, read them as a young man when Kon-Tiki first came out, but they had not meant anything like what they meant now. Holderlin had marked most of the next page. When the first Europeans came to the Pacific islands, they found to their astonishment that there were "whole families conspicuous for their remarkably pale skins, hair varying from reddish to blonde,

blue-grey eyes, and almost Semitic, hook-nosed faces."
A few lines later, Heyerdahl described reading the "Inca
legends of the sun-king Virakocha, who was the supreme
head of the mythical white people in Peru."

"Mythical!" Darnell cried, laughing out loud.

Virakocha turned out to be the name of fairly recent
date. The original name was Kon-Tiki, the "high priest and
sun king of the Incas' legendary 'white men' who had left
the enormous ruins on the shores of Lake Titicaca."

A few pages later, in the last marked passage,
Heyerdahl quoted a museum director in New York, "'It's
quite true that South America was the home of some of the
most curious civilizations of antiquity, and that we know
neither who they were nor where they vanished when the
Incas came to power. But one thing we do know for certain
– that none of the peoples of South America got over to the
islands in the Pacific.'"

Heyerdahl proved that in fact those ancient people
did get to the islands in the Pacific. But if he proved where
they had gone, he never asked where they had come from.
Darnell put down the book. It seemed incredible that neither
Heyerdahl nor anyone else had asked why, if these white
men were so mythological, so much the stuff of legend,
Heyerdahl not only went looking for them, but found them,
on the islands of the South Pacific. Heyerdahl had made
a great discovery and, though it was staring him right in
the face, let a far greater one slip away. Millions had read
his book, and no one, including especially the author, had
known what it really meant until a young German had been
given a copy of it by his father, an archeologist who hoped
to encourage in his son a sense of the mystery of ancient
places.

Through the open shutters of the French doors that led
to the verandah, Darnell watched soft silver clouds, blown
by the eastern wind, drift past the moon and move down
toward the sea. He would be there himself tomorrow, on the
ocean for the first time since he had been a young man sent
to war, a voyage to seek a city that no one was supposed to

find. He felt a strange contentment in the knowledge that while he might have only a few more years to live he had seldom felt so alive. He fell into a deep, dreamless sleep.

He awoke with a sudden sense of terror to a tremendous, ear-shattering noise. It was as if the earth itself had exploded. He sat bolt upright, bracing himself as the whole building began to sway. It was an earthquake, a major one. Darnell sprang out of bed and was immediately thrown to the floor. The glass windows began to shatter and huge cracks started twisting down the heavy stucco walls. He crawled across the bedroom floor to the bathroom doorway, the safest place to be, and then watched in stunned amazement as the French doors began to sink, slowly at first, as if they were just slipping a foot or two, and then, before he knew it, the entire wall fell away. The floor began to buckle and he felt himself start to slide. Then, suddenly, it was over and everything stopped moving. There was a long, agonizing silence, and then the screaming started, people trapped under rubble calling for help, people paralyzed with fear screaming at the almost total devastation that had in less than one long unbearable minute taken place.

Darnell's heart was racing; his eyes, his face, were full of dust. The windows and the outer wall were gone. The building, though still standing, had been turned into a living, breathing thing, a half-dead monster that at any moment might lose its balance and fall flat over on its side. Darnell grabbed his clothes and started out the door. He met Holderlin in the hallway.

"Are you all right?" he asked Darnell as they hurried down the stairs.

"I've been in earthquakes before, but never one like this. I thought I was going to fall right down the floor into the street."

They got outside and, standing among the crowd of dazed hotel guests, made sure they were each in one piece. The earthquake had struck just before dawn. With the first rays of sunlight, the line of crumbled buildings and stone littered streets stretched out as far as the eye could see.

There did not seem to be a single structure that had escaped unscathed. The front of the hotel had been ripped away, each of the rooms now open like the back of a doll house, with beds and chairs all tangled together just waiting to plummet down to the ground. It was difficult to breath for all the smoke and dust. Clutching their few belongings, they picked their way through the rubble to the beach on the other side.

The marina and most of the boats in it had been destroyed, but the larger craft, anchored off shore, had come through it safely. The captain of the boat they had chartered was waiting for them near what was left of the dock.

"I'm glad you're safe, gentlemen. We better go. There may be another one, and the aftershocks will be bad enough. It's a miracle you're both alive."

A few minutes later, they were safe on board the sixty foot motor craft headed out into the Pacific. The captain, a small, meticulous man who was always apologizing for imperfections no one noticed, kept them informed about every new development. The earthquake, he reported that day at lunch, had registered 8.0 on the Richter scale.

"A colossal power of destruction," he explained with the peculiar pride of those who, having survived a disaster, wish it to be remembered as one of truly legendary proportions. "Greater than anything seen in years."

"Where was it centered?" asked Holderlin with more than normal interest.

The captain was embarrassed that he did not know.

"Somewhere offshore, somewhere in the ocean," he replied, averting his gaze. "The radio reports didn't say anything more than that," he added defensively, as he began to concentrate on the food on his plate.

Holderlin seemed to grow tense, and more pre-occu- pied, as the days passed and they drew closer to the island. Darnell thought it must be the weight of anticipation, forty years living alone, not just physically, but morally and spiri- tually; forty years living with a secret he had not been able to share, a discovery that, if he could have revealed it, might have changed the way the world thought about itself and altered in the most fundamental ways what people believed. Forty years living in that book-cluttered apartment, working feverishly on that dictionary of his; a dictionary which, even if he were ever to finish it, would probably never be published, a strange unintelligible manuscript detailing a language which, more than forgotten, had never existed. That without question would be the judgment any expert would pass on it. Atlantis? – A legend. The language of Atlantis? – A literary hoax, an academic fraud; the made up language of a man who, judging by the effort, might be a genius, but was certainly demented.

"When we get there, what do you intend to do?" They were standing at the starboard railing under a blistering sun. Holderlin, who did not seem to mind the heat, was bareheaded; Darnell was wearing a floppy straw hat.

"What do I intend….? Whatever they want me to do. There is a reason they went to all this trouble, a reason they wanted you to find me. I just hope we're not too late."

"Too late? You think the earthquake might have…?"

"All we get out here is what the captain learns on the radio. There's so much destruction, so many people dead or injured, no one on shore is going to take any time to find out what might have happened on a tiny island a thousand miles away."

Something was missing. Squinting into the blinding sun, Darnell tried to grasp what Holderlin had failed to say.

"It's more than the fact that the earthquake happened, more than the damage it might have caused. You think…?"

"That they knew it was coming, that they knew it was only a matter of time. Yes, why not? This modern science of ours – we think it can tell us everything, teach us how to conquer nature. These people know better than that. They don't want to conquer nature – they're not such fools as that – they want to learn from it. So could they learn when the earth was about to change, to make some new adjustment, the way our own bodies do? – In the twelve thousand years since Atlantis disappeared, in the countless generations that

Atlantis was one of the dominant powers in the world, are you certain this is something they could not have learned?"

On the morning of the seventh day at sea, Holderlin woke Darnell to tell him that they were almost there.

"It's just a few miles ahead. Come on deck and see for yourself."

Darnell dressed as quickly as he could. The sea was calm and the morning air cool and clean. He looked ahead, but there was nothing there.

"Farther ahead, on the horizon; see it – the fog bank? The island is just the other side of it. Forty years, and now, coming back, it's just the same."

Holderlin gripped the railing, searching the horizon, waiting for the fog to lift and he could see for the first time in forty years the island that through all the years in Berlin he had never really left. They drew closer, and the fog swirled all around them, a dense, gray curtain. Suddenly they were through it, on the other side. The sky above was a brilliant blue and the sun as bright and golden as any Darnell had ever seen. He turned to Holderlin, whose face now wore all the marks of a death-like disappointment.

"It isn't here," said Darnell. "It's disappeared."

"Vanished into the sea," replied Holderlin with stoic resolve. "Just the way Atlantis did."

Holderlin's eyes traced a line across the empty blue water to another fog bank, the other side of the circle that masked the next horizon.

"Look there!" he cried.

At first Darnell did not see anything, but then, a moment later, he saw what in the distance looked like angel's wings, moving toward them and moving fast.

"Tell the captain to turn around, that we're going back," said Holderlin.

Darnell ignored him. He kept looking at what he now realized were three sailing ships. What had looked like angel's wings were canvas sails billowing in the wind. The ships, not very large, thirty or forty feet, danced across the surface, barely touching the sea, as they came on, faster by the moment. Then, when they had come within a few hundred yards, they stopped. A man stood on the bow and waved his arm. It was Holderlin's old friend, the one who had taken his name, the one that Darnell had met.

"Tell the captain to turn around," said Holderlin. "Tell him to take you back." He shook Darnell's hand and thanked him for what he had done. "They've come to take me with them. They promised I could come back. You'll keep the secret, won't you? It's important that no one knows."

Before Darnell could even think what to say, Gerhardt Holderlin, with an agility that made a liar out of age, plunged headfirst into the water and with a powerful stroke began to swim the last short distance of the journey that had taken all his life.

A week later, when Darnell flew home to San Francisco, Summer was there to meet him at the airport. She did not try to hide her surprise.

"You look better now than when you left. How is that possible after what you went through, an earthquake that could have killed you and a long trip at sea?"

"The sea is the answer. In all the years I practiced law, I never felt quite so good, so alive, as I did when I was out in the Pacific during the war. I thought it was because I was so young and didn't have to worry about what was going to happen next. But now I know that it wasn't that at all. It doesn't have anything to do with how old you are. When you're out there, everything is different, more intense, and in a way, more fundamental. You don't much care what anyone else thinks about you, only what you think about yourself. Out there you come closer to the truth of things. If I learned nothing else from Gerhardt Holderlin, I learned that."

Darnell was home and he felt good about that. He liked having Summer near, he liked the long talks they had, but as the days wore on he found himself thinking more and more about Holderlin and about Adam and the girl. Summer would ask him where he thought they were, but all he could tell her was that he was certain they were somewhere no one would find them, somewhere they could live the way they always had for at least a few more hundred years.

"And you're the only one who knows, now that Gerhardt Holderlin has vanished with them?"

"Yes, and you're the only person I'll ever tell. Who would believe me if I did?"

"Your friend, Henry Hammersmith, would."

"Maybe I should tell him. He deserves to know the truth, after what he did."

"It changes everything, though, does it? It's hard to think of anything the way we did before."

Staring out at the lights of the city, the city in which he had been born and which he had always loved, remembering the easy comfort of what he had always thought he knew, the granted certainty that he had lived, if not at the end, then at the pinnacle, of history, Darnell laughed out loud at the vanity of things. For the first time he felt a stranger, a brief visitor, in a place that had all the time belonged to others.

A Note from the Author:

Thank you for reading <u>The Dark Backward</u>. Please let me know your thoughts about the book. You can send me email, sign up for my newsletter and get updates about new releases by visiting my web site at www.dwbuffa.net.

- D.W. Buffa

OTHER BOOKS BY D.W. BUFFA

The Defense

The Prosecution

The Judgment

The Legacy

Star Witness

Breach of Trust

Trial by Fire

The Grand Master

Evangeline

Rubicon
(Released under pen name
"Lawrence Alexander")

The Swindlers

CPSIA information can be obtained
at www.ICGtesting.com
Printed in the USA
BVHW081801050121
596841BV00003B/106